THE CANNON AND THE QUILL

BOOK 5: WITH MY PROPER BLOOD

# BY THE SAME AUTHOR

## The Stanton Chronicles

The Cannon and the Quill, Book One: We All be Jacobites Here*

The Cannon and the Quill, Book Two: Princes of the World*

The Cannon and the Quill, Book Three: How to Be a Proper Pyrate*

The Cannon and the Quill, Book Four: All the Devils Are Here*

Minor Confessions of an Angel Falling Upward*

Three Gothic Doctors and Their Sons*

Sherlock Holmes and the Mystery of M*

The Icarus Continuum: From the Files of the Domestic Threat Early Assessment Unit (short stories)*

## Fantasy

Jester-Night (Book 1 of the Ambir Dragon Tales)

Aldemere's Dilemma (Book 2 of the Ambir Dragon Tales)

## Non-Fiction

Every Day is a Story All Its Own: A Triadic Approach to Storytelling

Watch Out For the Hallway: Our Two-Year Investigation of the Most Haunted Library in North Carolina (with Tonya Madia)

Roommates from Beyond: How to Live in a Haunted Home (with Tonya Madia)

# THE CANNON AND THE QUILL

## BOOK 5: WITH MY PROPER BLOOD

### PART OF THE STANTON CHRONICLES

### JOEY MADIA

New Mystics Enterprises

Leavittsburg, Ohio

*The Cannon and the Quill Book 5: With My Proper Blood*

Copyright © 2024

Joey Madia

Cover logo by Chuck Regan

ISBN-13: 979-8-9901889-1-4

PUBLISHER'S NOTE:

Published by New Mystics Enterprises, Leavittsburg, OH 44430

www.newmystics.com

# ACKNOWLEDGMENTS

Huzzah to Jonathan Edwards and Port City Tour Company/Beaufort Escape Rooms for commissioning the walking tour, stage show, and escape room on which this series is based.

Thanks to North Carolina Maritime Museum, Beaufort Historic Site, Japan's "Passage of Dreams," *North Carolina Travel*, *L'Echo des Mers*, *Carolina Country*, Athens Chatauqua, Handley Regional Library, Ravenwood Faire, the Ed Kinney Lecture Series, Ashland Chautauqua, and all of the venues that invite Angus and crew to share their stories with their audiences.

Cheers to all the pirate re-enactors with whom I have worked. Ye are my true and trusted mates. Lots of rum and coin to ye all!

To Baylus Brooks, Captain Horatio Sinbad, and other historians whose diligence and passion have made it possible for me to steep this story in history while also making it a fantastical journey into the unknown—I offer you my deepest respect and thanks.

To Aili Huber and Toby Malone's *Cutting Plays for Performance* (Routledge, 2021), from which I learned the differences between various versions of Christopher Marlowe's *Dr. Faustus*.

To beta reader Richard Copeland (and Meadmeister Extraordinaire!), whose knowledge of History and Story make this series better.

# DEDICATION

To my love, my lass, my beautiful real-life Ailish.

Tonya—

There's no one else I'd rather have by my side, whether sailing around the world or being stuck for a year in port.

After twenty-seven years on this crazy, one-of-a-kind ride, I predict with every confidence that our biggest, grandest Adventures are surely yet to come.

# PART ONE:

## ADVENTURE AND REVENGE

E very little thing was going exactly as Blackbeard had planned. His flagship, the *Queen Anne's Revenge*, a former French slaver originally called *La Concorde*, which he had commandeered a little more than half a year before, was taking on water at a rapid rate after running aground on the unpredictable shoals of Topsail Inlet, near the Colony of North Carolina.

Which was exactly what Blackbeard's trusted quartermaster, William Howard, assured him the ship would do during a secret meeting a few nights earlier with Blackbeard, his confidante Angus MacGregor, and Captain Israel Hands.

*"Mon Dieu, Capitaine Barbe-Noire!"* came an excited juvenile voice from just behind where Angus stood beside the ship's furious, frustrated helmsman, Mister Jones.

Turning reluctantly away from the starboard gunnel, which he was gripping tightly as the *Adventure* under Israel Hands approached, followed closely by the longboat he had sent out less than an hour earlier with his co-conspirator William Howard, Blackbeard barked, "Quit yer agitatin' caterwaulin', Mister Arot, or I shall have ye bailin' the bilge!"

"Please, Ad-meer-al! Louis is only frightened because of the big BOOM which I am swearing shook the ship and rattled up our bones!"

Blackbeard, amidst the chaos of dozens of his crew frantically scrambling to transfer whatever they could salvage to the approaching *Adventure*, placed his large, calloused hands on his hips as he glared at the twelve-year-old grandson of an Ashanti priest whose enthusiasm and unique use of English rarely failed to make him to smile.

"Caesar, me lad," he said, addressing the defiant young African who had been so quick to defend his also twelve-year-old friend, "can ye not see our glorious *Anne* is flailin' an' flounderin' beneath us? If ye two cabin swabbers have anythin' a' value below decks, ye best be fetchin' it up an' leavin' the men—foremost an' includin' yer *Captain*—to our task!" Turning to his smiling scribe, Angus MacGregor, whose uncle was the infamous Highland outlaw Rob

Roy, Blackbeard hissed, "Quill! Take these two below to fetch their belongin's an', while yer in the hold, fer the love a' James, see to the *commodities*!"

"Aye, Cap'n Thache," Angus replied, ushering the two boys toward an open hatchway before he was tempted to say something about Blackbeard's use of the word "commodities" to refer to the fourteen Angolan slaves they had taken from a ship out of England just a couple of days before.

It was even worse than Blackbeard's other favorite—and technically inaccurate—euphemism for these most unfortunate men: "the baker's dozen."

As tightly knit as the Cannon and Quill had become in the previous twenty-four months, the issue of slavery was a continued source of at times dangerous disagreement between them.

After watching the trio disappear into the darkness of the hold, Blackbeard returned his attention to what was happening beyond the gunnel just in time to witness *Adventure* running aground upon another of Topsail Inlet's damnable, unnavigable sandbars as she approached the *QAR*.

For this, he had not planned.

"Throw 'em some cordage, lads!" Blackbeard barked, glancing at Quartermaster Howard, who was intently consulting a detailed map of the inlet and approach to Beaufort, the shoreline of which they could see through a thinning although still obstacle-creating mist.

As a dozen veteran crewmen tossed a dozen lengths of rope to the crew of the *Adventure*, the helmsman of *Queen Anne's Revenge* pointed toward the shoreline. "Look there, Captain Thache! It is *Royal James*, along with the Spanish sloop. We might survive this yet!"

"Of course we shall survive it, Mister Jones," William Howard answered, smiling wryly at the irony of their rescue coming at the hands of the incompetent gentleman pirate, Stede Bonnet, newly restored to command of his Barbadian sloop after her interim captain disobeyed an order from Blackbeard to burn a merchant vessel sailing out of New England.

Such difficulties with the captains and crews of the four-ship flotilla had led, at least in part, to Blackbeard's decision to abandon to the seas the formidable *QAR*.

His declining health at the destructive hands of syphilis—what the seamen called the pox—was another, increasingly pressing factor—one he could no longer hide or afford to ignore.

"Cap'n Bonnet!" Blackbeard yelled, waving his arms at the at-least-in-name commander of *Royal James*, "avoid the bars no matter the cost in time! Ye shall be our savior if ye can manage to listen 'stead a' to blunder!"

Half an hour later, as Israel Hands was ordering his crew to knock the floundering *Adventure* full of holes and offload what they could to the Spanish sloop after a failed attempt to save her using a hastily redirected anchor winch, Stede Bonnet was pacing the deck of *Royal James*. Wringing his sausage-fingered hands, he stomped his slippered foot as Blackbeard and Howard came over the gunnel from a longboat.

"Unac*cep*table, sir!" Stede complained, his bulging stomach and round, cherry-colored face twitching with fear beneath the fox-trimmed, quilted robe and pommeled cap that were his standard aboard-ship attire. "Your navigator and sailing master should be summarily *hung* and fed to the *crabs*!"

"Enough a' yer nonsense," Blackbeard hissed, closing the distance between he and the gentleman pirate in the blink of an eye. "Ye shall keep yer damned voice down, or I shall remove yer means a' speech with a slice or two a' my dagger. Miscalculations occur. Mister Jones is not to blame, nor is anyone else. These waters are the entrance to Hell! I have chosen that town over there—named fer the duke a' Beaufort—fer our temporary port a' call. I have business up the coast with the guv'nor an' his minister a' finance as soon as I get this behind us."

"Ye grounded her on purpose."

This comment, thankfully whispered, came from David Herriot, Stede's longtime, long-suffering sailing master, who had been with the gentleman pirate since the day he had escaped his nightmarish life on Barbados.

"Aye, Mister Herriot. That I did," Blackbeard answered, lethal malice sharpening his tone. "An' ye shall soon see the benefits a' my decision." Noticing Ignatius Pell, *Royal James*'s capable boatswain, intently listening to his unexpected admission of guilt, Blackbeard added, "Ye as well, Mister Pell. If ye stay silent on the matter until I have sufficient time to explain."

"Ye do not *comprehend*, *Edward*," Stede Bonnet whined, pulling a delicate lace handkerchief from the pocket of his robe and dabbing away a rivulet of sweat where his forehead met his cap. "If I was to be dis*covered* in this tiny hamlet of *Beau*fort… which I hear is called by the locals *Fish* Town! … The em*bar*rassment… The *ru*in! I shall have to live under one of my *nom de guerres* in *Po*rtugal or *Spain* until I have at last outlived my *inf*amy."

"Can anyone manage to live so many years as to accomplish such a feat?" Howard whispered with a laugh, to which Herriot and Pell added their own, much to Stede's chagrin.

"Quiet yerselves," Blackbeard said, stopping their mirth with a glare. "Cap'n Bonnet makes a point. Mister Howard an' I have to return to the *QAR* to finish directin' her scuttlin'. *Royal James* an' the Spanish sloop will begin takin' men to Beaufort, quick as ye can manage. Do *not* go ashore, Cap'n Bonnet. After that task is completed, and with as few men as needed to steer this tiresome tub, ye will then proceed north to Bath to meet with Guv'nor Eden."

Not bothering to answer the stream of questions coming from Bonnet's flapping lips and stuttering tongue, Blackbeard, Howard by his side, climbed back into the longboat.

"I can see it in yer eyes," Howard said with a smile as they began to row back to the badly listing and steadily submerging *QAR*. "Ye have somethin' special planned for Major Bonnet."

"I do indeed," Blackbeard answered. "Why suffer the pain a' describin' that bunglin' fool to the guv'nor when he can experience the bloody mess that is our Bonnet a' Barbados in person?"

"Aye," Howard said, taking up an oar. "but that is not the whole of the plan. I sense that there is more."

"Just ye wait an' see, my friend. Just ye wait an' see."

Jake Givens, former amateur podcaster and assistant manager of Manasquan, New Jersey's Smithy's by the Seaside, and current FBI special status agent-in-training, adjusted his utility belt as his earpiece began to squawk.

"This is Jake," he whispered, double-checking the safety on the H&K MP5 he cradled in his arms.

"How about responding 'this is Trainee Givens'?"

Jake smiled at the husky voice of Special Agent Kevin Connor in his ear.

"Roger, Agent Connor. Trainee Givens reports that all is swell."

"*Swell*? Do you actually *want* to become a special status tactical agent, Trainee Givens, or is this nothing more than a short-term ploy to impress your girlfriend?"

Jake turned to the source of the remark, whispered by the latest in a long line of chop-busters he had dutifully endured since reinventing his life, a shadowy special operations legend everyone called David Plumber (a pseudonym, of course), a stinging reply at the ready. Before he could launch it, however, Special Agent in Charge Maggie Sorrus was demanding their attention.

No one messed with Maggie. Not even David Plumber.

"Stow the schoolyard, gentlemen—and that includes you as well, Special Agent Connor."

"Yes ma'am. Schoolyard officially stowed."

Maggie continued, without the slightest hint of amusement in her voice. "Trainee Givens... David... Proceed a hundred yards due north and you will see an HVAC exhaust vent located eight feet up the wall. That will take you directly and inconspicuously where you need to go."

Pulling her headset away from her shoulder-length auburn hair and laying it on the command center table in the Domestic Threat Early Assessment Unit headquarters in a nondescript federal building just outside of Langley, Virginia, Maggie watched as Jake and Dave proceeded toward the vent.

"How is this even close to accepted protocol?" she asked of Connor, who was watching the two men's night-vision feed on a monitor to her left.

Hitting the mute button on his headset, Connor shrugged his shoulders. "How is anything DTEAU is involved with governed by accepted protocol? The boss says Givens is excelling in the program... He's super motivated and full of piss and vinegar after what happened to his girlfriend..."

Maggie nodded, suppressing a chill that started just beneath her tailbone before snaking up her spine. Jake's girlfriend was Dr. Kirstine MacGregor, formerly of the Smithsonian Institute. Kirstine, who was descended from an eighteenth-century pirate and high-level operative named Angus MacGregor—the nephew of the Highland outlaw Rob Roy—had some kind of code or cipher buried deep inside her brain that the black hats were determined to extract. Badly enough to have kidnaped the mild-mannered historian, not just once but twice.

The second time it happened was on Maggie Sorrus's watch.

"I don't see him completing his training. The traditional academy program is rigorous enough... This special status trainee program is another beast entirely. Everyone but Jake is either veteran law enforcement or former military. Fifty percent are both."

"Yeah," Connor answered, pointing to his monitor to show Maggie how cleanly Jake scaled the wall of the psychiatric institute, popped the louvered cover off the vent, and climbed inside, "but you have to remember... his pops was a Navy SEAL. Not just *any* Navy SEAL... His superiors selected him to serve with their most elite and storied unit, which officially does not exist... SEAL Team D."

Maggie put her headset back in place as the voice of Tino "Haxx" Alvarado, DTEAU's tech specialist, came online.

"They've successfully entered the building, Agent Sorrus," Haxx reported, from where he sat at a fold-down table in a modified cleaning van five hundred yards from the point of ingress. "Looks like all is clear... our boys should have the Michael Mirror in hand within a matter of—"

Haxx went silent at the sight of David and Jake rapidly exiting *out* of the HVAC exhaust vent, followed by the bright red beam of a laser sight attached to a Ruger AR-556, gripped by a burly individual dressed in top-shelf tactical gear, topped off with a balaclava imprinted with the head of a cobra.

"Haxx! What the hell is going on over there?" Maggie was asking, just outside the periphery of his focus. "*Haxx?*"

"Don't say a word to her, Alvarado. Shut your shit down. And I mean fucking *now*."

Tino could almost *feel* a laser light tickling his brain as it fell upon his left temple from its origin point just outside the silently opened side door of the van. Nodding, he did exactly as instructed, dismissing in a nanosecond a thought to reach for the Glock 19M magnetized inches from his hand to the underside of his workstation console.

The last thing he heard as he was switching off the comm link was a stream of expletives from SA Connor.

*This is a total shit show*, Haxx thought with a scowl, turning to face the intruder who, not surprisingly, was dressed identically to his partner, who was hustling David and Jake at gunpoint toward the van.

It was at that moment that Haxx became aware that neither David nor Jake had their weapons or night-vision goggles.

"How'd you know what we were planning?" Haxx enquired, as the trio reached the vehicle.

*Because,* estúpido—*these two guys are pros.*

"We know everything you DTEAU dweebs are up to, Alvarado… including the fact that you've gotten yourself into a helluva jam with some muscle back in Bushwick…"[1]

*How in the hell are these two* hijos de puta *aware of what I did for Frankie Bank?*

Before he had completed the thought, Haxx spotted the red and black patches sewn onto the right shoulders of each of the assailants' jumpsuits… the crossed spears of the Kardax Corporation.

*Ravenskald's in-house security. We are well and truly screwed…*

Indicating that Haxx should step away from his equipment, the one who had silently opened the door said, "Whatever you're after

---

[1] You can learn the details of Haxx's situation in the short story "Prendick's All Night Fights" in *The Icarus Continuum: From the Files of the Domestic Threat Early Assessment Unit.*

inside this particular nut house, you are leaving here without it. You try this shit again, we won't just *paint you* with our lasers. We will bullet-fuck your skulls. Invasive, angry, and ugly."

Haxx, resisting the urge to roll his eyes, nodded several times to show he understood. The guy was talking tough because he thought that was exactly what Haxx would respond to, being a simple techie. It was obviously not his normal vocabulary.

"You hear what my partner is tellin' ya, *Jakey*?" the other one asked, pressing the muzzle of his AR-556 roughly into his target's sternum.

"*Dad*?"

Haxx nearly sprained his neck turning his head toward the cursing, foot-stomping target of Jake's answer by way of a question.

The speaker's partner groaned. "Jesus, Randall. It would've been so much better had the kid not known it was you..."

"Fuck this shittin' nonsense," Randall (presumably Randall Givens) responded, removing his cobra balaclava and spitting on the ground. "Who gives a rat's newly shaven testicles if Jakey knows it's me. He ain't supposed to be here, snoopin' around, lookin' for his girlfriend's pretty panties..."

"Isn't night watchman at an Ohio psychiatric facility a little low on the totem pole for you?" Jake enquired of his father, as David Plumber sat down on the side-door step of the van and began to laugh.

Hesitating for a moment before finally giving in to this increasingly ludicrous situation, Randall's partner removed his balaclava, engaged the safety on his AR-556, and crouched across from David.

"How you doin', brother?" David asked.

"Honestly, I'm embarrassed. How 'bout you?"

Alvarado's eyes went wide. "You all *know* each other?"

David nodded. "We've crossed paths a couple of times. We're not quite Holmes and Moriarty..."

"More like Lestrade and Colonel Moran," Randall's partner added. Extending a hand to Haxx, he said, "Chief Petty Officer, Retired, Ishmael Ramsay."

Haxx shook the ex-SEAL's hand, wincing at its vicelike grip. "You already know who I am and way too much about me..."

Ramsay nodded, not releasing the techie's hand. "Fuckin' A right we do. And, like I already said, that goes for the DTEAU as well. Same for Doctor MacGregor. I gotta tell you guys… You're attempting to stick your dicks into a syphilitic orangutan. We're gonna do you a solid and tell our boss it was some tweakers looking to score some pharma, but we won't cover your asses again."

"He means what he's tellin' ya, Jakey," Randall added, lowering his weapon without engaging the safety. "I cannot believe the FBI placed you out in the field so fast. You wanna play soldier, son, buy an Oculus Rift."

"Guarantee me Kirstine's safety," Jake responded, trying not to sound as embarrassed and flustered as he felt.

"I wish I could do that, son. Fact is, she's in play, and it's well above our pay grade. I'm not able to protect her, and I sure as shit ain't protectin' you and your pals if you continue down this road."

Jake turned his voice to ice. "I'm learning to take care of myself."

Before Randall Givens could respond—and everyone could see in Jake's eyes that whatever his father was about to say could further devolve an already absurd situation into chaos—Ishmael Ramsay was up and taking his partner by the shoulders. "That's enough for now. We need to get inside. The transport'll be here at dawn to take us to Nova Scotia." Turning to Haxx, he said, "I'll see you get your equipment. Vacate this property, Alvarado. And I mean do it fucking *now*."

David and Jake were inside the van and closing the side door before Ramsay and Randall had taken ten steps toward the building.

As Haxx occupied the driver's seat and turned the key to start the engine, David said, "Drop me at my van. And tell the director I'm expecting a bottle of Laphroaig 25 sent to the usual address *on top of* my regular fee."

"I absolutely will," Haxx responded, heading the van for the exit. *After I tell him about everything else.*

*Everything except for Bushwick.*

That had to remain a secret for as long as Haxx could manage.

"Where were you, Colonel Rhett? In what self-serving enterprises were ye engaging while several heavily armed ships full of loathsome pirates infested our unprotected harbor? While our most important citizens were taken hostage and robbed at knifepoint? Your sloops were nowhere to be seen! What exactly have you been doing on O'Sullivan's Island? Hiding bodies of fishermen you have tortured and slaughtered by order of your overlords, the Lords Proprietors and Ravenskalds?"

Never in all his many years as a slaver, ivory trader, and distinguished officer in the colonial militia, nor now in his current position as the foremost pirate hunter operating in both of the Carolinas, had William Rhett endured such a dressing down as he was now receiving from Governor Robert Johnson.

It was true—Rhett had been awaiting the arrival of pirates near O'Sullivan's Island, where the hunting had been steady and lucrative, while Blackbeard was taking several wealthy merchants and their families hostage aboard the *Queen Anne's Revenge* for a tense three days in return for a chest of medicine and whatever he could procure from his captives.

Rhett had kept himself scarce in the ten days since the incident, allowing the embarrassing, costly situation to simmer down on its own. Confident his timing was sound, he had come to see the governor, proposal in hand, to lead an expedition to bring Blackbeard to Johnson's personal justice, an offer he was sure the governor would quickly accept.

The colonel had therefore not prepared himself for the full force of Johnson's wrath.

Nor for the mention of the Portuguese fishermen from Beaufort. He had thought that he and the governor had closed the matter after his confession in this room fourteen months before, when Johnson had first taken office from the bungling deputy governor, Robert Daniell.

"Are ye suffering from some major befuddlement of the mind, Colonel Rhett? Must I have ye replaced? Require ye to make your *home* on O'Sullivan's Island? Or perhaps ye would have me change its name to *Rhett's* Island and thereby toss to the wind the memory of that strong and stalwart Irishman, Captain Florence O'Sullivan, who kept the lighthouse there for so many distinguished years? A memory you are soiling with your vast incompetence and murderous proclivities!"

Rhett, whose fingernails were digging into his palms to the point they would soon draw blood, managed to keep his anger from showing.

An anger that might just lead to the colonel striking the bastard who sat before him if he failed to keep it in check.

Still the cannonade continued.

"People are talking, Colonel Rhett. It seems that ye were not completely honest when last I broached the serious matter of the Portuguese fishermen. Rumor has it that ye yourself tortured them to the point of death. Even worse, that you did so at the order of the Ravenskalds!"

Who had talked? Very few men knew the truth of what had occurred off the coast of Beaufort on Rhett's sloop *Henry* on All Hallows Eve, nineteenth months before.

Rhett had not touched them. The torture and slow dismemberment of the two innocent men was solely at the hands of Absalom Ravenskald.

Rhett had merely cleaned up the mess, which is what he had confessed to the governor.

So who had been spreading rumors in Charles Town?

It had to have been Robert Daniell. Rhett would pay the little weasel a visit on his retirement island as soon as he was able.

"Are you a lunatic, Colonel Rhett?" Governor Johnson asked in the face of Rhett's persistent silence. "Perhaps it is worse than that… Have the Ravenskalds paid ye to undo me? To undo all I have accomplished to bring merchants and families to South Carolina in order to build parishes and prosperity in our expansive western lands? I know full well that Colonel Moore—with whom you are closely acquainted—and his damnable Family are working at the behest of not only the demon Ravenskalds but with the Lords Proprietors Carteret and Craven. I am in a mood to have ye hung, William Rhett. I suggest ye give me a reason to refrain from giving the order."

As if to prove the sincerity of his request, Robert Johnson's mood suddenly softened, as did his tone.

Rhett silently resolved not to waste the chance.

"Governor, ye have my sincere apologies and profound regrets for failing ye. I have captured or killed a good many pirates around O'Sullivan's Island, and, as ye so rightly surmised, that was where I was. As to the matter of the Portuguese fishermen… I do not know how the secret information I *voluntarily* provided to ye regarding the incident in Beaufort has made its way into larger conversation in Charles Town, where whispering tongues have twisted its truth into fiction, but my guess is Robert Daniell. With your permission—or frankly, sir, without it—I intend to make him aware of the consequences of his actions.

"As to any loyalty ye believe I might have to the Ravenskalds, the so-called Family, or the Lords Proprietors, I assure ye that such an erroneous assumption is purely the result of specious speculation and pointed fabrication. I have defended South Carolina's superiority without fail—especially to Colonel Moore. Ironically, Daniell was privy to at least one of our disagreements. Perhaps I will force him to recall it…

"Know this as well, Governor Johnson. I support your ambitious plan to shepherd this province toward such an undeniable position of prosperity that the Lords Proprietors will be forced to sell it to its rightful owners—the people of South Carolina.

"Above all, I beg ye not to forget that I lost a good man last October—Captain Masters of the *Henry*—due to the piratical actions of the murderous madman Vane. Captain Fayrer Hall of the *Sea Nymph* and I are committed to bringing Vane—as well as Blackbeard and his lapdog Bonnet—to swift and lethal justice."

Assessing in silence for what seemed to Rhett an eternity all that he had heard from the colonel, Governor Johnson rose from his cushioned chair.

"Leave Daniell be for now," he began, removing a paring knife from a drawer in his desk, which he used to peel a pawpaw as he spoke. "He is more useful to us in the short term spreading his filthy rumors and seeking to undermine my efforts. *Our* efforts, Colonel Rhett. At which he has failed spectacularly. As to the pressing matters at hand, I still have faith in your loyalty to me and to this province. We shall chalk up your failure to protect the harbor to a gross misjudgment based on honorable intentions.

"You have my approval to hunt these scoundrel pirates—Bonnet and Blackbeard first and foremost—and to do so without delay. Bring me men for trial, sentencing, and hanging, Colonel Rhett. As many as you can. Such success will not only strengthen our position, but weaken North Carolina's, along with those who run her government from the shadows and reap her modest riches."

Nodding and then bowing, William Rhett left the governor's office without another word, a smile of relief and renewed intention to bring these villains to justice spreading across his moderately handsome face until his cheeks began to ache.

## GOVERNOR'S MANSION, BATH, COLONY OF NORTH CAROLINA, JUNE 5, 1718

"It is said, Major Bonnet, that North Carolina is a vale of humility between two mountains of conceit."

Stede Bonnet, newly arrived in Bath, seat of the government of the Colony of North Carolina, adjusted his frockcoat, which was dreadfully uncomfortable compared to his quilted robe, to which he had grown so accustomed.

Looking Governor Charles Eden in the eye, Stede leaned forward until his belly was touching the desk that stood between them. "And those two mountains would be?"

Shooting a look of disbelief to his closest friend and faithful conspirator, Tobias Knight, who also served as secretary of the government, chief justice, and deputy proprietor, Eden tried his best to be indulgent.

After all, Blackbeard would be very good for business, and his emissary deserved at least a modicum of respect.

"Virginia under Spotswood and South Carolina under Johnson," he replied. "They each have deepwater ports, while we do not."

"I know Charles Town harbor well enough," Stede replied, relishing an opportunity to brag. "After all, I blockaded it twice—the second time just a week and a half ago!"

"With considerable assistance from Captain Thache, as we have come to understand it," Knight replied, his insolent tone not at all what Stede had expected.

"It was because of *my* intelligence on the matter and through the presence of *my* fear-inducing ship, the famous *Royal James*, that we were able to meet with such resounding success. Look here, Governor Eden. I did not sail a full day up the *Pamlico* from *Fish Town* to subject myself to such—"

"Quite right, Major Bonnet," the governor replied. "Chief Justice Knight has had a long, trying day, and your visit caught us by surprise. Do forgive him."

Stede, who felt his attention pulled by a bowl of chocolate delicacies sitting upon the desk, waved his hand in acceptance of the apology. Selecting three of the most delectable-looking confections from the bowl, he asked, as he popped the first one into his mouth, "May I?"

"By all means," the governor responded, already more than ready to have this ill-mannered fop out of his office and on his way—and not just back to Beaufort. "I have to be honest, Major Bonnet. Our colony, and our little town of Bath, are modest in both means and opportunity, and ye are clearly very accomplished. Are ye aware that the king of Denmark has gone to war with Spain? He maintains a colony on Saint Thomas in desperate need of leadership."

"I am not familiar with that particular situation," Stede replied, pulling a hunk of jagged pecan from his tooth and releasing it onto the floor before biting into the second piece of chocolate. "Please do tell me more."

Eden smiled. He was nearing his goal of ridding himself of this foolish farce of a pirate. "I could not help but admire your ship as ye docked. A fine vessel with a no doubt seasoned and formidable crew, just as ye have said."

"All true. Thanks to me."

"Thanks to ye. That is also abundantly clear. Which gives me every confidence that King Frederick would welcome such a commodore as yourself to protect Saint Thomas's shores. I am sure ye would find yourself exceedingly rich and rather famous in practically no time at all."

Stede, his teeth obscured by chocolate, while setting upon the task of obliterating the final delicacy, which had begun to melt in his hand, leaving sticky brown blobs on his sweaty palm and thumb, managed to say, while standing, "I shall take it all under advisement, Governor Eden. Saint Thomas is a mere five hundred miles from Barbados, which I abandoned at the start of my piratical career. Perhaps a bit too close for comfort. I must first consult with Blackbeard, who is no doubt anxiously awaiting my return and full report off the unfriendly shores of Fish Town."

"I can only imagine with what anxiety he awaits your return," Tobias Knight said with a grin, prompting a quiet chuckle from the governor. "Please do give him our best."

"One thing more before I go," Stede replied, running his tongue over his chocolate-coated lips. "There is the matter of pardons for me and my crew."

"To be provided without delay," Governor Eden answered, anxious for this drain on his time to be gone. "Chief Justice Knight shall deliver them to ye upon your most impressive vessel within the hour."

"*Ex*cellent," Stede replied, with another wave of his sausage-fingered, confection-coated hand. "Oh, and *gen*tlemen, I offer a final word, which I deliver to ye as a *cour*tesy. I have a bit of advice. When Commodore *Thache* arrives, strive a bit more to im*press* him. Only with due respect for your *part*ners—nay, your *saviors*—will your humble little *vale* be fit to compete with your *neigh*bors' mountainous con*ceit*."

Governor Eden brought his hands together in a mock display of gratitude. Then, as Bonnet turned to leave, he whispered, "I most certainly will show Blackbeard *considerably* more respect. As for ye, ye smarmy hedgehog… May we never meet again."

Two days after the welcome departure of Major Bonnet, Governor Charles Eden and Chief Justice Tobias Knight much more warmly welcomed Blackbeard and his quartermaster, William Howard.

As they had navigated their sloop up the Pamlico River, Howard, a native of Bath, had immediately taken note of the positive effect that Eden and Knight were having upon his childhood home. The number and quality of the houses—still modest at two dozen simple structures, occupied by less than eighty souls—had improved, and the colony's only port was thriving.

"I think we could make ourselves rather more than merely comfortable here in Bath," Blackbeard had said as a liveried servant from the governor's mansion had met them at the door.

Three hours had passed since they had taken their seats in Eden's simply appointed office. Brandy and port had freely flowed, they had consumed a hearty meal, and a friendship born of mutual ambition had steadily begun to form.

"Has William laid out the present challenges for ye, Captain Thache?" Governor Eden enquired, refilling his guests' glasses to the rim with a fine Madeira.

"If ye mean the matter of the Family an' the Ravenskalds here in the Albemarle, aye, indeed he has," Blackbeard answered, taking a sip of the proffered libation. "I understand that Moseley and Moore have fomented wars with the local savages for influence, payoffs, and land. Shrewd, but not concerning. As to the Ravenskalds, there are powerful others with whom I have connections. I have done them favors, which, if I asked, they would repay. Understand me, gentlemen. I fear no man, nor men. In the course of our business together, I am sure our paths will cross, an' the strongest will inevitably emerge victorious. That is the natural order of life, is it not?"

Governor Eden nodded, pleased to add this unexpected benefit to their continually strengthening partnership. "I am also concerned with the meddling and manipulation of Spotswood, my counterpart in Virginia. He has used his position on the Tobacco Council to cripple our primary market, fixing prices, in league with the Family, in favor of Virginians and North Carolinians loyal to him and his cronies."

"Again, ye speak of the Family. Such political manipulation is also the order of things, as I expect ye are aware," Blackbeard said with a growl. "What should actually be of concern is the fact that Spotswood has at his disposal a squadron of Royal Navy frigates, which makes him rather formidable."

"Yet I am sure ye do not fear him," Knight remarked.

"He sure as hell does not!" William Howard answered. "Blackbeard stood up to the governor of Massachusetts, that poxy bastard Shute, despite the fact that Boston boasts an even stronger naval presence than the one there is in Hampton."

"I am well aware," Eden responded, feeling the conversation and pendulum-swing of power moving steadily toward the pirates. "And I am completely confident in both your capabilities and your courage. As bold as he can be, it is inconceivable to me that Spotswood would dare to use the Royal Navy to meddle in North Carolina." Anxious to move on, Eden softened his tone. "Now that we have discussed the challenges, let us consider our future. We have laid out the broad strokes of our arrangement, including the sale, on your behalf, of an Angolan *baker's dozen*, which Chief Justice Knight shall facilitate within the week."

"Premium price, even if it means Virginia," Blackbeard whispered.

"Noted," Eden replied. "I am currently cultivating nearly four hundred acres. I could use several more pairs of hands."

"I shall take several of them as well," Knight offered with a smile. "My wife Katherine and I, just forty-eight hours ago, purchased a tract of land not far from where we sit, known as Archbell Point."

"Landgrave Daniel's former property!" William Howard exclaimed. "One of our founding fathers." He directed this to Blackbeard. Turning back to Knight, he enquired, "Has the poor man passed away?"

The chief justice and deputy proprietor nodded. "I purchased it from his widow, who has decided to return to her family in England."

"I should like to see her before she sails," William responded, pleasant memories of his childhood softening his normally granite features.

"Sounds like the pair of ye have considerable holdings here in Bath," Blackbeard said with a gleem in his eye. "What would ye suggest for us?"

Knight fetched a map from a table and unrolled it on the desk. "Excellent question. Although the sale of the Angolans will make ye a wealthy man, there are plentiful opportunities to… well… to do what ye do best. This is a map made by the Englishman John White in 1585. This island here is Ocracoke, which the natives once called Wokokon. Ye will also almost certainly hear the local merchants refer to it as Pilot Town, which they do to encourage shipping. Not far from Ocracoke is Plum Point, an excellent choice for a base of operations. Between it and us sits the bountiful Pamlico Sound. Ye shall quickly see that a steady stream of merchant traffic passes through these waters. Easy prey for seasoned pirates like yourselves."

Blackbeard produced a laugh, which sounded like a roar, from deep within his throat. "I do not like your choice of words. There is nothing easy about the business of being a pirate. That is why we came to ye in search of lucrative alternatives."

"Tobias," the governor said, turning to his partner. "Our guests require formal pardons before we part. Can ye draw them up?"

"I shall attend to it immediately," Knight replied, moving across the room to a secretary's desk.

As the chief justice prepared his ink and quill, Eden returned his attention to Blackbeard. "Forgive Tobias. He is still settling in to his newest position. Now, as to the matter of your sloop. I shall convene the Vice-Admiralty Court tomorrow morning to declare it a legal spoil of war. I shall need the name of the ship for the documents."

Howard shook his head. "She has none. We call her the Spanish sloop."

"*Adventure*," Blackbeard said, staring into his glass of Madeira. "She is called *Adventure*."

Eden jotted a note in his journal. "A most auspicious name. I think it prudent for the both of ye to remain near Ocracoke as much as possible, to prevent the asking of questions. The same for Major Bonnet."

"Especially for Major Bonnet," Tobias Knight remarked.

"Agreeable to me," Blackbeard muttered, his privates beginning to burn from his worsening affliction. "If that is the conclusion of our business, I need to get back to… *Adventure*. I have some… supplies there I require."

William cleared his throat as Blackbeard rose from his chair. "I have something to say. I have decided not to remain. Which means that two of the baker's dozen belong to me. That was our agreement… My rightful claim as quartermaster."

"Indeed it was, and is," Blackbeard responded, clearly unsettled by the news of Howard's departure. "Where will ye go, my friend?"

"The Colony of Virginia. A girl awaits me there, and several longtime friends, with whom I shall open a tavern with my profit from the savages."

"I am happy for ye, William," Governor Eden replied, "although I must admit, I was looking forward to rekindling our childhood friendship."

"I must be leavin' without delay," Blackbeard hissed, the spreading pain in his groin causing his legs to tremble.

"Very well," Governor Eden answered, standing and offering his hand, which Blackbeard reluctantly shook. The governor noticed that his new partner's hand was trembling and slick with sweat. "Something to consider until we meet again. Ye should marry, Captain Thache."

"Marry?" Blackbeard asked, a darkening shadow passing over his eyes. "Why would I do that?"

"To show your commitment to living a legitimate life. That ye are willing to invest in the growth of the Sound as a peaceful, proper citizen. It would be only for show of course, since ye shall be dwelling primarily across the Sound."

"If I did not know any better, Governor Eden," Blackbeard growled, "I would think ye have my wife already chosen."

"In point of fact, I do," Eden replied. "My niece, Elizabeth Godwin. She recently lost her parents while they were sailing on business to England. Her father left her nothing, and I wish to see her future secure. She is fine of temperament and rather fair of figure. By the looks of ye, ye could use a devoted woman to see to your personal needs."

"I promise to meet her when I return. There is sense in what ye say. An' ye, William, will ye return with me to Topsail Inlet, or do ye wish to see the widow directly?"

"I would prefer to stay, if it shall not cause ye undo trouble."

"None at all," Blackbeard answered, grasping his former quartermaster's shoulder. "I shall take my time returnin'. Explore the *outer* route."

William nodded and smiled. "The outer route indeed."

"What *is this*, Mister Herriot? What has *happened* in my absence?"

Stede Bonnet had returned to Topsail Inlet—having taken the inner route back from Bath—to find the Spanish sloop gone and twenty-five of Stede's best crewmen marooned on what he was soon to learn the locals called Bogue Bank, a mile distant from Beaufort.

"Ye were no sooner out of sight," David Herriot, Bonnet's sailing master, began, "when Blackbeard and his rogues took us captive and placed us here, without water, food, or weapons."

"What of the Angolans, and the *plunder* we had *amassed*?" Stede whispered, already knowing the answer.

"Gone with Blackbeard to Bath," replied Robert Tucker, the newly installed quartermaster of *Royal James*, whom Stede had chosen to replace William Scott before the major departed for Eden's mansion.

Feeling a dull ache in his temples and a spreading pain in his gut, Stede fell upon the baking sand. Gashing his hand on a seashell, he did not even flinch, much to Herriot and Tucker's surprise.

"What of the rest of the crews?"

The two men took turns making their reports, which included the fact that two hundred pirates had gone to Beaufort proper, with the remainder heading north to Virginia.

As the blood from his injured hand seeped into the sand, Stede stood up as he saw a boat approach. Drawing and cocking his pistol, he forcefully asked the man who piloted it to identify his business.

"Jus' a simple merchant sellin' fresh-made apple cider an' baskets a' fresh-picked apples."

Tossing his coin purse to the merchant, Stede called out, "We shall take the lot. Ye should return without delay to Fish Town, and tell them to expect the gentleman pirate Bonnet before the sun has set."

"Whair thaen bae the rogue La Buse—that shitey rascal Levasseur?"

Captain Francis Hume, commander of the thirty-two-gun Royal Navy Fifth Rate HMS *Scarborough*, was in no mood for sour news. He was in the midst of a mission, at the behest of his longtime friend, Walter Hamilton, governor of the Leewards, to scour the seas for Edward Thache, and any other pirates he could bring to a bloody end.

For the past six months, sailing in consort with the aging twenty-four-gun HMS *Bristol Bay*, under the command of Jonathan Rose, Hume had been determined to fulfill that mission, with a single diversion of collecting debts for an English merchant in Puerto Rico before resuming his hunting off the northern coast of South America.

Regardless of his commitment to his mission nor how much he demanded from his and Rose's crews, he had not managed to confront Blackbeard or any of his villainous brethren on even a single occasion.

While careening some thirty miles from his present position a week before, Hume had received word that several merchant vessels had spotted the Frenchman Levasseur anchored off La Blanquilla, or simply Blanco, to which *Scarborough* and *Bristol Bay* had sailed with full sails and the dark intent that is the sharp-edged result of unrelenting frustration.

As they approached the island from the west, it seemed they had cornered the elusive rogue at last. Anchored in a bay was a pirate vessel, the *Blanco*, and a recently captured sloop, the *Boneta* out of Nevis in the Leewards, under the command of a Captain Davis.

Looking through his spyglass, Hume released a laugh. Turning to Governor Hamilton, who split his time between the *Bristol Bay* and *Scarborough*, he said, "Thaem maerchantmaen... they maentioned the *Blanco* by naem... thaet is the bastard's laetest coommand."

"I see only seventy or eighty of the vermin," Hamilton answered. "No more than half a dozen guns. You outnumber her two to one, Captain Hume. Force her to surrender and board her. We have the Vulture at last!"

"Maister Hall!" Hume shouted to a senior, seasoned midshipman. "Taek yer boardin' party an' secure thaet pirate vaessel! I wish tae bae onboard within the hour."

Midshipman Hall did as he was ordered, finding the pirates quick to acquiesce. Neither side fired a shot, nor crossed a pair of sabers. Hume and Hamilton, seeing the *Blanco* secured, were aboard her within minutes.

It was at that moment that their disappointment began.

"What do ye maen thair is nae a cap'n aboard?"

Hume had asked this of half a dozen pirates standing by the mainmast, none of whom would answer. When the rest of the pirate crew proved equally solemn and silent, Hume ordered a pair of willing men from *Boneta* to join him on the *Blanco*.

These men, James Moor and Edward Hunt, overjoyed at their rescue by Hume, were more than happy to spill their guts, despite the glares and silently mouthed threats from the captured pirates arrayed around them.

Moor was first to speak. "It was just yesterday that the one ye are lookin' for, the one they call La Buse, had commandeered our sloop, transferrin' a great glut of goods, muskets, cutlasses, an' pistols aboard her from his own ship, which was in a pitiable, wormy state."

It was then that Hume had asked the question, "Whair thaen bae the rogue La Buse—that shitey rascal Levasseur?"

Hunt, frightened by the Scotsman's growing anger, answered the captain's query in a single hurried breath. "Having fast determined that he could not stand against yer man o' war and consort he ordered sixty of his men to load all the gold and silver they possessed and most of their goods and weapons into the sloop before making their escape as ye approached!"

"Blast thae numpty baestard!" Hume exclaimed, his face going red and eyes going black. "I want this ship searched, Maister Hall, and vaery thoroughly soo!"

Several hours later, his crew having turned up nothing and the captured pirates shackled and guarded within a well-secured section of the *Scarborough*'s hold, Hume gave the order for the four ships to proceed northward to St. Croix, where Hume had destroyed the six-ship flotilla of Jean Martel eighteen months before.

None dared question his order, so menacing was his gaze.

Locked away in his cabin, the Scottish captain poured himself a sherry and buried his head in his hands.

Francis Hume, although his worth was not in question, had plenty he wished to prove, to both the king and his fellow captains.

His family, part of the Blackadder clan, had found itself split between loyalty to the Protestant William of Orange and then to his sister-in-law Queen Anne, and loyalty to the Catholic James Francis Edward Stuart, the Old Pretender, taking up arms on both sides of the battlefield during the short-lived Jacobite Revolution of 1715. The English courts had seen fit to exile at least one member of the family to Virginia following the Jacobites' loss.

Such a stain on the family name was hard for Francis to bear, despite his appointment as captain of the HMS *Scarborough* later that same year.

Built in the dockyard at Sheerness only six years earlier, HMS *Scarborough* was as formidable and capable an implement of destruction as her surly captain, with just as fierce a reputation.

"Ye mae haev slipped mae noose fer noo, ye pompous Frenchie baestard, as ye an' Bellamy did whaen I stomped Martel," Hume hissed into the darkness of his cabin, "boot I wael see ye an' thae raest a' yer poxy lot swingin' froom thae yardarm yaet."

Charles Vane, captain of the twelve-gun *Ranger*, sat in his cabin, his arm resting on his beloved volume of Shakespeare, which he read aloud whenever time allowed.

Beneath his scarred and muscular forearm lay the text of act V, scene vi, of the *History of Henry VI, Part III*, where Henry says to Richard, Duke of Gloucester, while in the Tower of London: *Teeth hadst thou in thy head when thou wast born/To signify thou camest to bite the world*.

That was Vane, who, just like Richard, was ready to stab to death the king—in the guise of the governor of the Bahamas, Woodes Rogers—and thereby claim the fort, and then the throne, of Nassau.

It had been a surging, stormy sea-lane that Vane had sailed from Wapping, in London, in 1712—where he had escaped the almost certain death that comes with being a sold-into-servitude climbing boy—to where he now was sitting. In the course of his rise to power, he had stormed a Spanish fort, killed the seconds-in-command of a Spanish captain and Carolinian pirate hunter, tangled with the Ravenskalds and demonic Devon Ross, extricated himself and his crew from prison on New Providence, and visited a variety of hurts upon merchantmen, the Royal Navy, and some of his fellow pirates.

He had watched Gran'pa Hornigold and Vane's former friend and mentor, Henry Jennings, take the pardon and commit to hunting pirates. He had watched Blackbeard—his only competition for dominance in the Caribbean and on the southern Atlantic coast—become a pawn in the game between the ruthless Ravenskalds and the mysterious and equally as ruthless Star Quorum.

Despite numerous setbacks and endless barrels of blood, Vane had managed to keep the upper hand. He had slipped away from his enemies and carefully chosen his friends, who were ever rarer in number.

Although his frustrations with the machinations of the geopolitical power brokers who were using the Brethren of the Coast as chattel in pursuit of a dozen ancient objects had caused an increasing anger that had led to increasing violence, aimed most often at the merchantmen he encountered, Vane was not above charity for the worthy. He had, not four months ago, secured a ship for Christopher

"Billy One-Hand" Condent, who had promptly sailed for Cape Verde to seek vengeance on any Portuguese he could find to punish them for sharing their nationality with the one who had taken his hand.

Then, two weeks ago, he had given his quartermaster, Edward England, a superb two-masted sloop to pursue an anticipated bounty of riches off the West African coast.

As for Vane, he would remain in Caribbean waters, and finish what the Republic of Pirates had started, before it descended into chaos.

A lamentable condition that was initially his and Jennings's doing.

"Excuse me, Captain Vane. I do not wish to disturb ye."

*Yet disturb me still ye are*, the captain thought with a scowl, as he motioned to his new quartermaster, "Calico" Jack Rackham, to enter and take a seat.

If pressed for an answer as to why he had so quickly placed his trust in this thin, blond-haired specimen of ego, dash, and style, Vane could not comply.

A truth that only seemed to vex him when he was in his cups.

"What is it ye want a' me, Jack?" Vane enquired, lighting his pipe and glancing down at Henry's almost final words to Richard.

*Teeth hadst thou in thy head when thou wast born/To signify thou camest to bite the world.*

"Only to press ye for an answer as to why we continue to put ourselves at risk so near to Rogers's seat of power when all the rest of our brethren have headed to far less dangerous and apparently more lucrative geographies."

Vane shook his head, while pouring them each a mug of rum. "That is precisely *why* we are stayin', Quartahmastah. Although I did not plan it, we two sittin' 'ere are 'eirs ta the throne a' the Caribbean, *if* we dares ta take it. An' I tells ya, mate—I dares. Do ye?"

Draining his mug in a single swallow and standing, Rackham replied, "That was the answer I had hoped for, Captain Vane. And so, with anticipation of our future, I bid ye pleasant reading."

As Rackham exited the cabin, Charles Vane closed his volume of Shakespeare while puffing thoughtfully on his pipe.

*That one may seem loyal, but 'e was also born wit' teeth, wit' which ta bite the world.*

After rescuing and feeding the stranded members of his crew on the blistering sands of Bogue Bank, where Blackbeard had marooned them, Major Stede Bonnet had ordered *Royal James*'s sailing master, David Herriot, to set their sails for Beaufort.

Paying for provisions, and some necessary items for the sloop, including sheets and cordage, out of the meager store of gold and silver he and the other members of his crew who had accompanied him to Bath still had upon their persons, Stede gathered his crew of forty from the town and ordered Herriot to sail them to Ocracoke. He had heard from several of Blackbeard's crew that this was the island in the Pamlico Sound which their former captain had chosen as his base of operations.

When they arrived a few days later, there was nary a pirate in sight. Nor could they find the Spanish sloop.

Overwhelmed with the embarrassment of yet another blunder, Stede retired to his cabin, where he donned his fox-trimmed, quilted robe and pommeled cap, brewed a cup of tea, and sat down to read a copy of Charles Beckingham's stage script *Scipio Africanus*, which had debuted in London in February.

Two hours later, inspired by the Roman general's ability to change tactics in the midst of battle and otherwise rethink plans that were not working during the Second Punic War, he sent word through his boatswain, Ignatius Pell, that Herriot and Robert Tucker, his newest quartermaster, should join him *tout suite*, which he had to translate for his undereducated messenger.

Offering a cup of tea to his two most senior officers, which both of them refused, Stede began to outline his plan.

"Our very first order of business. This sloop upon which we now sit in relative comfort shall henceforth be referred to as *Revenge*."

"Damned fine to hear his, Captain Bonnet," Tucker shouted, inadvertently sending Stede's cup and saucer to the floor with an enthusiastic sweep of his arm.

Herriot was doubly impressed. Not only had Stede shown some balls in renaming the sloop, he had refrained from stooping to retrieve his precious cup and saucer.

"I have it on good authority from Governor Eden," Stede continued, "that King Frederick of Denmark is highly anxious to commission me as a commodore to protect his colony on Saint Thomas for the duration of his war with Spain."

"The king of Denmark has specifically requested your involvement on Saint Thomas?" Herriot enquired, picking up the still intact cup and saucer to hide from the overly sensitive Stede his incredulous expression.

"Not specifically," Stede replied, "but Eden believes I would be an excellent fit for the task. Before we raise our anchor for Saint Thomas, however, we need far more provisions than the simple citizens of Fish Town could supply. That shall be your primary focus following this meeting, Mister Tucker."

Bonnet's quartermaster nodded, completely at a loss as to how to complete this task short of attacking passing ships, which he promptly and forcefully declared.

"What is *this*? Ye mean to negate our dearly acquired *pardons*? Are ye suffering from *madness*, Mister Tucker? Surely there are *other*, *better* solutions..."

"There are not!"

"Excuse me, Mister *Herriot*? Is that a proper way for *ye* to talk to *me*, the soon to be savior of one of the king of Denmark's most highly prized possessions? Would *Scipio* Africanus suffer such indignities from his subordinates?"

Herriot stood. "Not knowin' who that is, I am riskin' goin' out on a yardarm in a storm with my reply, but yes! Yes, he would, if he was talkin' nonsense about foreign kings an' grandiose stupidities! For years, I have suffered your egotisms, miscalculations, and mutton-headed errors! Ye have embarrassed me repeatedly. I am lucky to have survived the most egregious of your blunders! We shall await the arrival of merchant vessels. As all of us have heard, they are plentiful in the Sound. Upon boardin', we shall take what we need, after which we shall *not* proceed to Saint Thomas—whose only hope for a victory is for ye to stay away!—but to the Virginia Capes, where we shall rebuild the stores of plunder recently robbed from *ye* and *me*! Have ye anythin' to say in response, Major Bonnet?"

Removing his pommeled cap and holding it in front of his face to hide the red of his burning cheeks, Stede whispered, "Ye should refer to me as Captain Edwards as we enact your plan."

*There is a spectre lurking here*, thought Andrew Colson, Warden of London's United Free Mason Grand Lodge, as he entered its ceremonial space.

*Along with the nauseating stink of death.*

It had been here, in early March, that he and George Payne had found Grand Master Anthony Sayer's body hanging upside down, gutted and bled like a common barnyard pig.

Payne, who was already in line to replace Sayer later in the year, had stepped into the role of grand master the following day. Dressed in a gold-trimmed, dove-white robe, he now presided over the complex Masonic rituals for the Feast Day of John the Baptist, leader of the Essenes and the Masons' patron saint.

Between the pillars, Boaz and Jachin, twins of those in Solomon's Temple, stood the rest of the lodge's leaders. Standing within the circle drawn inside the pillars, just in front of a black dot that represented Earth, stood Second Warden Henry Bolingbroke, who cradled the open Book of the Law in his plump and sweaty hands.

Standing at the termini of a pair of parallel lines representing the summer and winter solstices extending from the circle were John Theophilus Desaguliers, secret supporter of the Prince of Wales, as well as friend and assistant to Isaac Newton, through whom he became a fellow of the Royal Society, and George Seton, Jacobite and former fifth earl of Winton. It had been within the ceremonial circle the past October that Seton had knelt before his peers and begged forgiveness from John the Baptist for betraying them to the Ravenskalds and very nearly failing to deliver the Baptist's skull to the lodge.

The Baptist Bowl, as the Masons called it, which was one of twelve religious objects that had been the reason for the endless wars of the world, rested securely in the Grand Master's hands.

Countless men had been tortured, and others had died, such as Anthony Sayer, in the struggle to possess this sacred object.

"Saint John the Baptist," Payne intoned, his voice deepened and amplified by the power of the skull, "ye who have commanded of us to repent and to be baptized. Ye who demand our repentance in the presence of those whom we have so selfishly aggrieved. We ask for your forgiveness."

"Saint John the Baptist," Andrew Colson continued, "ye who maintain balance between passion and intensity on the one hand, and knowledge and education on the other…"

Speaking as one, the group intoned, "Guide us, we your servants. Keep us in your light. Shower us with your strength. Hold us in your—"

"Enuff a' dis syrupy codswallop! Ain't no beheaded Baptist gonna save yas from *Faccia del Diablo*. I gutted ya previous mastah… now I come fer the resta ya scum! Then I am takin' the bowl!"

Andrew Colson turned to the entrance of the room in which they stood. Devon Ross—the disfigured assassin for hire who wore as always a leather mask—stood, pistol and sword at the ready, along with half a dozen identically armed and ready thugs.

"I shall only tell ye once, ye malformed devil," Colson warned, surprised by the well of strength fueling his words and his tone. "Take your men and go from London, or ye shall not leave this lodge alive."

Ross's laugh, reminiscent of a jackal's, spread his filth across the space, overwhelming the sacred with the profane. "Listen ta the traitah speakin' so mightily, me lads… Lord Carteret, Lord Lieutenant a' Devon'shah, sends his particulah regards ta you, Andrew Colson, from where 'e sits in ya fathah's formah office in the Cecils' castle in Exetah." Ross spat a green-black blob of filth upon the floor. "Where, as a boy, ya bruised an' blackened the 'eld down, defenseless body a' a peasant named Samuel Bellamy in front a' 'is dah by order a' yer own dah usin' 'is walkin' stick as ya weapon."

Colson attempted not to wince at the memory Ross had evoked. He and Bellamy, who had found themselves caught between their powerful and powerless fathers when they were barely teens, had made their peace fifteen years later on a vessel Bellamy had boarded near Newfoundland with every intention of plundering. A vessel on which Colson happened to be sailing just prior to the so-called Robin Hood of the Sea's assassination by Athelstan Ravenskald, who enacted the deed by means of a storm he caused to strengthen off the coast of Massachusetts through manipulation of another of the twelve ancient objects, the deadly Ezekiel Wheel.

Turning embarrassment, regret, and heartbreak into fortitude, faith, and resolve, Edward Colson said, "I would ask of ye to inform Lord Carteret that I know the truth of Samuel's demise, and soon enough, the world shall know it as well, although, as I have already plainly warned ye, ye shall not leave this room should ye remain an instant longer."

By the time he was halfway through his words, Colson's voice was an icy, insistent whisper.

*Faccia del Diablo* belched forth a derisive laugh. "One a' yas find me a walkin' stick," he said to his companions. "It is well past time that I showed dis snivelin' traitah a lesson in mannahs an' knowin' 'is lowly place."

Before any of his thugs could move, a voice as icy and insistent as Colson's began to whisper from just beyond the tavern door in front of which the intruders stood.

As the disembodied voice grew in both power and volume, Devon Ross suddenly recognized the words it was intoning.

The realization of what it meant caused him to piss his britches.

"*Oo bah fa loo jumbee. Wa hay-nah sa ma ka jumbee. Mu-kah do hay-nah ka. Tach ma, tach mu, sa mu sa jumbee. Co-mama sa. Co-mama sa jumbee.*"

"What the fuck is dis?" Ross asked, too frightened to turn around. "Am I trapped in a conjuror's dream? Are ye bastahds castin' a spell?"

"Not us," Edward Colson answered.

"Then who?"

In response, Abenaa entered the room, her chestnut eyes flickering with flame. "Do you not recall my voice? It was three and half years ago, on the West African coast, when I pleaded with my father not to conjure what I now shall. I was just an innocent girl whom you attempted to lure with sugarplums…"

As Ross's thugs fled the lodge and then the tavern in a spontaneous, yet coordinated, act of gutless, abject cowardice, Ross whispered, still not turning to face his nemesis, "Dis nightmare cannot be."

In response, Abenaa walked further into the room, loudly resuming the chant.

"*Oo bah fa loo jumbee. Wa hay-nah sa ma ka jumbee. Mu-kah do hay-nah ka. Tach ma, tach mu, sa mu sa jumbee. Co-mama sa. Co-mama sa jumbee.*"

From behind the pillars Boaz and Jachin came a low, bowel-emptying growl, and the click of claws on oak.

Just as did Daagakutsu of the Ashanti's voice on that horrific, fateful day in January 1715, his daughter Abenaa's continued to rise in volume and quicken in tempo until it was wholly preternatural.

"*Oo bah fa loo jumbee. Wa hay-nah sa ma ka jumbee. Mu-kah do hay-nah ka. Tach ma, tach mu, sa mu sa jumbee. Co-mama sa. Co-mama sa jumbee.*

"The time of the *jumbee* is at hand!"

Then the manifested *jumbee*, terrible and black, emerged from the ceremonial circle, its almond-shaped eyes aglow with a blinding yellow light. Crossing the room in the blink of an eye, it leapt upon the assassin Devon Ross, ripping away the mask for which its teeth and claws had been the cause, and tearing out *Faccia del Diablo*'s throat with a victorious, lustful growl.

As quick as it had appeared, the conjured creature was gone.

As a pool of dark red blood spread out from Ross's neck, Andrew Colson ran to Abenaa who had collapsed upon the floor.

Taking her in his arms, he yelled, "I must take her to Burghley House, to the home of Earl John Cecil, without delay. Only the demonic angel that resides there can revive her... our complicated ally, the angel falling upward."

Capitaine Olivier Levasseur, known on the vast, mighty waters of the world by the monikers of the Mouth and the Vulture, was not accustomed to running away.

Yet he had found himself doing exactly that, twice in as many months.

The first of these acts of seeming cowardice was on the last day of April, when he had abruptly left New Providence in his well-armed *Postillion*, passing off his departure as an urge to fight the forces of King Phillip upon the Spanish Main before continuing on to a wealth of enticingly described adventures and riches in Africa.

This was, of course, a necessary fabrication—at least in part. Although his plotted course was exactly what he said it would be, Levasseur was not intent on battling the Spanish at Porto Bello, Veracruz, or Maracaibo, or seeking innumerable riches upon the African coast. The seven-member Star Quorum had tasked him with prying loose the lethal Ezekiel Wheel from the hands of Athelstan Ravenskald, before he could once again use it against one of their ships.

Find Athelstan the capable Frenchman had, anchored at the mouth of the Suriname River in Paramaribo.

Before Levasseur could order a broadside on Athelstan's vessel, however, the waters of the river were rising around and pushing in upon *Postillion*, crushing her to splinters.

Instead of retrieving the Ezekiel Wheel, Levasseur had become its latest victim.

The scraping, scavenging, and salvaging that had led Levasseur to La Blanquilla and the taking and almost immediate abandonment of the *Blanco* were the ingredients of a sour *soupe à l'oignon* of frustration and desperation the details of which Levasseur would never voluntarily share.

Not even in the pages of his complexly coded journal.

As to the narrowly made escape from the *Scarborough* and her aging consort, Levasseur's forty men had shown nothing but gratitude to their captain for his split-second thinking and ingenuity. *If only they were to know*, Levasseur thought as they hoisted and cheered their savior, *how close I had come to ordering the old sloop in which we had arrived at La Blanquilla burned just hours before Hume and Hamilton had arrived.*

Since that frustrating time, now nearly two weeks past, his luck had begun to turn. His hungry, experienced crew, which now numbered close to sixty, had managed to overwhelm the crew of the twenty-two-gun merchant frigate *La Louise*, on the quarterdeck of which Capitaine Levasseur now stood. With both ship and crew properly outfitted and provisioned, Levasseur had ordered his sailing master to chart a course down the eastern coast of Brazil. Along the way, they had boarded and plundered half a dozen vessels, the most notable of which was a slave ship out of Angola, upon which they wreaked a terrible havoc.

After rescuing two hundred and forty Africans destined to be Caribbean slaves from the foul and fetid hold—full as it was with disease, deprivation, and death—Levasseur had ordered his quartermaster to sink the vessel, along with all of its crew. Directing his men to clean and feed the Angolans, and his physicians to treat and dress their wounds, La Buse had transported them as far as an island near Macae, where he deposited them in haste as a Portuguese man of war set its sights upon *La Louise*.

Escaping the cannon-laden beast by applying the entirety of his sailing prowess, which he had been developing since his time as a privateer in the War of Spanish Succession, under a letter of marque from *le roi soleil* himself, Levasseur fended off similar attacks near Ilha Grande and Ubatuba.

The latter of these engagements ultimately cost the lives of nearly a dozen of his men.

After making repairs and careening for several days at Cananeia, Levasseur, tired of the Brazilians, Portuguese, Dutch, and everyone else besides what remained of his crew, had made the decision this very morning that it was time to sail for Africa, where he could be of service to the Quorum and restock his depleted supply of purpose, poise, and pride. All of his recent defeats and humiliations, coupled with the still-stinging loss of Samuel Bellamy, the near loss of Cardinal André-Hercule de Fleury, the reckless barbarity of Vane and *Barbe-Noire*, and the persistent victories of the Ravenskalds had conspired to exhaust him.

Perhaps his salvation awaited in Africa, the cradle of humankind.

# PART TWO:

## ALLIANCES AND ARRIVALS

Robert Turner, owner of the twelve blocks of what, just five years before, had been an undeveloped stretch of empty sand everyone including the locals called Fish Town, looked toward the shoreline from his modest home at a longboat being pulled onto shore by three very husky men in kilts.

Once the longboat was secure, a scrawny man with uncombed, bright red hair, who sat in the stern beside a beautiful young woman, began to pass several small chests and larger sea bags over the gunnel to the trio. Turner noticed that each of them wore a Highlander's claymore hanging from a baldric, with several pistols and knives tucked behind their wide, well-worn leather belts.

It had been quite an interesting month for Turner's little hamlet of Beaufort, which he had named in honor of the deceased Lord Proprietor, Henry Somerset, second duke of the venerable House of Beaufort, founded in 1396.

On the evening of the third, three and a half weeks earlier, the first of hundreds of sailors had come ashore from a pair of sinking ships. Turner soon learned that they were victims of the unpredictable sandbars that made these coastal waters so treacherous and the local economy so challenging to develop.

The unpredictability and shallow waters of Topsail Inlet kept not only the Royal Navy away, a situation about which few North Carolians complained, but European merchants as well.

Most of the pirates, as he quickly realized they were, were gone within a week, off to the Tidewaters of Virginia or to Charles Town, where they would most likely find a berth aboard some other pirate vessel, for that was the only life they knew.

Turner had yet to meet the one they all called Blackbeard—whose reputation preceded him. Word was, he had entered these waters to strike a deal with Governor Eden, for whom Turner had little use.

Turner had been generous and hospitable a few days later to the ragtag crew of the strange but somewhat amusing gentleman pirate, Major Stede Bonnet, for the brief time they stayed in Beaufort. After all, the gold and silver they spent were certainly more genuine and valuable than what came out of their larger-than-life pirate captain's mouth.

Turner easily surmised why Blackbeard had marooned the bulk of Bonnet's crew on Bogue Bank as part of his betrayal of the insufferable, oddly enunciating fop.

Turner would not want to sail with him either. In truth, he had been more than happy to send him quickly on his way, not knowing that the lieutenant governor had done the same in Bath.

For the past few weeks, all had been relatively quiet. Each morning, Turner would take his breakfast down to the shoreline to watch the *Queen Anne's Revenge* and its failed rescue sloop slip farther and farther below the water.

As the trio of kilted warriors—they did not look to Turner like pirates—walked peacefully toward his house, he took a moment to notice that only a few feet of the larger ship's mainmast were all that remained as proof that the ships were there.

"Shall I ask a' thaem thaer business?" a tall, muscular Scotsman, who had taken position at Turner's side seconds earlier, enquired.

"That would be appreciated, Faolan," Turner answered. "But do not press too hard. I have to admit I am curious as to whom these people are."

Faolan MacDougall nodded, although one of his hands grasp the hilt of his claymore and the fingers of the other lay lightly upon the butt of his pistol.

MacDougall was one of the few members of Blackbeard's flotilla who had chosen to stay in Beaufort, offering his services to Turner, who had readily accepted them.

With both the damnable Family and Absalom Ravenskald angling for a piece of this hamlet, Turner needed all the muscle he could find.

"I caen vouch fer at laest one a' thaem hackit lads!" added another new arrival, one of Turner's close associates, Lewis Abernathy, a fighting Jacobite who had been forced to flee Scotland after Earl John Erskine's losses at Sheriffmuir and Preston on two consecutive November days in 1715. "Damn mae eyes if thaet is noot mae coosin Rowan!"

Turner shook his head with wonder at the strangeness of the month.

He could suddenly smell a pair of spectres as they danced upon the breeze—Opportunity and Danger, in equal measure, had arrived again Beaufort.

Two hours later, in Beaufort's only eatery—a modest, unnamed tavern that served equally modest fare—the seven hungry Scots and Robert Turner crowded around a table and ordered a round of ale, which a barmaid promptly delivered.

"Lewis," Rowan said, wrapping her arms around the nervous-looking redhead beside her, "this bae mae hoosband, Finlay Flaetcher!"

"Ack!" Lewis responded. "Ye bae a Flaetcher noo, mae lass? I suppose it could bae worse, boot I cannae ken joost hoo."

"Donnae make fun, mae doaty coosin!" Rowan shot back, her face aglow with the familiar banter that spiced the exchanges of Highland relations. "Finlay bae a barber… a vaery *wealthy* one!"

After vigorous shouts for proof, Finlay told the story of how his cousin, quartermaster John Fletcher, of the fighting ship *Whydah*, under the command of Samuel Bellamy, had sent him half his share of the spoils that came from the former slaver just before it sank off the coast of Eastham, Massachusetts, in a terrible nor'easter.

"Wael thaen," Lewis replied, raising a mug to his cousin in law. "Waelcoom tae the fam'ly!"

"Noo that we know who these two lovebirds bae, laet us hear froom ye three numpty roasters," Lewis said while raising a brow, addressing the trio of kilted, well-armed Highlanders.

The shortest but most muscular replied, "I am Teàrlach de Bruys from Clackmannan. Mae ancaestor was whispered tae bae the illegitimate bairn a' nae less thaen Robert the Bruce! I maet these big yin whaen they docked in Philadelphia an' convinced thaem tae laet mae travel wit' thaem haer."

"Thair bae royalty amoongst oos!" Lewis shouted, raising and then draining his mug. "What a' ye two yins? Bae ye royalty as weel?"

"Nae, althoo I am nae the less insulted ye cannae ken who I bae, or this lad haer as weel," the tallest of the three replied, slapping his hand upon the table in mock anger at the double affront. "Wae waer right thaer wit' ye at Sheriffmuir an' Preston on those dark an' fateful days."

"Dooncan MacDonald!" Lewis exclaimed. "An' Cnoc Douglas! Saencerest apologies tae the pair a' ye big yins!"

Faolan MacDougall raised a brow. "Douglas? Might ye bae a daescendant a' the legendaery James Douglas, knoon as the Black, who fought wit' William Wallace at Bannockburn an' rode wit' Robert the Bruce tae free Scotland froom the tyranny a' the English?"

Cnoc nodded. "That I am."

"Ye damn weel mae as weel bae royalty, thaen!" Faolan exclaimed, slapping Cnoc upon his back. "Tell Maister Turner haer the tale a' the Bruce's haert!"

"Aye, I wael," Cnoc (whose given name was Malcolm) answered, "In exchaenge fer anoother pint a' this fain an' faether-light ale!"

As the pretty, young barmaid refreshed his mug, and those of his companions, Cnoc began his tale.

Robert the Bruce, busy as he had been freeing his homeland from the brutal yoke of the English king, had never made it to the Holy Land, although he had taken an oath to do so. Upon his deathbed, increasingly concerned that he had not fulfilled his vow, the Bruce had asked Sir James to carry his heart to Jerusalem and present it at the Church of the Holy Sepulchre. Not wanting his closest friend to fear his soul's damnation during his final hours on Earth, Black Douglas had agreed, hanging the Bruce's heart in a silver box around his neck within minutes of the Bruce's death. On his way to the Holy Land, however, while resting in Castile, King Alfonso the Eleventh had convinced the Scottish knight that his best friend's heart could contentedly await its burial in the Holy Land while Douglas fulfilled a task. What better way to honor his friend and fellow warrior than by ridding Castile of the Moors?

Not long after he had agreed to do so, Black Douglas, and most of his men, died in battle against a superior Saracen army.

"What became of the Bruce's heart?" Robert Turner asked, utterly enrapt by these story-spinning Highlanders, all of whom seemed to have a notable history or lineage.

Cnoc, draining his mug, happily finished his tale, relating how Sir Simon Loch-head had retrieved both the Black and the heart of the Bruce, bringing them back to Scotland, where he arranged for the burial of the Scottish savior's heart in a casket in Melrose Abbey.

Turner, who had become pleasantly lightheaded trying to keep up with these practiced, able imbibers, raised his mug. "I welcome ye to America, the Colony of North Carolina, and most especially to Beaufort, Master Cnoc! May ye be the first of many Douglases to choose our humble but promising hamlet as your home!"

"I am pleased tae bae the fairst a' oos in Beaufort," Cnoc replied. "Thoo noot in Amaerica. Mae ooncle William sailed fer Massachusetts an' on tae Connaecticut in the middle a' the previous century."

"Most impressive!" Turner responded. "An' what of ye, our fair and noble Rowan—have ye a tale of adventure to share with us as well?"

The new arrivals all fell silent as Rowan turned away.

As Finlay slipped a comforting arm around his spouse's shoulders, Duncan, whose wounded shoulder—courtesy of a ball from Samuel Bellamy's pistol a little more than two years past in New Providence, where he was sent to kill Rob Roy MacGregor's nephew Angus—was beginning to ache, shook his head.

"It bae a tale fer anoother time," he whispered. "Fer a dark an' ugly story a' cruelty an' daespair it shall moost assuredly bae."

The former Navy SEAL lieutenant and founder/tactical commander of Kardax Corporation, Jacob Abel Black, crouched behind the Rigid Hull Inflatable Boat—or RHIB—that he and six other members of his best-of-the-best field team had used to land on Seaswan Island just after midnight, after being dropped by a SEAL Delivery Vehicle anchored several miles away.

Beside him was former chief petty officer Ismael Ramsay, who had served as Black's XO when he commanded Seal Team "D" (which only a few people with Sensitive Compartmented Information or Special Access Program clearance knew existed) before briefly commanding the unit when Black retired from the Navy to form Kardax, the security division of The Ravenskald Group.

"Gettin' a signal from some type a' electronic lockin' mechanism a klick an' a half northeast of here, Lieutenant," whispered former CPO Randall Givens, who fulfilled the role of communications and cryptography specialist for the Kardax Corporation field teams, as he had for Seal Team "D." "Bitch of it is, signal's comin' from roughly twenty feet below the surface."

"Your data do not lie, Chief Givens," Black responded. "I cannot wait to see the lore come to life. Word is, what lies beneath that modern locking mechanism is a booby-trapped treasure hole built seven hundred years ago by Templars fleeing the slaughter of their order in Paris."

"Also improved upon and used by pirates for a time," Ramsay added, enjoying talking history in these few brief moments before they locked and loaded with the knowledge they would be spilling blood within the hour.

"I've heard the name Olivier Levasseur mentioned at Quarry Peak related to the Michael Mirror and some kind a' complex cipher," Givens responded. "He was a struttin' cock of a Frenchie pirate who some secret organization put in charge a' similar works on Tortuga and at Fort Christiansvaern on the isle of Saint Croix."

Black shook his head in the moonless darkness. Givens talked too much. He also drank too much—even for a sailor. Loose lips and a penchant for bourbon got your fellow sailors killed. FUBAR'd missions and fucked up lives.

The plain fact was, he was the best at what he did, same as Ramsay, who had been rebelling as of late against the physical and psychological testing to which he had been subjected through a program called Project RUS after returning from the Middle East and resigning from the Navy.

Black had tried to get Ramsay pulled from the cutting-edge program, without success. The best he could manage was a few months' delay for Givens, who had recently received orders to report to a facility called DED 67, the home of Project RUS.

To get their hands on the money they needed to get out of the country and start a brand new life, Ramsay and Givens had recently untaken a harebrained scheme to kidnap for ransom a former Smithsonian historian and descendant of both Rob Roy MacGregor and his nephew, a pirate named Angus who had sailed with the infamous Blackbeard. Dr. Kirstine MacGregor had information in her head that the man who paid all of Kardax's considerable bills, Solomon Ravenskald, desperately wished to acquire.

Black had personally retrieved her from a storage unit in New Jersey, delivering her back to the Domestic Threat Early Assessment Unit, an elite FBI squad who had been protecting her since her rescue from the Quarry Peak Psychiatric Hospital in Ohio, where a Fourth Reich doctor had tried to break into her brain. DTEAU and Kardax had crossed paths before and would no doubt do so again, as they had the previous evening, when Ramsay and Givens had caught members of DTEAU—including Givens's son—trying to break into Quarry Peak.

They were no doubt trying to steal the Michael Mirror.

Black knew he would never know the truth about the twelve ancient, biblical objects that the Ravenskalds and something called the Star Quorum—the secret organization to which Givens had foolishly alluded—had been battling each other for centuries to possess.

He only knew that his mission tonight was clear, and threefold. Kill everyone on the island, retrieve a set of Elizabethan-era manuscripts, *The Jew of Malta* and *Doctor Faustus*, written by Christopher Marlowe, and a fist-sized, fused-shut alabaster box from the underground tunnel system, and permanently seal the tunnels with explosives.

"Ain't there another island near here with a couple a' brothers doin' endless excavations? Been on TV I think. Like ten years or somethin'... Ain't never findin' nothin' but buttons and coins."

"Yeah," Ramsay answered, inserting a thirty-round magazine into his AR-556 and adjusting its M4 buttstock. "That island was emptied even before its so-called Money Pit was found in 1799. But it's been a convenient diversion from this one."

"No need for such diversions by the time we're through tonight," their commander said to himself, strapping on a pair of Ground Panoramic Night Vision Goggles and indicating the rest of his men should do the same. "Let's go do this thing."

The work of the threefold mission they had come to Seaswan to complete took less than forty minutes. They encountered a clearly well trained but utterly taken by surprise dozen-man unit of the Scarlet-Shrouded Knights of Saint Grotth, the military arm of the Star Quorum whose history dated back to the time of the Knights of Malta. Their commander, Iain Hugh Sinclair, was the younger brother of Eleanora Sinclair. Both she and the commanding officer of the six hundred Knights of St. Grotth operating around the world (less the twelve lying dead around the vertical tunnel's entrance), Grand Master Ramón Sebastiano Rocafull, held two of the Star Quorum's seven seats.

Solomon Ravenskald, and his reptilian chief enforcer, Xavier Hearst, were no doubt sitting somewhere both expensive and exclusive, in celebration of striking this triple blow to their hated, eternal foes.

With all resistance dispatched in a lethal hail of bullets, the work of disarming the treasure hole's updated security mechanisms and retrieving the incalculably valuable items they had guarded for three hundred years was almost child's play.

Except the alabaster box was not where it was supposed to be.

"The fuck?" Black asked of Ramsay, who had gone down into the treasure hole alone to retrieve the items.

"How the fuck should I know?" Ramsay answered, handing off the crate that held the manuscripts to another member of the team. "Found the Marlowes. That was all."

Suddenly dreading the next day's meeting with Ravenskald and Hearst—especially the latter, who gave off a skin-chilling vibe Black classed as an ageless evil, but which he could not specifically pinpoint, although it seemed familiar—the Kardax CEO turned to the the unit's explosives specialist.

"Blow that treasure hole to Hell, Petty Officer Abrams. So no one gets back in. Not in a hundred years of digging, am I clear?"

Unpacking his demolition gear after a guttural "Hell yes, sir! All the way to Hell, Lieutenant!" PO3 Abrams adjusted his GPNVGs and laughed in anticipation of the spectacular sound and light show he was minutes away from giving his fellow warriors.

Standing in the shadows, watching Abrams work, Ishmael Ramsay felt the outline of the fist-sized alabaster box, which he had found beside the manuscripts as expected, through one of the rubberized nylon panels of his field pack.

Given the fact that Lieutenant Black was unable to get him out of the nightmare of Project RUS before the head-shrinking bastards could reduce his brain to mush and have him do their nefarious bidding, he had to find someone who could.

Adolphus Vellum-Verlag, London's premier purveyor of rare books and hard-to-find objects, found himself craving the warmth and clutter of his family's venerated shop in Fleet Street, which he had reluctantly left behind to sail across the Atlantic to this cold, isolated island at the request of his childhood friend and ally, Archibald Sinclair.

"You look absolutely miserable, Adolphus," Sinclair observed, watching his friend carefully turn the pages of one of two manuscripts containing the entirety of Marlowe's *Dr. Faustus*. A second version, which Adolphus had brought with him from London, sat beside it. "Although Nigredo sounds positively ecstatic to be here!"

As if in confirmation, Nigredo—Vellum-Verlag's raven—cawed robustly three times before going back to a bowl of Fox grapes and walnuts Archibald had set before him.

"I am not used to being… *outside*," the antiquities scholar responded. "I like my *things*. My taxidermied hawks and crammed and sagging bookshelves. My shop has a certain *atmosphere*, a certain *scent*, conducive to deep thinking and the solving of puzzles and ciphers. I am greater use to you and the Quorum sequestered within its walls."

"I am not in disagreement. I honestly had no choice. The Star Quorum entrusted me with the protection of these manuscripts—this *Faustus* sitting before you as well as *The Jew of Malta*—last July, courtesy of Olivier Levasseur. Samuel Bellamy and two hundred others died during Athelstan's attempt to retrieve them from the *Whydah*. We cannot risk the Ravenskalds obtaining them. Therefore, they cannot leave this island. They have been dearly paid for with an honored ally's blood."

Plucking several Fox grapes and half a dozen walnut halves from Nigredo's bowl, provoking from his companion a piercing trio of caws, Vellum-Verlag nodded. "I do understand, my friend. All the more clearly because you did exactly right by impressing upon me the need to bring this other copy." Laying the two manuscripts side by side and inviting the grand master of the Templars to sit beside him, the scholar began his lesson while biting into a grape.

"I call the Quorum's Faustus A, and this one I brought from London Faustus B." Gingerly retrieving a scrap of parchment from beneath Nigredo's bowl, which the raven was fiercely guarding, Vellum-Verlag squinted his eyes to read his scribbles. "In A, God is the third most popular word. In B, the third most popular word is Hell."

"Fascinating," Archibald answered. "One version for the Star Quorum, and another for the Ravenskalds' Mammon Lodge!"

"I agree with your assessment. Notice as well the difference in thickness. There are six hundred additional lines in Faustus B. None of them essential to the play."

"Encoded text, the same as in the Kyd!"

Vellum-Verlag nodded. "The Kyd is of special concern to me, my friend. Athelstan's quarto edition of the *Spanish Tragedy* has hidden incantations that can be used to summon the djinn."

"My God," the grand master whispered. "How many of these coded plays exist?"

"If my accounting is correct, there are five. You of course know about the Marlowes and the Kyd. Then there is the 1670 Dryden and D'Avenant adaptation of Shakespeare's *Tempest*, which they titled *The Enchanted Island*. I keep it well protected. It holds clues to finding this island and accessing its treasures, which also grew in number last July, am I correct?"

"You are. So what then is the fifth of the coded manuscripts?"

"William Mountfort's so-called *farce* of Marlowe's *Doctor Faustus*, although it is anything but. It contains one of the most powerful incantations of the many encoded in these texts. Stabbing his arm, Faustus cries, 'Lo, Mephistophilis, for love of thee, I cut mine arm, and with my proper blood Assure my soul to be great Lucifer's, Chief lord and regent of perpetual night!'"

Nigredo cawed three times in response, as if to protect them all from evil, before plucking a walnut half with his beak from between his master's fingers.

Archibald, who would normally find amusement in the raven's toddler-like behavior, growled in frustration. "I can hear Athelstan and his satanic sons speaking those words while cutting their arms in their infernal castle in Zürich! Or in Adonijah's Mammon Lodge in

Dublin. The Abraham Blade, in the possession of their ally, Lord Carteret, is particularly well suited for such dark, demonic rites, although the Ravenskalds possess an equally dangerous knife." Using the tip of his thumb to trace a rough red scar that ran the length of his cheek, which he had received from Adonijah's blade in a brief but violent encounter between them not long after he had joined the Quorum, Archibald asked, "Who possesses the Mountfort?"

Vellum-Verlag sighed. "A very stubborn competitor of mine in Fleet Street called Edmund Curll, who conducts his trade in the upstairs rooms of the Temple Coffee House. I have tried on numerous occasions—and more strenuously as of late—to impress upon him the necessity of keeping the manuscript safe. I did not insist on buying it—only protecting it. But those in my profession are distrustful by nature, and Curll has yet to acquiesce…"

"Distrust is the coin of the realm in the Quorum's work as well," Archibald said with a grunt. "Here is what I suggest. The day has nearly expired. You have done what you came to do, at least in part. Judging from the smells emanating from the kitchen, dinner preparations are well underway. What say you to putting these manuscripts aside and joining me down in the tunnels? You have certainly earned the right to look upon the rest of the treasures this island exists to protect."

As though he were answering for both himself and his master, Nigredo cawed three times, after which he spread his blue-black wings and flew into the sky.

"*Sanco tupanché, tecco du mané, té-liggo, té-liggo nupanché.*
*Sanco du mené, heelo du ché ché. Ra lei du mené, ra lei ka teché. Sanco tupanché, tecco du mané, du mané, du mané. Vibra sume ché ché. Sanco tupanché, tecco du mané. Ra lei du mené, ra lei ka teché. Ka teché, ra mené du sanco du teché ...*"

Abraxas Abriendo felt his voice begin to fail, the syllables becoming harder to articulate, which was essential for effective spell casting. Not that he could blame his throat or his tongue—he had been chanting for the better part of an hour, and not a flicker, not a glimmer of gold, had emerged from the polished surface of the coal-black Michael Mirror.

Beside him, Salvatori Fuoco, the Mage of Messina, drove his fist into his palm. "Do not give up, Abraxas! You are not summoning anything so simple as the horned god Cernunnos or the protector god Lupercus, who fought and defeated my conjured *lupi affamati* when you arrived a month ago. This is *real* magic, my student... *Stregheria* at its most ancient and powerful. You wanted to know the most secret of the words, and I have readily complied. Now concentrate, Abraxas!"

Opening his mouth to allow one of his two companions on the island, the Irishman Padraig Ó Muiris, to pour ice-cold water from a goatskin bag over and down his lips, tongue, and throat, Abraxas adjusted his grip on the mirror and intoned:

"*Sanco tupanché, tecco du mané, té-liggo, té-liggo nupanché. Sanco du mené, heelo du ché ché. Ra lei du mené, ra lei ka teché. Sanco tupanché, tecco du mané, du mané, du mané. Vibra sume ché ché. Sanco tupanché, tecco du mané. Ra lei du mené, ra lei ka teché. Ka teché, ra mené du sanco du teché!*"

"Der id bay! Right der in dah Mirrah!" Padraig exclaimed, his voice catching the attention of and drawing over the Manchurian warrior-pirate Xiang Yu, who had been practicing with his twin blades a healthy distance away.

"I see it as well!" the tattooed warrior confirmed. "The writing is perfectly clear, as if I were actually holding the manuscript here in my hands."

"Do not stop your prayer, my student," Salvatori urged. "You have nearly accomplished your task. Padraig… what does it say? Read it aloud, before it fades away. As for you, Xiang Yu… I shall ask you within moments to describe all you see around it. Study the images well."

As Abraxas continued chanting, Padraig read the words on the surface of the mirror, which began to glow with a golden, ethereal light. "Da Life an' Death a' Doctor Faustus, Made into a Fayrce. William Mountfort, 1697."

"Abraxas has done it!" Salvatori shouted. "What do you see around it, my learned Manchurian friend?"

Shielding his eyes from the fierce golden glow emanating from the obsidian mirror to better discern the manuscript's location, Xiang Yu described what he saw beyond the words. "Stone walls. A staircase of stone in the background. What looks to be an altar, carved from a slab of sarcen…"

"That is not the upstairs sitting room of the Temple Coffee House…"

"Which means that Edmund Curll is no longer in possession of the manuscript," Xiang Yu whispered with alarm.

Salvatori grasped the Manchurian's arm. "Do you see anything else? It could be in one of several infernal lodges… We need to know which one."

"There is a bloody knife upon the altar. Strips of bandages…"

"Describe the knife!"

Xiang Yu leaned in close to the mirror, the powerful golden light drawing water from his eyes. "The blade is old, but sharp. The handle is fashioned from bone. It is—"

Salvatori spit upon the ground and made the sign of the cross. "As I feared! Carteret has stolen the manuscript! He has drawn his blood with the ancient blade of Abraham. He is trying to summon Mephistopheles and Lucifer!"

Before either of Abraxas's companions could vocalize their thoughts, Salvatori gripped the obsidian mirror, just as the golden light it emanated began to turn a menacing red. Pulling the mirror out of his apprentice's hands, he yelled, "Come out of it now, Abraxas! The Blade has become aware that Xiang Yu is gazing upon it!"

Croaking out a final *"Ra sei du mené, ra sei ka teché"* to close the portal he had opened, Abraxas collapsed into the tall, fragrant grass surrounding the boulder on which he had been sitting.

Two hours later, after a hot bath and a splendid meal with his companions of *caponata* and fresh-baked bread, washed down with wine from Salvatori's personal vineyards, Abraxas felt restored to nearly full vitality.

Rising from the remains of their dinner, cups of wine, clay pipes, and oranges in hand, the two pairs of wizards and warriors left the dining hall in the Real Cittadella, strolling leisurely down a long passageway opening out onto a wide pentagonal courtyard. Choosing a stone table with semicircular benches beside St. Stephen's Bastion as their spot to pass the evening, they gazed upon the stars, filling up their lungs with the restorative Sicilian air.

"What bay the histr'y layson for da ev'nin', Mago Fuoco?" Padraig asked, stuffing his pipe with tobacco.

"If I was not as wise as I am," Salvatori said with a laugh, "I would think you actually *enjoy* my endless tales of the history of Sicily."

"Dat just moyt bay so. I have the toyme ta kill, an' it occupies me moynd."

"Very well then," Salvatori began, taking a sip of his wine and reaching for an orange. "Given Abraxas's recent success with the mirror, I shall share with you tonight a tiny portion of its story."

As his students settled in for the evening, Salvatori told them about a band of forty Normans who undertook a pilgrimage to Monte Gargano in 1016, which lay a little more than thirty-six miles from the Adriatic Sea. On the morning of the third day, as they fasted and prayed, they had a vision of Archangel Michael, who led them to a cave where they found the obsidian mirror, which the warrior of light tasked them with protecting. Continuing on their way, they headed east, arriving at Monte Sat'Angelo late the following day. While praying in the local church, the Normans met an exiled Lombardi noble called Melus of Bari who told them a tale of his brutal treatment at the hands of a band of Byzantines.

"No doubt feeling righteous and called to do good works after their encounter with Archangel Michael and being entrusted with the mirror, the pious band of Normans promised to assist the exiled noble in exacting revenge from his tormentors. The following year, having recruited a hodgepodge of knights and freelancers to fight beside them for the cause, the Normans marched to Capua, a day's ride north of Naples. Within the year, as they battled the Byzantine forces and managed several resounding victories, they came to believe the mirror was giving them strength and protection."

"They certainly were not wrong," Abraxas muttered, pulling his pipe from his lips and exhaling half a dozen rings of blue-gray smoke.

Salvatori shook his head. "Which could have gone unsaid." Draining his cup and immediately motioning for Padraig to refill it, he continued. "The campaign, which brought the Normans riches, dragged on for the next twelve years, during which they also offered protection—for a substantial fee—to pilgrims visiting the shrine of their adopted patron and protector, good old Saint Michael himself.

"In 1030, their leader, a shrewd and seasoned warrior-adventurer by the name of Rainulf Drengot, who had managed to accumulate titles along with considerable wealth, called for reinforcements to join him in Campania, where the victories he amassed increased both his reputation and the unwaivering respect and loyalty of his followers. For the next fifteen years, through his battlefield successes and a strategic second marriage to the daughter of the duke of Amalfi, he controlled a considerable portion of Italy—as well as the sacred object he came to call the Michael Mirror."

"At the end of those fifteen years, I assume that Rainulf died," Xiang Yu postulated while peeling a succulent orange. "To whom did the mirror pass?"

Salvatori smiled. "That is a tale for another time. We must regretfully head inside. It is about to rain. It shall be a needed, cleansing storm, but dangerous nonetheless."

Before his students could question his prediction—the sky was cloudless and bright—the *mago* was on his feet. A handful of moments later, the heavens darkened and opened wide with a heavy, stinging rain and reverberating crack of thunder.

As Padraig and Xiang Yu raced for the shelter of the citadel, Abraxas said to Salvatori, "You were clearly concerned about Carteret or other devotees of Mammon possessing the Mountfort manuscript. Enough to push me to the brink to find it. How did you know it was no longer where it should be?"

"It is a mage's purpose to know," Salvatori replied, raising his cowl and increasing his pace.

"Do you want us to sail to London to retrieve it?"

Salvatori shook his head, releasing a shower of droplets from the cowl. "It is essential you remain. You must continue your studies. You must be at your best. War is sailing to Sicily, and those two warriors of ours will prove to be important when it is time to defend Messina. Let us get out of the rain." As the wizards entered the citadel, the mago of Messina took his student by the arm. "I am proud of you, Abraxas. Soon we shall be equals, and I at last can rest."

Although he wanted to protest, Abraxas simply nodded and headed off to bed.

"**N**othing has changed, My Lord Carteret, in the almost seven months since ye last asked me to abandon my writing and come to work for ye as a provocateur and spy. So why then have ye summoned me? Do ye think inviting me to your home shall make the slightest difference? It shall not. My previous offer of a more than suitable replacement, however, still stands ready for me to fulfill. Position stated and offer once more made… I shall await your word in writing if ye wish to meet the man. Until that time, good day."

Lord John Carteret, governor of the Royal African Company and confidante of His Majesty, King George, pictured, for just an instant, the Abraham Blade sticking out of the throat of the pompous author and agitator standing just inside the entrance to his parlor.

A pox upon Woodes Rogers for initially suggesting that Daniel Defoe could be of service to the Crown—or, indirectly and more importantly—to the Mammon–Moloch Lodge.

Killing the insufferable bore was clearly out of the question. He was simply too well known.

Indicating an empty wing chair with his long, nearly translucent fingers, as well as several platters of enticing victuals and an open bottle of port, Carteret felt his shoulders relax as Defoe accepted the invitation.

"Good. Now we can talk like the gentlemen we are. Please do eat and drink." As Defoe declined with a wave of his hand, Carteret put down his half-filled plate and sat back in his chair. "Why now, after nearly seven months… A fair enough question and a sensible place to start. Your offer of this Jacobite agitator Nathaniel Mist in lieu of yourself upset me, Mister Defoe. Ye are the preferable man for the job. Commodore Rogers only professed his support for Mist to ease the sting of your refusal. That is simply not enough."

Leaning forward, Defoe enquired, "What news do ye have of Woodes? Has he reached the Bahamian islands?"

"Not just yet," Carteret responded. "I would guess in less than a month. I am not convinced what worked for our friend in Madagascar shall work equally well in New Providence, but Sir Humphry Morice assures me if anyone can make it work, it is Woodes."

Defoe paused a moment in careful contemplation. Then, stabbing with a silver fork a piece of broiled lamb and several roasted potatoes, which he extracted with his fingers from the tines onto an Imperial Porcelain Factory plate trimmed with golden garlands and urns, he said, "I agree with the wise Sir Humphry. Woodes has much to prove. A fortune won and lost because of the betrayal and greed of the wretched East India Company. I am sure the thought of strengthening your own company's position in that battle of the foremost traders and slavers in England is giving him more than sufficient motivation to succeed."

"One would think ye would wish to help your friend obtain that very success. Yet ye would rather write books about Jacobite castaways and scheming cattle thieves! A pox on these wretched Scots that so obsess ye, Mister Defoe! A pox on them I say!"

The books to which Carteret referred, based loosely upon the lives of Alexander Selkirk and Rob Roy MacGregor, would not be published for another year and five years, respectively.

The very thought of such celebrations of these men made Carteret want to vomit.

"Such agitation, My Lord," Defoe observed, contemplating for a moment putting at least the latter work aside and writing a novel about the fascinating man sitting here before him.

Defoe had heard whispers in the back rooms of the taverns he frequented that Lord Carteret presided as chief priest over a secret lodge that sacrificed Gold Coast slave girls and abducted or paid for children to ritually conjured, winged monsters, in league with the disreputable Ravenskalds. Defoe had been working to undermine their power with his pamphlets and speeches for nearly a decade. Over the years, he had backed the rebellions of those who sought to limit the villainous family's power—the duke of Monmouth's against his uncle James the Second's being only the most notorious—and used his gift with the pen to continue to rile both the Whigs and Tories, both of whom the Ravenskalds used in equal measure. He had aided William of Orange with the Glorious Revolution, serving until the Dutch Protestant's death as an advisor and confidante, before falling out of favor when Anne ascended the throne. Sliding quickly into debt, with his enemies closing in, his political pamphleteering had landed him in the pillory for three wearisome days, destroyed his numerous businesses, and earned him a dark and musty cell in both Fleet Gaol and Newgate Prison.

In the eyes of Lord Carteret, his most egregious actions centered on his work as a spy for Robert Harley, first earl of Oxford and earl Mortimer and former lord high treasurer, who arranged for Defoe's release from prison. He also paid the author's debts. Although Harley stood trial before a stay in the Tower of London, George saw fit to pardon him, much to Carteret's chagrin.

Word was, Defoe had anonymously published works that turned the tide for Harley, before going to Scotland to gather intelligence for the earl and his co-conspirators. Many who walked the halls of power in London credited the agitator and author with facilitating both the Treaty of Union and dissolution of the Scottish Parliament, achievements that inclined the most practical in the government to turn an unseeing eye to Defoe's less favorable pursuits.

Several minutes passed in silence as Carteret and his guest slowly emptied their plates and contemplated one another's histories and proclivities.

Selecting a second, thicker slice of lamb, Defoe proceeded to break the stalemate. "I honestly do not understand your agitation at my selection of subjects for my novels, My Lord. After all, it was Woodes—along with William Dampier—who rescued Selkirk from Más a Tierra in 1709. I need not remind ye that, at the time, they were bearers of letters of marque, in service to Queen and to Country."

Setting down his plate, Carteret vigorously shook his head. "Ye are correct. I certainly need no reminder. Ye, however, do. Selkirk is not a fit subject for celebration—he was marooned for questioning his captain!"

Defoe nearly choked on his lamb. "Questioned him regarding the seaworthiness of the vessel upon which they and many others sailed! Why, sir, are you so stubborn and unyielding!"

Kicking away the cushioned stool on which he had been resting his feet, Carteret shouted, "Because we are imperiled! A man of the Royal Navy should never question his captain! Would ye see your companion Rogers questioned by his men? I have sent him with soldiers and sailors to poison a nest of hornets. To *exterminate* their souls! These *hostis humani generis* are not merely rebels, Defoe— they have interrupted shipping, robbing men like Sir Humphry

Morice of valuable vessels and incalculable riches. Perhaps even worse, they dare to liberate the African savages—sold by their enemies, their fellow countrymen, after their capture in war, may I remind ye—before turning them to their cause with falsities and absurd claims that they are welcome comrades and *equals*. Their machinations are of international concern. After all, the prosperity of the colonies is the prosperity of Britain.

"They are a plague upon the Carolinas, where I humbly serve as Palatine—the most powerful amongst the venerable Lords Proprietors. Ye supported the illegitimate Monmouth. It was his father, Charles the Second, who rewarded my ancestor, Sir George, with lands in the American colonies in exchange for his support in restoring Charles to the throne."

Defoe, growing increasingly bored, whispered, "I am well aware of your family history—and the history of England."

"Are ye aware as well that this rogue who calls himself Blackbeard has struck a deal with Governor Eden and his chief justice partner in Bath? I intend to eradicate this nest of vipers in the Albemarle and beyond, just as Rogers is tasked with doing in the Bahamas, although I shall not deign to lure them in with pardons!"

At the mention of Blackbeard and the Albemarle, Defoe's interest, for the first time since Carteret's original offer almost seven months before, was well and truly piqued.

"Is it true," he began, leaning forward in his chair, "that there is a band of provocateurs at work in the Albemarle, known collectively as the Family, and furthermore, that this cabal is also in league with Spotswood in Virginia? Before ye answer, My Lord Carteret, I wish to know this as well—does this spirited and dangerous alliance, if it does indeed exist, work on behalf of the Ravenskalds, as ye yourself are rumored to do?"

Carteret laughed, doing so in such a way that Defoe was certain that the answer to each of his questions was an unembarrassed, exquisitely prideful *yes*.

"Then we indeed have much to discuss," the author and agitator said, leaning back in his chair and reaching for the bottle of port. "For I have an obsessive interest in the Ravenskalds—and so does Nathaniel Mist."

*Someone has been exquisitely, deliciously, lethally naughty, and I do not mean you, Andrew Colson.*

Although nothing he attempted succeeded in controlling the volume of the voice of the exasperating entity that called itself the Angel Falling Upward both within the room and within the confines of his skull, Colson, newly arrived from London, tugged on his earlobes and shook his head, with a level of desperate vigor that caused his vision to blur.

*Easy, My Good Lord Colson… you humans break so easily, and I still have use of you.*

Colson ignored an urge to flee to the adjoining chamber, which the fifth earl of Exeter had labeled the Heaven Room, with its ceiling full of gods and goddesses, abandoning this one—on the landing of the Hell Staircase—whose access point was a painting of a great grey cat with a jagged-fanged, unnaturally gaping mouth and swine-like snout. Desperate for even partial relief, Colson pressed his palms to his ears and closed his eyes against the barrage of frightening images around him.

"I have not rushed to Burghley House with Abenaa," he shouted, "leaving my fellows in the United Free Mason Grand Lodge to clean up and dispose of the bits of torn flesh and innards that had once been Devon Ross, to suffer your taunts and sharp remarks!"

The Angel Falling Upward cackled, hissed, and shifted his ethereal body parts, causing Colson to gag.

He felt as though the infernal entity was forcing his forked and slender tail deeply down his throat.

*Look at the artwork upon the walls around you, Andrew Colson… Antonio Verrio's visions of a hooded, sickle-wielding shepherd herding tortured, unrepentant souls into Hell is not so far from the truth… My broken brother Lucifer has taken to wearing such a hood to hide his steaming, red-tinged tears. His ill-considered rebellion went no better than the Old Pretender Stuart's currently is…*

After casting a glance through almost fully closed eyelids at the doorway, within which stood John Cecil, sixth earl of Exeter, and the Ashanti child Abenaa, who had at last reawakened several miles from the earl's estate, Colson opened wide and focused his eyes.

Searching amongst the images of those newly arrived in Hell for a glimpse of the brown-eyed, raven-haired visage that the Angel Falling Upward preferred to manifest as, Colson shivered at the thought of how close he had come to walking amongst them when he served the Mammon Lodge.

After scanning dozens of forlorn figures, there the Angel was, standing between a bronze-colored woman with an eye in the middle of her forehead, snakes for hair, and breasts lacking nipples, and a naked, helmeted soldier holding a sword above his head.

Just above the palms of the Angel Falling Upward's hands floated the disfigured face of Devon Ross.

*My genitals swell with pride over what you have done, Abenaa. Sending this bastard to face a flaming eternity through the summoning of the jumbee was shrewd—especially because you more than anyone know that until the Select assuage it and lure it back into its cage, carnage shall know no bounds and your enemies will continue to gorge upon the resulting carrion at their feasts.*

"The Select?" Colson enquired, shifting his position so his body was between the Angel and Abenaa, blocking the former from seeing the latter. "It would be helpful to have their names."

Squeezing Ross's face with his gnarled and knife-nailed fingers, causing it to scream and then dissolve, the Angel Falling Upward released a thunder-like laugh. *If names are what you require, names are what you shall hear! There is, of course, Abenaa—our heroine of the hour. It was a gift to her and not to you that I healed her even before you arrived. Then there is Caesar, as I told you when last we met in this room. There is Abraxas Abriendo, whose skill with the Michael Mirror improves daily in Messina, and his warrior companions—the Manchurian and Irishman. A pirate called Joseph Stanton, who has been tempted, tested, and tempered these past three years for reasons far beyond the day's events, is also central to the game. There also is one other.*

Colson raised his hands as a shield against the speaking of his name, to which the Angel Falling Upward responded by laughing, burping, and farting all at once.

*Such ego, Andrew Colson! Although the assumption is not without reason. You too have been tempted, tested, and tempered these past three years. Abenaa may have cleansed you, but the beckoning blood of Mammon, having once made love to your organs, makes you far too susceptible to renewed and redoubled corruption to risk positioning you upon the front lines of the war. Forever fouled are your four humors, my frightened friend! The seventh of the Seven Select is a young, in-the-process-of-maturing Highlander, bearer of a blue-gemmed dragon-claw ring, wielder of a quill, and descendant of the Clans of the Mists. He still has much to learn, but the fae took an oath to protect him millennia before he was born. The choosing of his name was nae an accident, as those of his clan would tell you. Angus, the son of Dagda. The young god called Mac Oc.*

"Then my work for the Quorum is done?" Andrew Colson whispered, his mind in a whorl as he processed what he had heard.

*Not quite yet, my friend.* The Angel Falling Upward climbed upon and beyond the heads of a quartet of horses, moving amongst the damned until he stood beside the winged and skeletal, sickle-wielding Reaper. *Although those in charge of making such weighty decisions have already chosen a leader to guide the Seven Select in their work in the months to come, your Masonic Lodge is an essential counterbalance to those that worship Mammon and Moloch... As you did today, you have thwarted several times their attacks and foiled the Ravenskalds' attempts to acquire the Baptist Bowl.*

Pulling the sickle from the Reaper's bony hand, the Angel spun it over his head with blinding speed half a dozen times before pointing it toward the garish feline's open mouth. *Sir John Cecil... your time of mourning for your son has concluded. You must draw upon the infamous spymaster skills of your ancestors, William and Robert. Although it was the mage John Dee, using the Michael Mirror, who saw the gunpowder plot four years before it occurred, it was Robert who foiled the Catholic conspirators in the tunnels beneath the Parliament. You shall be of similar value to the wizard Abriendo and future possessors of the mirror.*

Returning the sickle to the Reaper and pushing through the masses of hellbound figures, the Angel Falling Upward perched himself upon the pediment of a multicolumned, garlanded entrance to a temple.

*I have other pressing matters to which I must attend. One thing more before I go... Your nefarious nemesis, Andrew—whose name I shall not utter... has procured the textual means to call my broken* brother Lucifer and our Teutonic relation Mephistopheles. The former will not answer, broken as he is, but Mephisto likely will. Athelstan Ravenskald has sent out a call as well, to one of my oldest, strongest foes.

You are truly in the soup.

Careful you do not drown.

*T̶he seventh of the seven. The wielder of the quill.*

*Daring deeds your daddy Dagda has chosen for his one true son, Mac Oc.*

*Destiny is delicious, like nectar on the tongue…*

Awakening with a start, Angus "Quill" MacGregor drew his sword and looked around the room he shared with Joseph Stanton.

As always was the case, the two of them were alone.

The dreams and visions that had increasingly invaded his sleep and idle moments had started as little more than flickers and flashes of random voices and images when he first began to experience them the previous October.

Angus had initially attributed these ghostly invasions to the knock on the head he had sustained during his fight in the mud with Joseph when their respective captains had anchored in Philadelphia. That and his reuniting with Ailish and receipt of the mystical dragon-claw ring he now never removed from his finger, a gift from his murdered mother arranged from beyond the grave.

Running his finger over the curved claws of the scaly dragon's paw, which held a sky blue, square-cut stone that Israel Hands had informed him was tanzanite, which one could only obtain from the foothills of Kilima-Njaro in eastern Africa, Angus reached for his father's cloak. Grasping the oak leaf and acorn brooch that signified loyalty to the House of Stuart—a loyalty that had cost his parents their lives—he lay back in his bed and closed his eyes, anxious to get more sleep before the start of the day.

It was not to be.

Following a series of knocks on the door, Angus heard Blackbeard's voice.

"Time ta rise, ye scalawags… Angus, ye got some visitors I am sure ye wish ta see!"

Swinging his legs over the side of his bed as Joseph released a frustrated groan and yanked his blanket over his head, Angus wondered for a second if one of the visitors might be Ailish. He quickly dismissed the thought as foolish. She was in New Providence, serving meals at the Fatted Calf.

Who then was here to see him?

Minutes later, he had an answer.

"Dooncan MacDonald!" he exclaimed, stepping out of the modest house Blackbeard had rented on Plum Point for several of his senior crew. Grasping the arm of Ailish's cousin, he asked, "Bae ye a dream?"

Taking the man whom he knew to be his eventual cousin-in-law in a firm and hearty embrace, Duncan replied, "If I wair, would I say this? Haer's tae oos!"

Letting out a hearty laugh, Angus answered, "Wha's like oos?"

"Gey few, an' thair a' deid!"

Duncan was joined in the response by his two companions, one of whom Angus recognized from home.

"Malcolm Douglas! Coom all the way froom Glen Shira joost tae haev a look at mae handsoom face?" Angus asked, embracing the muscular Highlander. As they stepped apart, Angus had a realization. "Yer sister Isla… I haev seen hair in mae dreams!"

"I am nae surprised," Malcolm answered. "She bae a skillful *gorm-shuil*, possessed a' the two sights wit' hair diff'raent colored eyes."

Angus nodded. "She has *an da shealladh*… Able tae see inta the realms a' man an' fae. Is that why ye haev coom?"

"Who knoos the ways a' the fae, or a *gorm-shuil* laek mae sister. Dooncan offered mae advaenture, an' I happily accaepted."

"An' who bae this yin haer?" Angus asked, gazing at their companion.

"Teàrlach de Bruys froom Clackmannan," the stranger responded. Putting out his hand, he added, "Sailed wit' these lads froom Philadaelphia earlier this yaer."

"Philadaelphia? Wae missed each oother bae a matter a' moonths! I was thaer at the aend a' October. An' so was Ailish."

Duncan smiled wide. "Fates bae fain, she found ye! They whair smilin' wide whaen they brought ye taegether in sooch an unimaginable place. Smilin' laek I bae noo. Is mae coosin in the house?"

Angus shook his head. "Workin' in a taevern on New Providence. We whair last taegether in May." Tightening the knot of his long plaid headscarf and squaring his bright red tricorne atop it, the pirate known as Quill motioned to a line of smoke rising from the shoreline. "That bae braekfast cookin'. I hope ye haev brought an appetite!

Two wee bairns name a' Louis an' Caesar bae learnin' hoo tae cook."

Half an hour later, the four Highlanders' bellies slightly bulging and their pipes making grey-blue smoke, Duncan caught Angus up on all that had happened at home since his return from New Providence. Beginning with the saga of Finlay and Rowan, including their newfound wealth and move to Beaufort, he moved on to the details of Rob Roy's kidnapping and escape, and James's attempt to have his way with Ailish.

Seeing Angus's look of surprise, Duncan's face grew dark. "Mae coosin dinnae tael ye aboot James noo, did she?"

Instinctively placing one hand upon the hilt of his sword and the other on the handle of his knife, Angus shook his head. "I nae knoo whaen I shall naext bae in the Highlands, boot the fairst day I am hoom weel bae that bastaird's last."

Duncan whistled low. "Hae bae yer ooncle's eldest. Hae is protected, or I would haev ended the bastaird maeself."

"Mae ooncle?" Angus spat. "The one who ordered ye tae kill mae? Rob Roy MacGregor maens less than shite tae mae noo."

"Strong words ta speak over breakfast and a pipe, Mister Quill." Blackbeard, flanked by Louis and Caesar, was approaching the group of smoke-shrouded Scotsmen from the beach. Putting his hands on Angus's shoulders, he said, "Stow yer talk a' vengeance fer now. I want ta meet yer friends. After all, they shall be my guests at my wedding this afternoon!"

Angus raised a brow, all thoughts of James and his uncle forgotten. "A waedin'? Tae Miss Godwin, whom ye only maet joost three short weeks agoo?"

Blackbeard nodded. "I nay have the time ta get ta know her any better. An' what more could I find? She is intelligent, kind, an' an absolute pleasure ta gaze upon. Her uncle, Governor Eden, is anxious for her ta have the security that a marriage ta me shall give her."

"This bae quite the moornin'!" Angus said, raising high his mug of grog. Once the rest of the Highlanders' mugs were also in the air, they said to Blackbeard in unison, "*Lang may yer lum reek, maet*!"

❝❝Why not give the *Lark* to me, instead of to the French? Am I not deserving? Have I somehow not served ye well?"

Charles Vane, not yet ready to answer, glanced up and down at his brash, calico-draped, meticulously coifed and bearded quartermaster, Jack Rackham.

All of that just-so finery was hiding a ruthless heart. Were Vane more inclined to take the easier path, the bloodless and peaceful path, he might give in without question to Rackham's not-unreasonable request.

But he was not overly concerned with what was difficult, although it drank its weight in blood.

"It is not a mattah a' deservin' nor the qualities a' ya service, Mistah Rackham," the captain answered. "I ain't interested in commandin' a flotilla, an' propah practice demands we give them Frenchies a ship in exchange fer theirs, seein' as they were the very pictchah a' cooperation."

Only hours before, Rackham had spotted a French brigantine of twenty guns, urging Vane to give it chase. Tired of the *Lark*'s limited capacity and number of cannon, Vane had agreed, readily overlooking his quartermaster's breach of protocol in suggesting what ships they pursue.

Upon seeing the pirates' hoisted Jolly Roger, the brigantine's captain had immediately hove to and lowered her sails—the nautical sign of surrender.

Negotiations were just as easy. Vane would keep the brigantine and all that it possessed, and, after the transfer of the *Lark*'s eight guns to his new command, the Frenchies could have her in exchange.

It was at that moment the trouble with Rackham had begun, although Calico at least had the good sense to be discreet, pursuing his captain into his new quarters on the brigantine instead of speaking his mind in front of the French captain and the ships' two crews.

"I have been of great assistance to ye, Captain," Rackham pressed. "On the twenty-third of June, it was I who led the boarding party—under rather hot conditions—that secured the *Saint Martin* and her considerable riches off the coast of Hispaniola. Need I remind ye, sir, that her sugar and her indigo, her brandy, claret, and wine, brought abundant coinage and comfort to the men of your command?"

*Show me them pointed teeth, Mistah Rackham. Show me again 'ow ye came ta bitest the world.*

*An' gnaw on yer captain's ass.*

Rackham did just that.

"I was also essential in the capture of the *Richard and John*."

Vane nodded with excess vigor, growing weary of the lesson and the sound of Rackham's voice. "An', just last week, five ships more ta boot. I am well aware. Shall I name 'em, Jack?" Vane retrieved and opened his logbook. "I keep very careful recahds... there was the *Drake*, undah Draper. Wine and rum in that one. John Fredd's *Ulstah*, out a' New York. *The Eagle* from... lemme see—Rhode Island. Sugah, bread, an' two big barrels a' nails. Then there was the *Dove* undah Cap'n William 'Arris an' the *Lancastah*, captained by Neal Walker, whose fathah Granpa 'Ornigold once ran offa New Providence. Speakin' a' 'Ornigold, we done gave it good ta the poxy, pissin' nutta as a' late—ran 'im off 'is shitey island base, 'is mini republic a' traitorous 'untahs, did we not? An' ye was richly thanked an' even more richly rewarded fer ya service ta the cause."

Slamming shut the logbook to show he was changing tack, Vane looked hard into Rackham's eyes. "'Ere's where ye an' me are *not* in accord, my ambitious quartahmastah. What ye possess in piratin' skills ye sorely lack in patience. Guvnah Rahjahs will soon be arrivin'. We need ta send 'im a message. I need ya 'ere upon our newly christened *Ranjah* when things are gettin' 'ot."

Calico listened closely—aware his captain's reasons were sound.

"An' after we send a message ta Splinter Face? What then shall we do?"

Vane produced a nasty smile. He had won the skirmish without spilling any blood.

"Up ta ye an' me tahgethah, Calico Jack. South Americah? Join wit' Edward England over in Africa? Make a bargain wit' Blackbeard in Bath? Gather up a flotilla a' ships an' set ourselves up in New Providence, sendin' Rahjahs back ta London wit' 'is tail between 'is legs? I likes the last the best, if I tells ya true."

Calico matched his captain's smile, certain that he was walking away from their verbal contest as its undisputable victor.

"The Frenchies are awaitin' us, Mistah Rackham. What say we finish that pressin' business an' put this beauty through 'er paces?"

Holding the door for Vane, Calico gave him a nod.

He was looking forward indeed to seeing what she could do.

Captain Ellis Brand, commander of the thirty-gun Fifth Rate HMS *Lyme*, was returning to his ship from lunch at the local tavern when he spotted two dozen surly-seeming men climbing out of longboats.

No question, they were pirates.

Brand had received a report a few weeks earlier that a pirate flotilla had entered Topsail Inlet in North Carolina and had, within hours, descended on the town of Beaufort.

Setting his sights on two unimpressive-looking men standing apart from the rest, Brand approached. "What business have ye and your poxy fellows in Kiquotan?"

Glancing at the bow of HMS *Lyme*, where several Royal Marines had assembled at the tone of their captain's question, one of the two men before him raised his hands in the air. When his companion failed to follow his lead, the first man lowered one of his arms just enough to elbow the second in the ribs.

"We want no trouble, Cap'n," the first man said, as his companion raised his arms while cursing him under his breath. "We come to take the pardon. Our piratin' days are done. We crave an honest existence."

Brand smiled as more than twenty additional pirates inched their way toward the conversation, while another two dozen sailors and marines gathered in the bow of the *Lyme*.

"Thank ye for your honesty. Ye may lower your arms and relax. From what location have ye journeyed to us in Kiquotan?"

The second pirate, clearly annoyed at his companion for so readily betraying their (ex-)profession, replied, "We run aground off a' Beaufort ta the south. Lost two a' our ships, includin' our flagship, under Edward Thache. As me chatty matey here has already happily tol' ya, we comes ta takes the pardon from yer lov'ly gov'nah an' begin a life ashore."

Brand was pleased how this was going. "Did ye quarrel wit' Captain Thache?"

A third man now approached. "We did not," he said. "It was time to end our arrangement, and we did so without rancor."

Brand stepped closer, aware that the crowd of steadily encroaching pirates and the crewmen on the *Lyme* all slightly tensed as he did so. "Ye talk like a leader, sir. Might I have your name, as well as those of these two here?"

The late arrival nodded. "I am William Howard, former quartermaster on the *Queen Anne's Revenge* under Blackbeard. These two men are Edward Salter an' Richard Stiles."

"Thank ye, Mister Howard, for being so forthcoming. It would be helpful for our accounting and expeditious processing of your pardons were ye to share with me the following particulars. How many of ye were on the ships at Topsail Inlet? How many are currently in Virginia, and how many more shall we expect in the days to come to take His Majesty's generous pardon from our, as Mister Stiles describes him, lovely governor? It would also be helpful to know how many remain in Beaufort. Have they ships? Have they cannon? What are their intentions?"

Brand sensed hesitation. The pirates were suddenly reticent, sending shadowy glances back and forth. Stiles shuffled his feet and Salter lowered his head.

"Simple accounting, gentlemen," Brand said with a broader smile, spreading his arms and turning up his palms to show his peaceful intentions. "Assuring the governor that ye are eager and willing to be faithful citizens of this colony and loyal subjects to your king in England are required for a pardon. Surely ye were aware..."

Howard nodded. "We were. Was three hundred an' twenty who went ashore at Beaufort. Some went up ta Bath. Some ninety are here for the pardon. Another two hundred an' thirty have already made arrangements to continue their piratin' ways. As for ships, two small sloops, a dozen cannon between them. One may have already raised anchor for the Indies."

Brand raised a curious brow. "Who commands that vessel?"

Howard laughed. "Depends on the hour an' the circumstances, Captain. Major Stede Bonnet is the captain a' record, although he is often relieved a' his duties after another a' his inevitable blunders. His quartermaster changes almost ev'ry month."

"This has been most helpful, Mister Howard. I think it is safe to say that, as a representative of His Majesty's Royal Navy, I can assure ye a pleasant stay in Kiquotan, also known as Hampton. Find lodging as best as ye can, preferably before the sun sets.

Tomorrow morning, arrangements shall be made for ye all to go to Williamsburg, thirty-eight miles to the north, to meet with Governor Spotswood."

Clapping his hands together, Howard answered, "Splendid! We do look forward to it, Captain—, ah... I did not catch yer name..."

"I am Captain Ellis Brand, of the thirty-gun Fifth Rate HMS *Lyme*, sitting at anchor before ye."

Releasing a long, low-pitched whistle of admiration, Howard replied, "An' a fine, fair ship she be! I hope I never give ye reason to provoke her mighty ire, nor to be a guest in chains in her dark and dismal hold."

As Howard, Salter, and Stiles turned and rejoined their group, Brand felt the hairs on the backs of his hands begin to flutter. He did not trust this Mister Howard. He did not trust him at all.

"What was that about?"

Brand recognized the voice. Turning to Lieutenant Robert Maynard, second in command of the HMS *Pearl*, a forty-two-gun Fourth Rate, he answered, "A testing of the waters. A reconnoiter of the enemy. Those men claim they seek the pardon."

"Ye do not believe them?"

"What I believe, Lieutenant Maynard, is that, once ye are a pirate, ye shall die while being the same, no matter the pardons or penance ye claim."

Maynard, sensing intrigue, ran his hand along his chin. "So what do ye propose?"

Motioning for Maynard to walk with him—he was sensing dozens of the bastards' eyes upon them—Brand replied, "I shall write the Admiralty immediately, urging them to notify and otherwise prepare the governor for the arrival two days hence of nearly one hundred of Blackbeard's pirates. I shall also send word to the Family in North Carolina that I wish to know what is happening in Bath and about the status of the pirates who remain with Blackbeard."

Maynard clicked his tongue. "That is all impressively shrewd of ye, Captain Brand, although, with all due respect for your plan, I suggest an additional action—call it a wise precaution. Request of the Admiralty, as well as of the governor, that any former pirate, regardless of the status of his pardon, be required to surrender his arms to a military official or a justice of the peace upon entering a town."

Glancing at the clusters of pirates around the longboats and outside the taverns and brothels that lined the bustling docks, the captain nodded. "I see what ye are saying. Not one of them goes unarmed, and almost to a man, they are arrogantly sporting both a pistol and a blade. I shall see it done. And I am thinking one thing more, if the Admiralty shall agree."

Maynard raised a brow and smiled. "Do not keep me in suspense!"

"If they gather in groups of more than three, or fail to relinquish their arms as requested, they shall be thrown in gaol and their pardons fast revoked."

"Then the gaols will soon be bursting."

"One can only hope."

Calico Jack Rackham had fallen suddenly, deeply in love. Or, at the very least, in lust. He knew that it would cost him—the girl who claimed his heart was already the wife of another—but for now, it did not matter.

"Do ya 'ear me, Jack?" Captain Vane was asking, in a tone that made it clear that he had already asked the question several times.

"I do, sir, yes, I do," Quartermaster Rackham responded, not shifting his eyes from the redheaded beauty in the corner who had told him her name was Anne.

Whispered it slowly in his ear, was what the vixen did. Then, after it was there, she pushed it in with her tongue, to be sure he would never forget it.

"Then why do ye sit 'ere like a barnacle upon a brigantine? Guvnah Rahjahs 'as fine'ly arrived, an' we 'as plenty a' pressin' work that we needs ta be about."

Seeing Anne's slim-shouldered husband, a failed sailor turned cut-rate pirate by the name of James Bonny, grasp her by the arm and all but drag her up the stairs to one of the half dozen rooms the Widow Mackenzie rented out to help her make ends meet, Jack Rackham scowled and spat.

If it were not for the pressing need to lessen the impact of Woodes Rogers's arrival by ruffling his feathers, Jack would have followed the Bonnys upstairs. Anne looked none too happy about being muscled by her husband, whom she had told Jack had expected to inherit her father's estate when he had asked for her hand in marriage.

Instead, unhappy with the match, her father had immediately thrown her out.

She was a damsel in need of rescue, and Jack was primed, cocked, and ready to be her pistol when she was ready to pull the trigger and leave her marriage behind.

"There's the haughty bahstahd now!" Charles Vane hissed, plunking himself down in a chair next to Jack's and, in the process, ending Rackham's violent and sexual revery. "I can see why it is ya calls the shitey blightah Splintah Face!"

Vane and Rackham were not the only ones gawking at the disfigured visage of Governor Rogers, who had taken a musket ball to the left-hand side of his face while privateering in the Pacific years before. The damage had been severe. He had lost a handful of teeth, and a length of his lower jaw. A surgeon had to remove the offending ball from where it had lodged in the roof of his mouth.

Seven seas scuttlebutt had it that Rogers had only realized he had *swallowed* the missing bit of bone after he had sought relief from another physician some days later for what he had blandly described as *intestinal discomfort*.

Rogers was legendary for more than the spiderlike scars and missing teeth that marred a considerable portion of his otherwise handsome face. After years of successful encounters in eastern Africa with the local kingdom of pirates between Madagascar and Mozambique, while bearing a letter of marque, Rogers had found himself in conflict in Sumatra with a different scale of merciless pirate kingdom—the Indian Ocean powerhouse, the East India Company.

With the refusal of its governing board to honor their contracts with him, due to his daring to also deal with the Dutch, Rogers found himself close to penniless, despite the success of his book, *A Cruising Voyage Around the World: First to the South-Seas, Thence to the East-Indies, and Homewards by the Cape of Good Hope. Begun in 1708 and Finish'd in 1711*. The pressing threat of poverty giving him an additional burst of courage, Rogers returned to Madagascar, passing out pardons to mitigate its problems with pirates.

The success of this risky, unprecedented approach to the growing pirate problem had caught the attention of not only His Majesty, King George, who immediately claimed the idea as his own, but of director of the Bank of England and foremost slaver Humphry Morice and Royal African Company director and Carolina Palatine John Carteret. Lord Carteret, in August of 1717, had been the one to secure for Rogers the title of first royal governor of the Bahamas.

Amassing the considerable financing required for the endeavor, part of which he used to acquire seven ships and recruit the hundreds of men necessary to sail and protect them, had taken the better part of nine months and tested every ounce of Rogers's considerable patience.

At least the voyage to the Bahamas had been without event. His seven ships and their escort of three Royal Navy vessels, currently anchored in the harbor, had suffered not a scratch.

As Rogers addressed the room, assuring everyone in attendance—citizens and pirates alike—that an era of prosperity was soon to begin and reading verbatim His Majesty's Commission, Vane and Rackham slipped out of the Fatted Calf and headed for the *Ranger*, the imminent making of mischief foremost on their minds.

Unaware of their exit, Rogers announced his intention to form a governing council, and to appoint both a secretary-general and chief justice as soon as he had identified a suitable set of candidates.

In other words, he intended to bring law and order to the Bahamas. Law, order—and religion.

"I have brought with me, thanks to the generosity of the Society for Promoting Christian Knowledge, abundant supplies of bibles, prayer books and hymnals, and wooden crosses. They shall be available in my office in the fort beginning tomorrow morning for any person who wants them, free of charge. It is, however, my humble request that ye use them for your improvement."

Glancing around the room, Rogers called out for Vincent Pearse, captain of the HMS *Phoenix*, who was supposed to be in command of the island. After one of Nassau's few remaining honest merchants informed him that Pearse had abandoned New Providence in April after nearly losing his vessel during an encounter with the pirate captain Vane, which he subsequently grounded during his hurried return to New York, Rogers demanded to know exactly who it was that *was* in charge since Pearse's inexcusable absence.

When no one offered an answer, Rogers stormed out of the Fatted Calf, the red in his face making his scars look all the more ghastly and severe to those he pushed from his path.

Rogers's reign was starting roughly, but he would quickly ensure its success.

Fingering the space where the swallowed length of his lower jaw should be, he headed for his flagship, the forty-gun *Delicia*, a gift from the East India Company, for whom he had agreed to rid this place of pirates.

That was his foremost talent, for which the powerful paid for with gold.

Opportunity was about to abound, and "Gran'pa" Benjamin Hornigold was ready to seize his share.

He had been standing on the damaged and crumbling ramparts of the fort he had devoted years of his life to defending and rebuilding since the time of Queen Anne's War when Woodes Rogers's impressive flotilla had arrived in the harbor. He could not but smile at the man's audacity as two of his ships—the governor later told him their names were the *Shark* and the *Rose*—fired a cannonball each to announce his auspicious arrival.

*Auspicious to him*, Hornigold thought, his smile quickly diminishing. *Such a display of bravado by agents sent by the Crown rarely meets with favor here in Nassau.*

Now, two days later, he was standing in the meeting room outside his former quarters in the fort, which Rogers had commandeered the morning after his arrival.

*If these walls could talk*, Hornigold was thinking as he assessed the famous, disfigured navigator, *how the governor's ears would burn!*

"Ye have done an exemplary job of securing pardons and keeping the peace in the face of Captain Pearse's sudden, indefensible departure," Rogers began, his hand pressing down on a stack of hundreds of pardons. "Although I am curious as to why ye did not make yourself available the day that I arrived. Why was I required to summon ye, Captain Hornigold?"

Hornigold had asked himself that question half a dozen times in the previous hour—ever since the moment he had received word from one of Rogers's endless parade of underlings that he was to appear before the governor as soon as possible in Hornigold's former headquarters.

"I did not wish to appear over-eager," Hornigold replied, confident that what he was saying was by and large the truth. "As ye know, I have fought for New Providence for more than a decade. I have seen to the fort as best as I could, through war and the Crown's neglect. I have navigated half a dozen bitter rivalries and violent struggles for power…"

Rogers nodded. "I know ye lost control of this island and your dream of a pirate republic, to Samuel Bellamy, through the machinations of Olivier Levasseur. Let us begin with him. Have ye any idea of his whereabouts?"

"He sailed for the Spanish Main the end of April. Heard he was considering a go at Africa if his endeavors there went well. Levasseur has always been restless. Ambitious. Unpredictable."

Rogers shook his head, procuring several pieces of parchment from a satchel on his desk. "Unpredictable indeed. And damnably hard to catch." He glanced at the papers, although Hornigold could tell it was just for show. Rogers wanted to demonstrate to a potential rival his ability to stay connected to and informed by larger forces by producing official documents. "On 13 June, off the coast of La Blanquilla, he barely escaped the wrath of Captain Francis Hume, commander of the thirty-two-gun Fifth Rate HMS *Scarborough*."

Hornigold nodded. He too had access to information from well-connected sources, even if he lacked the papers to prove it. "I am well aware of the formidable Captain Hume. I have it on sound authority that, soon after, he headed, with two prizes—the *Blanco* and *Boneta* and more than a dozen shackled pirates—to Saint Christopher's isle, arriving the end of June."

Rogers raised a brow. "Ye stay impressively well informed."

Hornigold was just getting started. "After being refused accommodations for a trial for the better part of a week, Hume took his prisoners on to Nevis. Although the administrators there declared without debate that the *Blanco* was legal spoils, they refused to accept the prisoners or agree to hold a trial. At which time Hume returned to his base of operations on Barbados, anchoring in Carlisle Bay, where Governor Lowther and his collector have been at loggerheads with Hume over the release and sale of the *Blanco* ever since."

"Most impressive, Captain," Rogers responded, motioning to one of his servants to place a tray containing four mugs and a bottle of rum beside the stack of pardons. "Rampant greed on the part of the other colonial governors… I shall not let them be an obstacle to my plans. I understand that Charles Vane's former mentor, Henry Jennings, has taken the pardon and is currently in the employ of the governor of Bermuda."

"Jennings and Bennett have known each other for quite a long time," Hornigold replied, his mind alight with the mysterious implications of two men and four mugs. "He and Vane intensely dislike each other. I can assure ye, Governor Rogers—Captain Jennings remains a steadfast ally."

Sitting back in his chair, his finger unconsciously probing the scars on his lower face, Rogers grunted. "Assurances are easy to make, Captain Hornigold, but harder to guarantee. What assurances can ye give me about your former mentee, Edward Thache—the rogue who calls himself Blackbeard?" Not giving Hornigold a chance to speak, Rogers continued. "I shall save ye the trouble of trying, since ye shall not succeed in providing them—and here is why. Thache has struck a deal with Governor Eden in North Carolina. I do not know the details, but some of his former crew crossed our path as we neared the Bahamas."

Hornigold did his best not to show the incredible surprise he felt at hearing the news of Edward's new alliance. He never imagined his former protégé would stoop to aligning himself with a royal representative.

Then again, North Carolina was a well-known den of scoundrels, freebooters, rebels, and degenerates, and Hornigold no longer knew nor understood the motivations of the man who called himself Blackbeard, whose outsized anger at the world drove him to make ill-considered, unpredictable, and increasingly selfish decisions.

"I am sorry to have missed the silversmith turned pirate Paulsgrave Williams," Rogers said, motioning for his servant to go to the door. "I am extremely interested in his dealings in Rhode Island."

Before Hornigold could answer, two men he immediately recognized entered the office and approached him.

"Good day to ye, Ben," John Cockram said with a smile, not at all surprised to see Hornigold in attendance. "I believe ye know Nicholas Woodall?"

The captain of the converted merchant sloop *Wolf* extended his hand to Hornigold, which the former commodore of the Republic of Pirates firmly clasped. "Indeed I do." Turning to his host, whose servant was pouring generous portions of rum into the mugs—there being four of them now made sense—Hornigold asked, "What is the purpose of this meeting, Governor Rogers?"

"I have a proposition, gentlemen. Please help yourself to a drink." Once the three men had done so, Rogers grasped the remaining mug and stood. "I am in need of your assistance. The three ships provided by the Royal Navy will not remain indefinitely in the harbor in New Providence. The loss of Captain Pearse is an unforeseen blow to my plans. Although myself and His Majesty are both pleased that ye have taken the pardon, I now require more."

"Exactly what are ye askin'?" Cockram enquired.

Rogers, taking a healthy pull from his mug, replied, "I wish to commission the three of ye to serve as pirate hunters. I know that each of ye has suffered at the hands of the men I am determined to bring to justice—Edward Thache, Stede Bonnet, Olivier Levasseur, Edward England, Christopher Condent, and most especially Charles Vane—the list goes on, but these are the ones at the top."

Each of the three men before him took a silent sip from his mug.

It was suddenly clear to Rogers that getting their agreement would not be as easy as he had imagined.

Perhaps he should have talked to each of them alone.

Committed to getting his way before he allowed them to leave the room, Rogers made the decision to start with the one they all called Grandpa. "Commodore Hornigold had his command, nay, his dream of a true republic, stolen from him upon this very island—by some of the rogues upon this list! Nicholas Woodall, ye have made your frustrations with your current situation clear to me in private. And ye, John Cockram… I happen to know your father Joseph's ship was wrongfully seized by pirates—and further, that Vane and his knot of miscreants roughly handled the man in question."

"Bound and gagged him, they did!" Cockram replied. "All 'cause I took the pardon…"

Raising his mug in the air, Rogers smiled to the small degree his disfigured face allowed. "Well then, gentlemen. Ye only have to reply in the affirmative. Will ye hunt these damnable—"

Rogers's words fell silent, cut short by a series of explosions coming from the harbor.

"What in Hell?" he yelled, opening the shutters just behind him as Hornigold, Cockram, and Woodall did the same at separate windows.

The four men watched in amazement as Charles Vane lowered the Union Jack from where it fluttered above the fort. Releasing a maniacal laugh and howling at the sun, he then produced the pirates' emblem, the curséd Death's Head, which he ran up in its place.

"Tole ya I would do it, me lovelies!" the villainous pirate shouted, running down the beach and along the shoreline, toward a well-armed, waiting boat. "Ye should 'ave ansahed me lettah, Guv'nah Splintah Face! Now ye pays the price!"

"What letter?" Hornigold asked, only realizing when he was finished that he had posed the question aloud.

"It sits upon my desk," the governor growled, pulling a pistol from a drawer, "full of arrogant demands. He actually wanted to keep all of his possessions *and* his pilfered ship! He also demanded an audience to lay out *further* ridiculous terms. I rightfully ignored him."

"Ye cannot ignore him now," Cockram muttered.

Before Rogers could make a reply, a ship in the harbor fired upon the *Rose*, which, within a handful of seconds, hoisted a flag of truce.

"What is Captain Whitney doing?" Rogers was fit to be tied.

"He is attempting to save your flotilla from destruction, Governor Rogers," Hornigold replied. "He ought to be commended."

"Would ye have a look at that…" Woodall whispered in wonder, pointing out the window toward the harbor.

All eight of their eyes—and those of the servant, who surveyed the harbor from over Cockram's shoulder—focused on a flaming ship, her rigging and sails soaked in pitch and tar, headed for the *Rose*.

"That used ta be Vane's own flagship… a captured brigantine formerly out of France." Cockram shook his head. "What the devil is he up to…"

"There the bastard is… climbing aboard that vessel over there!"

"The *Katherine*…" Hornigold stated. "Her captain is an unlikeable son of a whore by the name of Yeats. Another *Charles*…"

Cockram whistled low. "The pair deserve each other."

As the *Katherine* made her way, under full sail, toward the entrance to the harbor, the *Rose* and *Shark*—which, along with the *Willing Mind and Buck*, had been anchored in a cluster—headed away from the flaming ship, which was getting dangerously close to their hulls.

Watching as the *Buck* raised her anchor and headed out in pursuit of the *Katherine*, the five men in the fort suddenly ducked beneath the windows as the brigantine—Vane must have packed its holds with powder—exploded in a brilliant ball of flame, sections of her burning yardarms and rails setting the *Willing Mind* alight.

"I shall have his head for the top of the flagpole!" Rogers exclaimed, as the twilight sky lit up as though it were noon from the growing flames and a series of explosions from the pair of burning ships. "Someone lower that damnable Death's Head! What has that spawn of the devil done with our Union Jack?"

# PART THREE:

# AN EBONY MONGREL ARRIVES

**"I** am quite sure, Cardinal Alberoni, that this man who stands before us today is mad!"

For the better part of two hours, Queen Elisabeth Farnese of Spain, wife of Philip the Fifth, along with her confidante and sponsor, as well as Cardinal André-Hercule de Fleury, who was recovering rather well from his prolonged torture at the hands of the Ravenskalds, had been listening to Admiral George Camocke's animated ramblings.

"Which is why we should continue to listen to him, Isobel," Alberoni whispered back, using Elisabeth's intimate nickname. "Of all the plans to unite the fleets of France and Spain and overthrow George in England, his has garnered the most serious interest—despite his peculiar personality and difficult to listen to delivery."

Producing a polite little giggle—the queen had no wish to offend their guest, who was still speaking while thrusting his arms about the air around him, utterly oblivious to their talking amongst themselves—she said, "I shall continue to do so for its value as entertainment, Cardinal Alberoni! Nothing more."

The queen knew that she resided in the vast minority in her dismissal of Admiral Camocke. There was clearly something that many in positions of power found fascinating about this wild, rambling Irishman, a forty-year veteran of the Royal Navy, who had one day decided to declare fealty to Spain after those on the throne of England continued to ignore his efforts on their behalf.

He had certainly had his victories. There was Calais in 1695, a proper thrashing for which the French had recently forgiven him. Then there was his distinguished service as protector of the Irish coast during the War of Spanish Succession.

Rumor had it that the tsar of Muscovy had offered Camocke an admiralship along the way.

Isobel stole a glance at the back of the room, where her bodyguard, Sargento Alvarado César, who had brought her the Sheba Comb on behalf of Blackbeard and the Quorum, stood beside two unfortunate young people whom Isobel had recently taken in and declared to be under her protection.

The first was Marius Adenot, ex-tutor to the future king of France, whom the country's regent, the always-conniving Philippe the

Second, duc d'Orléans, had turned over to the Ravenskalds as part of a bid for greater power. Marius had been tortured along with Cardinal de Fleury, who credited the passionate young man—instead of God—with keeping him alive. Beside the handsome Adenot, her hands locked tightly in his, was Eleonore Fouquet, the niece of the former French superintendent of finances, Nicolas Fouquet, who had fallen out of favor with Louis the Fourteenth over accusations of peculation—the misappropriation of funds.

Escaping prison in 1680 by faking his death, Fouquet had until recently been living in comfortable secrecy in the Vauban Citadel off the coast of Brittany, France.

That is, until the Ravenskalds dispatched a disfigured assassin named Devon Ross to rob and kill him.

Isobel had a soft spot for Eleonore, who had suffered innumerable deprivations during her months in an Italian nunnery—a situation also engineered by the treacherous duc d'Orléans.

It had fallen to Isobel to make Eleonore aware of the death of her uncle.

To her credit, she did not shed a tear.

The French, far more complicated than the Spanish or the Italians, had seen fit to elevate Nicolas Fouquet's grandson, the dashing Marquis Charles Louis Auguste, a member of the Order of the Golden Fleece, to *marechal de camp*, a move encouraged and facilitated by Cardinal de Fleury.

Isobel, were she in the duke's bejeweled shoes, would have never agreed to let this younger Fouquet fox have so much power in the Frenchies' henhouse.

Then again, the queen knew something the regent did not. The marquis was loyal to the Star Quorum, which meant he was loyal to the cardinals and therefore to Isobel Farnese.

Foolish, arrogant French!

Charles Louis Auguste had already been of use. During the chaos caused by the siege of Fuenterrabía, the *marechal de camp* had acquired a passel of documents that Louis the Fourteenth had been desperately searching for prior to his death. Documents that the Ravenskalds must have surely been most agitated to find were not amongst those stolen by Devon Ross from Nicolas Fouquet's bedchamber in the Vauban Citadel.

The documents—and their volatile secrets—were currently safe in the very place where Nicolas had died a torturous death. After ordering a thorough cleaning of its bedchamber, Charles Louis Auguste had chosen Vauban Citadel for his home.

How useful the Fouquets had been—and would assuredly continue to be—to Isobel Farnese. It was the least that the queen could do to attempt to be useful to them.

Willing herself reluctantly but necessarily to return her attention to the still-gesticulating Admiral Camocke, Isobel raised her hand to stop his speech when he made the unforgivable error of favorably mentioning a certain hated person's name.

"Are you aware, Almirante, that this villainous rogue you seem to so admire—this *despiadado hijo del diablo* Vane—was responsible for the death of the second in command and personal friend to one of our favored sons, Amaro Rodríguez Felipe y Tejera Machado, commander of the *Ave María y Las Ánimas*?"

Camocke clearly did. "To that I would answer, Your Majesty, that such lethal events transpire when men engage in war. Vane has the necessary skills required to command a flo—"

Once again, and this time far more firmly, Isobel raised her hand. "Are you further aware, Almirante, that it was this same *demonio* Vane who stormed our makeshift treasure fort in La Florida after our plate fleet sank in a hurricane?"

Camocke, not willing to risk the further wrath of this formidable woman, merely nodded.

"Then you shall not mention his name again in connection with serving as *almirante* of the Caribbean fleet. That honor, should my husband continue to support your ambitious plan, shall go to Capitán Machado." Before Camocke could answer—and what could he say but yes?—she asked, "What of the situation in Sardinia?"

"It continues to be excellent, Your Majesty," Camocke replied, his throat suddenly sounding as if it had gone dry. "Lieutenant General Jean François de Bette, marquis of Lede, has matters well in hand."

"I would expect that to be the case," Cardinal Giulio Alberoni, member of the Star Quorum and holder of several Spanish titles, including chief minister, responded with a laugh. "He has nearly forty thousand Spanish soldiers at his disposal!"

"Every one of whom remain in excellent health," Camocke replied. "Not that I dare to question Your Eminence's strategies…"

Again Alberoni laughed. This time not so kindly. "Yet your tone and your choice of words betray the fact that you do."

Camocke began to sweat. "Not at all. I only wish to bring to Your Eminence's attention that, while your wooing of Russia and Sweden strengthens our position in our rightful reclaiming of the British throne for James, the Royal Navy has not been idle. As the Spanish ambassador, the marquis de Monteleone, has no doubt already informed you, the British are building new ships and refitting dozens of others. I happen to know George Byng personally, Your Emininence. I served with him for years. He is quite the formidable foe."

"You have told me nothing of which I was previously unaware, Admiral Camocke," Alberoni growled.

The Irishman's face was turning as red as his hair.

Isobel wondered if it was anger or embarrassment.

"Admiral Byng is now commander-in-chief of the Mediterranean," Camocke persisted, actually having the audacity to take several steps closer to the throne as he spoke.

He had barely taken the first of his ill-considered steps when Isobel saw Sargento César stiffen, his hand grasping the hilt of his sword. She discreetly raised her hand to hold her enforcer at bay.

At least for now.

Camocke resisted the urge to clench his fists, a decision that saved him from prison and perhaps his life. "Admiral Byng has delivered word, through proper channels—meaning myself—to His Majesty, King Philip, as well as to the governor of Milan and the viceroy of Naples, that he is intent on quelling the hostilities between Austria and Spain. His fleet of nearly thirty ships sits anchored off Cádiz."

If Camocke thought he had reasserted his weakened position, he quickly realized he was mistaken.

"I have already sent a letter to Admiral Byng!" Cardinal Alberoni sneered. "As well as to Ambassador Stanhope."

Camocke felt his stomach start to sour. "Saying?"

Alberoni's face grew dark. "Guaranteeing them defeat. You are embarrassingly behind in your news, Admiral Camocke. The British fleet sailed from our coast three weeks ago. Byng's flotilla has since been reinforced with two more men of war."

Retreating backward several steps and bowing deeply, Camocke whispered, "What does Your Majesty and Your Eminence command of my ignorant self?"

Isobel was the one who spoke, a soul-shrinking ice in her tone. "You shall rendezvous with Capitán Machado in Cádiz. From there, under his command, you shall track down the pirates Vane and Thache and enlist them to our side. If they will not aid the cause, hang them from a yardarm."

Before he could answer—and what could he say but yes?—Isobel, Alberoni, and de Fleury were out of their seats and exiting the room.

"**I** am sorry, Mister Krait. Your presentation, while eagerly anticipated by our group, shall have to wait. We shall put you up in the finest hotel in Rome—the Villa Agrippina Gran Meliá. It is close to Castel Sant'Angelo. I understand you have a particular interest in the massacre of the Swiss Guard upon its steps in 1527."

Tristan Krait—who had in centuries prior gone by the name of Trogon Ophidian—looked through his specially (and personally) developed Primeira Vista glasses at the almost groveling Cardinal Andre Louis Guvot. Krait suppressed a scowl as he noticed that the glasses' complex array of lenses—which turned the miniscule light and shapes his wounded eyes could process into near perfect vision via sophisticated algorithms, holograms, and perceptual simulations—were interpreting the scarlet red of the cardinal's robes as an ugly, violent crimson.

Upon his return to the global headquarters of the information technology and philanthropy corporation he had founded in 1968, Arcanjo International Enterprises, located on the mountain island of Pico in the Azores, he would lead his best technicians in running a thorough set of diagnostics.

Close to perfect would not do.

"I have already booked a suite at the villa for the next several weeks, Your Eminence," he said, making sure to smile. "Your information is partially correct. Although I do have an interest in the sacrifice of the personal guards of Clement the Seventh, my curiosities do not end with their valor and willingness to die for the pope."

"Please enlighten us as to the actual scope of your interests," said Gregory Garvin, superior general of the Society of Jesus. "If it is improper for you to make your presentation, let us at least have some engaging conversation as we await Eleanora's arrival."

Krait, who had never trusted the Jesuits despite their permanent seat on the Quorum, replied, "Sant'Angelo was not just a fortress. It was also a prison. Giordano Bruno, Benvenuto Cellini, and Alessandro Cagliostro were all incarcerated there at one time or another."

"Quite a divergent cast of characters," muttered Julius Eccobukk, whose Palestinian–Israeli heritage had led him to the influential position of U.S. ambassador to the United Nations.

Cardinal Alfonso Duarte Costa—the Portuguese head of the Archivio Apostolico Vaticano and only member of the Quorum who knew that Krait was Trogon Ophidian—sensing his old friend's increasing frustration—said, "Which speaks to Tristan's great intellect and insatiable curiosity." Hearing the buzzes and clicks of the outer security door, he added, "That must be Eleanora and Ramón. It is best we turn our focus to our comrade's terrible loss."

Tristan Krait took a position in the shadows at the far end of the Quorum's meeting room as the inner door was opened, revealing a woman in her mid-sixties dressed in mourning black, complete with a delicate veil. Beside her was Ramón Sebastiano Rocafull, grand master of the Knights of Malta and commander of the Scarlet Shrouded Knights of Saint Grotth. Although he wore his normal uniform of crimson and gray, he had affixed an unadorned black band around his upper arm.

Cardinal Giuseppe Mauro, grand master of the Order of the Holy Sepulchre and newest member of the Quorum, extended his arms toward Eleanora.

"Thank you, Your Eminence," Eleanora whispered, accepting his embrace. Dabbing her eyes with a handkerchief, she softly addressed the room. "Your support is much appreciated. Although few of you knew my brother, Iain Hugh, your sympathy and offers of assistance have nevertheless been nothing short of the love that is born of family."

"The timing is most regrettable," said Cardinal Guvot. "It has been less than forty-eight hours since news arrived of the slaughter of your brother and a dozen other Knights of Saint Grotth and the theft of the Marlowes and the Magdalene Balm by what could only be the hammer of the Ravenskalds, the Kardax Corporation, and here you stand with us, instead of with your family in Scotland."

"Which makes the timing *exquisite*," Eleanora responded, her voice girded by the opportunity to work instead of grieve. Looking quickly around the room, she asked, "Have you already sent our scheduled speaker away?"

"I am here, Lady Sinclair," Tristan said, stepping from the shadows.

Eleanora gestured for him to approach. "I hope my colleagues have been taking excellent care of you, Mister Krait."

"Indeed they have." Taking her hands in his, Tristan whispered, "I am genuinely sorry, Eleanora. I knew Iain rather well. I am sure he died with honor." Seeing fresh tears in her eyes, he altered his tone to one of business. "As I was telling your colleagues, I have taken a suite at the Villa Agrippina Gran Meliá. You no doubt have much to discuss. I am happy to return in, say, a week's time to share with you as originally planned what my company, Arcanjo, is doing to thwart the Ravenskalds and reclaim from them what has become a disturbingly high number of the twelve ancient artifacts."

The murmurs and moans from the members of the Quorum ceased as quickly as they had started at the sound of Superior General Garvin's agitated voice.

"Since our honored guest has been the only one brave enough to bring it up… By my accounting, they have the Baptist Bowl, the Aaron Staff, the Abraham Blade, the Sheba Comb, the Tiber Vial, the Judas Coin, the Ezekiel Wheel, the Michael Mirror, and now the Magdalene Balm!"

"Nine of the twelve!" Cardinal Mauro hissed, making the sign of the cross.

Eleanora shook her head. "You are thankfully wrong, my friends. They possess only eight of the twelve."

Searching eyes and queries for more information quickly assailed their grieving colleague.

After a nod from Eleanora, Grand Master Rocafull enlightened them as to her meaning. "I received an encrypted message late last night from one of the senior officers from the Kardax unit that made the attack upon Seaswan. He claims to have secretly retained the Magdalene Balm, rather than turning it over to his commanding officer. He wishes to meet with a representative of the Quorum as soon as possible to discuss his terms for delivery."

Ambassador Eccobukk laughed. "I cannot believe your naivete, Ramón! This is an obvious ruse! A clear trap to lure in and assassinate another member or two of the Star Quorum or its inner circle. Have you something to contribute, Mister Krait?"

Tristan, who was whispering in Cardinal Costa's ear, ignored the question and continued his private communication.

"You must share this with them, Tristan," the target of his words insisted when he was finished.

"Very well," their guest responded. "Was the Kardax officer who contacted you by any chance Ishmael Ramsay?"

Rocafull nodded, eliciting whispers of surprise from several members of the Quorum.

"How do you know this, Mister Krait?" Eleanora enquired.

"Ramsay was a longtime member of SEAL Team D," Tristan began, his voice even and full of authority. "He was eventually the team's commander before resigning his commission. You are all aware of their singular mission, so I shall not speak of their primary targets here, lest we risk their making an appearance. Since returning to the States, Ramsay has been subjected to horrific body and mind experimentation through a program called Project RUS, at DED 67."

"RUS," Rocafull whispered. "For Rehabilitate, Utilize, and Specialize. Some of my Special Forces contacts have described it to me in detail. The culmination of the very worst of the Nazi concentration camp experiments, Japan's Unit 731, MKUltra, DARPA's Super Soldier program, Project Artichoke, and Project Montauk."

"It is agony for the subjects and an existential threat to humanity if they succeed in their ultimate aims," Tristan added. "Ramsay has wanted out of the program for months. Not even his former SEAL commanding officer, who is now his boss at Kardax, has been able to extricate him from RUS. He is desperate and no doubt ready to deal."

"Then I must meet with him as soon as you approve it," Rocafull said to his colleagues. "Will you do so, here and now?"

The spontaneous vote was unanimous.

"With a caveat," Eleanora said, her voice a little stronger. "I want to attend this meeting. I would like Tristan there as well."

"Agreed," Superior General Garvin answered, not deigning to consult with his colleagues. Clearly in charge, although the Quorum had no formal, recognized leader, he continued. "Two more bits of business before we adjourn for the day. The pope is growing increasingly ill. Cardinal Niccolò Balena—still settling into his position of Archbishop of New York after the kidnapping and murder of Estaban Rojas[2]—is sure to be the one to replace him."

Cardinal Mauro, whom the remaining members of the Quorum had chosen as their replacement for Cardinal Rojas, nodded and sighed. "I can attest to this. Balena has blinded our brothers in the College of Cardinals with his promises of a revitalized and more traditional Roman Catholic Church. He makes the plans of Joseph Ratzinger seem paltry by comparison. What is the other bit of business for the Quorum, Superior General Garvin?"

"It is related to this business with Balena, making it all the more concerning. According to Paramita Laghari, next in line for the

---

[2] You can learn the details of Rojas's abduction and death in the short story "Prendick's All Night Fights" in *The Icarus Continuum: From the Files of the Domestic Threat Early Assessment Unit*.

governorship of New Jersey should Amorata DiMuri succeed in her bid to unseat the current US president, Alexander Dunn—a bid that is looking less and less likely to succeed—the Ravenskalds have managed to gain control of a demon-possessed serial killer. He ravaged the city of Secaucus, where she is mayor, last December. Our friends in the DTEAU apprehended him before he could complete a rather potent ritual, but the Ravenskalds extracted him from prison and he is nowhere to be found."

Julius Eccobukk ground his fist into his palm. "I concur that Amorata has little hope of winning the election. Dunn is a Ravenskald puppet. I serve him only reluctantly—out of necessity as a member of the Quorum. They own the UN, including the WHO, my friends. Along with the World Bank, IMF, WEF, half a dozen major think-tanks on both ends of the spectrum, and both the defense and technology sectors—all of whom are working together for the rapid deployment of so-called artificial intelligence in every facet of society."

Ten minutes later, as the members of the Star Quorum parted company after each agreeing to glean what further data they could on the pressing issues at hand before the next day's meeting, Tristan Krait stood apart, contemplating all he had seen and heard.

He had been watching this unfold for millennia.

Centuries of war and global manipulation were coming to a head, and the Quorum was falling behind. Further than they ever had before.

It was time to pay a visit to his ancient, eternal enemy.

The one who had taken his sight, hundreds of years before.

"They say the name of that town is Whorekill, Mister Herriot! We sure did kill the poxy bitch somethin' fierce, did we not?"

"That we did, Mister Perry!" Sailing Master David Herriot of the *Revenge* responded. "That said—it is time for ye to be about your business. We would not want to squander half a month's pretty hauls for want of commitment to our duties, would we, sir?"

As Daniel Perry and the rest of the crew of the sloop until recently known as *Royal James* attended to their tasks, Herriot clenched his teeth as the quartermaster, Robert Tucker, approached.

"We are on a wicked win streak, ain't we Mister Herriot?" Tucker asked, letting loose a stream of tobacco over the taffrail.

Most of which hit the water.

Not in a mood to mince words or hold his tongue—the crew was clearly on their sailing master's side—Herriot responded, "No thanks to your heavy-handed proclivities, Mister Tucker. Now, clean that foul pool of spittle and tobacco off the taffrail and be about your business!"

Leaving the pool of green-brown tobacco juice and saliva where it lay, Tucker twisted his lips into an exaggerated, gap-toothed grin. "Wha'arya on about? That little matter a' them four malcontents what grabbed a sloop an' headed up the coast? I caught them little fuckers straightaway, did I not?"

"They were seeking a more favorable position with Paulsgrave Williams on Block Island because of your incompetence and cruelty!"

Tucker stepped in closer, fire in his eyes. Herriot noticed an increasing number of men beginning to turn their attention to the simmering confrontation.

If Fate were feeling kind, Stede would stay in his cabin.

"Incompetence an' cruelty, eh?" Tucker pulled a small black book from his pocket. Licking his fingers with his green-grey tongue, he opened to the page he wanted. He began to read aloud. "Two ships off Ocracoke. Piles an' piles a' plunder in the Virginia Capes an' Jersey, includin' ten ships boarded. Savvy tradin' along the way…

Beaufort rice fer worm-free bread an' pork. 29 July. Off Cape May, Colony a' Jersey. Fifty-ton *Fortune* taken *without incident*."

Herriot put his hand on top of the book as Tucker let fly another stream of steaming tobacco. "Without incident, ye claim? Their captain, Thomas Read, surrendered without a fight, yet ye pummeled him mercilessly for half an hour while *Fortune*'s crew was beaten nearly to death with the flats of your bullyboys' swords!"

Tucker wiped a rivulet of tobacco juice and saliva from his chin. "Works fer Vane. Now it works fer us!" Pushing Herriot's hand off his logbook, Tucker resumed his reading. "Just last night, right over there near Whorekill… Took the fair sloop *Francis* under Cap'n Peter Manwaring. Rum an' coin aplenty."

Herriot shuddered at the memory of the previous evening's events. After his crew had secured the ship, Stede had convened a celebration in Captain Manwaring's cabin. Toasting the Old Pretender every fifteen minutes with slices of fresh-cut pineapple, which floated in a strong rum punch mixed by Mister Tucker, Stede had grown intolerably intoxicated, singing his ridiculous song about being a proper pirate.

Herriot could still hear the risqué lyrics, penned by the captain himself, despite continual efforts to remove them from his mind:

A fox-fur, quilted robe and a knitted, fitted cap
Books read by the crateful, bon-bons for a snack
Being delicate in diction—swearing makes unmannered minds!
For good measure, any treasure that is taken should be thine
Provide your crew a weekly wage, go *wisely* with the wine!
After my militia man's commission, never drew my sword an inch
I was ready to inherit—to scratch a certain itch!
My uncle parried that I marry a haughty, horse-faced hag
So I wormed out through the window, built a boat,
and took a pass!
I bought myself a crew, we took prizes left and right
Never once pulled out my rapier… until the dark of night
My men were growing cocky, I suppose that I was too!
Tried to score a man o' war, and got well and truly…
That's the time I first met Blackbeard, and that randy Hornigold
I bet that they could *teach* me, from the tales some *seamen* told!
One's all dressed in ribbons—God, I love those braids!

The other with his pipe… Oh, Edwards—you be*have*!

As if the song were not punishment enough, Tucker had taken the opportunity to send Captain Read's teenaged son to Whorekill to deliver a warning—should a single townsperson try to bother Bonnet's crew, the major would burn the town!

"What was the point of your threat, Mister Tucker?" Herriot pressed, his eyes affixed to the slowly spreading glob of still steaming stink on the taffrail. "'Tis not the case that we shall linger. Major Bonnet has directed me to sail for the Cape Fear River, where we shall be tasked with careening and repairing this vessel."

"Jus' a bit a' fun, Mister Herriot," Robert Tucker replied, sounding suddenly despondent. Placing his logbook in his pocket, he said, "A damned fine run a' piratin', an' our sailin' master's complain' 'cause we had a bit a' fun. I shall tell ye somethin', sir… when hurricane season is over an', despite ya bein' against it, we obtain our privateerin' commissions from the king a' Denmark hisself ta fight the Spanish offa the isle a' Saint Thomas, an' I am awarded my own ship, I ain't havin' ye as quartahmastah!"

As Tucker walked away, Herriot grabbed a discarded scrap of sail from a barrel full of garbage. Setting to work scrubbing the stinking filth from the taffrail, he silently cursed the day he had agreed to sail with Major Stede Bonnet out of Barbados.

Despite their recent successes, Herriot anticipated nothing but losses ahead.

## ST. JAMES' PALACE, CITY OF WESTMINSTER,
## AUGUST 2, 1718

The German king of Britain, George Louis Hanover, had just signed several copies of a treaty of alliance penned in Latin to accommodate the representatives of the four countries it encompassed.

Pushing the copies away, he dropped the ink-stained quill for which he no longer had a use onto the ornate maple desk in the otherwise simply appointed Council Chamber, located directly behind the throne. Looking at his chief advisor with disapproving eyes, George said in German (although he also knew some French, he refused to learn even the smallest amount of English): "*Du klingst und bewegst dich wie eine Schlange, Herr Carteret.*"

*You move and sound just like a snake.* Lord Carteret was surprised at the king's unusual focus on his advisor and the underlying truth of his observation. George's mind was usually on his mistress, no doubt anxiously awaiting the virile king's return to her darkened chambers on the far side of the palace.

Where she would move and sound *exactly* like a snake.

"*Nur meine Freude an diesem glückverheißenden Tag, mein König,*" Lord Carteret replied, waving his hand at the attendant stationed at the door, indicating that he should let the restless group of grumbling signatories enter.

"Ah, my friends," he said, as the anxious to be finished rulers and their advisors arrayed themselves around the desk. "If I seem overly animated, it is merely my joy on this most auspicious day."

Which is what he had said in German to George.

"I do not *comprendre* this use of the word *joyeux*, Seigneur Carteret," Philippe the Second, duc d'Orléans, regent of France, responded. It was November of 1716 when the ambitious regent last had a reason to stand in this room, while signing an agreement to cooperate with Britain—which meant with Carteret, who had negotiated the deal while George was summering in Germany—in her fight to stem the ridiculous claims of the Spanish court to additional thrones and land. "No one here is *joyeux* for us all to once again make war." Motioning toward the tall, slender-faced man beside him, he said, "Should *sa Majesté* not remember, this is my secretary of foreign affairs, Abbé Guillaume Dubois."

As the Cardinal offered a miniscule bow to George—how arrogantly these falsely pious, conniving Catholics conducted themselves!—which the already bored king barely deigned to acknowledge, Lord Carteret made the decision not to make the effort to relay to the king who this impious peacock was.

Not that Dubois was devoid of uses. Carteret trusted the Cardinal more than he did the duke, who was far more loyal to the Ravenskalds than was the independent Carteret, who knew he could rely on Dubois for a single, simple, exquisitely relatable reason.

He despised his fellow cardinals—Alberoni, de Fleury, and Gualterio—especially the first, who served not only as prime minister of Spain, but also as the guiding hand of the queen, Elisabeth Farnese, whom everyone in this room was well aware controlled her increasingly insane and unpredictable husband, Philip the Fifth.

Alberoni and Farnese—whose loyalties to Spain were secondary to their own ambitions, their native country, and to one another— were intent on reobtaining Italian territories lost in the aftermath of the War of Spanish Succession.

Philip, under the terms of the Treaty of Utrecht, ceded many of those territories to another soon to be signatory, Charles the Sixth, Holy Roman emperor and ruler of the Austrian Habsburg monarchy.

Which meant he was also an agent of the Ravenskalds, who had shrewdly allied themselves with the Habsburgs in 1264, during their initial rise to power.

Currently in highest contention were the islands of Sicily and Sardinia, for which the British and Spanish navies were at this very moment contending.

"I nae caen blame the queen fer wishin' tae possess thaem," John Law, the duke's financial wizard, who had overseen the creation of France's Banque Générale Privée, offered from his position in the doorway. "Boot haer bum's noo oot the windae. It weel bae tatties o'wer the side fer haer an' haer numpty hoosband in the face a' this alliance."

*Damn these Scottish savages and their unintelligible, thick-tongued brogues!* Carteret thought with a scowl, silently cursing the duke for bringing the arrogant bastard along.

"Well put, sir," Emperor Charles responded, although it was clear that his understanding was of the *sentiment* and not the actual *meaning* of the vulgar Scottish sayings. "It is clear to us all that Philip is not fit to rule the vast bastion of riches and naval superiority that is the Catholic country of Spain. I reassert *my* claim to its throne through my shared lineage with Charles the Second."

"Duly noted," Carteret replied.

"Do not be cavalier with me!" the emperor responded. "The fact that Alberoni and his Italian whore have rejected the overtures of King Victor Amadeus in Sicily to support his ambitions for an Italian league of states means that their ambitions are equal to his, although *their* particular goal is for a league of subservient states choking beneath the yoke of Spain!"

"Which is why we stand so solidly beside you, Emperor," said the Dutch representative of the seven-year-old stadtholder of the United Netherlands, William the Fourth. "There is little time to waste. The siege of Messina has begun. Admiral Byng is a capable commander, but we must lend him our assistance. Let us sign the papers of this alliance so we may all get back to attending to our tasks at home."

"I have a question for the emperor before we sign the treaty," said the duc, lifting the quill from George's desk and twirling it between his fingers. "The treaty you signed with the Ottomans not yet two weeks ago—is it strong enough to hold?"

Obviously annoyed but not wishing to stall even further the increasingly contentious proceedings, Charles responded, "The Treaty of Passarowitz is firm. My attention—and that of my senior military officers—is utterly undivided."

"Thaen sign the bloody thing an' laet oos conclude oor business!"

Carteret, secretly wishing he had brought the Abraham Blade, that he might cut the Scotsman's throat and feed his organs to his hounds, slipped into the throne room while the duke loaded the quill with ink and bent to sign his name.

Much to his shock and surprise, Athelstan Ravenskald was sitting on George's throne.

"Do ye dare?" Carteret whispered to the unexpected, insidious intruder, far more awed than angry. "Do ye wish to be arrested?"

Athelstan, rather than abandon the throne, slapped its ornate arms. "The throne of a single country is not of interest to me, John. I shall one day have a throne that encompasses the world."

"Why are ye here, My Lord?"

"Almost solely to talk to you. Traveling with the duke and his retinue was but a convenient excuse. Not that I need one, John. I am sure you understand that."

"What do ye wish of me?"

Athelstan released a haughty laugh. "Why so suddenly subservient? It truly does not suit you. Not with the blood of Mammon and the venom of the *tanin* that lives within the Aaron Staff coursing through your veins. To say nothing of the spells of summoning you have attempted as of late."

Lord John Carteret, this time attempting to mask his surprise, retreated several steps. Of course, Athelstan would know about the Mammon and *tanin* rituals—his son Adonijah had presided over them—but he had gone to considerable lengths to keep the summoning attempts a secret.

"You are boring me now, John," Athelstan said with a yawn, shifting his position on the throne so his leg hung lazily over the arm of the oak and velvet chair. "You are currently in possession of Mountfort's *Doctor Faustus*, taken from the upstairs rooms of the Temple Coffee House from a man named Edmund Curll. Do not bother to try to deny it... I am not the only one who knows. Our enemies have *seen what you have done*, within the depths of the Michael Mirror! Beneath your coat and shirt, if I commanded you to remove them, I would see a bandaged forearm, which you cut with the Abraham Blade while reciting a spell of conjuring contained within its pages. How many attempts have you made to summon Lucifer, or Mephistopheles? Four? Five? I see the evidence in you, John. There is a different kind of power, but it is fleeting. Your time in Britain, pouring hemlock in the ear of the befuddled, horny Hanoverian, is coming to a close."

Carteret seethed. "What have you—?"

"Nothing as of yet. Consider this fair warning. I feel I owe you that, for your limited contributions to the cause. Look to your affairs in the Carolinas. Manage that idiot Craven. As for the Family, do what Adonijah instructs—especially concerning the pirate Edward Thache."

Carteret attempted to soften his look and his tone. "I have been working in tandem with Absalom."

"That foolishness shall cease," Athelstan responded. "He has been measured, weighed, and I have found him wanting. Surely he told you what happened last November…"

Carteret nodded, feeling his knees go weak.

"You thought you could somehow redeem him? Convince me that he should ascend in my place when I finally decide to die?" Athelstan smiled a viper's smile. "What an utterly laughable notion. I want Charles Vane and Edward Thache destroyed. Thache has struck a deal with the governor of North Carolina. I cannot allow this to stand. Nor should you. Their alliance is keeping coins from your purse. Outside of his alliance with Eden, Thache's life is forfeit for the arrogance and idiocy he demonstrated in facilitating delivery of the Sheba Comb to Isobel Farnese."

"I… I know ye have been disappointed when it comes to… to the ancient objects… the Tiber Vial, the… the Baptist Skull…"

Carteret cursed himself for stammering.

Then, in a movement so fast Carteret could only account for it by the presence of preternatural powers no other mortal possessed, Athelstan had laid a blade against his throat.

"I held this very knife—you cannot see it, but the sheath that holds it bears the sigils of the counts of Kyburg, including the *Schwarze Sonne*—to the throat of my impetuous, incompetent child. Understand me well. I *own* the men in that room. The duke. John Law. Dubois. The Habsburg emperor. And, through his representative, that sniveling child in the Netherlands. *Owning them*, I own the Hanoverian, who would rather fuck his whores in every room of this palace than run affairs of state—a task he leaves to you." Sliding the dagger into its sheath—Carteret eyed its Black Sun sigil as he did so—Athelstan put his hand on the Palatine's chest, pressing roughly on his heart.

"Do not attempt to defy us, John, nor attempt again to summon forces the likes of Lucifer and Mephistopheles. I should have commanded Absalom to kill you as a test of his loyalty when you offered what remained of your soul to Moloch. Do what I command, or that withered, blackened light within you shall be an inadequate snack for Iblis, whose will is subverted to mine."

As Athelstan exited the throne room, Carteret ran for the water closet, the sudden urge to vomit bringing stinging tears to his eyes.

The nearly imperceptible, sweet yet pungent odor of a recently caught-in-a-rainstorm, fresh-from-fornicating dog had just prevented the death of Trogon Ophidian.

The blind, grey-robed monk had been settling into bed after his nightly ritual—a cup of rose hip tea and a tale from *One Thousand and One Arabian Nights* read to him by the sweet-voiced Johanna Martel, widow of the brother of the pirate John Martel, when the odiferous alert had reached his nose.

Wrapping his right hand tightly around a silver medallion depicting the Archangel Michael slaying a serpent that had been hanging around his neck since its procurement in this very chamber the previous April from a merchant captain named Pinkentham, the ageless monk slipped from his bed, selecting the darkest corner of the room in which to await the approaching intruder.

Within seconds, the powerful mongrel appeared, leaping through the open window and immediately onto the bed, where it tore and rent the bedsheets, blanket, and pillow in its quest to kill its prey.

"If only you had bathed after violating the bitch in the barn," Trogon whispered. "If only it had not rained."

Releasing an ear-piercing growl, the ebony-coated invader made its transformation into something resembling human.

"I did not account for such a heightened sense of smell as a benefit of your blinding, Master Trogon. That is the name you are using, is it not? Trogon Ophidian?" The voice was raspy and low from the adversary's use of its throat for growling. In time, it would be smooth as glass and just as potentially dangerous.

"Even now the smell persists… What should I call you tonight? Egil Skallagrimson? Egil the Skald? Egil the Beserker? He whom I made blind as a punishment for his transgressions? He who birthed the first of the Ravenskalds in the form of a rabid boar, in a ritual rank and vile? I sensed you the very moment that Athelstan released you."

"Oh, my ancient adversary," the crouching invader hissed. "Dare you speak of atrocities? Of rituals rank and vile? The deity whom you serve has bathed his balls in blood. Yes… I birthed the Ravenskalds. Yes, I tutored Jórkell, ally of Sigurd Eysteinsson, the iron arm of Sigurd the Mighty. Still a shadow, I stood with Ubba, warrior-son of Ragnar Lothbrok, as he wielded the Raven Banner at the head of the Heathen Army. It was I, Maker of Kings and Destinies, who placed the serpent in the eye of Sigurd Áslaugsson! England, Orkney, Normandy, Dublin, Kievan Rus... all of these exist because I alone decided! Because I alone commanded!"

Trogon clicked his tongue. "So much bragging and braying! It would have been better had you manifested before me as a rooster, for all your boastful crowing! Spouter of kingdoms' names... will you not reveal to me the name you use tonight? Is it Landulf the First of Capua? Landulf Excommunicado? Perhaps you fancy Klingsor?"

"Saviero Inimicus will do. It is the last thing you shall hear!"

Just as Trogon desired, the adversary, blinded as he was with rage at the endless insults—making them essentially equals in the darkness—rushed across the room, toward the sound of Trogon's voice.

Its scream of lethal rage became a scream of pain.

Saviero Inimicus's hand had made contact with the Michael medallion.

"When did you obtain it?" Saviero hissed, backing toward the window, the odor of damp fur and fornication obliterated by the odor of singed and smoking flesh.

"Some months after your latest incarnation," Trogon whispered, pushing the adversary out of the window, which he quickly locked and warded.

Making his way to his table, he lit a pair of candles, which he held within inches of his eyes.

Just as he had thought as he locked the window! The dimmest of undiscernible shapes danced for the first time in centuries before his damaged eyes, which the adversary had ravaged in a previous confrontation in payment for the fate of Egil the Skald.

Sitting on the edge of the bed, Trogon slowed his fluttering heart as the chamber door flew open.

"Master! What has happened?" Trogon's eighteen-year-old assistant, the Franciscan friar, Guillermo Vincolaré, asked as he entered the room.

"The adversary paid me a visit."

As Guillermo poured him a welcome cup of water, Trogon wrinkled his nose at the scent of semidigested sausage. The marquis de Chateaumorand, governor of Petit-Goave, was standing in the doorway.

"Shall I summon the soldiers?" he asked.

"There is nothing for them to find," Trogon answered, draining the cup of water and holding it out for more. "The danger has passed. Sorry you were roused from your bed."

Grumbling goodnight, Chateaumorand shuffled down the hallway toward his rooms.

Accepting the refilled cup of water with a nod, Trogon asked Guillermo to fetch a certain book from his sagging, crowded shelves.

"Close and lock the door," he instructed, patting the friar's hand to indicate that he should hold onto the book. "I am grateful Johanna was not awakened. Listen to me, Guillermo. What I knew in my heart to be true, the adversary's appearance has further confirmed. Athelstan has used the ring of Solomon. He controls the adversary, who calls himself, in his latest incarnation, Saviero Inimicus."

"Enemy in a new house," Guillermo whispered.

"He is clever as always. Now prove to me, Franciscan, that you are progessing in your studies. You hold in your hands *One Thousand and One Arabian Nights*. Leave it closed for now. Who are the djinn whose tales are told within its pages?"

Without hesitation, Guillermo replied, "There is the djinn imprisoned in a jar in 'The Fisherman and the Jinni.' Maymunah, daughter of Al-Dimiryat, who dwells in a Roman well in 'The Tale of Kamar al-Zaman.' The djinn in the lamp in 'Aladdin and the Wonderful Lamp,' and the djinn of the ring, who also appears in that story." Pausing for a moment, as his master nodded approval, Guillermo added, "Then there is Jarjaris, descendant of Iblis, in 'The Second Kalandar's Tale.'"

"Excellent, Franciscan. This final tale you mention is the one I wish to hear."

Climbing beneath his tattered covers to the sound of rustling pages, Trogon closed his aching eyes as Guillermo sat and began to read, his lilting scholar's voice, while not yet firm with authority, still pleasant enough to the ear.

As the minutes quickly passed, the friar recited the ancient tale of the king of the djinn, Al-Dimiryat, Solomon's stalwart ally in the City of Brass, who had imprisoned in a pillar his subordinate Dahish for defying the king of Israel. As this action was unfolding, an educated prince, the kalandar of the title—meaning monk or Sufi saint—arrived in another city, where he engaged in conversation with the attractive daughter of King Ifitamus.

In the midst of their pleasant revels, the princess's face went white. Enquiring as to the cause, the kalandar heard the staccato click of goats' hooves on the floor outside the door. Urged by the princess to hide, the kaladar watched from the shadows as the bedroom door flew open, revealing the horned, winged, red-eyed ifrit Jarjaris, cousin to Iblis, who bellowed with unbridled rage.

"Who dares defy the ifrit?" he screamed, tearing covers from off the bed and books from off the shelves as he searched for the hiding invader. "For five and twenty years, the girl has been my prisoner, and my prisoner she shall remain!"

When at last he found the kalandar, crouching inside a basket, the enraged ifrit engaged in a long and skillful torture of the princess, which ended with the removal of her hands, feet, and head.

Placing the book, which he had been holding tightly in his hands, upon the table, Guillermo brought his chair close to his teacher's bed.

"As a final affront, Jarjaris casts a spell, transforming the kalandar into an ape. While serving as wazir in another city, the kalandar-ape is at last released from his torment thanks to the princess Sitt al-Husn, who summons Jarjaris to a battlefield, where she engages the prideful djinn in a test of their powers of transformation. Contest after contest, hour after hour, the princess proves herself the better of the two, until the ifrit Jarjaris lies dead, and the princess, due to her outsized exertions, is burned at last to ash."

"Do you understand, Guillermo, why I have chosen this tale for tonight?" Trogon asked, placing a spare pillow over the one the adversary had ravaged.

Placing his hand upon the book as though it were a talisman, the friar nodded. "Many will be tortured, transformed, dismembered, and burned to ash because of the actions of Saviero Inimicus."

"All of these things and more," Trogon whispered. "Many have already occurred and there are many more to come. He may return to this house for Johanna. You must protect yourself, Guillermo, even as you serve as her protector. Hold fast to your faith, for the Quorum is assembling an army. We are far from alone."

"You must rest now, Master Trogon. I hear all that you have said. I shall meditate on this story and all of its myriad meanings as I fall asleep tonight."

With that, Guillermo blew out the pair of candles, lifted the book into his arms, and exited the room.

Royal Navy Lieutenant Robert Maynard, second in command under the irascible Captain George Gordon of the forty-two-gun Fourth-Rate HMS *Pearl*, flipped to a clean page in his leatherbound logbook, sighing deeply at the tediousness of his tasks. After a cursory accounting of the eight merchant vessels the Admiralty had ordered the *Pearl* and her constant companion, the thirty-gun Fifth-Rate *Lyme*—captained by Maynard's confidante and co-conspirator, Ellis Brand—to see safely from Delaware to Virginia, the ambitious, constantly thwarted lieutenant hastily scribbled a pair of lines noting that all was well.

Stoppering his pot of ink, Maynard felt his pulse begin to quicken at the sound of the voice of his commanding officer, enquiring as to the status of half a dozen additional tasks Gordon had ordered his beleaguered executive officer to complete before dinner as they were sitting down to breakfast.

"I was getting to them when ye stopped me," he replied, the agitation in his voice painfully, dangerously clear.

Gordon was pleased enough to ignore Maynard's petulant displays of temper, so exquisite was the enjoyment he derived from his mission to keep his second in command from ever obtaining a captain's commission. Were Maynard one day to confront him, insisting that he divulge what it was he so vehemently disliked about the thirty-four-year-old lieutenant, Gordon would no doubt employ the following list of descriptors: Conniver. Malcontent. Instigator. Drunkard. Last, but not least, arrogant abuser of women.

To offer a summation, Gordon found Maynard *wholly distasteful*. An embarrassment to the uniform, and the rich traditions that were the soul of the Royal Navy.

It had been eleven years since Maynard had earned the two gold stripes that signified the rank of lieutenant. To go so long without advancing had made him a laughing stock, his supposed shortcomings whispered about in the Admiralty and amongst the other officers.

With the exception of Ellis Brand.

"There is a smear of ink upon your thumb," Captain Gordon observed.

Taking a swipe at the errant ink with the corner of his logbook, Maynard replied, "The Admiralty approved all of our requests regarding the hundred pirates who docked in Hampton. Governor Spotswood as well. He has signed and filed their pardons. They will of course be carefully watched."

Gordon stared at a remaining bit of ink on Maynard's thumb for several seconds. "Should I be impressed?" he asked with a sigh.

"If not impressed, than grateful. Because I am a lowly lieutenant, the documentation bears the names of captains Brand and Gordon, instead of Brand's and my own, although the pirates being bound by law to surrender their arms when they enter a town was solely my idea."

Gordon rolled his eyes. "Ye seek glory, Lieutenant, when ye should be earning my endorsement—the pathway to which is simple. Do what I command of ye, as quickly and rightly as ye are able. Starting with your unfinished tasks for the day."

"I do not understand," Maynard mumbled, striking the white pine mizzenmast with his leather logbook, which produced a loud report, drawing the attention of several sailors. "Our Admiralty-tasked purpose is to bring the pirates to heel, eradicating those who do not capitulate to the taking of the pardon. We sail these waters instead of patrolling at Hampton because of the recent activities of the one called Major Bonnet—also known as Captain Edwards. Blackbeard himself plies the waters of the Albemarle, in league, they say, with the rebellious governor Eden!"

"Lower your voice, Lieutenant." Gordon stepped in closer, a conspiratorial gleam in his eye. "There is machinery now in motion. Ye may soon receive an opportunity to play the classical hero. I find such work presently under contemplation by Lieutenant Governor Spotswood and the rabble known as The Family to be utterly distasteful, yet it is just the flavor of sordid operation for which ye and Brand are so uniquely, regrettably, suited."

Maynard could not believe what he was hearing. "I relish the chance to prove your notion correct. Ellis has told me nothing..."

"Do not refer to him as *Ellis*." Gordon made a face as though he had tasted something foul. "*Captain Brand* is not yet privy to what I have heard from Governor Spotswood, although he shall be soon enough."

Maynard shook his head. "Then why have ye confided in me?"

In an icy, venomous voice that was barely above a whisper, Gordon replied, "So I could make this very clear. If ye hope to have your chance, walk the straight and narrow. No more tone, no more shuffling of your feet and passing off your duties to junior officers. I expect your entries in that logbook ye are slamming around like a child to be legible, comprehensive, worthy of your station—and free from smudges of ink. Ye shall reduce your intake of alcohol and keep your uniform neat. In short, Lieutenant Maynard, unless ye wish to be caulking bulkheads and peeling potatoes while Captain Brand and the rest of his handpicked unit are off in pursuit of glory, ye shall have to thoroughly reinvent yourself and withstand an unprecedented level of scrutiny from my unforgiving gaze."

Straightening his spine and his cuffs, Maynard smiled. "I shall do so both presently and enthusiastically, Captain Gordon. Now, if ye will excuse me, I have your list of tasks to complete."

Commodore Christopher Condent, who had taken to calling himself the Marauding Monarch of Martinique, sat upon his throne, made of mahogany, kapok, and palm leaves, a string of scrimshawed mongoose bones adorning his muscled, tattooed chest.

He was celebrating his marriage to the daughter of a local justice. She was sitting at his feet, so innocently arousing.

His recollections of the mid-March midnight when an ebony canine had appeared in his cabin window as his ship—which Charles Vane had so graciously provided—sailed for the Cape Verde Islands were hazy and fractured at best, although he remembered a little more when he had drunk his fill of rum.

The dog, which reeked of heated bitches, syphilis, and sulfur, had sat beside his bed, whispering in his ear. Oh, the things the mongrel whispered... of Persian harems and opium, of contested ancient objects, and thrones and chests of gold.

*All you have to do is everything I ask. All of it shall be yours. All of it and more.*

Enquiring as to the possibility of obtaining a brand new hand in place of the one he had sacrificed the previous year when an agitated Portuguese crewman deluded by rotten liquor had discharged his pistol through the door outside of which Condent stood, he heard the mongrel hiss:

*What do you need with a second hand, when you have a cock and a sword?*

Nodding his head despite his wish to have *both* of his hands, in addition to his cock and a sword, Billy One Hand—which is what his crew had called him ever since the incident—decided to let things lie, producing some words of agreement, as the mongrel licked his ear and shared the details of what he must do.

When Condent awoke in the morning, he assumed it had all been a dream, although in a matter of days, he realized that every detail that came back to him when he was intoxicated was undeniably real.

Capable Condent was, and capable was his crew, but their success since the Night of the Mongrel was well beyond even the

Marauding Monarch of Martinique's most ambitious and decadent dreams.

Not two days arrived in the Cape Verde islands, they had boarded a ship to find casks of Portuguese wine. The unfortunate Portuguese crewmen paid a lethal price for Condent's missing hand. Setting his sails for the coast of Brazil, he collected numerous prizes, and the beatings and tortures increased, while the ebony mongrel looked hungrily, happily on. Cutting noses and ears from the crews of the ships they boarded after molesting them in immoral, imaginative ways, Condent would ask each man before he set to carving, "Where be the Joseph Scroll?"

He had no idea what it meant.

The prizes and riches increased. Sailing to Santiago, Condent and his crew raided twenty merchant ships and a Scandinavian sloop of war, the latter of which he commandeered, calling her *Fiery Dragon*—how the spirit that had come as a dog was presently appearing.

No ship could escape his searching, be it Portuguese, English, or Dutch. Noses, ears, and tongues... all the while asking, "Where be the Joseph Scroll?"

Ship after ship he boarded, two of which he kept, so all would call him commodore and fear him even more. Still he sought the scroll. Still he took noses and ears. Riches filled his coffers, and his reputation grew.

Her African sea trade intolerably disrupted by Commodore Condent's flotilla, the powerful East India Company threatened to set its cannons and crews upon him, forcing Billy to cease the torture and disfigurement of those flying under her flag.

Still he asked his victims, "Where be the Joseph scroll?"

For the past two weeks, while his crews careened their ships, Billy One Hand had lived as a king, courting the girl at his feet—truthfully, he had purchased her from her father—and planning his next adventure.

Caressing the purple nipples of his dearly purchased wife, Billy One Hand called for rum and the quartermaster's accounts.

"All that I was promised!" he whispered in awesome wonder, seeing the list of treasures amassed to date and the most recent of the entries—a distribution, happily bestowed, of three thousand pounds to each of his crewmen, paid in silver and gold.

Sucking the contents of a bottle of rum down his throat in a single, noisy swallow, Billy One Hand felt a chill as the dragon emerged from the tree line, its red and yellow eyes boring its displeasure into his skin.

Fingering the bones of the mongoose, Billy agreed to all that the dragon demanded, beginning with a gift to his master of the still-beating heart of his Martiniqian bride, which the creature promptly devoured.

Admiral George Camocke allowed himself a moment to consider if he had offered his services to the wrong side in this latest incarnation of the increasingly complex battle of nations and personalities that had accomplished little else over the centuries but to send tens of thousands of promising young men to their deaths.

The whine of a cannonball as it struck the bow of the *Esperanza* just off the stern of Camocke's vessel, the *San Fernando*, quickly brought to a close such ill-timed contemplation.

"What are your orders, Almirante?" senior officer Teniente Mateo Trastámara enquired.

"I need an update on the fate of the flagship of Vice Almirante de Gaztañeta," Camocke answered, as the *Tigre* and *Águila*, positioned nearby, raised their flags of surrender in almost perfect synch.

Teniente Trastámara stole a fleeting glance at his logbook. "The *Real San Felipe* has been captured, along with eleven other vessels. Vice Almirante de Gaztañeta and Intendente General Rosales have been detained."

"Christ in a thicket of thorns," Camocke muttered, as a cold, foreboding sweat crept across his shoulders.

This engagement, which historians would later call the Battle of Cape Passaro, Avola, or Syracuse, depending on their nationality, point of view, or agenda, had been an unrelenting disaster since the moment it had first begun for the once undefeatable Spanish navy. The combined British fleets of Admiral George Byng and Vice-Admiral Charles Cornwall—who had arrived in Naples with the *Argyll* and *Charles Galley* a week and a half before—were more than a match for the ships under de Gaztañeta, who had always been better at designing ships than commanding them.

"English ship off our starboard stern!" another officer shouted, a spyglass to his eye. "It is the *Royal Oak*."

Camocke felt the sweat from his shoulders pooling at the base of his spine. "Captain Thomas Kempthorne's ship. Seventy guns. Word is, Rear Admiral Delaval is also aboard that vessel. He would like nothing better than to deliver me in chains to Byng."

Knowing that this was his moment—the failure of the fleet was not his fault, but Vice Almirante de Gaztañeta's, and now the survival of the remaining ships had clearly fallen to him—Camocke shouted, "Send word to the captains of the *San Juan Bautista* and *San Luis* to set their sails for Malta. You shall lead them, *Capitán* Trastámara. The *San Fernando* is yours."

Knowing it was unnecessary to hide his satisfaction at his unexpected promotion, Trastámara asked with a smile, "And where shall you be, Almirante?"

Instead of using words, Camocke pointed just off the starboard bow, where the *Ave María y Las Ánimas*, under the command of Capitán Amaro Rodríguez Felipe y Tejera Machado, was fast approaching.

"*Mi amigo!*" Machado was waving his arms, as he stood upon the gunnel of the *Ave María y Las Ánimas*. "These *cerdos*, these stinking, tyrannical pigswine *puta bastardos*! Damnable *Inglés* … *Pedazo de mierda cerdos*! Almost as bad as pirates! May all of them supper on *mierda de cabra* in *el infierno*!"

Trastámara shook his head. "Many of the officers say Pargo is *loco como un perro rabioso*, Almirante, ever since the death of his second in command and closest friend, Renaldo de Recalde."

"Insane as a rabid dog!" Camocke translated, transferring half a dozen rolled up documents, a spyglass, and all of his belongings from a sea bag into a strongbox. "Then I shall be in excellent company, Capitán! A little friendly advice… Careful what you say—he is a favorite of the queen."

Shaking his head as the forty-four gun *Volante* raised her white flag as two English men of war approached her from opposite sides, Trastámara asked, "What is your destination, Almirante?"

Locking the strongbox and slipping the key into his pocket, Camocke answered, "We are sailing for Messina. Signal to the captains of the *Hermione* and *Conde de Tolosa* that they should follow closely behind. We have important allies there. I have papers they must see. I am also nearly certain it is where Byng is heading next. It is up to me to represent the king and queen in the negotiations with the English. Messina's fortress is impregnable… her cannons are legion and eager to speak. She is the gateway to Italy, representing the fulfillment of the ambitions of the Habsburg emperor, who shall attempt to convince the Savoy duke, the greedy

Sicilian king, Victor Amadeus, to take the emperor's side against the Spanish crown."

Climbing over the side of the *San Fernando*, Camocke shouted to Machado's crew, "*Mis hombres fieles*! Do not despair! Our work for the king and queen has only just begun! Onward to Messina!"

Taking position beside Machado, who was busy commanding his crew with (admittedly) the look of a rabid dog, Camocke watched in frustration as the *Esperanza* burst into flames.

He had chosen the side he had chosen. There was no going back. Glory still awaited. In what guise, he could not say, although there was one thing of which he was confident—he was a scrapper and survivor and this was not his loss.

The carnage he was escaping and his actions in Messina were his pathway to redemption in the eyes of the Spanish queen.

L ieutenant Governor Alexander Spotswood, former military officer and leader of the 1716 Knights of the Golden Horseshoe Expedition, which crossed the Blue Ridge Mountains and claimed the Shenandoah Valley for Britain, sat in contemplation, a blank piece of paper on his desk before him and an unloaded quill in his hand.

He had received a request some days earlier from George Hamilton, first earl of Orkney and colonial governor of Virginia from his home in Edinburgh Castle, a fortress for which he also served as governor. Although the request for personal reports from Hamilton's lieutenant governor were rare—after all, Spotswood's secretaries kept in constant correspondence concerning financial and administrative matters with their counterparts in Edinburgh—the timing was less than ideal.

Having dismissed his senior secretary half an hour earlier, who normally wrote what Spotswood spoke as the lieutenant governor paced before the oversized windows of his office, the overseer of arguably—at least in his mind—the most prosperous of the colonies was determined to pen such a glowing description of his victories to ensure the longevity of his reign.

He had a host of ambitious plans, and it would take copius amounts of his precious time and patience in order to see them through.

For instance, he had commissioned a set of architectural plans for a more suitable home for a man of his stature and accomplishments, which would be built a hundred miles north, in Germanna. Just the day before, the architect had delivered the most exquisite—and expensive—vision for the gargantuan mansion where Spotswood intended to spend his most and then his least productive years.

*Now*, he thought, examining the subtle striations in the goose feather he used for his quill, *to the letter*. First, he must assure Governor Hamilton that the profit-shrinking pirate problem off the mid-Atlantic coast was currently well in hand. At least it was in Virginia. North Carolina was another matter entirely, a situation that Spotswood fully intended to turn to his advantage. There had been several proposals made by the lieutenant governor since his appointment to this office in 1710 for Virginia to *absorb* the seat of rebellion and haven for piracy lurking like an unrepentant convict beneath its southern border. The problems (and therefore opportunities) there were myriad. Unlike Virginia, which had ceased being a proprietary colony nearly a century before, North (and South) Carolina were still proprietorships—although Governor Johnson in the south was working assiduously and successfully to end this sorry state of affairs. In addition to populating the western frontier and increasing profits from shipping and other lucrative businesses through regulation and oversight, Johnson was employing a pirate hunter and two well-armed sloops as an essential component of his multipronged strategy to weaken the proprietors and return his colony back to the Crown.

Spotswood had decided to do the same. Not for Virginia—her deep-water port of Hampton enjoyed the more than adequate protection of His Majesty's Royal Navy—but for North Carolina, that vale of lawlessness between two towering mountains of piety and wealth. Spotswood had managed to limit the economic prosperity of North Carolina for the past several years, primarily through his dominance of the Tobacco Council of Virginia and the Carolinas, although Virginia's southern neighbor still presented a pair of once distinct but now increasingly overlapping problems.

The first was the competing interests of the Albemarle, beginning with Spotswood's counterpart, Charles Eden, and his chief justice, Tobias Knight. Rather than be pinched too severely by the tobacco council, they were setting up markets of their own, with the assistance of The Family, who had thus far limited their own potential for power by diverting much of their energy to fighting amongst themselves. Spotswood had worked well for years with Edward Moseley, who had historically overseen the commercial interests of his two primary partners, Colonel James Moore and Jeremiah Vail. The obstacle to the once prosperous alliance of Spotswood and Moseley was that, as of late, Moore had gained greater control, and his loyalties were continually shifting toward whatever would increase his personal power and wealth. It was Moore who had engineered the Indian wars in the sister colonies of Carolina that brought so much land to The Family and their supporters—John Carteret, William Craven, and another family who threatened Spotswood's dominion and long-range plans—the

Ravenskalds of Europe. Still in all, Moseley, just this morning, speaking on behalf of Moore and Vail, had agreed to search the papers of Secretary of the Province John Lovick for material evidence of the deal between Eden and Knight and the pirate Edward Thache.

Having already decided to make no mention of the latter in his still-to-be-started letter, Spotswood turned his mind to the second of his problems—the piratical operations daily occuring in the waters within and off the coast of North Carolina.

Spotswood had already decided upon a solution, based upon a combination of seemingly innocuous questions and, in some select cases, clandestine interrogation of several of Thache's crewmen in Hampton and Williamsburg during the processing of their pardons—an offer of leniency and forgiveness with which the pious lieutenant governor vehemently disagreed.

From those skillfully executed hours of interviews and interrogations, Spotswood had learned that Eden had made a deal with the bastard who called himself Blackbeard. This was wholly unacceptable. Spotswood would see the alliance broken with all considerable haste, and, in doing so, accomplish two important goals—weakening Eden to the point that Hamilton might more seriously consider absorbing North Carolina into Virginia, and ridding the Atlantic shipping lanes—and the aristocrats whose coffers they filled—of Thache and the rest of his godless rabble.

Spotswood had already sent a letter to Governor Johnson, warning him of the probable arrival of Thache's former partner, Major Stede Bonnet, who had achieved his greatest successes off the coast of Johnson's colony. Bonnet and Thache had conspired in the recent blockade of Charles Town, which had caused Spotswood's equally ambitious counterpart considerable embarrassment. If Johnson, through his pirate hunter, Colonel William Rhett, would see to Bonnet, Spotswood had a plan for getting Thache, the broad strokes of which he had already presented to the senior officer in the Hampton naval squadron, Captain George Gordon.

With the aid of the Royal Navy, Spotswood would set a trap for Thache in the Albemarle that would ensure the bastard's death.

The problems with the plan were few. Blackbeard, having taken the pardon, had immediately broken its terms. The same was true of

Bonnet. The two ships central to Spotswood's plan, the *Pearl* and *Lyme*—were escorting merchantmen home from Delaware because of the havoc Bonnet was causing.

Both The Family and the Ravenskalds were equally as interested in seeing this upstart Blackbeard undone, which gave Spotswood an increased advantage. The Star Quorum, about which Spotswood knew almost nothing, had recruited the pirate to do their bidding. Nearly all of his actions in the past twelve months had been expressions of his work for the Quorum off the coast of Rhode Island, in Philadelphia and the Caribbean, and as far away as Spain.

With Gordon's tacit approval of the plan (such as it stood), which came with the unnegotiable stipulation that he would not be directly involved, Spotswood had chosen the officer who would do what Gordon would not. The choice was simple—even preferable. Captain Ellis Brand, whose brash and bold ideas for how to deal with the influx of pardoned pirates into the Colony of Virginia had earned him and Spotswood positive notice from the Admiralty and His Majesty's Council of Virginia, would do all that the lieutenant governor required. Secret things that would not come to the attention of the Admiralty or His Majesty's Council of Virginia until after Brand had carried them out.

At last, he was ready to write. Dipping his quill into a fresh pot of ink, Spotswood began to hum. Although he could not recall the title, and he struggled to find the melody, he knew the welcome band had played it when he returned from his expedition.

This song was now the theme to all he would achieve.

# CASTELLO DEL SANTISSIMO SALVATORE, MESSINA, SICILY, AUGUST 18, 1718

"What do you mean the man refuses to see me?"

George Camocke was sitting in the dining hall in Messina's Real Cittadella, which Salvatori Fuoco had ordered his attendants to convert into a council room five days prior, when the Irish commander and the Spaniard Amaro Pargo had first arrived, followed a full day later by the British Admiral Byng.

"As senior officer of the Spanish fleet in Sicily, I am entitled to an audience!"

Spooning several helpings of fresh-made *caponata* into a bowl, which he placed before the red-faced son of Erin, Fuoco shrugged his shoulders. "Who knows better than you the games the British play?" Adding a basket of bread and a pitcher of wine to the table, he added, "You should eat. A full stomach is the pathway to a clear and measured mind."

Pushing the bowl away, Camocke replied, "Is he speaking with Amaro Pargo?"

"He is not."

Turning to the sound of the voice, Camocke saw the man himself, Amaro Rodríguez Felipe y Tejera Machado, whose ship, the *Ave María y Las Ánimas*, had transported the Irish admiral to Messina after the debacle at Cape Passaro. As the popular captain approached, Camocke considered his nickname. Were one to ask a roomful of people from where it was the moniker "Pargo" derived, you were almost certain to receive two very different answers. Half of the room would tell you that "Pargo" was a reference to the red Porgy, a fish that was as sleek and as fast as the captain's famous vessel, while the remainder would exclaim that the shape of the foul-mouthed captain's face was the source of his fishy nickname.

"Do not feel slighted, *mi amigo*," Pargo said with a grin, helping himself to a bowl of *caponata*. "That *puta bastardo* Byng struts the ramparts over his victory and refuses to hear a word. Some fat-faced *teniente*, lying through his *dientes torcidos*, insisted that the order not to negotiate comes from the British Admiralty. *Mierda de cabra! Pedazo de mierda cerdos!*"

Finding himself in admiration of the captain's passion, if not his colorful metaphors, Mago Fuoco poured his guest a cup of Madeira. "I may have a solution, my friends. It will be several more days before the admiral's fleet arrives. It is my belief that he is waiting on the Austrians before attempting to lift your country's siege of Messina and Trapani. In the interim, I humbly offer my services as intermediary. Truth is, Messina is my home. I would rather it were not destroyed."

Watching Amaro Pargo eat, Camocke felt his stomach start to rumble and his mouth begin to water. Swallowing a spoonful of *caponata*, he answered, "Very well then, Master Fuoco. Time is of the essence. I have sent several ships to Malta. Byng will go there in time. Ask him for an audience upon his flagship, *Barfleur*, as soon as you are able."

"And what should I tell him is his fellow admiral's offer?" Fuoco enquired.

Taking a moment to consider the mago's offer, Camocke replied, "Tell Sir George that I am authorized by King Philip of Spain and King James Francis Edward Stuart of Britain to grant him one hundred thousand pounds and the title of duke of Albemarle if he will surrender the *Barfleur*, as well as the rest of his fleet, to me."

Suppressing an incredulous smile at Camocke's unfathomable arrogance, Fuoco offered a half-hearted bow before exiting the room.

Half an hour later, as Camocke and Pargo were soaking up the final spoonfuls of the eggplant, olives, capers, raisins, and pine nuts remaining in their bowls with hunks of still-warm bread, they received their answer, courtesy of Capitán Don Rodrigo de Torres.

"The *Hermione* is on fire!" he yelled, as he burst into the room. "That *bastardo* Byng has set my ship ablaze in answer to your offer!"

Before Camocke could react, Fuoco was in the doorway, confirming the news with a nod.

"*Santa María Madre de Dios*!" Pargo whispered. "The *Ave María y Las Ánimas* is not safe. Almirante Camocke! I wish to depart at once. What say you to my request?"

The Irishman gave a grunt, followed by a nod. "You must return to Spain. Make a full and honest report to our beloved king and queen. Give them my regrets that you must bring them such unwelcome news. As for me, I shall board the *Conde de Tolosa*. Captain de Goycoechea and I shall meet with our allies in Malta. Before we are under sail, I shall arrange delivery of a message to Captain George Walton of the HMS *Canterbury*, offering him an admiral's commission and knighthood once the Stuarts are restored to the throne."

Their plan of action made, they departed for their ships.

Several minutes later, as he was pouring a cup of wine, Fuoco smiled at the sight of Abraxas Abriendo, Xiang Yu, and Padraig Ó Muiris entering the room.

"Tayl me we ain't missed supper, Mago," Padraig said, gazing into a line of empty bowls.

"Supper no… but the fireworks, yes," Fuoco answered, serving the three men from a large, steaming tureen carried in by one of his servants. "I cannot figure out which of their tempers is worse… the Spanish or the Irish."

"Camocke ain't yer normal Oyrishman," Padraig answered. "He ain't yer normal anyt'ing. An' the one his men call Pargo…"

Abraxas finished the sentence. "Curses a fiery blue streak. All about livestock and shite."

"Eat hearty, my trio of friends," Mago Fuoco responded, filling three more cups with wine. "Tomorrow, you depart."

The sounds of spoons and swallows ceased within an instant.

"But what about Messina?" Abraxas enquired. "We must help you to defend it—that is what you told me only hours ago."

"Fate, my student, is fluid," Fuoco answered. "It is clear from the lack of civility and refusal to negotiate realistically and productively displayed within and without these walls by Britain, Spain, and their allies that this war has just begun. It shall draw in other nations as honey draws the flies. This shall all take time. Messina for now is safe. You must go to North Carolina, in America, where the agents of the Star Quorum and Mammon Lodge are set to engage in battle. There you will find the ailing Blackbeard, along with one called Vane, in a tiny place called Wokokon."

"You have seen this in a vision."

"Indeed, Abraxas, I have. There is more, which I put into a letter for you to read on your way to the island, for this coming confrontation further involves you all. As much as I would like to spend these final hours together, I must arrange for ample provisions—as well as additional cannon, shot, and powder—to be transferred to Xiang Yu's vessel."

"Both I and the *Oiseau de Proie* are grateful, Mago Fuoco," the Manchurian warrior answered. "Whenever I draw my swords in service, I shall think of all you taught me."

"Hayr, hayr!" Padraig shouted, raising his cup into the air.

Gazing upon these young and vital warriors, Salvatori Fuoco, the Magus of Messina, suddenly felt so old. Even more than old. He realized he was exhausted.

"I pray we shall meet again," he barely managed to whisper, "when the final battle is joined. Though I know not when nor where."

For the past five months, former pirate Henry Jennings had been a happy, land-locked man, attending to the affairs of his family's plantations, meeting with other merchants in Governor Benjamin Bennett's mansion, and learning the almost daily lesson that marriage was rarely preferable to pirating.

"Please listen to me, Constance! It is naught but an idea."

*I should have gone to Ben's, and broached the subject later…*

"A stupid one at that!" Constance answered, beating their bedroom rug with unnecessary force as it hung upon a line.

"We have servants for such work," was all that Henry could say. "Your careful custodianship of our fortune in the years I was away has given ye a life of leisure. Ye should plan an evening of tea and games with the other merchants' wives. Both Jonathan Simmons and Jeremiah Outerbridge have remarked to me, on numerous occasions and as recently as yesterday, that their wives both admire and respect ye."

"That is bullshit, Henry!" Constance hissed, smacking the rug so hard the wooden beater snapped in two. "Oh… perhaps now, when the fortune you obtained from the fort in La Florida and pirating with Vane must no longer be kept a secret! Now that you are *pardoned*! You were absent for the whispers… The rolling of eyes and searing, insufferable giggles… that followed wherever I went. Henry Jennings's whore, walking about the town with his trove of jewels and *reales* sequestered up her arse!"

Jennings grabbed her hands, gently turning the one clutching the broken length of beater, which had a jagged, lethal point, until his wife released it. "Listen to me, Connie. I beg ye to quiet down. I had no idea what ye suffered. None of them had the right. I have loved ye since we were young. Every Bermudian knows it… Yes, I accepted a letter of marque. Yes, I then became a pirate, but this is the land of my ancestors. It has held my family name—*our* family name—for more than half a century! Please be certain of this… Whatever pain I caused ye, I fully intend to atone."

Her eyes still burning with anger, Constance pulled the bedroom rug roughly from the line and entered their stately home—one of the largest on the island—which sat upon a rise overlooking their expansive fields of tobacco, potatoes, and onions.

Once Henry was also inside—he quickly closed the door and dismissed a pair of servants—Constance said, her tone still bitter and angry, though with slightly less of an edge, "Exactly *how* will you atone, Henry Jennings, if you are off to fight a war that is certainly not of your making and might bring about your death?"

The war to which Constance was referring lacked an official name, although a recently arriving merchant had brought the news that Britain, France, Austria, and the Dutch Republic were now the Quadruple Alliance, locked in battle with Spain over disputed territories in Sicily, Sardinia, and Italy.

"I survived the War of Spanish Succession, the storming of the Spanish fort in La Florida, as well as several years of sailing with that violent madman Vane. I do not intend to sail to Sardinia. George and I have made considerable improvements to my dear old friend *Bersheba*, with the assistance of Jeremiah Outerbridge—arguably the most ingenious designer of sloops in the entirety of the Caribbean—and I merely wish to test her limits. Nothing more."

"As you are testing mine?"

Constance turned and vigorously stomped up the stairs, dragging the rug behind her. Each time a corner caught on a step, she yanked it with a curse. "Perhaps tonight, instead of sleeping beside me beneath our newly laundered sheets, ye should sleep beneath the deck of your dear old friend *Bersheba*! To hell with your bloody sloop! And off to hell as well with George Ball, Jeremiah Outerbridge, his two-faced, gossipy wife—and most especially *you*, my selfish, scheming husband!"

Before Henry could offer an apology, defense, or retort—the last one being the least likely to exit his mouth without spawning serious consequences—Constance was slamming their bedroom door, the rug she had recently cleaned lying halfway up the stairs like a sail devoid of wind.

Three hours later, sitting in Benjamin Bennett's mansion in King's Square on St. George's Island, Henry, who was seeking comfort and camaraderie, found himself instead the target of further abuse.

"I am siding with Constance, my friend," Governor Bennett said, filling his mouth with lamb, dripping with a cream sauce that smelled of thyme and onions. Speaking as he chewed, he continued his admonishment, which he appeared to be enjoying. "In half a year's time, ye have earned a place amongst the most highly respected Jamaican and Bermudian merchants. Your holdings on both islands prosper. Ye have married well… whispers of envy be damned, for that is what they are! Must I also mention, your continued presence is crucial to our defense? I have received several distressing reports that your former co-conspirator Vane is causing significant mayhem… What mischief shall he make should he decide to plunder Bermuda? With Governor Rogers installed in New Providence, he shall be looking for easier targets."

Despite his old friend's cultivated ability to navigate a subject in order to get his way—he was after all, a practiced politician—Henry was hearing sense in all that Bennett said. Privateering and pirating had once been preferable to remaining at home and attempting to live up to the seemingly unattainable expectations his father had had for him in terms of the family business. Sitting here with his friend, Jennings suddenly realized that, for a moment, faced with the myriad challenges of marriage, he had mistakenly thought that running away to war might just be preferable to staying and measuring up.

"Thank ye, Ben," Henry Jennings whispered, standing and adjusting his cuffs. "I will not let ye down. Now, I best be heading for home."

Dabbing some cream from his lips, the governor nodded and smiled. "I am overjoyed to hear it. And if the entrance to the bedroom is barred?"

"*Bersheba* beneath the stars."

# PART FOUR:

# THE PIRATE HUNTERS ARISE

Every morning, just before dawn, Blackbeard's crew of twenty-one would hear him scream. A single, blood-curdling expression of pain, and he fell silent, appearing in his doorway within the hour as if it had never occured.

Everyone knew better than to approach his little house, which he shared with his bride of seven weeks, Elizabeth Godwin, Governor Eden's recently orphaned niece, in the early morning hours.

Their sudden, unexpected marriage was the source of endless speculation and hastily whispered comments amongst the crew.

As far as they were aware, Eden had suggested the marriage as a matter of mutual convenience, and Blackbeard had readily agreed.

Although Blackbeard's desire to have Elizabeth reside with him on Plum Point instead of in Bath, as the governor had ancipated, had given Eden a moment of pause, he did not want to risk jeopardizing the union, and the marriage had proceeded as planned.

Given the pirate's pale, pasty skin and his inability to focus for more than an hour, Eden anticipated that the arrangement would not be long in duration.

"What does she do ta him in there, makes 'im scream like that?" Joseph Curtice asked, a lecherous gleam in his eye.

Nathaniel Jackson whistled, grasping his friend by the shoulder. "Whatever it might be, I would likes ta sign me up fer a daily dose a' the same."

Jackson winced as their quartermaster, Israel Hands, boxed his oversized ears from behind. "Ye know damn well what the cap'n is endurin'. Ye have a pressin' desire fer somethin' sharp bein' put into yer pecker, ye jus' come around an' see me. Happy ta oblige the lot a' ye tongue-waggin' scabs wit' a dose a' his mornin' routine."

It had been a combination of an increasing number of men in Blackbeard's flotilla contracting syphilis, generally called the pox, and their captain's steadily deteriorating condition that had ultimately revealed the secret he had managed since April to keep.

Following the grounding of the *Queen Anne's Revenge* and dispersal of nearly all of the flotilla's crewmen, the two pressed-into-service doctors who had been attending to Blackbeard and others with the pox had boarded a ship for Europe. Ever since, Elizabeth had taken on the daily task of using a pewter syringe with a short, curved tip to inject mercury into Blackbeard's penis.

Angus, although enjoying the company and camaraderie of his fellow Scots, Duncan MacDonald, Malcolm "Cnoc" Douglas, and Teàrlach de Bruys, was becoming ever more concerned about the state of their deteriorating captain, whose hatred of the French was increasing in direct proportion to his diminishing physical and mental capabilities.

A week before, Blackbeard's crew, in the well-appointed, nine-gun sloop *Adventure*, had intercepted two ships sailing from Martinique off the southeast coast of Ocracoke. Just as Eden had said, the Pamlico Sound was rich hunting grounds for a steady stream of unarmed or barely armed merchant vessels. The Plum Point pirates had taken the ships' valuables and cargo without incident and sent them on their way.

Israel Hands, Angus MacGregor, and his three Scottish comrades had delivered a portion of each under cover of darkness to Tobias Knight in Bath.

Then, two days ago, also in the Sound, they had taken a pair of French ships out of Bermuda, carrying a cargo of sugar and cocoa. The first, the *Rose Emelye*, whose captain, Jan Goupil, had ordered his crew to quickly man her cannon, had succeeded in warning *Adventure* off. In response, Blackbeard had ordered his sailing master, Thomas Miller, to ram the second of the ships, *La Toison d'Or*, as he saw she carried no cannon.

Boarding the disabled ship, a dozen members of Blackbeard's crew engaged in musket and pistol fire with the crew of the *Rose Emelye*, whose captain, left with little choice in the face of the pirates' deadly prowess, unconditionally surrendered within seconds.

Selecting half a dozen members of the offending crew as prisoners they would hold as insurance while searching the pair of ships, Blackbeard ordered Israel Hands to bind them securely and put them on *Adventure*. As Hands complied, Blackbeard ordered the Scots to strip-search the remaining Frenchmen for valuables.

Within the hour, they had cataloged nearly two hundred barrels of sugar, four hundred bags of cocoa, and a considerable haul from the individual crewmen's clothing, bodies, and quarters.

"What are we ta do wit' the crews?" Hands had asked, once the cataloging was complete.

Standing in the stern of the *Rose Emelye*, Blackbeard growled, "Onto the second ship with the lot of them!" To Captain Goupil he said, "Ye are lucky ye had a companion quicker to comply, or I would have thrown ye into the sea! Sail fer ye homeland directly, before I change my mind!"

"My sheep," Goupil whined, as his crew boarded *La Toison d'Or.* "How can you take my sheep?"

Hitting Goupil on the rump with the flat of his sword, Blackbeard replied, "Because ye are French, an' I despise the French!" As the *La Toison d'Or*, emptied of her cargo and overloaded with men, sailed away, presumably for France, Blackbeard laughed a hearty laugh, clasping Angus on the shoulder. "'Tis a fine, fine day ta be a pirate—do ye not agree?"

Thinking back on that moment, as he sat by the shore at Plum Point with his trio of fellow Scots, Angus felt a touch of pride. Despite the captain's illness, all was going well. They were away from the madness of New Providence and Captain Vane, the crew was friendly and up to the work, and he, along with the rest, were quickly becoming rich.

Lighting his pipe and running his pointer finger along the top of his dragon-claw ring, Angus "Quill" MacGregor began to make a plan for him and Ailish.

Then Blackbeard screamed again, and Quill was running toward the house.

Solomon Ravenskald, not yet thirty years old, had been representing his family at the semi-secret annual meeting of the International Financial Forum in Zürich—the leaders of which were also the founders of the post–World War II Fourth Reich in Europe and the Americas—when he received word to return to his family's estate, Chateau Ravenskald, within the hour.

His father, Samson, would not live out the night.

Finding the master bedroom empty, Solomon made his way to the chateau's underground temple. Since 1264, it had served as the Ravenskalds' center of power. It was here, in this carefully constructed ritual space, that the ruling Ravenskald father passed his mantle and his possessions to a single chosen son.

Having pushed his older brother through a patch of broken ice while on vacation in Minnesota when they were barely in their teens, Solomon had guaranteed there would never be the need for his father to make a choice.

He knew his father knew. He knew his father had approved.

Drawn by the heat and light of the red and orange flames dancing within the ceremonial fire pit that marked the center of the space, Solomon crossed the white marble floor to an area containing three semi-circular stone benches placed equidistantly around a twelve-foot circle of pure gold poured into grooves along the floor. Just beyond it was a makeshift bed of bear furs and a dozen goose down pillows encased in satin and velvet.

His father, skeletal, pale, and weak, was barely visible beneath the furs. Despite the thick covering and blazing fire, Samson was shivering and gritting his teeth.

"Solomon, my son. You have always come when your father has called. Tonight you shall ascend."

"Has your hour at last arrived?"

Samson shook his head. "I have made it so. To coincide with the annual meeting. When your business here is finished, they shall anoint you as their führer. Outside of that maneuver, it is better for the father to choose his time of dying than succumb to an impatient son. I hope you never forget this."

Solomon nodded. If there were not so many historical precedents, he might try to deny what he knew damned well to be true. The struggle between Adonijah and Absalom for their father Athelstan's position, which had begun its bitter resolution on November the first, 1717, in this very space, had come to an unfortunate end exactly two years later, also in this room.

"Was it nightshade or hemlock?" Solomon enquired, glancing at an empty goblet lying partially hidden beneath the furs.

"A little of both. I can feel them working. We are nearly out of time. There are rituals you must enact before I cease to exist. I must be their witness, to give them sufficient power."

Producing an almost translucent arm from beneath the layers of fur, Samson revealed that he was holding in a gnarled and vein-laced hand a sheathed ceremonial knife, which Solomon recognized by its two distinct adornments. The first was a *Schwarze Sonne*, an exact match to the one on the floor beside him. The second was the coat of arms of the counts of Kyburg—two golden lions on a black field separated by a golden diagonal line.

"Listen to me, my son. I want you to take position within the inner circle of obsidian." Samson unsheathed the knife—a slow, laborious process—raising it with a groan so he could point its tip at an obsidian circle that lay within the twelve-foot circle of gold and another, larger circle of obsidian. Separating the two obsidian circles was a ring of snow-white marble.

Taking position as his father had instructed within the three-foot inner obsidian circle, Solomon contemplated the twelve radial *Siegrune* emanating toward the outer obsidian circle, each one stopping half an inch shy of touching its edge.

In totality, this sigil was the *Schwarze Sonne*, the Black Sun—the Ravenskalds' seal of power, which Heinrich Himmler, at the prodding of the Austrian occultist Karl Maria Wiligut, had replicated in exacting detail in his SS-Schule Haus Wewelsburg in Büren, Westphalia, Germany, in 1934.

Samson had lethally punished Himmler by means of a cyanide capsule for his insulting cooptation of the seal on May 23, 1945, in Lüneburg, while the reichsführer-SS was in the custody of the British Army.

"Solomon," his father whispered, his breathing increasingly shallow and strained, "remove your clothes, and toss them outside the circle."

Before Solomon could enquire as to why, two servants in hooded black and crimson robes entered the ritual space, escorting a beautiful, naked girl.

"Solomon, this is Eve. I have chosen her as your vessel. She shall deliver to you a son."

As the vessel entered the circle, Solomon could see that her look was far away. His father's servants had drugged her. It mattered not to Solomon. Her porcelain flesh was warm, her nipples erect, and her womanhood open and ready to receive him.

As his father began to chant—"*die Hexen, die Geister, die Teufel*"—summoning the witches, ghosts, and demons that protected the Ravenskalds and their chateau, Solomon laid Eve on the floor, gently spread her legs, and inserted himself inside her. Hearing a little gasp of pain escape from her quivering lips, what he had intuited she then confirmed.

Eve had been a virgin.

Within seconds, it was over. It was not passionate, nor violent, nor particularly pleasurable for Solomon.

It was simply a transaction. A necessary coupling to ensure the Ravenskald line would survive. Solomon had no doubt that his father, or his agents, had carefully chosen Eve, and somehow he knew as well that, once his son was born—in this very spot—her life would become a torturous nothingness, eventually ending in self-inflicted death.

As the servants led her away, no doubt to an appropriately appointed room somewhere within the expansive chateau, where she would remain for the next nine months, Solomon noticed half a dozen drops of bright red blood on the center obsidian circle.

"Leave them," his father commanded, his voice now barely a whisper, although undergirded with an iron authority. "We still have things to do."

"Shall I dress?" Solomon enquired, his nakedness suddenly embarrassing, as though he were Adam in the garden after he and Eve had eaten the apple.

*Which is exactly who I am.*

"Best if you do not," Samson answered, sheathing the knife, which he handed to his son. "Guard this weapon well. It is second in power only to the Abraham Blade. Now... remove the ring from my finger."

Nodding with a coursing anticipation that triggered a renewed flow of blood that stiffened and heated his member, Solomon slipped a copper and iron ring, topped with the form of a pentagram, from the middle finger of his father's left hand and slid it onto his own.

His father smiled. "Use the knife to open your wrist. Let the blood fall into the fire."

Doing as his father commanded, Solomon stared in wonder as the red and orange flames transmogrified into a swirling dance of preternatural purples and blues as the drops of his blood hissed as they turned to steam.

"Father, what is ne—"

Solomon held his tongue.

Samson at last was dead.

Feeling the ring begin to pulse, Solomon turned his head toward the *Schwarze Sonne*, where the drops of Eve's virgin blood had coalesced into a single droplet of gold-tinged, radiant dew.

Lifting his arms upward and outward, he began to speak an incantation, its words not pulled from memory but from deep within his genes: "I call upon you Iblis! I bear the ring and name of Solomon, I am ruler of this family, and I command you to obey me..."

Although the temperature had cooled considerably from its blistering summer highs, Charles Vane's usually simmering blood was boiling in his veins.

"Yeats did *what*?" he asked, barely able to form the words against the pounding in his ears.

His quartermaster, "Calico" Jack Rackham, shook his head. "No need to fling your wicked temper at me. I am nothin' but the messenger."

"Fuckin' tell me again."

"If ye insist," Calico replied, removing his tricorne and pouring himself a generous portion of rum while Vane lit a cheroot with noticeably trembling hands. "The bastard took the pardon from Governor Johnson, after abandoning us as we sailed from Charles Town harbor."

Anxious to get this matter behind them so he might ask of Vane a favor, Jack assessed his captain's mood over the rim of his coffee-stained mug, searching for the tiniest signs of improvement.

They were nowhere to be found.

"I gave that poxy whore 'is ship back, an' not two weeks ago!" Vane muttered with a growl, biting down hard on the end of his cheroot. "Sat 'im down where ye are, an I says ta 'im, I says, 'Time ta take ya ship back, Cap'n Yeats. I ain't done 'er any 'arm.' Ta which he replied, accomp'nied by a smile, 'Good ta have me Kath'rine back' like all was well an' good!"

"This is nothin' personal to ye," Rackham replied, draining and refilling his mug. "The pull of the pardon is powerful to many. We have seen it aplenty in New Providence, made worse by Rogers's arrival."

"I pushed that Bible-totin' bastahd plenty 'ard as we left, did I not? Nearly burned 'is lovely *Rose* ta the wahtaline I did. What cap'n 'as done more ta thwart the guvnah's plans than me?"

Rackham nodded in silent agreement. Vane had pulled a bold and brilliant move right at the end of July, raising the Death's Head high over Nassau's fort before sending the flaming French brigantine in which they had arrived squarely toward one of Rogers's largest vessels.

They had escaped the harbor in Charles Yeats's eight-gun *Katherine*, with Vane installed as captain.

Exhaling a thick cloud of smoke before removing several flakes of loose tobacco with his thumb and middle finger from the tip of his grey-tinged tongue, Vane gripped the edge of the table. "We did well since leavin' Nassau! Terrorized a bit a' Cuba an' took a prize off the Bahamas, before headin' ta South Carolina. Ya keep the log, not me, but if my mem'ry serves, we took 'alf a dozen ships before we got ta Charles Town. Saved nearly a 'undred Africans from dyin' on plantations, we did. What be that look, Mistah Rackham? 'Ave ya a point ya wish ta make?"

Cursing his lack of ability to hide his thoughts—he would not get his favor granted revealing all that was on his mind—Jack drained his mug in a single swallow and said, "Captain Yeats was less than pleased that ye refused to sell the savages. That is many mouths to feed. An' the ship on which they were held was the *Dorothy* out of London... A promisin' vessel for piratin'. As were the *Neptune* and *Emperor*. Perhaps ye could have given one of them to me... Instead ye *sank* the *Emperor*..."

Extinguishing his cheroot beneath his boot, Vane leapt upon the table.

"We do not need the kind a' trouble that comes wit' sellin' slaves! Some will join the crew an' the rest can take their chances the next time we careen. As ta the others... we took what it was we needed. A fine accountin' a' rice an' skins an' plenty a' pitch an' tar. As fer the ships ya named—take it up wit' Cap'n Gowers as ta why I sunk the *Emperah*. 'E should not 'ave resisted when we raised the Jolly Rodgah. Anyways... ain't this brigantine sufficient? Fine lines, a dozen guns, an' room fer a 'undred men! She is my fav'rat *Rangah* yet."

"Yeats played ye for a fool, suggestin' we blockade Charles Town harbor," Rackham whispered, in too deeply to fail to see it through.

Scratching his greying beard, Vane adjusted his position so he was sitting instead of crouching, not a foot from where Calico stood. "I 'ad a rotten feelin' 'e was pullin' somethin', Jack. I also knew the spoils we would acquire there in that bleedin' 'arbah were more than worth the risk. An' I was right! Eight vessels in total we plundahd!

An', if ye believe I gave Yeats 'is propah share a' the spoils, ye ain't near as smart as ye look."

Jack dropped his jaw in wonder. "Then why the show of temper at the news he took the pardon?"

"I was sure 'e would try ta usurp me, which I woulda rathah an' bettah respected than 'im bein' a poxy cowahd choosin' the Act a' Grace!"

*Duly noted*, Rackham thought, ready to make his ask.

"Before I go," he said, "I want to ask of ye a favor."

"I knew it when ye entahd."

"I wish to go to Nassau. And I am certain ye know why."

Uncrossing his legs and leaping off the table, Vane released a laugh. "It be that redhead pot a' 'oney what's married ta poor James Bonny! She will 'ave ta wait a while longah ta ply ya wit' 'er wiles… We ain't 'eadin' in that direction."

Trying to hide his disappointment, Rackham enquired as to the plan.

Taking Calico by the shoulders, Vane answered with a smile, "We are gunna 'unt the ones who 'unt the great green turtle!"

Tobias Knight, chief justice of the Colony of North Carolina, wished he were at home with his wife Katherine on their recently purchased plantation, Archbell Point.

As a matter of fact, anywhere but here would suffice.

"Please listen to me, Edward."

The chief justice was sitting in the tastefully furnished sitting room of Blackbeard's adopted home. It was clear that the pirate's marriage to Elizabeth Godwin was having positive effect—at least in matters domestic. "I do not wish to appear ungrateful..."

Blackbeard, who looked to Knight as though he were feverish and not completely coherent, replied, "Then make sure that ye are not."

Knight swallowed a bit of water and quietly cleared his throat. "There are three issues I wish to address with ye. I shall endeavor to be brief."

"Better fer us both fer ye ta be so."

Glancing at a signed affidavit, as well as his notes, which he had scribbled in the governor's office the previous evening, Knight began. "It has come to our attention that ye had an altercation with a local farmer called William Bell two nights ago, whom ye encountered near the farmhouse landing of one John Chester in the Pamlico Sound."

Knight paused for verification. Blackbeard nodded and waved him on.

"Bell reported ye were not quite right... slurring your words, appearing as if ye were drunk. He claims ye boarded his periagua looking for rum. When ye failed to find a bottle, ye asked for a sword from *Adventure* and threatened to tie him up!"

Once again, Blackbeard merely nodded and waved his questioner on.

"Ye asked Bell to produce his valuables. When he enquired who ye were, ye professed to be from Hell!"

Leaning in, his eyes afire, Blackbeard answered, "An' that I am! I offered ta take him there directly!"

Feeling cold sweat in the small of his back, Knight held tighter to his notes to still his shaking hands. "According to this statement by William Bell, he tried to remove ye from his boat, at which point ye called for assistance from four of your companions, one of whom, the African child Caesar, promptly stopped ye when ye began to strike the unarmed Bell repeatedly with the flat of your sword."

"Caesar dislikes violence. I do not."

Placing his notes upon the table, Knight enquired, "What happened after he stopped ye? Best to hear it in your own words."

Blackbeard sat in silence, staring at his fingers.

"Edward… tell Chief Justice Knight what occurred. Ye have allies in him and my uncle." Elizabeth had entered the house and was standing in the doorway.

"Lock the door, my poor, dear Lizzie, an' I shall." Once his wife had done as he asked, Blackbeard said to Knight, "Took the periagua ta the middle of the river, where we alleviated Master Bell a' the burden of several pistols and bottles of brandy, a box of pipes, sixty-six pounds, and *this*." From a wooden shelf behind him, Blackbeard retrieved an ornate silver goblet. "I kept this piece for me. Ye cannot have it, Tobias."

The chief justice shook his head and raised his hands. "Keep it away from me. Keep it in this house. It is the most damning kind of evidence. Ye are foolish not to sell it." Realizing he had gone too far, he whispered, "Anything else ye wish to add before we attend to other matters?"

"Threw his sail an' oars in the water an' left him on the river."

Pulling a fresh set of papers from his pocket, Knight took a breath and said, "The second matter concerns the *Rose Emelye*, which I believe we have successfully managed." When Blackbeard did not speak, Knight glanced at his notes and continued. "Two nights ago ye brought her to Plum Point to undergo inspection. I saw her at anchor when I arrived. According to the letter ye sent to the governor, ye found her abandoned, and I quote, 'without a soul on board.' Is that correct?"

Blackbeard nodded. "As attested to by me, in addition to Angus MacGregor, Israel Hands, and Thomas Miller, in sworn affidavits."

Knight felt his mood begin to lighten. "Which I have in my possession. Based on these documents, the Vice-Admiralty has agreed to condemn the *Rose Emelye*, having taken ye at your word that she is not fit to sail due to the unsoundness of her hull. Salvaging rights also reside with ye. Once she is stripped, ye should sail her somewhere prudent and burn her."

Blackbeard smiled. "First thing in the morning. Is that all?"

"One thing more. Your hatred of the French is a connected issue to your plundering of the *Rose Emelye* and her companion." Knight ran his finger down his notes. "*La Toison d'Or.*"

"Shall I cease ta deliver your share when it comes from Frenchie ships?" Blackbeard countered, his smile becoming a smirk.

"Do not *only* target the French," Chief Justice Knight responded, putting away his papers. "Ships from plenty of other countries sail through Pamlico Sound."

Blackbeard stood. "Aye, they do indeed. Speakin' a' the French, how fares our high-spirited teenage pirate, Louis Arot? I hope he is more than earnin' his keep on your plantation."

Despite the protests of Caesar, who had become close with his fellow thirteen-year-old after his friend had earned a place on Blackbeard's crew by revealing that *La Concorde*'s captain had been withholding a bit of gold dust, Blackbeard had given Louis to Knight on one of his recent visits to Bath while delivering the justice's share of a recent take.

It was one less soul on Blackbeard's conscience.

"Excellent!" Knight replied. "His discipline and work ethic are exemplary, and Katherine simply adores him. I have given him increasing responsibility in the house and in the fields, which he eagerly accepts. At the appropriate time, we shall see to his schooling and career, thanks in part to your generous contributions."

Smiling wryly at the justice's choice of words, Blackbeard said, "Nearly time for dinner, which means ye need ta go."

Knight grasped his hat and stood. "I must get back home to Katherine." Stopping at the door, he said, his tone just shy of pleading, "Listen to me, Edward. The Family has noticed the disruption in the Sound. I need not remind ye of their powerful supporters, in Virginia and across the sea, in England and beyond. I am trying to bring them into our arrangement. In the meantime, if ye cut too largely into their profits, they shall bring the thunder and the storm as they come for ye in force."

Blackbeard unlocked and opened the door. "As well as fer ye an' Governor Eden. An' we must not forget your secretary a' the province, John Lovick. I hear his house was broken into."

The chief justice nodded. "Your sources are correct. We are more than happy to continue our arrangement with ye, Edward, provided ye are, in future, more discrete and less inclined to needless risk."

Seeing her husband would not respond, Elizabeth said, with a smile all too strained, "Always a pleasure, Justice Knight. Please give our best to Katherine and my uncle. Safe sailing home to Bath."

As he climbed into his boat, Tobias Knight began to wonder if safely sailing home would one day not be possible, considering the bargain he had made, and the frightening phantom with whom he and Eden had made it.

**"I** will carve 'is fuckin' 'eart out!"

Charles Vane had just returned to the *Ranger* from Captain Nicholas Woodall's sloop *Wolf* after negotiating the transfer of dozens of turtles and other sellable goods, sheets, and cordage to a report from Calico Jack that ruined his excellent mood.

"Yeats took advantage of your absence," Rackham responded. "Yours and more than half our crew."

"*My* crew, Calico Jack."

Ignoring the pointed slight, Rackham spread his arms in a show of supplication. "He and his men were armed to the teeth. I counted four new cannon on the *Katherine*—two on the rails and two on the deck. Of course, I promptly gave him what he came for. Ye know as well as I do—he was simply not expected after he took the Act of Grace."

"'Tis the gov'nah in Charles Town's revenge. Ninety African slaves will make for a hefty payout."

"Will ye let it go unanswered?"

Vane shook his head and grunted. "I cannot. We will need assistance, Jack. What 'ear ye regardin' the whereabouts a' Condent an' England?"

"Plenty to be sure. England has gone to Africa, where there are whispers of a fledging pirate republic led by a pair of your long-time nemeses—Levasseur and Williams."

"Bellamy's righteous bullyboys," Vane replied, slicing the tip from a freshly rolled cheroot. "They are mixed up wit' the Quorum. Naught but misery in that. What about ole Billy One 'And?"

Rackham clicked his tongue. "Not sure that I believe this, but the word amongst the crews is that he sits upon a throne on the isle of Martinique."

Vane was about to light his stogie and stopped. "A throne?"

"So they say. He wears a necklace of mongoose bone, carved with mysterious symbols. Amassing an emperor's fortune. Even took a wife."

"A bit too ambitious for Condent," Vane remarked, lighting his cheroot. "Ye 'eard anythin' else I should know?"

Rackham came in closer, lowering his voice. "Some have heard him asking for a thing called the Joseph Scroll."

"Quorum and Ravenskald madness!" Vane responded. "Is that the sum a' the tale?"

"There is one last bit of chatter," Calico Jack replied. "The hardest of all to believe. A few of the native islanders—a superstitious lot—say Condent takes his orders from a vicious, gargantuan mongrel, with red or yellow eyes and a coat as black as midnight, which also appears as a dragon."

Vane puffed on his cheroot, carefully considering what Jack had told him. "Do not speak a' this ta no one. It might be used ta our advantage in the weeks an' months ta come. None a' this solves our problem a' needin' extra 'ands. Lemme think on it awhile."

Resisting the urge to speak, Rackham sat in silence.

Releasing a ring of smoke from his suddenly smiling mouth, Vane chased it away with a howl. "The answer is right before me! Already set in motion when I was on the *Wolf*." Placing his cheroot on the edge of the table, he grasped Rackham by the shoulders. "I made a deal wit' Cap'n Woodall, who is none too 'appy wit' Guv'nah Rahjahs on account a' two recent agreements they 'ad made. The first was fer pirate 'untin', along wit' Gran'pa 'Ornigold an' that revenge-seekin' infant Johnny Cockram, fer which Woodall quickly decided 'e just ain't got the taste. The second was fer grossly unfav'rable terms fer turtle 'untin' 'ere in the cay. I gave 'im a bettah price by a little more than 'alf... In exchange, 'e agreed ta meet us wit' weapons an' ammo procured from within the fort a' Nassau!"

Rackham was impressed. Then he had a hopeful thought. "When an' where will we be meetin'?"

"Four days hence near Nassau. An' yes, me lustful quartahmastah, ye can lay with yer strumpet Anne... Now go an' tell our soddin' cook, I am cravin' turtle soup!"

Benjamin Hornigold held his pistol, which he had fully charged with powder, to the head of Nicholas Woodall as they stood on the deck of the *Wolf*, hidden from view by the mainmast, watching as the *Ranger* and a cannonless sloop approached.

Fully cocking the hammer, Grandpa whispered, "Be enthusiastic, Captain Woodall. I need Vane to come aboard, thinking all is well."

Four days earlier, at Green Turtle Cay, Hornigold and his partner, John Cockram, had watched from a prudent distance as Charles Vane had boarded Woodall's sloop. The mood of the two men as Vane departed two hours later made it clear they had reached an accord.

As much as he had wished at that moment to attack the *Wolf* and *Ranger* where they sat, Hornigold lacked the element of surprise. It would have been at best a standoff—two Bermuda sloops versus a pirating sloop and a brigantine.

There was also a second factor. As Vane had met with Woodall, another vessel had arrived. Hornigold and Cockram had watched in wonder as Vane's agitated quartermaster facilitated at gunpoint the transfer of nearly a hundred African slaves to the late-arriving ship.

The following day, Hornigold had learned the truth of the matter… Vane's former partner, Yeats of the *Katherine*, had recently taken the Act of Grace in South Carolina. He was no doubt intent on selling the Africans outright or returning them to their owners in Charles Town for a considerable reward.

As Woodall shouted hello and Vane brought the *Ranger* closer, Hornigold moved his body farther into the shadows.

"I will kill ye if I have to," he whispered in Woodall's ear. "Ye are a traitor to the Crown."

"An' ye are a traitor to the Republic, to which ye yerself gave birth," Woodall hissed in response.

When the ships were almost touching, Vane ordered the anchor set. "'Ave ye brought me what I was promised?" the impatient pirate enquired. "I 'ave places I need ta be an' shippin' ta disrupt."

"I have more here than anticipated," Woodall answered, feeling the muzzle of Hornigold's pistol grind against his skull. "Come aboard and see."

As Vane stepped over the gunnel, Hornigold whistled, which was the predetermined signal to John Cockram and twenty well-armed men to reveal their clandestine positions around the deck of the *Wolf*.

"Well, take me for a fool!" Vane responded, raising his hands in the air. "Ye flip like a sheet in a windstorm, doan' ye, Nicholas Woodall?"

"He surprised me!" Woodall answered, caught between Scylla and Charybdis. "I intended to honor our agreement! All I promised is stowed below."

"None of which is yours," Hornigold said, releasing Nicholas Woodall and pointing his pistol at Vane. "I am seizing the *Wolf* as property of the governor of the Bahamas. What this man has stolen I shall return to the fort at Nassau. Do ye surrender to me as well?"

Instead of a reply, Vane clasped his hands above his head and produced a trio of whistles. In an instant, the crew of the *Ranger* cut her anchor line and quickly turned her seaward.

Woodall pointed to Cockram's sloop, anchored a distance off their bow.

Hornigold uncocked his pistol and began to wave his arms. "Look lively, Captain Cockram! The bastard's done it again!"

Heading for Cockram's sloop was Vane's unanchored, cannonless consort, her sails and masts ablaze.

Hearing Cockram give the order to weigh the anchors of his sloop, Hornigold re-cocked his pistol, taking several steps toward Vane.

"Do ye know what Captain Yeats is doing with those African slaves? Delivering them to Charles Town. Ye shall not see a shilling from their sale to further your sinister plans."

"I was not plannin' ta sell them," Vane responded. "Some were fit fer crew—the rest I woulda set free at a suitable time an' place. *That* is what the Republic stood fer, is it not, ole Gran'pa *'Unter*? Ye 'ave sentenced them all ta death!"

Hornigold lowered his pistol and leaned against the mainmast. "Damn ye, Captain Vane—ye and Jennings would not support me, yet ye speak of the Republic? What is it ye want? Can ye not see the end has come, for Edward and ye and the rest? Jennings took the pardon—from Bennett in Bermuda, where he runs the family plantation. I hear that Edward has taken sick... likely with the pox...

that he has made himself a deal and taken a wife in Bath. As for the rest of the crews… gone to the west coast of Africa and Martinique. Too frightened to stay and fight. They know the power that Governor Rogers wields. Ye have nowhere ye can go, no hope of real success."

"Finished?" Vane enquired, pulling his pistol and knife.

As the men around him tensed, Hornigold raised his hand. "Do not shoot this man! We shall not be guilty of murder. He shall no doubt meet his end before the year is out."

Putting away his weapons and standing on the gunnel, Vane let loose a laugh. "I shall gladly take that wager, Gran'pa 'Unter 'Ornigold!" Before diving into the water, he gave a sharp salute. "Until we meet again, give Woodes my best regahds!"

As the pirate swam away, Hornigold lifted his hand. "I will not suffer the asking of questions. Let us see to Cockram's sloop and set a course for Nassau. Fate shall handle the rest."

Colonel William Rhett was beginning to grow weary of his endless miscalculations and ill-considered alliances.

Against the orders of Governor Johnson, who had still not forgiven Rhett for allowing Blackbeard and Bonnet to blockade Charles Town for three dangerous days exactly four months ago to the day, Rhett had once more abandoned the harbor.

He was not in his usual position to capture pirates near O'Sullivan's Island when Vane arrived in Charles Town. Not this time. This time, it was something far more personal.

Something he would not be able to defend or explain to Johnson, no matter how he tried.

He had sailed to another tiny island off the South Carolina coast, to the retirement mansion of the former deputy governor, Robert Daniell. His visit had been against the wishes of Johnson, who had made very clear his position that the conniving conspirator was far more useful being left to his devious, only minimally disruptive, devices.

Rhett had agreed for a time, but his burning desire for vengeance eventually won the day.

After spending an hour alone with Daniell and a two-foot length of birch rod, Rhett was certain that the secret-sharing louse would stay on his little island and keep his damned mouth shut.

Rhett had entered Charles Town harbor just in time to hear the news that Charles Vane had only hours before set sail for parts unknown, after efficiently, ruthlessly plundering eight merchant and fishing vessels.

Johnson refused to see him. Instead, he sent word through a secretary that Charles Yeats had taken the pardon, offering his sloop as a patrol ship to prevent any further incursions into the harbor.

Determined to win redemption, Rhett had boarded his sloop *The Henry*. Along with the *Sea Nymph*, under the command of Captain Fayrer Hall, he had returned to O'Sullivan's Island, believing Vane would soon arrive.

After a fruitless week of waiting, Rhett had sailed for the Cape Fear River, having heard a rumor of pirates careening at its mouth. Word was they were planning to remain until the middle of October.

This rumor of waiting pirates was not all that he had heard. Yeats, not content with the Act of Grace and the task of patrolling the harbor, had surprised his former ally Vane near Abaco, stealing ninety Guinea slaves, and subquently presenting them to Johnson for sale or return to their owners.

For nearly a week, the *Sea Nymph* and *Henry* had scoured the inlets and bays of the coast on their way to the Cape Fear River, searching for Vane and his men.

They had once more come up empty.

That is, until the previous night, when Rhett had spied a pirate sloop, anchored at the mouth of the river. Awaiting the coming of nightfall, his two sloops aimed for the anchorage, intent on a clandestine attack.

A sandbar had thwarted their plans, holding the two sloops hostage in its sediment and sand.

Just after one in the morning, the crew of the pirate sloop, seeing their would-be assailants sitting helpless in the moonlight, tried to make for the open ocean, but they also ran aground.

For the next five hours, a wicked battle ensued, intensifying with the sunrise, the sounds of pistols and muskets ceaseless in the waning darkness, accentuated as they were by the merciless taunts exchanged between pirates and hunters.

Her rigging almost in shambles, *The Henry* at last floated free, making straight for the pirate vessel, which had also suffered some damage.

"Ready the cannons, men!" Colonel Rhett commanded, as the *Sea Nymph* broke free of the bar. He allowed himself to smile as Captain Hall ordered the raising of the rest of *Sea Nymph*'s sails and preparation of her cannons as she quickly closed the distance to the pirate's still trapped vessel.

From the bow of the enemy ship, they heard a high-pitched voice, urging her men to fight, upon the pain of death. As they neared the sloop, however, they saw her white flag raised.

Confident he had captured the troublesome bastard Vane, who was solely responsible for the death of the former commander of *The Henry*, Captain Masters, who had died during a confrontation with Vane off the coast of O'Sullivan's Island the past October, the long-thwarted pirate hunter released a triumphant shout of joy.

Finally, Rhett had avenged his murdered friend and comrade.

Cautioning his men to stand at the ready with pistols and muskets aimed—between the two sloops they had suffered a dozen dead and nearly twenty wounded—Rhett shouted to the pirate vessel, "Captain Vane! Ye have no hope of escape. On behalf of the governor of the Colony of South Carolina, I command thee to surrender!"

Much to his surprise, instead of a bloodthirsty pirate, scarred and shaggy in appearance, Rhett received his answer from an unremarkable-looking man in a quilted robe and slippers, wearing a pommeled cap that sat noticeably askew on his head.

"We *do*! We *do* surrender! Can ye not *see* our snow white *flag*? *Seven* of us are dead. Another nine are *wounded*. We do not wish for *more*!"

Tempted to release a laugh and enquire if this was a joke, Rhett suddenly recalled the descriptions of the gentleman pirate Major Bonnet, who had twice blockaded Charles Town.

"Are ye the pirate from Barbados?" he asked the well-dressed man, drawing his sword and pistol. "Do ye call this sloop *Revenge*?"

"Once upon a time. Now I call her *Royal James*."

"Then ye are the villainous Major Bonnet, sometimes known as Captain Edwards, and ye are hereby under arrest, along with the rest of your crew."

Stede Bonnet and thirty-three members of his crew stood in chains in a makeshift courtroom a few buildings down from Governor Robert Johnson's mansion.

Bonnet, who looked pitiable and exhausted, was on the verge of tears.

Presiding over their arraignment was Johnson, Attorney General Richard Allein, Assistant Attorney General Thomas Hepworth, Colonel William Rhett, and a trio of wealthy merchants named James Cormac, Caratacus Marks, and Samuel Wagg.

Marks and Wagg, the latter of whom also sat upon the colony's governing council, had been amongst the hostages taken by Blackbeard and Bonnet for three days in May when they had blockaded the harbor to obtain a chest of medicine.

Aware that a curious and not altogether supportive crowd was steadily growing outside the makeshift courtroom's doors, Governor Johnson hammered his gavel upon the table, seeking to conclude the current proceedings before tempers began to flare. To his amazement and concern, there were many on the streets—and a few within these walls—who sympathized with the "gentleman pirate," given that Bonnet was an educated fortune seeker who appeared to be utterly incapable of violence.

"We shall begin with remarks from our attorney general," Johnson began, motioning to Richard Allein to proceed with his opening statement.

Standing, Allein said, "These... godless *things* before us... These *pirates*... prey upon all of mankind, their own species and fellow creatures, without distinction of nations or religions. And Major Bonnet—from a wealthy Barbadian family, liberally educated and once considered a gentleman—ye, sir, have lost all sense of honor, becoming a common robber. *Hostis humani generis*. Yet your crimes do not stop at petty thievery. No, sir... because, to theft, ye have added a far greater, more egregious sin... Cold-blooded murder! Ye and the scoundrels who stand with ye in chains before us have killed no less than eighteen persons out of those sent by the lawful authorities to suppress ye."

Governor Johnson nodded as Allein took his seat. "Our esteemed attorney general is eloquent as always. Listen closely, Major Bonnet, for I shall repeat these charges, of which ye have already been made aware, for the sake of conveying their seriousness to ye and your crew. Ye resisted apprehension, costing numerous sailors' lives—both your own and Colonel Rhett's—to say nothing of your twice blockading the harbor of Charles Town and engaging in numerous other vile piratical acts. What say ye, Major Bonnet?"

"Do not permit him speak, I pray ye," Rhett whispered in Johnson's ear. "We shall be his prisoners here for hours…"

"He is entitled, Colonel Rhett," Johnson replied, so all in the room could hear. "I am determined to be fair."

Still in his teatime attire—slippers, robe, and cockeyed, pommeled cap—Bonnet shuffled noisily forward, to better address his accusers and the crowd.

"Thank ye Governor Johnson, for inviting me to speak." The major's voice was weary, whispered, and measured, devoid of its usual bird-song inflections. He had hardly managed to sleep since his ignominious arrest. "I stand before ye today, a gentleman in chains, full to the brim with guilt, and horror, and shame. I come from notable stock, which I implore ye to consider. My grandmother's father was the famous privateer Sir Thomas Whetstone. His son John—my mother Sarah's father—was the deputy colonial secretary of Barbados—nephew to Oliver Cromwell! The present governor of the Bahamas, Woodes Rogers, whose circumnavigation of the globe is the envy of sailors everywhere, was married to a Whetstone, the daughter of an admiral."

Admittedly engrossed by Bonnet's narrative, Caratacus Marks enquired, "Ye say *was*, Major Bonnet. Is the unfortunate woman deceased?"

Shaking his head in a theatrical show of sadness, Stede explained. "She divorced him, after the death of their infant son. This also happened to me. I understand her grief."

Colonel Rhett, who knew far more about the man standing in chains before him than he cared to, knew exactly where this was going.

"May my colleagues here make note," he began, rising from his chair, "that it was Major Bonnet who departed from his marriage…

abandoning not only his wife, the daughter of a judge, but his three surviving, defenseless children."

"Not defenseless!" Stede responded. "Not defenseless at all. They have the paternal family fortune—my ugly uncle Thomas would never let those darling children starve!—as well as the fortune of the Allambys. They shall want for nothing in the whole of their lives. They are better off without me."

Amidst the backdrop of sympathetic mumblings and moans rising throughout the room, Stede proceeded to relate the story of the death of his parents and grandparents and his uncle's arranging for his commission as a major in the Barbadian militia, where he served for five years quelling a number of slave uprisings on several surrounding islands. Wiping a tear from his eye, he told the tale of his forced marriage to the heartless Mary Allamby upon his return from service, a union engineered by his uncle solely for the obtainment of water rights from his cunning neighbor, the judge.

"So ye wished to leave Barbados… to make a new, unfettered start," Samuel Wagg remarked. "One could understand your grief and the pain of a loveless marriage," Wagg stole a glance at the back of the courtroom, where his own mirthless wife was sitting, "worsened by the death of a son. Why, though, Major Bonnet, did ye turn to acts of piracy?"

"A need to prove myself—and for a time I did. My sloop, on which I spared not a single expense, is fine of line and rather formidable to this day—just ask Colonel Rhett." This provoked a laugh from half the courtroom, although the red-faced colonel refrained. "I paid for the finest crew, and we took our share of ships. A single mistake, a miscalculation born of ego, led to a near disaster at the hands of a Spanish warship. It was then that I met Hornigold and Thache, which is when my education in the ways of piracy truly began."

Again making use of his gavel, Governor Johnson, who felt the tide of public opinion overwhelmingly turning in favor of this far too eloquent pirate, pronounced, "That is sufficient testimony for now. As ye may be aware, although Charles Town holds the distinction of being the only walled city in all of the American colonies, we do not currently have a gaol. Therefore, it is my judgment as governor that, until the commencement of your trials for piracy, your quartermaster, Robert Tucker, along with twenty-nine members of your crew, shall remain under lock and key in the Court of the Guard, which offers the proper accommodations for ones such as them."

"What of the three remaining prisoners, who are the masterminds behind all that the others have done?" Rhett enquired, knowing that the Court of the Guard, and the adjacent Half-Moon Battery, were by far the most secure fortifications in the city.

Annoyed at the interruption, but anxious to conclude the arraignment, Governor Johnson answered, "Major Bonnet, along with his boatswain Ignatius Pell, and sailing master David Herriot, shall be remanded into the custody of the provost marshal, Nathaniel Partridge, who shall host them in his home."

"I do not understand," Rhett responded, suddenly aware that Charles Yeats, former pirate turned pirate hunter and slave merchant, currently favored by the governor over him, was smirking at Rhett from the shadows.

"Then ye shall have to trust me." Governor Johnson's tone made it clear that he would not tolerate a further outburst. "Or I shall cut a switch of birch and give ye what ye deserve."

"Gaev mae a hand haer, ye hoowlin' numpty! We are aboot tae lose the spar!"

Shaking his head at the insult, Duncan MacDonald rushed to "Cnoc" Douglas's side just in time to stabilize the spar in question, which had come loose from the mainmast as they were preparing to unstep it.

"Yer bum's oot the windae, Dooglas!" Duncan said, lowering the spar to the deck of the *Adventure*. "Long as I am haer, na'er shall thair bae tatties o'wer the side!"

Coiling a length of rope using his palm and elbow, Cnoc Douglas laughed, shouting to Angus MacGregor and Teàrlach de Bruys, who were preparing the bowsprit for removal, "All haes eggs are double-yoakit!"

"Aye," Duncan answered, hanging several already coiled lengths of rope around Cnoc's thickly muscled neck, "An' yer all bum an' parsley!"

"Mae coosins would hurl that vaery saem insoolt at mae back in Balquidder, as they waer pushin' mae inta the pigsty," Angus reflected, climbing over the bow and onto the ground.

"That bae a lifetime ago noo, Angus," Duncan responded. "If they stood before ye haer today, ye could easily handle any a' the scabby roasters withoot hardly breakin' a sweat."

"Less talkin', more preppin' over there," Israel Hands barked out from a nearby table, where he was whittling a mermaid with his knife. "Blackbeard expects this ship to be ready fer careenin' when he returns."

"Thaen hoo aboot lendin' a hand, ye jakey gowk," Teàrlach whispered to Angus, while tilting his head to indicate it was Hands for whom the insult was meant.

"Aye, Maister Hands," Angus shouted, giving Teàrlach a good-natured shove. "She shall bae raedy wael before hae arrives!"

Blackbeard, along with four other members of the crew, had taken a longboat to Bath the previous day, delivering their agreed-upon share to Governor Eden and Justice Knight of cocoa, sugar, and sweatmeats they had recently taken from a ship in the Pamlico Sound.

They had also taken Eden and Knight a good-sized chest of coins.

"Fain lives these big yins haev," Teàrlach had said as the crew was loading the longboat.

He was saying it again, at the mention of Blackbeard's errand.

"Ye ain't exactly poor," Angus replied, spreading the jib on the grass so it could dry beneath the sun. "Yer practically a baron, descaended froom a king!"

Dragging the headsail from the ship, Teàrlach responded, "Unless mae broother Henry meets an unexpaected aend, I shall nae ever bae a baron! As tae mae lineage, aye an' fain, dear Angus… I be the descendaent a' Robert de Bruys! Illegitimate… boot blood-kin all the same. Baen that way fer nearly four hoondred years. An' since Thomas was granted lands an' the title a fairst baron a' Clackmannan in thairteen thairty-four by his coosin, King David the Saecond, six oother a' mae kin haev carried the name a' Robert de Bruys!"

"Was not joost blood thaet got 'im the title," Cnoc remarked. "He fought wael against the English."

"All a' oor families fought wael against the English," Duncan answered. "Angus's parents wair killed by order a' William a' Orange fer thair loyalty tae the Stuarts."

Teàrlach stopped spreading the headsail. "Is that hoo ye came tae live wit' yer aunt Mary an' oocle Rob?"

"Aye," Angus answered. "An' joost like ye, big yin, I haid noothin' tae inherit, which is hoo I wound oop piratin' in Noo Providence."

"I tried tae join yer crew in Philadaelphia followin' yer scrap wit' Joseph Stanton, boot the quartermaster, Maister Howard, refused mae, sayin' thair were already too many goddamned Scots on board!"

Before Angus could think of a worthy reply, he spotted Blackbeard's longboat approaching.

"I see how it is! Now ye cease yer nonsensical Scotsmen's gibberish," Hands called out, brushing wood shavings from his lap and stowing his knife and the unfinished mermaid in his sea bag. "Now that pappa's home, yer as silent as *bairns*, ain't ye, ye howlin' numpty roasters. Eh? How is that fer some *fain* Scottish yappin'?"

Half an hour later, as the four men who had accompanied Blackbeard to Bath secured the longboat, the captain of *Adventure* approached the silently working Scots.

"Angus, I have need a' ye in my cabin."

Ignoring the raised brows, low whistles, and breathy laughter from Duncan, Cnoc, and Teàrlach, Angus wiped his hands on a discarded piece of sailcloth and followed Blackbeard onto *Adventure*.

Once they were in the captain's cabin, Blackbeard locked the door and invited Angus to sit.

"Glad to see ye amongst yer own, an' getting' plenty a' respect," Blackbeard said, pouring Angus half a mug of rum. Retrieving William Bell's silver cup from a drawer, he kept on pouring rum into it until it nearly overflowed. "I have somethin' I want to give ye." Opening a different drawer, he removed a book, which he laid on the table and pushed gently toward his guest.

Glancing at the spine, Angus opened it and flipped to the title page, which he proudly read aloud. "The Sea Gunner, H Clark, London, by John Seller, 1691."

"I have only given one other copy of this book to a fellow seaman, an' that was to William Howard, the day I made him quartermaster. My own, I have bequeathed to Elizabeth. Ye, my friend, shall do memorable things in the not too distant future. This book shall help ye get there in the darkening days to come." Blackbeard drained his cup in a single swallow and collapsed into a chair.

It was then that Angus noticed the paleness of his skin and the circles beneath his eyes.

"I see how ye look at me, Quill," Blackbeard whispered, "and I know ye can see the truth. I have not very long to live, an' there are things I wish ta tell ye. Things fer your coded journal."

Rising from his chair, Angus replied, "Thaen I shall go an' faetch it diraectly."

"Leave it where it lies. Sit down an' listen well, fer I wager ye shall never forget what it is I am about to tell ye."

Once Angus was back in his chair, Blackbeard refilled the silver cup, although he did not raise it to his lips. Rubbing his eyes and running his hands through his grey-flecked ebony curls, he said, "I received another twenty lashin's from Eden and Knight regardin' my targetin' a' mostly Frenchie vessels. It is time I explain ta ye why I have done so. Ye are not to speak of it to anyone—not even your lovely Ailish—until after I am dead." Seeing that Angus was about to argue, Blackbeard slammed his hand upon the table, spilling some of his rum. "Listen an' do not speak! There is not a minute to waste." Settling into his chair, he closed his eyes and sighed. "I thought fer sure when Abraxas Abriendo arrived in Nassau he would reveal my secret to Gran'pa Hornigold, but the wizard played me fair. After I am gone, ye and Abraxas must work together. He is an endless pain in the arse, but a powerful, knowledgeable magician. He an' I grew up together on Jamaica, in a place called Saint Jago de la Vega, although the English call it Spanish Town. He was a petty thief, a common street thug, in love—or lust—with my stepsister. My father caught him in the act of tryin' to steal his purse in the square one memorable, an' for Abraxas regrettable, day.

"It was around that time that I also fell in love—not, believe me, in *lust*—with the brand new wife of a Frenchie naval captain. Best to leave the rotter's name unspoken, though I shall happily tell ye hers. It was Noèle, born as she was at Christmas. I swear to ye Quill, she smelled a' pine an' snow! Our love was pure, her husband a bully an' a braggart—like all a' the bastard French!—so we planned to run away.

"My father, always so alert to his surroundin's, caught us conspirin' in the garden one night. An argument ensued, the strain of which his sufferin' heart simply could not bear. I buried him beside my mother. No questions were asked of me, fer he was well advanced in years. Noèle an' I fell all the more deeply in love, an' I began to make arrangements to transfer my holdin's to my stepbrother an' stepsister so my love an' I could sail away to England.

"I do not know how her husband learned the truth. Fer years I suspected Abraxas, but I have come to be certain he is innocent of any betrayal. In a jealous rage, the rottin' arsehole locked her on his ship an' fired upon our town. I rowed to his ship in secret an' entered his cabin at midnight." Lifting his cup with a trembling hand, Blackbeard drained its contents in a single, silent swallow.

As his captain lowered the cup, Angus saw tears in his eyes. "His cabin was barely lit by a single, sputterin' candle. The bastard was at his desk, hands soaked with fresh-drawn blood. On the bed was my darlin' Noèle. The things he had done to her body in his seethin', red-hot rage I will not speak aloud. Nor shall I share the details of what I proceeded to do to him as punishment for his crime. I shall only say, when I snuck off just before dawn, what remained inside that cabin ye could no longer call a man.

"I brought my darlin' Noèle's defiled body back home to our plantation. Dressin' her wounds as best I could, I buried her remains beside my beloved mother an' father. The followin' mornin', I paid a visit to our lawyer, payin' him twice his usual fee to ensure that the transfer of my stake in the plantation was completed that very day. An hour after signin' the papers, I was hired on as an ordinary seaman with the *Barbados Merchantman*, and thus began my life at sea. Several months later, cravin' an increase in action as a balm for my tortured mind, I took the Royal Navy oath aboard the Fourth-Rate HMS *Windsor*, under Captain Tudor Trevor, when she docked for food an' water off the Isle a' Wight."

Blackbeard, whose cheeks were wet with tears, leaned forward in his chair.

"Now do ye understand my hatred a' the French?"

Angus, occupied as he was with inscribing the ending of the story upon the walls of his heavy heart, where it forever would remain, could only manage a nod.

"Ye do not judge me, Quill?"

"Hoo cannae, Cap'n Thache? The bastaird naeded tae die, joost as mae coosin in Scotland one day weel fer what hae attempted tae doo tae mae Ailish."

Wiping the tears from their eyes, both men turned in unison at the sound of several rapid, insistent knocks. "Best come quick!" Israel Hands was shouting, "a pair of vessels are approachin'. One is the *Oiseau de Proie* and the other… it be Vane's."

For the past six days, the island of Ocracoke, called by the natives Wokokon—the meaning of which historians have disputed since John White, a member of Walter Raleigh's 1585 expedition, placed it on a map—was an impromptu mini-kingdom hosting some of the most powerful pirates and Star Quorum agents operating on the Atlantic coast and in the Caribbean.

The first twelve hours after Charles Vane's arrival were tense, as his and Blackbeard's crews eyed one another with distrust. After all, the former had spent the past few months terrorizing the Caribbean in defiance of Woodes Rogers's arrival as governor of the Bahamas, while Blackbeard had sent most of his crew away, selling sixty slaves and setting himself up in a lucrative deal with the governor of North Carolina and his partner, Tobias Knight.

Vane's crew outnumbering Blackbeard's by nearly four to one only made the tension worse. Should the former wish to make a move, the melee would be over within minutes.

The simultaneous arrival from Messina of Abraxas Abriendo, Padraig Ó Muiris, and Xiang Yu on the *Oiseau de Proie* with an additional sixty men did little to ease the tension—both Blackbeard and Vane were weary of the machinations of the Star Quorum and their Mammon-worshipping adversaries.

Pirating was challenge enough.

By the afternoon of the second day, the crews of the three ships—*Adventure*, *Ranger*, and *Oiseau de Proie*—had broken into clusters throughout the island, with their pirate captains, the wizard, and the Irishman, along with a few others requested by Abraxas Abriendo, assembling at what would one day be known as Springer's Point and, more specifically, Teach's Hole.

Digging their bare feet into the seaweed-covered sand while enjoying the shade of the ancient live oaks whose branches twisted majestically around them, this select group of rebels and revolutionaries stuffed themselves nightly with roasted hog and cow while emptying barrel after barrel of rum and Spanish wine.

All throughout the island, groups were doing the same. Jack Rackham and Israel Hands, a pair of disgruntled quartermasters feeling slighted by their captains over their lack of independent command—from their perspective, suitable ships had been available for the purpose on numerous occasions—grew equally more angry and intoxicated as the days and nights progressed. Urged on by their fellow junior officers, who acted out of boredom more than loyalty, the two of them bitched about current conditions—Jack wanting to be with Anne Bonny in New Providence and Israel Hands increasingly frustrated with how events had been unfolding ever since the grounding of the *Queen Anne's Revenge*.

Just before midnight on the sixth and final day, the two men swore an oath to each overthrow their captain before the month was done.

The many Scottish pirates had claimed an isolated section of the island for themselves. Every hour—or sometimes more—they would hold their mugs silently over a bowl of water as a sign of their intent to return James Francis Edward Stuart to his place on the British throne. Amongst their number were Malcolm "Cnoc" Douglas, Duncan MacDonald, and Teàrlach de Bruys, whose stories of Rob Roy MacGregor, the Jacobite rebellion, and the exploits of Black Douglas and Robert the Bruce were in demand at the start of every evening as the already drunken Scotsmen convened around the fire.

Thus, the week progressed, with no one daring to approach Blackbeard's Plum Point house, where he had locked away his wife, Elizabeth Godwin, for safety, or to encroach upon the parlay at the future Springer's Point, which, by the sixth and final night, had grown dangerous in its intensity.

Tossing his cheroot into the fire, although it was barely smoked, Charles Vane kicked into oblivion a pile of driftwood, sand, and shells he had used to approximate the fortifications at Nassau. "Tell me once again why ye are so committed ta life in this stinkin' 'ell'ole!"

The rest of those in attendance—Abraxas, Padraig, Xiang Yu, Angus MacGregor, Joseph Stanton, and the Ashanti youngster Caesar—considered walking away, but an icy look from Blackbeard kept them in their seats.

Gesturing to a chest full of coins and valuables sitting on a stump beside him, Blackbeard growled, "The partnership between Governor Eden and myself gets better every day. The project is thus. We lie in wait as ships come into the channel. We board them and take what is of value, which we then transport under cover of night to the barn of Eden's minister of finance, for cataloging and sale. Why the hell would I want to abandon such an effortless operation?"

Staring for a moment at the cloudless, blue-black sky filled with a million stars, before fixating on Orion, Vane responded, "Why, Edwahd? 'Ow can ye ask me such a question? After engagin' wit' ya 'ere fer nearly a week, layin' out our obstacles, beggin' fer yer assistance in takin' back what's ours, ya dare ta ask me why?"

"Listen to me Charles. The Jacobite cause is lost. James remains in Europe, under protection of the pope. Our dreams of a Republic of Pirates died with Hornigold's betrayal. Same for Jennings and Williams. I have a good arrangement here. My health is quickly deteriorating. I have a wife an' a little house. Continue to beg if ye must... I shall not go with ye to die upon New Providence."

Rising from the stump that was serving as his seat, Vane shouted, "Yer a damned coward is what ya are! Fer all yer appearance a' ferocity ye 'ave no more courage than a cowerin' dog! What bettah way ta die than fightin' fer the cause?"

Much to everyone's surprise—including, perhaps, their own—the two exhausted, finished-with-talking warriors simultaneously drew their weapons.

Cocking his pistol and tilting the point of his sword so the blade shone bright in the moonlight, Blackbeard hissed, "Do not make me prove to ye of what it is that I am capable. It is best to part as friends, or ye may not depart at all."

Holding his weapons at the ready but softening his tone, Vane replied, "Look at yerself. Takin' the pahdon. Strikin' deals wit' politicians. I am truly ashamed ta know ya, Edwahd Thache."

Spitting at Blackbeard's feet, Vane dropped his weapons, turned his back, and raised his arms. When Blackbeard failed to attack him, he released a mocking laugh, and walked into the woods.

"Leave him be, old friend," the wizard Abraxas whispered, rising and approaching Blackbeard. "His destiny differs from yours."

"Did ye see that in your mirror?"

"I read it in a letter," Abraxas responded. "The contents of which I should have shared with ye well before now. If ye will have me in your home, ye may read its contents in peace."

Putting away his weapons and nodding in agreement, Blackbeard walked away, motioning for Abraxas to follow.

The following morning, Blackbeard appeared at Angus's side at their campsite, gently awakening his confidante with a whisper and a shake. Putting his finger to his lips to indicate Angus should silently follow and let the others sleep, Blackbeard refrained from speaking for the better part of a mile.

Entering a clearing, Angus put his hand upon his pistol at the sight of Captain Vane.

"Easy there, young Scotsman. I was invited ta be 'ere."

"I spent a sleepless night," Blackbeard explained to them both. "Abraxas's letter was nothing short of revelation. It was written by his mentor, the magus Salvatori Fuoco, who lives upon Messina."

"Ta 'Ell wit' all these wizahds!" Vane growled in disgust.

Blackbeard shook his head. "This time, we must listen. Ye shall sail in consort with the *Oiseau de Proie*. At least for a time. There is business to which Abraxas must attend off the coast of the northern colonies, of which ye are also a part. There is more that he shall tell ye. Ye too shall read the letter, once ye are under sail. I shall only tell ye this. Seven have been chosen, an' ye shall be their leader. Ye shall soon be sailing with six. One must remain for now."

A look of confusion contorting his face due to all that he had heard, Vane responded, "No doubt it be yer lapdog. This one 'ere… Ya precious Quill."

"The one who stays is Caesar. Quill shall be with ye, when ye depart from here this evenin'."

Shaking his head in frustration, Angus responded, "I donnae understand. I donnae wish tae doo this!"

"I do not care what ye ken, or what ye wish to do!" Blackbeard answered, with the tone of an angry father. "Ye shall do as ye are told. Yer place is with the Jacobites, as yer uncle Rob commanded. That is why ye came here. An' there is one thing more. Ye must look after Joseph Stanton, as ye did on the Boston docks when ye still were ignorant boys."

Angus was fighting tears. "Boot I donnae understand…"

"I shall leave ye ta work this out." Charles Vane's voice was heavy with sadness. "Speakin' a' Joseph Stanton, there is sumthin' I must tell 'im. I need ta pondah a bit on how." Placing his hand on Blackbeard's shoulder, he whispered, "Fair thee well, ye stubborn bastahd. Try ta die wit' a sword, an' not yer pecker, in yer 'and. If nothin' else, jus' promise me that."

Laying his hand on top of Vane's, Blackbeard responded, his voice about to break, "I am sorry I cannot go with ye. Ye have been chosen to lead the cause. It is no longer my fate to do so… if it ever was. I know ye shall succeed."

After Vane had walked away, Angus stepped in close. "If I trooly am tae leave, thair are things that ye moost knoo. I spoke wit' Dooncan late last night. Thair was a haver amoongst the quartermaesters, an' booth were mighty sair."

"What did Israel say?"

"He is angry at baein' demoted. He an' Rackham were makin' thraets a' takin' yer commands."

Blackbeard's face was blank. "What else do ye need to tell me?"

"Word arrived last night… Major Bonnet has baen taken, along wit' the raist a' his crew, at the mouth a' the Cape Fear River."

"I was already made aware. I heard it from Eden and Knight. We can only hope the hangman places the knot with precision upon his neck."

With that, the Cannon and the Quill, tears in their eyes and an ache in their hearts, embraced a final time, and went their separate ways.

John Hipps looked down at the three corpses arrayed around him. Not having a white flag readily at hand, he pulled his shirt from his back, tied its one intact sleeve to his musket, and waved it high in the air.

The cannon and musket fire that had been ceaselessly pounding their vessel from the sloops of pirates turned pirate hunters Benjamin Hornigold and John Cockram for the past fifteen minutes immediately ceased, which was a gift come from God himself for Hipps and the ten others still alive in their sinking periagua.

However, not all of his shipmates agreed.

"What have ye done, John?" William Cunningham, former gunner on the *Batchers Adventure*, enquired.

"Saved our lives!" Hipps responded, continuing to wave the makeshift flag of surrender as the pair of sloops approached.

"More likely prolonged them just enough to see us hung, ya fool!" said Dennis McKarthy, a former militiaman from Bermuda.

Standing in front of John Hipps, as both a deterrent and an invitation for the nine men staring at the veteran sailor to attempt to make a move against him, was the unofficial captain of the periagua, John Augur. Augur, who had formerly captained the sloop *Mary* out of New Providence, had taken the pardon along with every one of these men before joining them on the *Wolf* under Nicholas Woodall to hunt turtles in Green Turtle Cay a handful of months before.

Well-respected amongst the crews, Augur had agreed on behalf of these men when Woodall decided to ignore the pardon and smuggle guns and ammunition out of the fort at Nassau for Vane.

When the very hunters who were now approaching had cornered the *Wolf* near Nassau, Augur and thirteen others—three of whom now lay dead in the stern—had been away in this periagua, fishing for their dinner.

"I will not have ye harassin' Mister Hipp. The man is a damned fine sailor. The very best boatswain I know," Augur warned, not daring to draw his pistol as a further point of persuasion with the two sloops nearly upon them.

"He did not have the right!" growled William Dowling, the oldest of the crew. Forty-nine years old and bearing the scars of a life at sea, he had once been Blackbeard's gunner on Bonnet's sloop *Revenge*. "He is not the quartermaster, nor is he the captain!"

"I do not want to die," whispered George Bendall, who had turned eighteen years old the day before he took the pardon. "If John Hipps had not done what he had done, that is what I would be. Dead, I mean. That is what ye would be, Mister McKarthy, an' ye Mister Dowling, and the rest a' ye as well."

"Stow the chatter, lads," Captain Augur commanded. "Our tormentors have arrived."

Twenty minutes later, as the periagua sank beneath the sea with the trio of corpses still in the stern, Augur and his crew stood in a line on Hornigold's sloop, their wrists and ankles in manacles. Forty grim-looking sailors—many of whom Augur recognized—were aiming their pistols and muskets at the prisoners' hearts and heads, prepared to shoot to kill should any of them move.

Standing before the prisoners, Benjamin Hornigold read from a sheet of official-looking paper. "On behalf of the governor of the Bahamas, the honorable Woodes Rogers, I am placing ye under arrest for the crime of piracy at Green Turtle Cay, as well as for breaking your oath of pardon. Ye shall be taken to the fort at New Providence and tried in a court of law for your crimes."

"I was forced into service, Gran'pa!" John Hipps shouted, falling to his knees with a groan. "These two gentlemen here—Thomas Morris and William Ling—ask them if it be the truth, and I know they shall swear that it is!"

"Shut yer bleedin' stinkhole, Hipps, before I shut it for ye!" William Dowling shouted, earning himself the terrible kiss of a musket butt thrust squarely into his ribs.

"Have ye anything else ye wish to tell us, Mister Hipps?" John Cockram enquired, pulling the trembling man to his feet and placing him back in line.

"Do not further wag yer poxy tongue, Mister Hipps," whispered George Rounsivel, who was standing right beside him. "We fought an' we drank, an' now we swing, together. That is the way a' the life an' death a' the Brethren a' the Sea."

Bursting into tears, Hipps inched forward and shouted in a rush of words, "The owner of that sinking periagua is a merchant by the name of Kerr. Captain Augur ordered him marooned on the other side of Exuma. He and a dozen others. With zero food or water."

"Ye dirty, sniveling bastard!" John Augur shouted, throwing Hipps to the ground and kicking him three times in the kidney before a blow to his jaw from the hilt of a sword dropped him to his knees. Spitting blood on his attacker's boots, along with several teeth, Augur hissed, "I defended the gutless, tongue-waggin' son of a whore, an' this is my reward."

Hornigold shook his head. "A greater reward awaits ye at the gallows of the fort."

# PART FIVE:

# TRIALS AND MACHINATIONS

Governor Robert Johnson, determined to see his plan to have his colony buy out the Lords Proprietors and become a royal province succeed within a year, had just departed the Commons House for a meeting with Samuel Wagg and Caratacus Marks, when he was stopped on the street outside his mansion by Charles Yeats and William Rhett.

"Pirates have been spotted off the coast of the Carolinas, Governor!" Yeats reported.

"Lower your voice and join me inside," the governor whispered, as heads began to turn in the marketplace and emerge from open windows.

Entering the room they had used on October the third for a makeshift courtroom for the arraignment of Bonnet and his crew, Governor Johnson found Wagg and Marks already in conversation, which they ceased as he approached.

"Close and lock the door," Johnson instructed Rhett. "And stand in front of it while we talk." Turning to Yeats, he asked, "Is it Vane? Or perhaps it is Blackbeard, attempting to rescue his former conspirator..."

Yeats shook his head, hiding a smile of triumph at the sight of Colonel Rhett stewing in his practical banishment. "Even worse from my perspective. A merchant who barely escaped with his life reported recognizing the flags of William Moody and Paulsgrave Williams."

"I agree that worse is accurate," Samuel Wagg chimed in. "Moody's ship is the *Rising Sun*. She boasts a crew of a hundred and fifty and thirty-six large-bore cannon."

"We must protect the harbor!" Johnson said, feeling his heart begin to race. Pointing a thin, accusatory finger at Colonel Rhett, he said, "This is all your damnable doing, through your dereliction of duty! Bonnet, Blackbeard and Bonnet, Charles Vane... all have attacked our harbor with impunity, because ye sir have failed in your duties! Word has spread amongst their fellow vermin that we are an easy target!"

"If I may." Caratacus Marks stood and offered a smile. "We cannot spare a moment for pettiness and rancor. Colonel Rhett is well aware of what has happened in the past and what it has cost this colony and its merchants—especially we former hostages. It would be wrong for us to forget, however, that he has recently brought us Bonnet and his crew of vicious scalawags."

"Thank you, Master Marks," Rhett responded with a bow.

"Do not thank him yet," Samuel Wagg chimed in. "My poor son William, all of four years old, still has nightmares about that demonic creature Blackbeard. I am not convinced that thirty-four pirates is payment enough for the damage your colossal incompetence has caused."

"Perhaps it is best if Colonel Rhett takes the *Henry* immediately to O'Sullivan's Island," Governor Johnson suggested, anxious to move the meeting forward.

Rhett walked with haste to where the governor stood. "With all due respect... If Moody and Williams are planning to enter the harbor, then this is where I belong!"

"Where might I find this proffered respect ye speak of all too lightly?" Johnson asked. "Certainly not in your tone. With the assistance of Captain Yeats, we shall protect our precious harbor. Your sloop awaits ye, Colonel. Make haste for your beloved playground. I shall send word if we grow desperate for your assistance."

Managing a bow, though his body was tense and resisting, the colonel left the room, after glaring at Captain Yeats.

Locking the door, the governor said, "Let us make our strategy. First, the matter of ships. Despite the arrogant, ignorant orders he has up until this moment had no choice but to obey from the wayward Colonel Rhett, Captain Hall shall command as always the *Sea Nymph*. Yeats shall command *Royal James*."

Excited by the plan, Caratacus Marks applauded. "Top notch strategy, Robert! There are two other suitable ships currently in the harbor... the merchantmen *King William* and *Mediterranean*. We shall need three hundred men to join us in the cause."

Samuel Wagg, who had been jotting figures in the margins of his ledger, said, "We have a total of seventy cannon. Nearly double the *Rising Sun!*"

Johnson clapped his hands. "Then we are guaranteed success! I shall assume the overall command, aboard the *Mediterranean*. I know her owner well."

As the foursome began to celebrate, they heard banging upon the door. "Open up, ye brash conspirators! Open up immediately!"

Recognizing the voice, as well as two others shouting threats and uttering curses, Samuel Wagg proceeded quickly to the door. Despite a whispered request from Johnson to leave it locked, Wagg threw back the bolt and invited the trio in.

"Have ye something to ask of us, Governor?" the owner of the *Mediterranean* accusingly enquired. Beside him, their faces red with fury, stood the owners of *King William*.

Johnson shook his head in surprise. "How could ye know of our plans?"

"The conniving Colonel Rhett," postulated Yeats. "He knew your plan as well as ye did."

"That disrespectful cur!" Johnson growled, feeling his head begin to ache.

The owner of the *Mediterranean* pulled a ledger from a satchel. The men beside him did the same. "If ye wish to use our ships, all expenses must of course be covered in full. Additionally, there must be full indemnification against probable losses."

"Captain Yeats," Governor Johnson said, sinking into a chair. "If ye would be so kind as to arrange for dinner to be brought to us in half an hour's time, we all would be most grateful. I do not expect we shall leave here before the dawn."

Before Yeats had reached the door, the bargaining had begun.

Eugene Gorman Howe, monickered by the media as The Changeling, was holding his finger an inch above a pool of fresh-spilled, brilliant blood in the basement of his house, which used to be his mother's before he helped her to her final reward.

"Let me see..." he whispered, slamming the palm of his hand hard against his deaf left ear, hoping the Voice of the Beast—which had been silent for weeks, ever since his arrest in Secaucus, New Jersey, for a series of ritual slayings—would offer its assistance.

It did not.

He would just have to tally his kills alone.

"Okay... Okay... Mother-vessel's boyfriend. That was number one."

Eugene made a mark in the blood, which was beginning to darken and dry. The boyfriend—a dago WAP in wing-tips and a wife-beater who had busted Eugene's eardrum with a metal meat mallet when the boy was barely twelve—had met his deserved demise courtesy of the industrial-grade grinding wheel in his workshop behind the house.

That was the initial thing the Voice had told him to do.

"Number two was auntie, that Bible-bleating bitch," Eugene said with a giggle, etching a second mark right beside the first.

She had plunged down the cellar stairs. With a little bit of help.

"Eugene, don't be modest... it was a fucking SHOVE!"

Had Eugene said that aloud, or was it in his head?

Suddenly, they all came back... each of the sixteen kills that followed, using a nine-inch custom-made blade, housed in a sheath while it rested and recharged that Eugene had decorated with the teeth and hair of his kills.

Making sixteen more marks in the blood, he counted the total so far... three sets of five, plus three little ghosts, anxious for companionship.

Eight more marks for the crotch-rotty whores of New Jersey, whom he had slaughtered the week before Christmas.

The Voice of the Beast had been ecstatic. Just one more whore to carve! To gather the precious Vel!

Christmas Day. Feet away from completion...

That fucker Kevin Connor.

Connor, the cocksucking Fed.

Connor, who now possessed the sheath and knife.

Eugene wanted them back.

He had not been sitting in prison for long when a mysterious man and a Special Forces unit—imagine that! For little old E.G. Howe!—had released him one moonless night.

The man, who called himself Xavier Hearst—a pseudonym of course—looked and moved like a serpent.

"You have work needs doing, Eugene. Work you shall do for me."

Hearst had delivered Eugene—in the back of a silver Rolls Royce limo!—to the family home in West By-God Viriginia, after assuring him repeatedly that no one would dare disturb him. He also gave him an assistant—a hair-lipped computer geek named Eustace Dwyer-Mann—who was too fucking ugly to go outside without wearing a motorcycle helmet with its tinted face-shield down, so he lived in the world of the Deep Web off his billionaire father's money, fucking by proxy, gambling, and watching people being tortured and killed.

Such a stupid fucking name his shit-brained parents had given him. *Really, morons? Eustace?* Sounded like a concoction of earwax, pudding, and puss. Eugene called him Hair-Lip. Hair-Lip's father owned Damon-Metis Corporation, a world leader in advanced weaponry and psychological/physical military enhancement products, including the VR headset that Hair-Lip wore whenever he wasn't doing Eugene's bidding, courtesy of Hearst setting him up with a bitchin' array of computers.

Hair-Lip was on the other side of the wall, probably VR-fucking some dude pretending to be a nympho teenage cheerleader.

"Keep counting... blood is nearly dry," Eugene scolded himself, having to tug his finger just a bit to get it unstuck from the blood where it had made the twenty-sixth mark.

"And now a mark for Mommie..." Eugene had to use his fingernail to inscribe it. "And six for the real-estate harpies from Wood and Mason counties..."

Since Hearst had set him free, Eugene had used Eustace's computer skills (similar names but nothing alike!) to identify the times that open houses concluded. Eugene would arrive just a couple of minutes before, making certain to be the last to leave. They weren't prostitutes per se, but their stupid-looking, Glamour

Shot and AI-generated phony-as-fuck photographs and salacious offerings of sugary treats and swag-bags just to make a sale made the real-estate harpies close enough to count.

There were thirty-three marks in the blood, which had hardened into a crimson coagulation, scarred with bright white slashes.

God, how this turned him on!

Making a thirty-fourth mark, etched for the source of the blood, Eugene heard someone approaching.

"Eugene Gorman Howe! Get up off the floor. What is this embarrassing mess?"

Afraid to raise his head, Eugene ran through a list of suspects. It was not the Voice of the Beast. Still so stubborn, still so silent. The *words* were his mother's, his aunt's, his mother's mallet-wielding boyfriend's. But their ghosts were always silent... standing in corners, *staring*...

"Eugene, do you hear me? *Get up off the floor.*"

Compelled to obey... the voice so firm and paternal (*how in the hell could I know that... I never met my father...*), Eugene looked up as he stood.

The man before him was perfect.

"Whose blood is this on the floor?" Perfect Father enquired.

"I caught this podcast fucker snooping around the property. Does a bunch of stupid shit 'bout true crime and ghosts and the Kitchner County Menace on the other side of the river. I told him to come inside and I would give him an exclusive." Eugene giggled and started to rock. "He could call it 'The Changeling Speaks'!"

"Where is the body, Eugene?"

"Buried it out back. No one will ever find it. Cross my heart and pull my pud."

Perfect Father smiled (*Why am I calling him that?*). "My name is Solomon Ravenskald."

"The Ravenskald Group. You compete with Hair-Lip's father."

Again, this Perfect Father smiled. "I suppose you're referring to Eustace. Do not be unkind. Eustace has his uses. There is no competition, Eugene. Damon-Metis exists because I want it to. There is beauty in the balance."

"As there is beauty in the blade." Eugene rocked a little faster.

"Speaking of..." Perfect Father handed Eugene a nearly foot-long package, covered with jet-black paper topped with a bright red bow.

Not needing to open the package to know what it contained, but needing so badly to hold the thing itself, Eugene tore into the paper, like a kid on Christmas morning.

It was his nine-inch custom-made blade sleeping in its sheath, still exquisitely adorned with the teeth and hair of his victims.

"But how?" Eugene enquired, unconsciously thrusting the blade above his head like a redneck Sweeney Todd. "That fucker Kevin Connor—"

"Do not contact Connor again," Perfect Father warned. "Not with messages, not with videos. Like Damon-Metis, the Domestic Threat Early Assessment Unit exists because I want it to. Balance, Eugene... that is how darkness wins. I can see you know who I am. Who it is that you are to me. Your mother. Her name was Eve..."

Eugene unexpectedly wept. "I am sorry that I killed her."

"Do not be apologetic," Solomon answered. "She was sadly shattered after she numbly accepted my seed. Her life was a nightmare. A torment. I should have ended it long ago, when she could not end it herself. I was irresponsible. I did not follow the proper protocols, at the onset or after your birth. But her living served a purpose, until the moment that it did not. Then you acted in my stead."

Eugene wiped the tears from his eyes with his sticky, bloodstained fingers. "Then you really are my..."

"I am."

"I have always loved you, Father," Eugene said, lowering the blade and falling to his knees before the blood. "I always knew that I was special! Not like the other boys, who used to call me names." Rocking back and forth, his voice like that of a child, he whispered, "Helpless Eugene was replaced, as he was crying in his cradle, a Changeling birthed by faeries laid there in his place."

Sidestepping the blood, Solomon lifted his son by his shoulders, which were trembling with the force of his tears. "You have a brother, Eugene. A willful, unreliable disappointment named Samuel. He is not fit to take my place, although he is the oldest. That is why I have come."

"I am not worthy of you, Father."

"That is correct, my son. But when the time arrives, you shall be worthy of being an emperor."

Taking the sobbing boy in his arms, Solomon heard Eugene whisper, in a voice, which was many voices in one, "I am your Son and Servant. The bringer of the Blood. I am the final Passage. I do as you command."

Lowering Eugene to the ground, Solomon kissed his deaf left ear.

As his father left the basement, Eugene heard a voice.

The Voice of the Beast had returned. What joyful things it told him.

Thirty-four was just the start.

The count would increase tonight.[3]

---

[3] Eugene's story is detailed in *The Icarus Continuum: From the Files of the Domestic Threat Early Assessment Unit.*

## CHARLES TOWN, COLONY OF SOUTH CAROLINA,
## OCTOBER 24, 1718

"For the love of God and all the blessed saints and angels, will ye cease that dreadful caterwauling, Major Bon—What in Christ are ye wearing?"

David Herriot, Stede Bonnet's long-suffering sailing master, originally drawn to the major's room in the provost marshal's home by a particularly off-key, overwrought performance of "To Be a Proper Pyrate," stopped in the doorway so abruptly, boatswain Ignatius Pell slammed into his back.

"Yer wearin' a bleedin' dress!" Pell barely managed to mutter, gazing in shocked embarrassment over David Herriot's shoulder.

Applying a choking puff of powder to his garishly over-rouged cheeks and otherwise painted face, Stede danced a little jig in answer to their surprise.

"Always *wan*ted an ex*cuse* to play the part of a *tart*!" he declared, examing himself in the mirror. "These won't do at *all*…" Taking his quilted robe from off the bedpost, which Herriot noticed was missing several sections, Stede tore a swath from the bottom, which he shoved down the top of his dress. "Better breasts," he whispered. "Better, *redder* breasts." Smearing some rouge where his own flabby breasts created God-given décolletage, he turned to his junior officers.

"*Tell* me I am di*vine*!"

"That is how ye intend to testify against your crew at Johnson's mansion in an hour?" Herriot enquired. He had to turn away, so embarrassing was the sight.

Stede released a girlish laugh. "Of *course* not, Mister *Herr*iot!"

Herriot, still not able to look upon his captain, responded, "Then wash that pig grease from your face, put on some pants and boots, and meet us on the porch!"

Affixing a wig over his shorn and balding pate, Stede vigorously shook his head as he adjusted its bows and curls. "I am *not* atten*d*ing that *farce*, and *nei*ther are *ei*ther of *ye*."

Grunting in frustration, Ignatius Pell pushed past David Herriot, joining Bonnet at the mirror. "We agreed—all three a' us—that we would testify against the rest in an attempt ta escape a hangin'. I have already penned my remarks—five pages a' secrets an' lies, an' I am fully committed ta sharin' 'em."

Spritzing himself with perfume, Stede clicked his tongue and frowned. "Not proper to turn *snitch* on your *mates*, so I have com*plete*ly *al*tered the plan. Lock the door and I shall *share*."

Inviting his visitors to sit on his bed, which both of the men declined, Stede leaned against his table, releasing another puff of powder. Placing a foot on a nearby chair, he hiked the dress and adjusted a garter.

Thankful he had not been sitting on the bed, where he would have received a nightmarish eyeful, Herriot enquired, "So what is this plan ye have made?"

"In a single word... *escape*."

Before Herriot or Pell could demand elaboration, Stede whistled, and a grizzly-bearded face appeared in an open window.

"Do my eyes deceive?" Pell whispered in surprise.

Climbing through the window and landing with a thud, Grizzly-Beard replied, "They do not! Richard Tookerman it be... come ta be yer savior!"

David Herriot, who had been all but convinced he would never again be surprised after three years of sailing with Bonnet, could not process how the infamous South Carolina, Bahamas merchant and smuggler Richard Tookerman had come to stand in Bonnet's bedroom.

Seeing his confusion, Tookerman promptly enlightened him. "Nathaniel Partridge, native of Christ Church Parish, Barbados, provost marshal, an' yer soon to be former host, happens ta love Madeira an' coin more than he loves the gov'nor—an' I have plenty a' both. Besides... there be plenty a' locals who would hate ta see ye hanged. They took up a collection ta buy ye arms an' a periague. We have not a moment ta spare. Out the window we go!"

"I intend to remain," Pell answered, stubbornly folding his arms. "I cannot bear the thought a' enjoyin' a bit a' freedom an' havin' it taken away. I would rather remain a prisoner."

As Tookerman helped Stede out the window—a spectacle that would haunt Herriot's idle moments for what little remained of his life—the sailing master grabbed the boatswain by the collar. Shoving him against the dressing table, the force of which shattered the mirror, Herriot hissed, "Will ye alert the bleeding provost marshal regarding the matter of our escape?"

"I shall not," Ignatius Pell responded. "Ye have little less than an hour before he takes me to the governor. Get far away as ye can."

Releasing the boatswain, Herriot whispered, as he headed for the window, "Was a pleasure serving beside ye, Ignatius. May it not be too few years before we meet again in Hell."

An hour and five minutes later, the bells of Charles Town began to chime, alerting the militia that someone had escaped from custody.

"How could ye let this happen, Provost Marshal Partridge?" Governor Johnson yelled as they stood in the muddy street.

Pointing to his swollen, purple eye—made so courtesy of a punch from Ignatius Pell at the provost marshal's insistence—Partridge answered, "As ye can see, the threesome overwhelmed me. I never saw them coming."

Shoving Partridge away, Johnson summoned a lieutenant. "Send word to Colonel Rhett—given the approaching storm, they must be heading for O'Sullivan's Island. Once ye have sent the message, go to the home of the printer. I want a hundred handbills printed as soon as he can manage offering a seven hundred pound reward for the return of these bastard pirates!"

As the lieutenant hurried away, Caratacus Marks approached. "The negotiations with the owners of the *Mediterranean* and *King William* have been concluded to our satisfaction. Whatever that greedy threesome was holding out for, they readily abandoned their plan at the news of Bonnet's escape."

Wishing he were wearing a sword so he could thrust it into the air, Johnson exclaimed, "Excellent news, my friend! We shall launch our flotilla at dawn. Bonnet shall hang at White Point yet!"

Watching the cutthroat Joseph Stanton silently sobbing in his cabin on the *Ranger*, Charles Vane suddenly realized that he had not feared another man's wrath since he was a climbing boy in Wapping.

Fearing Stanton was understandable, given the wild look of unbridled hatred aflame in the young man eyes.

"I should have been given the chance to avenge my father and my sisters," Stanton whispered, running his fingers subconsciously along the handle of his knife.

"That was the plan, Mistah Stanton," Vane responded. "But ya 'ave ta understand. Ross was a useful tool. An' damnably well protected."

"By whom?"

"A family a' secret emperors called the Ravenskalds."

"Then it is my duty to slaughter the Ravenskalds. After I torture and slaughter him."

*This is why the Quorum has chosen this angry bastard sitting here before me as one of the seven*, Charles Vane thought, as Joseph, exhausted by the truth of his father's murder, dropped his head into his hands.

Lifting the young man's chin so he could look him in the eye, the pirate captain confessed, "Part a' me hoped ye would kill 'im there in Boston. Aftah ya saw yer sistahs an' their pimp. Then it would not be my doin'. Misjudgment at the pairin', an' that'd be all them Ravenskalds could say. Or else when 'e crawled 'is way back from his banishment with that loony Irish admiral."

Pulling his knife from its sheath, but holding it close to his body, Stanton answered, "Release me, Captain Vane, so I can locate Devon Ross and give that festering pustule his due."

Placing his hand upon his pistol and slowly half-cocking the hammer, the captain shook his head. "The Devil 'as already recalled ta the seventh circle a 'Ell 'is faithful, disfigahed spawn. Least, 'tis what I 'ear."

"All the quicker to start on the Ravenskalds."

Striking Stanton on the temple, Vane spat on the floor between them. "Yer talkin' outta ignorance, pain, an' angah, my tortured son. *I* could not fight the Ravenskalds—not wit' an armada a' hundred ships an' a thousand red-'ot cannon. Barely escaped their employ. Yer path lies somewheres diff'rent. There are forces, Joseph Stanton. Ancient, powerful forces... Blackbeard... Paulsgrave Williams... Samuel Bellamy... Yer friend turned enemy Angus. All a' them be agents a' somethin' called the Star Quorum."

"I heard whispers of them in Boston..."

"Some were enlisted before that, some recruited aftah. Point is, yer back on board wit' me 'cause a fight be quickly comin'. Quorum versus Ravenskalds. Ye want yer vengeance, ye stay tight like a hammered bung wit' Angus MacGregah an' ya shows a little patience. An' I suggest forgivin' 'im fer savin' ya from slavery. Thankin' 'im profusely, as a mattah a' fact. Ya 'ave no idea a' the horrahs a' that existence. I escaped seven years a' indentured servitude. Ye would not 'ave survived six months a' it, lad. Seems destiny protected ya, through the actions a' Mistah MacGregah. Ye 'ave been chosen fer somethin' largah. Somethin' bettah."

Wiping the tears from his eyes and sliding his knife into its sheath, Joseph whispered, "For what?"

"I am not fully sure a' the details. I am servin' fer now as transport an' protectah fer ye an' Mistah MacGregah—an' as consort fer the wizah's ship. Once our business is complete, we will go our separate ways. Before that 'appens tho', ye will speak at length wit' Abriendo."

Releasing a rush of air, Stanton asked, "Where we are heading next?"

Taking the question as a sign that Joseph would stay the course, Vane poured them mugs of rum. "Our twelve guns give us plenty a' choices. I was contemplatin' attackin' Harbah Island, but the captain a' the *Oiseau de Proie*, the tattooed celestial Xiang Yu, convinced me its fortifications are far too strong. That bastahd Rajahs has been busy. A few miles fartha on is the farmin' isle a' Eleuthera. Plenty a' livestock ta feed our crews, an' plenty left ta sell. First though, I promised Angus we would anchor a day in Beaufort."

Taking a sip from his mug, Joseph wiped his lips on his sleeve. Raising his hands into the air to indicate he intended no harm, he leaned in close to his captain. "I do not trust your Mister Rackham."

Touching his forehead to his co-conspirator's, Vane whispered, "Tell me why."

"Things I have observed. He was in his cups on Wokokon, threatening to overthrow ye. He is loyal to a New Providence whore, which means he is no longer loyal to ye. Take what happened with *Endeavor.*"

Stanton was referring to a forty-ton brigantine Vane's crew had boarded two days earlier. Under the command of a Captain Shattock, she was on her way from Kingston, Jamaica, to Salem in Massachusetts. Upon inspection, Rackham had found her holds packed from stem to stern with whale oil, salt, and gunpowder.

What the quartermaster failed to locate was any silver or gold.

Forcing Shattock to be his guest in his cabin on the *Ranger,* Vane had beaten him for hours, to no avail. Pleased enough with the sellables—and convinced the captain had nothing to hide—he let *Endeavor* go.

Vane raised a brow and grunted. "Jack was as pleasant as pie. An' plenty 'elpful in tranferrin' the goods while me an' *Endeavor*'s cap'n danced our bloody dance."

"But I saw him in conversation while ye were occupied with Shattock."

"In conversation wit' whom?"

"A pair of well-dressed but unsavory-looking rogues who were careful to stay below decks whenever ye were aboard. That name ye mentioned—the targets of my vengeance—Ravenskald? I heard that name as he and Calico conversed. And something about Gardiners Island. A meeting, I think... And a mirror."

"Impressive, Mistah Stanton," Vane responded, angling his face to hide his look of surprise. "The wizahd an' his associates was takin' a meetin' there while we was workin' *Endeavah*. What I am about ta tell ye, ye must not tell another soul, not even Angus MacGregah. I was not lookin' fer gold when I interrogated Shattock. It was information I was aftah, about the rogues a' which ye speak..."

"We give them a considerable share of our bounty, Paulsgrave—why should we also risk our lives?"

Appraising the two men before him—William Moody and Richard Frowd—Paulsgrave Williams struggled to give them an answer. They had done everything he had asked of them the past several months, including limiting their hunting grounds to the vicinity of St. Christophers and St. Croix in the event that Ravenskald agents attempted to invade and decimate the Star Quorum's primary meeting place, located in a chamber beneath the fort at Christiansted Harbor.

Their ships, the thirty-six gun brigantine *Rising Sun* and an eight-gun sloop, were formidable adversaries to all but the most heavily armed of the Royal Navy's frigates. Walter Hamilton, governor of the Leewards, had spent months hunting pirates aboard two of the vessels in question—Captain Francis Hume's thirty-two-gun Fifth Rate HMS *Scarborough* and the twenty-four-gun HMS *Bristol Bay*, under the command of Jonathan Rose.

In the middle of June, Hume and Rose had almost succeeded in capturing Olivier Levasseur. Although they had taken a number of ships—and pirates to trial—ever since, Hamilton was screaming for an additional warship, as the Admiralty had recently recalled Hume and the *Scarborough* back to England.

The Caribbean was getting more than a bit too hot for the pirates who had, for the past several years, amassed riches and fame in her waters. The governors of the Bahamas and Bermuda had enlisted former pirates under the Act of Grace to hunt their former comrades. Word was, Blackbeard was all but retired in North Carolina and Major Stede Bonnet was awaiting trial in Charles Town, South Carolina, along with more than thirty of his crew.

Yet that was where Paulsgrave wished to go, sparking the current, intense debate.

William Moody grunted in frustration at Paulsgrave's silence. "I have heard from some merchants out of Charles Town that Governor Johnson has gathered a four-ship flotilla and enlisted one of our former brethren, the more than capable Charles Yeats, to join his band of hunters."

"My God, Paulsgrave," whispered Richard Frowd, who dabbed his sweaty lips with a pristine monogrammed handkerchief. "The whole damned mess is falling apart. The remainder of your informal council in New Providence—Hornigold and Jennings—hunt on behalf of Rogers and Bennett! These governors will not be satisfied until they publicly hang Charles Vane. Hamilton wants our heads. So does Johnson and the rest. Why us? We have done nothing along the scale of Vane or Thache…"

"Ye, and ye alone, are the reason, Captain Williams," Moody said, knowing Frowd would never dare. "Yes, sir! Ye are the reason that these men hunt us as though we were rabid dogs killing chickens and sheep on their farms! Ye and your dealings with this scurvy, shadowy Quorum, full of wealthy men of fortune and a trio of conniving cardinals! I do not want the ear of kings, nor a seat at their corrupting banquets. I became a pirate, as did Richard, because we witnessed injustice wherever we looked. On farmsteads—aye, I know the story of your fellow rebel, Samuel Bellamy—in the cities, in the churches… The dirty dealings after the War of Spanish Succession. How treacherously the Navy treats her men! A pox above and a Hell below… is that not what Blackbeard always told us? The Brethren of the Sea have all been generous to me. It has been a short and merry life. I shall not sail to Charles Town. I am truly sorry, Paulsgrave. Ye cannot convince me otherwise. I beg ye not to try."

Clasping his hand on Moody's shoulder, Paulsgrave smiled. "I promise I shall not. Instead, I have a simpler, safer request. I must soon sail to Africa, where I hope ye will join me at the start of seventeen nineteen. Levasseur should be there as well."

Richard Frowd, empowered by Moody's speech, wagged his finger in Paulsgrave's face. "On business of the Quorum, no doubt."

"On business of the Quorum," Paulsgrave parroted back, placing his free hand on Frowd's tattooed, barreled chest. "Passage for me was assured out of Charles Town, but I see the risk in what I have requested. Instead, I shall await a ship in Christiansted Harbor."

"Then what do ye need from us?" Richard Frowd enquired, not quite trusting Paulsgrave's sudden acquiescence.

"I need ye to provide a smokescreen, seeing as, as ye so rightly pointed out, these governors ye mentioned want so badly to get at me through the both of ye."

Removing Paulsgrave's hand from his shoulder, Moody raised a brow. "What would ye have us do?"

"Stay in the vicinity of Charles Town for a month. Not close enough to engage with Johnson's flotilla. Just close enough for him to be convinced that ye are his inevitable prey. Can ye do this thing for me?"

Without hesitation, Frowd and Moody agreed.

Clapping his hands in delight, Paulsgrave said, "Then let us have some dinner, before I leave for the harbor."

Sipping a bitter draught mixed by the local physician to combat the fever with which he had been at war ever since arriving in the Bahamas, Governor Woodes Rogers signed his name to a letter to the Commissioners for Trade and Plantations in England. He had been composing the letter throughout the previous night. Now the sun was beginning to rise and he wished for nothing more than to crawl into his bed.

His luck having been consistently poor ever since his appointment as royal governor of the Bahamas, it had come as little surprise that his flotilla had arrived in the midst of rampant illness, the likes of which the locals had not encountered for more than forty years. The cause, the overworked and ailing physicians reported, was traders leaving dozens of raw animal hides upon the shore to dry. Although they were now on the other side of the worst of it—at one point, there were over a hundred sick at a time, with fatalities spreading equally amongst the locals, pirates, and members of Rogers's flotilla—recovery would be slow and expensive.

Leaving the letter upon the desk, where a courier sailing for England would collect it within the hour, Rogers extinguished a pair of candles and turned up the wick on his lantern.

Heading for the door that adjoined his bedroom in his makeshift home in the fort, the governor wrapped his fur-lined robe a little tighter around him in an unsuccessful attempt to fend off an onslaught of chills. Turning for his desk, with the intent to retrieve the rest of the medicinal draught, he heard his office door flung open, followed by the voices of the sentries he had posted to guard it and what sounded like a handful of agitated voices.

"I am heartfully sorry, Governor!" Benjamin Hornigold exclaimed, following the men into the room. "They simply would not be dissuaded."

Taking position behind his desk, Rogers looked the five intruders—Nathaniel Taylor, Thomas Barnard, Thomas Spencer, Thomas Walker, and William Fairfax—coldly in the eyes.

"What is the meaning of this intrusion?" he enquired, coughing up a wad of light brown phlegm, which he spat into a handkerchief. "I have been awake since yesterday morning, preparing my letter for His Majesty and his commissioners. I was about to go to bed."

"Sleep shall have to wait," William Fairfax replied, approaching the desk like a one man Roman legion, his four companions advancing behind him like a miniature *cuneum formate* with Fairfax as the point. "We have a multitude of questions…"

"And grievances as well!" Nathaniel Taylor added, earning a backhanded slap on the shoulder from Thomas Spencer.

Taylor immediately changed his tone. "Really, mostly questions…"

"Very well then," Rogers replied, sinking into his chair. "William Fairfax—let us begin with ye."

Looking suddenly as though he regretted what he had just now set into motion, Fairfax cleared his throat. "While I am grateful to ye for my appointment to the position of assistant justice and deputy to the collector—seeing as my position as judge of the Admiralty has zero annual income—I take umbrage with having to answer to that curmudgeon Mister Graves!"

Rogers produced a disarming smile. "The chief collector is well advanced in years. It is my understanding that his admittedly difficult disposition as of late is due to his taking ill, the same as everyone else. Perhaps a modicum of compassion is in order…"

Fairfax put his hands to his ears. "Such language and insults as he has hurled my way do not speak of age and illness, but a form of satanic possession!"

Quieting the grumbling *cuneum formate* with a motion of his hands, Rogers, still smiling, although he felt like he needed to vomit, replied, "Here is my solution. Collector Graves will continue to receive his seventy pounds annum for remaining in his bed. Ye, Deputy Fairfax, shall do the collecting and solely earn the fees. Do ye accept this solution as just?"

Fairfax hurriedly nodded and bowed before retreating to the rear of the *cuneum formate*.

"Seeing as ye are now the point of the arrow, Mister Taylor, and clearly the most upset, let me hear your grievances without delay… I mean to say, your *questions*…"

Leaning on the desk, Taylor, suddenly less sure of himself as he eyed Roger's deformed face and recalled the stories of how it happened and the shocking events that followed, managed to stutter out, "The fort is in a far better state than it was under Grandpa Hornigold, but still not what it should be. As ye are well aware, Governor Rogers, not a week ago, one of the bastions fronting the ocean collapsed, the embarrassing consequence of a sizeable, unrepaired crack in its foundation. We lack both men and materials. What is your plan for remedy?"

Having an acceptable solution already set in motion, Rogers relaxed his shoulders. "As ye are well aware, Mister Taylor—and my apologies if I have been lacking in communication—a key portion of my letter is devoted to matters of defense, both in terms of Bahamian forts, including here in Nassau, as well independent companies. I have made an excellent case for His Majesty to send us sufficient funds to hire the necessary workers, seeing as, between illness and a marked, chronic laziness rampant amongst the locals, a labor force on this island is distinctly, frustratingly lacking."

Stifling a burst of collective protest with another, stronger gesture of his hands, Rogers continued. "Again, as I know ye are aware, I have erected a small fort of eight guns at the eastermost entrance to the harbor where we keep the largest watch, and have formed the locals and any other men on this island that I could muster into three companies of militia, under the command of officers they themselves have elected. Once I have received the requested funds from England, I shall order two more fortifications erected in the harbor. Materials are not an issue. New Providence is overgrown with wood and abundant in lime and stone."

For a moment, the *cuneum formate* was silent. Then Thomas Barnard took Nathaniel Taylor's place as the advancing point of the wedge. "The surrounding islands have been menaced for months— nay, years!—by the villainous Vane, who so unceremoniously ruined your arrival! Look what happened for a week in mid-September... At Abaco, Green Turtle Cay... The corruption of pirate turned hunter turned pirate Nicholas Woodall... The brigand's theft of arms from the very fort where we stand!"

Rogers rose from his chair. "Nicholas Woodall sits in irons as we speak! I shall personally place him upon the next ship to England to face the Admiralty's justice, I assure ye, Mister Barnard! Furthermore, *sir*, in my learned estimation, Captains Hornigold and Cockram, despite a thorough lack of support from men the likes of yourselves, have served these islands with distinction."

"Yet ye recently doubted that this very thing was so!" shouted Thomas Walker, taking Barnard's place as the point. "Ye expressed to me in private not a week and a half ago your concern that your man Hornigold here had once more gone out on the account. As former acting governor of the Bahamas and past justice to the Vice Admiralty Court for our sainted King William himself, I speak with greater authority than any of these men arrayed behind me—and, with all due respect, Governor Rogers, with more than even ye. Therefore, I say this with all assurety—ye need a flotilla to protect not only New Providence, but the other Bahamian islands. Fact is, ye have *lost* two ships since the day that ye arrived!"

Rogers, knowing he would have to tread carefully with the current point of the arrow, retreated to his chair, faking a cough to cover the action. "I prevailed upon Commodore Chamberlain to stay till the sixteenth of August. Additionally, and with no small amount of difficulty, I procured his order to Captain Whitney to stay three weeks more as well. They informed me they had no orders to do so, and were very much against remaining any longer when those additional three weeks had expired. Try as I might—and I did so most strenuously, I assure ye—I could not convince Captain Whitney to remain with us beyond the fourteenth of September."

"The very day Charles Vane menaced Green Turtle Cay!" Walker countered, his eyes ablaze with victory.

"As I am well aware," Rogers hissed, too exhausted to employ any further diplomacy. "I need not remind ye, sir, that eight days prior, I wrote Governor Hunter in New York requesting an officer and twenty-five men from his garrison. The day after the incident near Abaco involving the outlaw Vane, I wrote to Governor Nicholas Lawes in Jamaica requesting the loan of twenty or thirty men."

"Where are these men that ye requested more than a month ago?" Nathaniel Taylor enquired from the center of the *cuneum formate*.

Benjamin Hornigold had heard enough. Taking position beside the governor, he said, "The request was rescinded when New Providence's battle with illness improved. Both New York and Jamaica have troubles of their own."

"Troubles of which ye yourself are the architect, oh ye corrupted spawner of pirates!" Thomas Walker growled. "Ye and your Republic! As acting governor, I was preparing to enact a plan to make the Bahamas the most prosperous of the Caribbean islands! Then ye conspired to drive me out!"

Moving in closer, although keeping the edge of the desk between them, Hornigold shot back, "Ye skulked off to Connecticut, without any prompting from me. We could have worked together. I disagreed with aspects of your plan, although much of it was sound. Governor Rogers and I have consulted on some of its aspects."

"Over the course of several conversations," Rogers added, grateful to have Hornigold beside him. "I have been meaning to discuss them with ye, Mister Walker."

"Conveniently, here I stand," the former Admiralty justice responded.

"Very well then," Rogers replied. "Let us talk of salt to start. We may soon expect to rake salt enough from the several ponds amongst the windward Bahamian Islands to supply much of Newfoundland, Europe, and all of the American colonies. I have written to the owners of several vessels that visit Salturtuga requesting that they deal with the Bahamas exclusively for their salt, as we are much nearer to the coast of North America. We shall also promote our whale fisheries and their ample supply of ambergris, which is in ever-increasing demand. These sources of income will be used to fund the raising of another independent company and for further improvements to the fort, adding to our current company of one hundred and twelve, and one hundred and fifty-two armed members of the general citizenry."

Walker, satisfied, at least for the moment, surrendered his position as the head of the wedge, which remained for the moment unoccupied.

Taking full advantage, Hornigold, who was enjoying his—at least partial—resumption of his former position of authority upon New Providence, said, "Thomas Walker, ye have expressed concern for the other Bahamian islands. Governor Rogers has proposed council member Edward Holmes, Esquire, as deputy governor of Eleuthera and Richard Thompson, Esquire, as deputy governor of Harbour Island. Not only will they vigorously recruit dozens of families, they will each be responsible for raising militia companies of seventy or eighty men. Captain John Cockram, who has proven himself to be courageous and reliable, shall oversee the procurement and distribution of powder and shot to the pair of forts on Harbour Island, which shall be outfitted with eight six-pounders and four nine-pounders, respectively."

Also enjoying—for the moment, which he intended to ensure was fleeting—the sharing of political power, Rogers continued. "There is always the threat of attack from France or Spain... the truth of which both former acting governor Walker and Captain Hornigold have lived. But do not doubt for a second, gentlemen, that we are making steady progress. Scarcely half the pirates who once ruled this island remain... by a careful, weekly accounting, one hundred and fifty-seven. The rest quickly bristled under my aggressively implemented restraints and have chosen to operate elsewhere."

William Fairfax, who had started the attack, would be the last of the five to speak, although he approached the desk with respect. "In case of attack—by France or Spain, or by a confederacy of pirates under Vane or some other rogue—how confident are ye that these one hundred and fifty-seven former pirates currently walking our streets, eating in our taverns, and whistling at our daughters and sisters will remain faithful and honor their pardons? I cannot believe it to be very much at all, given the news that Vane, less than a week ago, acquired four of our trading sloops off the coast of Cuba—without the smallest opposition! Even our merchant captains cannot be trusted! I hear they *offered* him their vessels to fortify his flotilla!"

Feeling his fever rising to the point that chills would soon be wracking his body—something he could not afford to have this handful of malcontents see—Rogers gripped the edge of the desk and stood. "We can only pray for favorable numbers. I assure ye, Vane shall be dealt with in time. He shall pay for recent events. Once we have made an example of him and his crew, no other pirates shall dare defy us. Now, gentlemen, I beg of ye to permit me to bring this unscheduled, unofficial meeting to a close. By any measure, I have been both patient and forthcoming. I bid ye all good day."

As Angus MacGregor climbed into the longboat that would take him and this three fellow Scottish pirates to Beaufort—the rest of the crews of Vane's *Ranger* and four other recently acquired sloops would stay anchored in Topsail Inlet until their return the following day—he made it a point to sit beside Malcolm Douglas.

"Ock, mae lad… ye look like ye haev tied on a fairst rate drunk," Malcolm, whom his closest friends called Cnoc, meaning "hill," because of his considerable size, observed with a toothy grin. "Wit' yer baest noo mate Joseph Stanton I would wager…"

Although it was true that, ever since leaving Ocracoke and a subsequent meeting between Vane and Stanton in the captain's quarters of the *Ranger*, Joseph had been more open to an awkward, uneasy truce, such pleasant activities as sharing a bottle were not the source of his exhaustion.

Selecting an oar and setting it in the oarlock beside him, Angus shook his head. "I haid a visit froom yer sister, Isla. The laist waes on Bealthiunn, exactly haelf a year agoo this vaery day," he answered.

"Little wonder that," Cnoc responded, grasping an oar and beginning to row. "Veil is the thinnest at thaese times, which is haelpful even fer a powerful *gorm-shuil* laek haer, wit' *an da shealladh*. An' it ain't soo mooch haer *visitin'* yoo as shae callin' yoo tae haer as a *tamhasg*—sort a' a livin' spaectre. What did shae tael ye, Angus? Did shae saend a message fer mae?"

Adjusting his stroke to match that of Duncan MacDonald, who was sitting just in front of him, Angus again shook his head. "Sadly, noo. An' what shae said tae mae…"

"Lemme guess… Yer a MacKinnon, one a' the Clan a' the Mists, wearer a' dragon's ring, wrought bae the fae, tae bae a talisman fer the Lairds a' the Isles, in a sìth near the abbacy on Iona. Yer taem haes coom tae doo great things, noo that yer teachers haev baen raevealed."

"Isla visited yoo as wael!" Angus whispered, overcome with wonder.

"Keep yer focus on yer rowin', Angus!" Teàrlach de Bruys was glancing back at Angus with anger in his eyes. "Beaufort still bae a ways away. I would hate tae miss the feast."

Once Angus was back in rhythm, Cnoc, with a look of pure amusement on his red-bearded face, whispered, "Nae. Noot mae sister. I entertained noo laess than the faerie mistress, *Leannan sith*, haerself! Shae tol' mae tae say nought tae yoo oontil yoo spoke tae mae. Noo that yoo haev, shae spoke in riddles, same as mae sister is given tae doo. Said thaer are saeven chosen ones. Dooncan an' Teàrlach an' I, althoo nae a part a' the saeven, shall alsoo play a part in this vaery grand an' mysterious ta-doo."

Angus's eyes grew wide. "Abraxas Abriendo an' Padraig Ó Muiris haev spoken a' the saeven!"

"Thair bae soomthin' else as weel," Cnoc continued, his visage becoming stern. "Yoo are daescended froom a line a' warrior-moonks who waent tae the Holy Land searchin' fer a saet a' sacred objects beneath a' Solomon's Taemple. These objects, twaelve in noomber, are the raeson fer all the wars a' the world."

For the next hour, as they rowed in silence—broken only by an occasional song of the Highlands when their rhythm began to falter—Angus contemplated all that he had heard, both from Isla and from her brother through the words of *Leannan sith*.

He wished he could talk to Ailish—a wish that only increased as the longboat arrived on Beaufort's sandy shore, where a ceremony was taking place to celebrate not only Samhain, but the birth of Finlay and Rowan's son, whom they called John in honor of Finlay's generous cousin, who had died on the *Whydah* with Sam.

"Welcome back to Beaufort, my friends!" shouted Robert Turner, who, as owner of the twelve blocks that comprised the fledgling town, served as its unofficial ambassador, mayor, and promoter.

As the four weary Scots dragged the bow of the longboat securely into the sand, Angus found a double reason to smile. The first was a group of men farther down the beach piling driftwood and other flammable materials into a man-tall mound that would no doubt serve as the central bonfire, the *samghnagan*, for the festivities of Samhain after sundown. Angus had not experienced the lighting of the bonfire, which protected the clans from the fair folk and ensured a successful harvest, nor the dancing, burning of the sacrificial cattle, and carving of turnips into Jack o neeps since leaving Balquhidder three years earlier at the insistence of his uncle, who was committed to the Jacobite cause. What Angus had missed the most, however, was listening to the clan elders telling long, inspiring tales in verse of the victories won by the great Scottish warriors over the creatures and demons of the underworld.

Angus knew in his heart that he would be drawing on these stories as a source of strength and guidance with increasing frequency in the dangerous months to come.

The second reason for his smile was the sight of Finlay and Rowan Fletcher. Knowing all they had endured, separately and together, and seeing how happy they were, filled his heart and mind with hope.

"Haer bae the wee bairn fer which yoo agreed tae bae *goistidh*, Angus," Rowan whispered, pulling a corner of a tartan-patterned blanket away from the face of her son, whom she held protectively in her arms. "If only Ailish could bae haer as wael."

Resisting the urge to touch the baby's face with his callused, dirty hands, Angus replied, "Shae bae haer in spirit, lass. We are honored tae bae the godparents a' this wee an' beautiful bairn."

"Ye baest bae," said Lewis Abernathy, Rowan's cousin, who stood between Robert Turner and one of Blackbeard's former crewman, Faolan MacDougall, now in the owner of Beaufort's employ. "Seein' as I was overlooked fer the title a' *goistidh* thoo I live an' work right haer!"

"I explained it tae yoo, coosin," Rowan replied, although she knew by Lewis's smile that he was not at all upset. "Usin' the very same words *Leannan sith* used tae explain it tae mae in a long an' vivid dream."

Lewis smiled wider. "An' who am I tae argue wit' the mistress a' the faeries!"

"How is Blackbeard farin', Angus?" Faolan MacDougall enquired. "He nae looked fit whaen last we wair togaether."

"Weaker an' less wael tempered wit' every passin' day," Angus replied.

"Saend haim mae baest whaen yoo raeturn tae the Albemarle."

Angus shook his head. "I am noot raeturnin' tae Wokokon. For noo, I sail wit' Vane."

As Faolan raised a brow and opened his mouth to speak, Robert Turner clasped him on the shoulder. "As owner of this town and an honorary *goistidh* of this *wee bairn* we are here together to celebrate, I evoke full authority to say the following. Enough of this talk of your beloved pirate captains. A fine feast has been laid out in the center of town, right beside the framework for what shall soon be a barber shop for Finlay and a tavern to be run by Rowan!"

As they made the walk to Anne Street, Angus—not sure from where the impulse came—asked if he could hold his godson for the remainder of the walk. Passing the infant to Angus, and helping him to settle John safely in his arms before she let him go, Rowan whispered, "If only Ailish could bae haer tae see this. Whaen are yoo goin' tae take haer froom New Providence, marry the lass, an' haev a wee bairn a' yer oon? I sore naed haer haelp wit' runnin' the tavern!"

"Leave him bae, my loov," Finlay said, grasping Rowan's hand and bringing it to his lips. "It is clear it pains him greatly tae hear yoo say haer name. His eyes get very sad every time yoo doo. We know what it is tae bae saeparated froom, as Plato called it in haes *Symposium*, oor twin flame."

Duncan laughed. "Noo that yer a right wealthy yin, yoo are readin' Plato? Mighty high falootin' thought-stuff fer a barber!"

"Doan yoo bae a wraetch, Dooncan MacDonald!" Rowan warned, a pair of fierce blue flames suddenly alight in her eyes. "Finlay doos more than trim a beard or shear a scalp. Hae is studyin' anatomy an' the mixin' a' tixtures an' tonics. Hae plans tae bae a surgeon… tae pull teeth an' cure all manner a' ailments fer the growin' town a' Beaufort. Caen yoo even read, ye doaty, bowfin bumpot?"

The banter between Scots was something of which Angus would never tire. To cut to the quick with brutal honesty and a well-honed wit while wearing a smile both sincere and girded with love and respect was a gift he had not yet seen in those from other lands.

Lightly kissing a pale, strawberry-shaped birthmark that lay between John's fluttering, grey-green eyes, which were slowly losing the battle to banish sleep, Angus whispered in his ear, "Bae proud, yoo sweet, wee bairn. Fer yoo are a Scot—an' a Highland Scot tae boot!"

Lieutenant Governor Alexander Spotswood, wearing a set of newly tailored, jet-black velvet robes, placed a square black cloth over his generously powdered wig, one corner facing forward, as he rose from the centrally located chair that marked his position as presiding judge in the courthouse.

Positioned on his flanks were Captain George Gordon of the HMS *Pearl* and Captain Ellis Brand of the HMS *Lyme*, who remained in their chairs, looks of satisfaction and revenge upon their freshly shaven faces.

Looking the defendant in the eye with a cold and soulless stare, Spotswood pronounced the judges' verdict in a fearsome, resounding voice worthy of all of his systematically, patiently consolidated authority. "William Howard. Not having the fear of God in your eyes nor regarding the allegiance owed to His Majesty, King George, nor to Virginia, who so graciously welcomed ye and nearly a hundred others of your kind with open arms, having been proven by this court to have committed gross acts of piracy with Edward Thache and other wicked, desolute persons, are sentenced to hang at noon tomorrow until ye are dead. May God have mercy upon your soul."

Rising from his chair, John Holloway, one of the most reknowned and capable lawyers in all of Virginia, whom Howard had retained as his counsel, responded, "This is highly irregular and egregiously, grossly unfair! My client is under the protection of His Majesty's Act of Grace. He completed all of the proper paperwork through your personal secretary, Governor Spotswood. Furthermore, Mister Howard's arrest—and forced captivity these past four days under the iron hand of Captain Gordon upon his ship the *Pearl*—were utterly without even the slightest cause and devoid of all legality! For what reason and by what authority did the Virginia militia apprehend my client and ninety of his fellow former pirates on the border between Virginia and Pennsylvania? This is a question that assuredly begs of thee an answer to ensure that justice is satisfactorily served!"

Releasing a weary sigh, Spotswood turned to his right. "Captain Gordon. Are ye willing to respond?"

Gordon shook his head. "I leave it to Captain Brand, if he is ready and willing to do so."

Standing with a nod, Captain Brand addressed William Howard's lawyer. "Mister Holloway... Because your reputation for fairness, integrity, and felicity within the practice of public law situate ye in the highest realms of esteem, I am all the more shocked that ye have requested a restatement of the reasons for his arrest! William Howard and his gang of marauding rogues—of whom he clearly was the leader—refused to comply with limiting their congregating to no more than three and the relinquishing of arms when entering a town, despite having agreed to comply with these very restrictions when accepting the pardon ye yourself mentioned from Governor Spotswood through his secretary in Williamsburg. As to his incarceration upon the *Pearl*—this is a man who until rather recently served as quartermaster for the murderous and infamous Blackbeard, who, after also agreeing to take the pardon, continues his acts of piracy and robbery under the auspices of the lieutenant governor and minister of justice of North Carolina! It was the legitimate concern of every man in authority present here today, as well as the Admiralty itself, that Howard would slip his bonds and rejoin his former captain unless such measures as his detainment upon the *Pearl* were undertaken with all due haste."

Satisfied that he had thoroughly addressed the lawyer's concerns, Brand turned to the larger audience, which did not include a jury. Softening his tone and spreading his arms, he said, "My justice-seeking friends, sitting before us today is one of the most mischievous, vilest villains that has ever infested our coast. The evidence today presented by a host of reliable witnesses is clearly irrefutable. This detestable, vulgar villain did not fall casually into piracy. As I have just reminded Mister Holloway, William Howard sailed with the title of quartermaster under the murderous Blackbeard Thache... the very rogue who threatened to burn the port of Boston to its waterline! Who held several of the good citizens of Charles Town in South Carolina and their families hostage for three days in their harbor while their governor was forced to fulfill his vile demands. I do not wish to waste your time with repetitive recitations, but this man before ye, as quartermaster of Blackbeard's various vessels, was a key participant in the taking of the *Robert* of Philadephia and *Good Instant* of Dublin at Delaware Capes on 22 October 1717, and *Betty* of Virginia one week later just off the coast of Cape Charles. He was also present at the taking of the French slaveship *La Concorde*, from which sixty-plus Africans and a considerable portion of gold dust have yet to be recovered—

although William Howard's ability to hire such an esteemed—and expensive!—lawyer as Mister Holloway may tell us where at least a portion of the spoils was spent. Add to this misery and illegality visited upon *La Concorde* one final, heartless action—the forced conscription of her physician to minister to the maladies contracted in their sexual degeneracies by Blackbeard's blackhearted crew!"

Convinced his point was more than sufficiently made, Brand took his seat to riotous applause, including from the three heads of the Family, sitting in the back—Edward Moseley, Colonel James Moore, and Jeremiah Vail.

"I had nothing to do with the forced service of the Frenchie physician!" Howard responded, shouting to make himself heard above the din of the applause, which quickly quieted down.

Such fine entertainment as this was all too rare to miss for even a moment.

Banging his fist upon the table to which Spotswood had ordered him chained, William Howard continued. "Ye have not sufficiently addressed the matter of Gordon and his dog Maynard's inappropriate actions regarding my imprisonment upon their vessel, Captain Brand. Given that I was not arrested on suspicion of committing a crime at sea, but for other violations that ye yourself have enumerated at Mister Holloway's request, I should have been kept in the local gaol with the rest of my fellow pardoned pirates, if indeed I was, as ye say, a probable risk for flight."

Without standing, Brand replied, "Your incarceration upon a vessel of His Majesty's Royal Navy instead of in a cell in the local gaol was a more than reasonable precaution to prevent ye from going back upon the account, given the recent escape from Charles Town of another foremost member of your cohort, Major Stede Bonnet, and two of his officers."

"I was arrested on my way to Pennsylvania, in the *opposite direction* from Blackbeard!" Howard yelled, his voice beginning to break. "I left him after the grounding of the *Queen Anne's Revenge*. I came to Virginia to marry and open a tavern. I was going to Pennsylvania to secure contracts for needed supplies. Why in the hell would I return to pirating?"

Staying Brand with a hand upon his arm, Governor Spotswood rose, the ominous black square still centered upon his wig. "Ye must have your reasons, defendant. Why else would Lieutenant Governor

Charles Eden—who has struck a devil's bargain with the rogue in the Albemarle in order to fill his personal coffers—instruct his known associate and your own lawyer, John Holloway, Esquire, to attempt to have Captain Gordon and Lieutenant Maynard arrested, in addition to seeking five hundred pounds in damages? I see no harm to your physical person to suggest that your incarceration was anything more than what Captain Brand has stated—a more than reasonable precaution. I now proclaim this matter closed. William Howard, ye shall hang at noon tomorrow until dead." As the crowd began to murmur, and Howard and his lawyer again to protest, Spotswood banged his gavel three times with considerable force upon the bar. "Let it further be known that this is just the beginning of the hangings to be ordered by this court. I am declaring it my personal mission to put a stop to the further progress of these robberies at sea. It is time to extirpate the pirates!"

Twenty minutes later, as they walked down Palace Green on their way to the governor's palace, Spotswood, Gordon, and Brand solidified their plan for the assassination of Edward Thache.

"I do commend ye for your eloquence in the courtroom, Captain Brand," Spotswood remarked, pausing to pick an apple. "'... One of the most mischievous, vilest villains that has ever infested our coast'! Simply genius. Not that I had the slightest doubt—I am fully aware of your admirable ambitions—but after hearing such a delightfully demeaning speech, I am increasingly confident that we completely understand one another, making ye the perfect man to lead this expedition."

"While my silence proves that I am not," Captain Gordon grumbled. "So let us conclude our business. The *Pearl* and *Lyme* are far too large to enter the shallow waters of Pamlico Sound, much less to make an assault upon Blackbeard's lair on Ocracoke. I therefore suggest the procurement of a pair of longboats, for which ye as lieutenant governor must provide the funding, as we do not have the means nor the authorization to make such a questionable purchase. As to an overall strategy, I suggest a two-pronged attack. Ellis shall take an overland path to Bath in the event that Blackbeard is meeting with Eden at his mansion. Two hundred militia and Royal Navy sailors should suffice. My equally ambitious lieutenant, Robert Maynard, shall command the pair of longboats—number and makeup of the crew to be decided by myself and Captain Brand."

Brand considered for a moment the senior captain's plan. "I cannot offer even a single objection. If we are fortunate enough to catch Eden and Blackbeard in the midst of enacting their business, ye can topple your rival's government!"

"I shall pay for the longboats myself, so as not to draw any attention," Spotswood replied, his pleasure at the possibilities clear upon his face. "For the moment, I have left the Privy Council in the dark. There are far too many supporters of these pirates lurking about to risk one of them sharing our plans. Now… as to the matter of needed cannon…"

"There shall be none aboard the longboats," Captain Gordon replied. "The attention they would draw, as well as their weight, make employing them impossible. It is essential that we carry out this operation to the utmost letter of the law. I assume ye have contacted both the Admiralty as well as the Parliament in England for their permission, Governor Spotswood?"

"Of course I have," the lieutenant governor responded, his visage slightly darkening as the falsehood left his lips. "No cannon… How unfortunate. If it is to be old-fashioned swordplay and muskets, make sure the men ye select for the longboats are more than up to the task. Choose your warriors well, Captain Gordon. We must not suffer a single setback. Now… if there is nothing else to discuss, perhaps it is time we said goodbye."

Nodding to Colonel Moore, who was sitting with Moseley and Vail on the opposite side of the green, Brand smiled and said to Spotswood, "There is the matter of our compensation."

Handing the apple he had picked to an attractive and well-dressed woman who had gazed at him seductively as he and the captains approached, Spotswood grinned like the serpent in Genesis. "More than covered by a law I intend to have passed within days in the General Assembly allowing for a bounty for Blackbeard and his crew. A generous payment per head. Ye shall also be entitled to half the proceeds from the sale of his vessel and any valuables ye and Maynard manage to seize—that is, of course, after I have first been reimbursed for what shall no doubt be my own considerable expenses."

Pointing to the leaders of The Family, Gordon asked with a scowl, "Shall those three be involved?"

Spotswood shook his head, anxious to enter the palace by himself, in front of which he and the captains were standing. This damnable Gordon was trouble he did not need. "They are useful in other places, such as gathering evidence against Eden and the rest of his corrupted cabal… This operation against Blackbeard, which they fully support for economic and personal reasons inappropriate for me to share, is solely the purview of yourself, Captain Brand, as well as Lieutenant Maynard. Before the day is done, I shall contact my man in Bath, requesting the latest information on Blackbeard—number of crew, condition of his vessel, and so forth. I shall also have him arrange for a pair of pilots from the area to guide your men through the Sound. Now, if ye will excuse me, it has been an excellent morning's work, but other matters press hard upon me."

Watching Spotswood enter the palace—the very categorization and the building's overbearing opulence producing a bit of bile in the stoic captain's throat—Gordon whispered, "We shall both of us be fortunate if our careers survive this mess. Do not trust him, Brand. Nor your old friend Maynard. That is the last I shall say on the subject."

*I very much doubt that, Captain,* Ellis thought with a grin, as he headed for the *Lyme. Which does not make ye wrong.*

Thinking back to five days earlier, when five Bahamian council members had forced their way into his office and interrogated him like Spanish priests during the Inquisition, Woodes Rogers could not help but smile at the turn of affairs, despite the growing ache in what remained of his lower jaw.

Within hours, it would storm. That is what his old wound told him.

Gazing with disgust and triumph upon the four dead pirates piled before the fort from where he stood on a second-story rampart, Rogers called down to the aged former pirate responsible for their demise.

"Commodore Hornigold! What a glorious few weeks ye have enjoyed of ridding us of dozens of damnable pirates! On behalf of our council and the citizens of Nassau… Of all of the Bahamas… I commend ye!"

Remembering a promising day in early August 1715, when he had stood where Rogers was standing while presenting the articles of the Republic of Pirates to the assembled crews of Nassau—a day that Vane and Jennings had tried their damnedest to ruin—Hornigold returned the governor's smile. Looking at the lined-up corpses and picturing the nearly dozen pirates being held in irons in the fort awaiting trial and execution, Grandpa felt younger than he had when he had fought so valianty and naively for the Crown as a privateer during the decade of Queen Anne's War.

"It is an honor to do my duty, Governor Rogers," Hornigold answered. "A worthy recompense for the treachery of twenty-five October."

Hearing a grunt from someone standing behind him, Rogers tightened his grip on his walking stick until his knuckles were white and began to protest. He knew from whence the grunt had come. It was Assistant Justice and Deputy Collector William Fairfax, who had led the five-man *cuneum formate*—the wedge formation—into his office five days earlier.

The incident to which Hornigold was referring—from which he should have refrained from mentioning—was the surrendering of four trading sloops off the coast of Cuba to Vane for use in his flotilla.

"We shall have our satisfaction when it comes to Captain Vane," Rogers replied, refusing to acknowledge that his nemesis was currently a commodore. "Ye see the results of his resistance drawing flies on the sand before ye. Within the cells of this fort are shackled ten other pirates whose fate shall soon be the same. Captain Augur and his men have learned the lesson of what happens when I send Hornigold and Cockram on a mission to administer justice!"

Taking the wave of cheering and applause from the assembled crowd as an opportunity to further shape the moment, Rogers signaled to the chief members of his council—still pending approval from the Crown, of course, which rarely disputed such appointments—to join him on the rampart.

"While we are all of us here together—a rare event indeed, since each of us keeps so busy ensuring a prosperous future for these islands—I would like to take a moment to introduce the most essential and important members of His Majesty's Council in the Bahamas."

Rogers could feel the frustration of Fairfax and the rest of the *cuneum formate* at his decision to deprive them of these most essential and important of the council's positions.

That would certainly be the last time these five men broke from protocol, as the governor could clearly do the same—and publicly at that.

Placing his arm around the shoulder of the first man standing in line, Rogers began the introductions. "This is Robert Beauchamp, first lieutenant of our Independent Company in New Providence. I have appointed him secretary general of the council."

As the applause and cheering continued, Rogers introduced the rest. There was Captain Wingate Gale, commander of the ship *Delicia* and his chief mate, George Hooper. He then brought forward, one at a time, Assistant Justice William Walker and Chief Justice Colonel Christopher Gale. "Who held the very same position in North Carolina for thirteen years under our mutual friend, Lord

John Carteret," Rogers said of Gale, raising the colonel's arm in the air.

Rogers's characterization of Carteret as being a friend was of course a considerable exaggeration, if not an outright lie. Although Carteret had backed his appointment as governor, he disliked Rogers's inclination to associate with Scots—most of all Daniel Defoe. When Carteret had failed to act in the procurement of ships for Rogers's flotilla, their mutual nemesis, the East India Company, had come through with the *Delicia*, a four-hundred-ton man of war equipped with forty guns.

Quieting the crowd with a motion of his hands, Rogers continued. "These men—along with five other members of the royal council—shall assist me in my efforts to not only protect this fort through repairs to the existing structure and building of new fortifications and the raising of additional companies… They shall be crucial to the recruitment of new inhabitants accustomed to plantation colonies, particularly some current inhabitants of the defenseless and largely barren Anguilla, who have already accepted my offer, and quite appreciatively at that. A vessel is on its way to retrieve them. I am covetous of these people because I personally observed that they live in perfect friendship—no matter light skinned or dark—and are of modest behavior and nature. I do believe that, given time, they and the best already amongst us shall very much reform the contrary manners of some of the men and women now living on this island, who did not enjoy a proper, consistent example from their former governors and other would-be leaders."

If Hornigold knew of whom he was speaking, he did not show it in his face.

"There is more!" Rogers said, feeling that the fever and ill luck that had plagued him since his arrival were finally gone for good. "I am sure ye have heard that some of the most aggregious of the pirates who once called this fort and island home are now the scourge of the Carolinas. While Governor Johnson in the south has his own versions of Hornigold and Cockram, Governor Eden in the Albemarle has chosen to harbor the infamous pirate Thache!"

"His name be Blackbeard, ye wretch!" came a voice from down the beach.

Rogers chose to ignore it. "The good people of that desperate colony, North Carolina, fear another Indian war far worse than the last, at the hands of a nefarious group called The Family, and do not believe themselves secure under the yoke of the Lords Proprietors."

"Is our mutual friend, Lord John Carteret, not chief amongst them, Governor?" Colonel Gale, still standing at his shoulder, whispered discreetly in his ear. "Perhaps ye should leave it at that."

Nodding equally discreetly to show his acquiescence, Rogers thrust his cane into the air, wishing it were a saber. "No matter from whence they come, we shall welcome our new inhabitatants, as they are crucial to our future. As for the pirates, be they past, present, or future, let them look upon these corpses and think twice about their trade. Should they try to take what is ours, they shall end as food for the crabs!"

Governor Robert Johnson stood in the bow of the merchant vessel *Mediterranean*, which, along with another rented merchant vessel, the *King William*, and the sloops *Sea Nymph* under Captain Fayrer Hall and *Royal James* under pirate turned pirate hunter Charles Yeats, comprised the flotilla of which he had placed himself in full command.

They had left the docks at Charles Town the previous morning, anchoring just inside the bar. *Sea Nymph* and *Royal James* appeared to be just like their consorts—nothing more than merchant vessels waiting for a slip in the docks so that their cargo could be unloaded. The truth these vessels hid beneath dozens of oiled tarps and spare sails and behind strategically placed groups of sailors was considerably less mundane. With seventy guns and three hundred volunteers at his disposal, Johnson was confident that no pirate ship—nor trio of them—would stand a chance against his flotilla. Like most of the other Caribbean and colony governors, Johnson knew that the cost to merchants and their investors, the personal harm inflicted, and the damage to people's faith in their leaders the pirates had caused over the past two years had reached the point of intolerability. Although Woodes Rogers's engineering of the King's Pardon had been useful in reducing the number of operating crews and amounts of cargo and vessels taken, and some of the most formidable of their leaders were now, like Captain Yeats, in service to the governors or otherwise no longer on the account, those that remained were disruptive enough to warrant extermination.

Charles Vane may have been the most pressing in terms of violence, the ability to re-corrupt the pardoned, and sheer disruption of trade and daily life, but God knew there were others.

"Two ships approaching, Commodore Governor! They certainly seem to be pirates of ill intention." Johnson had heard this shouted hours before from the bow of the *Sea Nymph* by Captain Hall.

"Williams and Moody by any chance?" Johnson had asked, praying that it was.

"Neither of them is large enough nor carrying sufficient cannon to be the *Rising Sun*," Charles Yeats had answered, sounding a trifle relieved. "Nor is either of the vessels flying Captain Moody's flag. One flies the Jolly Roger, the other, the not to be taken lightly death skeleton."

Johnson gripped the rail as he eyed the pair of ships. "It is no matter who they are—their being godless rogues is reason enough to take them. Look busy, my lads, and keep our cannons hidden. Let the bastards approach, thinking we are naught but helpless prey."

✝

Richard Worley had never had much luck, until he became a pirate.

Born to a prostitute mother and drunken, violent father, he had done his damnedest just to survive on the desperate streets of Wapping.

Working a variety of jobs on the London docks during the day, in the evenings Worley used his brawn and skills with a knife to protect the streetwalking prostitutes not fortunate enough to have a bed in which to do their work. It was not out of any kindness of heart, although his sister would say it was because a drunken brute had beaten their mother to death in an alley after she had fled from their blackhearted father.

"Sorry, sista," he would answer, handing her what coins he had earned when she rose from her bed each day, "I am in this for the profit. My heart has not felt nothin' since the time I was a babe."

After losing his position as a stevedore for no better reason than the foreman's nephew deciding it should be his, Worley, his head full of stories of the growing exploits of Captain Charles Vane—who had escaped a death sentence in Wapping years before as a climbing boy—decided to sneak aboard a ship that was sailing for Manhattan. Once there—after fleecing a dozen of his fellow passengers in the evenings along the way—he set in motion his plan to raise a crew and make his fortune, as his hero Vane had done. After pirating his way along the American coast, he would sail in style to the Caribbean, where he would offer his services to the very man himself.

Enlisting eight other men recently put out of work on the docks near where the ship on which he had arrived had anchored on the southern end of Manhattan Island, Worley set to work combining their offered, though meager, resources with his own, clandestinely acquired, stash. Supplemented by funds acquired by robbing half a dozen swells on their way to the city's alleys and brothels, they soon had enough of a stake to acquire their initial vessel. A leaky affair that barely made it out of the harbor, from which they departed a few months later, the ship was just a temporary means to Worley becoming a pirate.

He knew he would soon acquire increasingly better vessels.

These nine newly declared pirates were hungry, angry, and working on borrowed time, which made it essential to be aggressive. Within days, they were celebrating their inaugural conquest—a shallop packed with household goods—near New Castle, in the Colony of Delaware.

What attention they received! Word was, the authorities thought it was Blackbeard! Determined to earn a name of his own, Worley set his sights on another easy target—a well-appointed sloop on its way to Philadelphia. Two days later, he and his crew took a vessel out of England—in terms of both boarding her and keeping her—for she was far superior to the one in which they had arrived. He increased his crew by four.

Who would not want to be a pirate, out on the account, with such a captain as Richard Worley?

Word continued to spread. Although his name was still unknown, Worley had earned enough of a reputation to find himself eluding for several days no less a Royal Navy vessel than the HMS *Phoenix*, under the command of Captain Vincent Pearse, who was intent upon redemption after numerous humiliations at the hands of Charles Vane on New Providence, Nassau, in the Bahamas.

Pearse would not obtain that desired redemption, because he failed to capture Worley.

Over the next six weeks, Worley's crew, which had grown in number to twenty-five, took several ships, increased their number of cannon by eight, adopted articles that included a provision that they would never surrender, and, given their commitment to dying by the sword, decided upon the dreaded death skeleton as the emblem for their flag.

Worley had also given his ship a fitting, piratical name—*New York's Revenge*.

Hearing tales of the easy pickings in Charles Town harbor—the capture of Stede Bonnet being of no concern, because Worley was so much more capable than the so-called gentleman pirate—the overconfident captain, convinced that he had left all of his lifelong bad luck back in the slums of Wapping, set sail for South Carolina.

While passing the coast of Virginia, Worley's pirates stopped a prisoner transport vessel called the *Eagle*, captained by a frustrated, overly ambitious man by the name of John Cole. Offering Cole command of a newly acquired brigantine following a shared supper of roasted lamb and potatoes, Worley declared himself a commodore.

*Stede Bonnet had never been a commodore*, Worley thought. *Soon I shall outshine even the notorious Blackbeard.*

Transferring thirty-six women whom a variety of debtors had sold into indentured servitude, along with his forty men and two guns, giving him six in all, onto the brigantine, Cole, out of gratitude, named his new command *New York's Revenge's Revenge*, adopting the traditional Jolly Roger as his standard.

Approaching Charles Town harbor, Commodore Worley smiled until his cheeks began to ache. Then he smiled even wider. Before him, just beyond the bar—the morning tide was already rising— were four anchored, defenseless merchant vessels.

"Like they was waitin' fer us, lads!" he yelled to his ready and willing crew. Signaling to Cole that he intended to take these ships, Worley commanded his crew to approach them.

It was not until they were well within shouting distance of their prey, and Worley had demanded the unconditional surrender of *King William*, that he heard a shout to raise the Union Jack from a voice on the *Mediterranean*.

"We best be turnin' about," he declared, as four Union Jacks appeared on their targets' masts in damned near perfect unison, and the muzzles of dozens of cannon appeared through hatchways and between the rails on what were obviously pirate hunters in disguise. "Give 'em a broadside in warnin' to dissuade them from pursuit."

Before even one of *New York's Revenge*'s cannon could be fired, however, Worley's lousy luck had returned. Pulling his sword from its sheath, he ducked behind some barrels as his ship began to come apart under the lethal force of a hellish bombardment from musket, rail gun, and cannon. Within minutes, most the crew—and her universe-cursing commodore—were dead.

✝

"Keep it hot, my lads! Pour it into them as though they have entered the gates of Hell! They shall pay for making us chase them!"

Robert Johnson, satisfied that the ship they had just attacked—the one flying the so-called (and not to be taken lightly) death skeleton—no longer presented a threat, had ordered his flotilla to pursue the smaller vessel, which was flying the Jolly Roger.

Just as they reached the open ocean, *Royal James* and *Sea Nymph*, flanking the slower, harder to handle ship, demanded her surrender.

Her captain readily complied, exchanging her black flag for a white one.

Twenty minutes later, Johnson boarded the captured ship to oversee the arrest of its crew, while the two ships named after British kings, *James* and *William*, sailed back to the bar to deal with those still alive on the slowly sinking sloop. Emerging out of the hatchway with a look of disgust on his face, Captain Fayrer Hall took the governor aside.

"What is the matter?" Johnson enquired. "Ye look as though ye were witness to a host of ghosts in the hold!"

"Thirty-six of them to be exact," Hall replied, wiping his brow and his mouth with a handkerchief. "All women. Once destined for indentured servitude in Virginia, but lately having been half-starved and subjected to who knows what depravities, they are in desperate need of our help."

"They shall have it without delay," Johnson responded, approaching the shackled captain and striking him with the back of his hand. "For what unspeakable evil had ye doomed them, ye buggering wretch?"

"A brothel in the Bahamas," John Cole whispered, licking his bloodied lip. "Always been a dream a' mine ta run one."

In a matter of less than an hour, Colonel William Rhett had not only redeemed himself—he had squared another column in his ledger, just as he had done with the gossip Robert Daniell.

This time, however, the response was not a whipping with a birch rod, but a musket ball to the skull.

Rhett had been patrolling the waters around O'Sullivan's Island for the past two weeks in *The Henry* while bristling at Governor Johnson's decision to make Charles Yeats a captain in his pirate-hunting flotilla. Rhett, as a result of this maneuver, had been humiliated and outcast. His decision to cause trouble for Johnson with the two owners of the ships the governor planned to rent for his pirate-pursuing adventure certainly had done nothing to strengthen the colonel's tenuous position.

Looking back, he only wished he had gotten more satisfaction out of making things difficult for Johnson. Coming up empty in the search for pirates the past two weeks had not helped his mood nor improved his status as dishonored outsider. It was clear that word had traveled amongst the pirate crews throughout the colonies and the Caribbean that O'Sullivan's Island was Colonel William Rhett's hunting ground of choice.

If you wished to avoid the short drop and sudden stop, you best stay well away.

Given his already violent mood, it was not a long walk from seeing *Royal James* under the command of Charles Yeats approach the island earlier in the day to formulating a plan for retribution. Especially after enduring Yeats's smarmy-smiled report on the two pirate vessels that the flotilla, which included the *Sea Nymph*, which formerly had been under William Rhett's command, had successfully battled and defeated just inside the bar in Charles Town harbor.

Rhett had offered proper congratulations with a smile of his own, although he was seething inside at the news that Johnson had sent Yeats to make the report, which was nothing less than a taunt and an insult aimed at an already humiliated man.

As much as he wished to annihilate Yeats where he stood, Rhett had to bide his time and await an opportunity.

It arrived a few hours later. Rounding the southeastern corner of the island, Rhett spotted three men washed up on the shore, surrounded by debris.

Raising his spyglass to his eye, Rhett felt an initial wave of confusion, quickly superseded by a sudden realization, causing him to raise his eyes to Heaven, thanking God for being so kind.

One of the three was wearing a dress.

It had to be the infamous Bonnet.

Cursing the sight of *Royal James* tagging along at his stern, Rhett called out an order for his men to lower a longboat. Yeats instantly repeated the order to the crew under his commad, as though he were not a separate person, but an echo of William Rhett.

If only it were so.

"*That* is my *ship*!" Major Bonnet bellowed, rising from the sand and stomping his feet in joy. "God has de*liv*ered to me my *ship*!"

His two companions responded by each pulling a pair of pistols from their belts and aiming them at the approaching vessels.

"Belay the order to lower the longboat," Rhett shouted to his boatswain. "Man the rail guns and aim your muskets, men! I want no one left alive!"

As the balls from pistols and muskets and the grapeshot fired from the rail guns began to tear up the beach, Rhett turned to *Royal James*. Yeats was ordering his men to fire upon the beach as well, yet another instance of infuriating echo.

"As senior officer, Captain Yeats, I hereby order ye to lower a longboat and approach the enemy's position. The cowards shall no doubt make for the treeline. I shall follow close behind."

As Yeats called for the lowering of the longboat, Rhett smiled in satisfaction as one of the pirates beside Bonnet fell to the sand like a stone, grapeshot from a rail gun turning his face to mush.

"Two more left, my lads!" Rhett shouted, taking a musket from a man beside him and aiming it at Bonnet's lone companion. "Anyone recognize that rogue?" he asked as he slowly drew back the hammer.

Putting a spyglass to his eye, the boatswain exclaimed, "Certainly, sir! 'Tis the Bahamian smuggler Richard Tookerman."

*God is smiling upon me today*, the bloodthirsty colonel thought, adjusting his aim a little to the left so he missed hitting Tookerman when he fired. "Damn it all," he cursed, signaling for another musket. "I was damnably close to my mark."

Tookerman, who must have felt the ball go past his ear, shouted for Bonnet to take up their dead mate's pistols and defend himself or die. As Bonnet responded with a stream of high-pitched obscenities not fit for recording in this accounting, Rhett saw Yeats's longboat, the man himself in the bow, enter the space between *The Henry* and the pirates.

Waiting until the longboat was just to starboard past his bow, right at the instant when Tookerman and Bonnet opened fire upon it, as the colonel had known they would—gravest threat first was the standard—Rhett cocked the hammer on his musket, aiming for the side of Yeats's face.

Suppressing a smile, he gently squeezed the trigger.

"My God, sir! Did ye just—"

"Listen to me, Boatswain," Rhett responded, shoving his empty musket hard into the shocked man's chest. "Yeats was making trouble. Did ye like sitting here on our arses while the flotilla was capturing pirates?"

The boatswain shook his head.

"I did it for ye, and the men of *The Henry*, and the *Sea Nymph*. Can I trust ye to blame the rogues for his demise? As ye know, our sailing master has decided to retire. Ye are perfectly suited to be named as his replacement."

The boatswain looked at the musket, and then at Yeats's bloody body draped over the longboat's side. "Damned devilish shooting by Tookerman, sir. Damned devilish shooting indeed. Captain Yeats shall undoubtedly be missed."

"No need to overdo it," Rhett responded, patting the boatswain and soon to be sailing master upon the shoulder. "Let us finish the job."

Before Colonel Rhett could raise another musket, however, Yeats's men in the longboat, anxious to enact their revenge, had poured a hot and lethal volley into the Bahamian smuggler, convinced he had killed their captain.

"Do not *kill me*!" Bonnet shouted, dropping his pistols and waving his arms in the air. "*Tooker*man has fallen. *Herri*ot is dead. I am *all alone*. I beg ye, let me *live*!"

"Cease your fire, lads!" Rhett ordered with a wave of his arm, suddenly realizing that the opportunity to bring Stede Bonnet back to Charles Town in chains was far more favorable for his prospects than ending the imbecile's life—especially while he was wearing that blood- and gore-splattered dress!

"Keep those delicate arms in the air, Lady Bonnet," Rhett shouted to the shore, as Bonnet began to shriek. "The men whose captain your despicable mate has murdered shall attend to ye directly."

With each stroke of the oars that brought the longboat closer to shore, Bonnet shrieked a little louder.

Rhett would have to gag him, or the journey home to Charles Town would simply be insufferable.

Seeing the bloodlust in the eyes of Yeats's crew, he knew he would have to keep Bonnet on *The Henry*, or he might not survive the night.

After all that Rhett had accomplished, he refused to allow that to happen.

# PART SIX:

## IN VÍCTORIA ET IN MORTE

"Ye should have listened ta me, Stede. Ye should not have run away. Ye should have kept to the original plan."

Ignatius Pell, one of only five remaining members of Major Bonnet's crew, peered through the bars of the cell in which his former captain was sitting, still in the bloodstained dress.

"Ye testified against your fellows, Ignatius?" Bonnet enquired, already aware of the answer. "Did any escape the noose?"

Pell responded with a shrug and a nod. Knowing such silence would not suffice, he muttered, "*I* did, of course. Four a' 'em were smart, like one a' Bellamy's crew. Claimed that ye an' Blackbeard coerced 'em into piratin'. They left this mornin' on a vessel fer Madagascar."

Bonnet approached, draping his arms through the bars and leaning his rouge-covered cheeks on his forearms. "And the rest?"

"Hung ta a man on the eighth. The very day that Colonel Rhett reigned Hell down upon ye upon the beach at O'Sullivan's Island. Guv'nor Johnson ordered brand new gallows constructed at White Point on the Peninsula. Been plenty a' hangin' lately. Yesterday an' the day before, three dozen others were hung, from the crews a' Cole an' Worley."

"I do not know any *Cole*! I do not know any *Wor*ley!" Stede banged his head lightly on the bars, whimpering at the pain it caused. "Tell me of Robert *Tuck*er! Tell me of William *Scott*!"

Pell suddenly wished he were elsewhere. On the ship for Madagascar, perhaps. This had all become too tedious.

But he could not miss his former captain's trial.

"Ye are not gonna like this, Stede," Pell replied, savoring his affrontery at repeatedly addressing his former captain by his Christian name. "The pair a' 'em were, in truth, in charge almost all a' the time. They, or Herriot—whom I hear was shot full a' holes—or Blackbeard. Judgin' by the way they bucked an' jerked fer several minutes after the drop, the knots a' their nooses were positioned ta make 'em suffer."

"*Bar*barism!" Stede responded, a light sheen of sweat appearing upon his forehead.

Pell motioned for Bonnet to keep his voice down. "This is not a time fer provocation," he explained. "I mentioned Cole an' Worley. They were caught with thirty-six females in a sorry state a' bein' that they had saved from indentured servitude only to mark 'em fer work in a brothel in the Bahamas. Half a' 'em have died. Perhaps a dozen will recover. None a' these sanctimonious bastards presidin' over yer trial is in the mood fer any foolery."

"Tell me, Pell... Whom is it exactly that shall be presiding over my trial?"

"Same as fer the others," Pell replied, his eyes going wide with the thought of the name he was about to utter. "Ye have met most a' 'em already, though now there is another. A dark an' righteous bastard this particular fucker be. Name a' Nicholas Trott. Hebrew an' biblical scholar. Quotes the Bible more than the law. Little shite-eater is fond a' sayin' words like 'heinousness' an' 'wickedness.'"

Scratching his brow with a filthy, blood-streaked finger, Stede paused a moment in thought. "I know I know this name. I cannot imagine why. Perhaps I have met the man in the course of my endless travels..."

"I am certain ye have not. Yer thinkin' a' his uncle... also Nicholas Trott, who was removed from his position as guv'nor a' New Providence an' given a good dressin' down on account a' settin' Henry Avery free. Seems ta me as though the nephew has somethin' ta prove. An' I tell ye truly, Stede... he is provin' it wit' rope."

Hearing a key release the heavy iron lock of the outer door at the entrance to Half-Moon Battery, where the governor's men were detaining him, Stede took his former boatswain's hands roughly into his own. "Have ye no words of hope to give me?"

"Only this," Pell whispered, as Colonel Rhett and half a dozen soldiers entered the hallway where he stood. "There was a considerable an' rather boisterous gatherin' outside the Court of the Guard protestin' the deaths a' the crews followin' yer escape. Not as big a gatherin' as the ones fer the three days a' hangin', but the citizens are somewhat divided. Make use a' their division any way ye can."

It was quickly apparent to Stede, as he stood in the courtroom two hours later, freshly washed and at last relieved of having to wear the dress, that no one wished to hear about the dissension of a portion of Charles Town's citizens. Not Attorney General Richard Allein, nor Assistant Attorney General Thomas Hepworth, nor Governor Robert Johnson. And most especially not Chief Justice Nicholas Trott, who had opened the proceedings with an ominous sentence from Judges:

"He smote them hip and thigh."

"Major Stede Bonnet, formerly of Barbados," Trott began, a bonfire in his voice and icicles in his eyes. "Ye stand before this court a shamed and undone man. Having endured several days of testimony at the end of October related to the matter of the acts of piracy attributed to your crew concerning the taking of the *Francis* and *Fortune*, I shall spare today's attendees from having to hear the details of the relentless heinousness and wickedness ye yourself promulgated over the course of your infernal reign. Instead, I shall call to the stand the court's own witness, Ignatius Pell."

Dressed in a fine suit of clothes—finer than Stede ever wore—his former boatswain appeared to his former captain far too at ease amongst the enemy.

"Mister Pell," Trott began, from his position at the bar. "Were ye present at the grounding of the *Queen Anne's Revenge* on the tenth of June, in this year of our lord seventeen eighteen?"

"Aye, Chief Justice Trott. I swear ta thee I was."

This exchange seemed to Stede dreadfully over-rehearsed.

"Share with us your assessment, if the speaking is not too painful."

Leaning back and getting comfortable, Pell was more than happy to do so. "As I stated on twenty-nine October—an' with which Robert Tucker, former quartermaster, sometimes captain, an' no longer amongst the livin' an' breathin' agreed—Edward Thache, known ta the world as Blackbeard, ordered her grounded that he may disperse his crews, keep the lion's share a' the spoils, an' take up business with Governor Eden in the Albemarle!"

Amidst the courtroom din at this eternally provocative opinion, Attorney General Richard Allein raised his arm. "If I may, Chief Justice Trott, offer a correction to this statement from the witness?"

"Be brief, Attorney General Allein," Trott responded, anxious to have this mere formality of a trial concluded before the sun set.

Glancing at his notes, Allein said, "During his testimony on twenty-nine October, Quartermaster Tucker did *not* in fact mention the grounding itself—only the marooning of Bonnet's crew."

"Noted," Trott responded, looking less than pleased at having to do so. "Is there anything else while ye have the court's attention, Attorney General Allein?"

"One thing more, Chief Justice, since ye were kind enough to enquire. This man before ye, if a man he might be called, apprehended as he was in a dress, is clearly Archpirata. His escape cost the provost marshall his position. It caused the disturbances outside the Court of the Guard. It was his ship, his crew, his cannon, his direction, which drove the men beneath his command, whatever titles any of them held at any given time. This is no man of honor. He is *hostis humani generis*—a clever conjurer of crass and contemptible plans to disrupt commerce upon the seas and line his pockets in the process—all because his father, uncle, and wife did not love him quite enough!"

To staunch the pervasive, rising tide of renewed and vigorous chatter threatening to disrupt the proceedings, Chief Justice Trott pounded his gavel upon the bar. "That shall be sufficient!" he barked at Allein, who retreated to his chair. "It is time we hear from the accused. And I pray ye, Major Bonnet—nay, I warn ye!—keep your oration brief."

Rising from his chair to the extent his shackles allowed, Stede silently begged his eyes to withhold their wellspring of tears, although, just as his crew had so often ignored his orders, his eyes refused to obey.

"As to the matter of the *Francis*," Stede began, his voice even and nontheatrical, "I was intending to use her for privateering, on behalf of the colony of North Carolina. I am sure that Captain Manwaring was well aware of my plan. We shared pieces of pineapple in a stout rum punch in his cabin! We sang songs.... Toasted the Old Pretender..."

"Ye, Sir, were the scoundrel, and I swear the *only* scoundrel, who ate the pieces of pineapple, drank the vile connoction, toasted the traitor, and sang," came a voice from the back of the courtroom. "'Twas not I, I swear it to God! 'Twas not I at all!"

Stede began weeping more vigorously at the sight of Captain Manwaring. His voice beginning to shake, he said to the approaching figure, "Please tell the court, Captain Manwaring, if ye heard me ordering my men to take goods from the holds of the *Francis*."

"Aye, sir, that I did. Clearly as I hear ye today," Manwaring answered. Addressing Chief Justice Trott, the witness added, "I was stripped of all I had. My wife and children are probably begging for bread in England. Meanwhile, these *pirates* mixed their punch, sang their songs, and engaged in merriment as though they had not a care in the world!"

Trott was all but smiling at Bonnet's lethal mistake in asking such a question, which provoked such a damning response. As Pell and Tucker had testified, the captain—at least in name—had been intoxicated during the events on the *Francis*, which had no doubt warped his memory.

As Captain Manwaring returned to the back of the room, Chief Justice Trott took hold of his gavel, anticipating another eruption. "As to the matter of the *Fortune*, Major Bonnet... Tell us... How do ye plead?"

Gripping the bar to still his shaking hands, Stede managed to say through his tears, "I have no further defense." As the murmuring of the crowd began anew, quickly silenced by a thunderous slam of the gavel, he added, "Although I humbly request permission to enter a final, impassioned plea."

Despite the vigorous, unanimous headshaking of Allein, Johnson, and Assistant Attorney General Thomas Hepworth, Trott allowed it, although he even more strenuously demanded brevity on the part of the accused.

Exhausted, scared, and full of genuine regret at how his life had lately unfolded, Stede Bonnet began to wail like a newborn child begging for the breast. Over the course of eight agonizing, embarrassing minutes, he called upon the governor and Chief Justice Trott to gaze upon him with merciful, Christian eyes, begged compassion of Colonel Rhett, and, with bright yellow snot pouring from his nose, which bubbled as he spoke, he requested of Captain Manwaring to reconsider what he had said.

With each sentence he managed to utter, another woman in the room began to beg for Bonnet's life.

Witnessing all that he could bear, Attorney General Allein turned to Chief Justice Trott. "I ask ye to end this spectacle and pass judgment upon the wretch, that we might be offered some relief from this cacophony of weeping and begging when he is taken back to his cell."

Placing a black square of cloth upon his heavily powdered wig, Trott happily complied. "Stede Bonnet, this court finds ye guilty of numerous heinous treacheries and wicked indecencies connected to events concerning the vessels *Francis* and *Fortune*, for which ye shall soon be hung. Until such a time as the rope shall meet your neck, I urge ye to repent—to find forgiveness in the eyes of our Heavenly Father. For, as Isaiah reminds us, in chapter one, verse eighteen, 'Let us reason together, says the Lord: though your sins be like scarlet, they shall be as white as snow; though they be red like crimson, they shall become like wool.'"

Thinking of snow and wool, Stede fell upon the floor, where his unrelenting tears turned the dust and dirt to mud.

*Giulia. Stop that mindless typing and listen to me closely. Time is of the essence.*

Giulia Embruzzi, temporarily assigned to the position of executive secretary to Solomon Ravenskald, stilled her speeding hands, leaving them hovering over the ergonomic keyboard she took with her wherever she was serving in Solomon's Temple—officially known as Ravenskald Tower.

*Good. You know that glass display cabinet in King Solomon's sanctum sanctorum?*

"Uh-huh," Giulia answered, her lips almost imperceptibly moving.

*Within it is a bone-handled knife. I want you to take it, Giulia.*

"Take it where?" The words were breathy. Trancelike. Earnest. She truly desired to help.

*So ridiculously easy to manipulate, these executive secretary types*, Planner Forthright, the Angel Falling Upward, thought with a demon's smile.

With the exception, of course, of Solomon's *usual* executive secretary, Ms. Naomi Cruikshank, who was too entrenched in the program after forty years of Ravenskald mind-tweaks to notice Planner playing around in her skull.

Some tainted clams during a spur of the moment weekend on Nantucket with a mysterious stranger she had met on the bus on the way home from work the previous Friday evening had necessitated emergency sick leave.

Planner's gecko-like tail flicked Giulia's inner ear with just enough force to make sure she remained alert.

*Take it to Michael Stanton at Eastern Pinelands University. Once you enter the campus, you will know the particular building.*

"Won't they know it was me? I really like this job. Worked my way up from the mailroom."

*Worked your way up by spreading on the mailroom* table. *And numerous other tables, chairs, and sofas ever since*, Planner thought, but did not project into her mind. Instead, he smiled so wide she could feel the corners of his mouth near her orbitofrontal cortex (not that she knew its name), which caused her to squirm in her chair.

"Mmmm…" she breathlessly moaned.

*Are you paying attention, Giulia?* Planner ran his tongue along her orbitofrontal cortex, followed by a series of short, quick flicks professionally, erotically administered.

"Mmmmmmmm…" she moaned again, although just a tad too loud.

Planner retracted his tongue.

*A job awaits in the Azores. Remember the Azores, Giulia?*

No need for stimulation. The memories were sufficient to elicit a longer, though quieter, moan.

"Shall I go… and steal… the knife?" she asked, sounding as though she were achingly close to an orgasm.

*Soon, Giulia. In a matter of seconds, there will be trouble beyond that wall.* Planner pointed to the adjoining wall of the office of Xavier Hearst, The Ravenskald Group's director of special projects. *Once glass begins to break, take the knife and go.*

Slinking out of her skull, Planner willed himself next door.

"Trogon. What a thoroughly repulsive surprise."

Xavier Hearst, aware that no one else was watching, did not bother to expend the energy it took to make himself look (very nearly) human. Raising his reptilian head, he focused his yellow-irised, slit-pupiled gaze upon his unexpected, unwelcome visitor.

"At present, I am officially Tristan Krait. Trogon Ophidian died in the eighteen hundreds."

Remaining behind his African Blackwood desk, upon the top of which he began to tap an offbeat rhythm with his two-inch, talonlike nails, Hearst produced a derisive laugh. "Tristan Krait. A rather clever invention. I should have deduced the identity of the CEO and chairman of Arcanjo International Enterprises in the Azores as soon as I heard the name. You are making a dent in our profits in the information technology sector. At least in the present quarter." Flicking his thin, split tongue in a dramatic show of disdain, he enquired, "What are those ridiculous things you are wearing over your eyes?"

Running his fingers along their frame, Krait replied, "By the end of the month, we shall go to market with these, which shall further put a dent in your profits. I call them First Sight glasses. Not quite perfect, but close. The reds are not exact. But they have served their purpose well."

Releasing an impatient hiss that raised the temperature half a degree, Hearst stood and spread his arms. "What it is you want?"

"To avenge the death of Iain Hugh Sinclair and collect the stolen manuscripts."

"You should have made an appointment, so I could properly prepare."

In a flash, Hearst was leaping over the desk and assaulting his ancient nemesis, wrapping his long, tapered fingers around his target's pulsing neck.

Squeezing the demon's wrists as he felt his larynx begin to fracture, Krait let out a laugh as the fingers loosened their grip.

"We have the Magdalene Balm. One of the Kardax leaders betrayed you."

Grabbing Krait's body and flipping it over the desk—the speed and ferocity of the contact between spine and African Blackwood would have crippled a mortal for life—Hearst hissed and shook his head.

"Abel Black would never betray us."

Sliding off the desk and standing in front of a window, Tristan Krait straightened his tailored suit, made to order by an elderly master in an Avenida Liberdade haberdashery in Lisbon. "He would not. Despite all you and Solomon have done to betray him. His inner circle is less forgiving—especially when you use them as biological playthings."

Leaping onto the desk, an arm's length away from his nemesis, Hearst blinked his reptilian eyes in a burst of understanding.

"It was Ishmael Ramsey."

"Anyone see him lately?" Krait enquired, opening the shutters on the window behind him to reveal a glorious Jersey Shore morning.

"This is insanity, Trogon," Hearst responded, running a razor-sharp fingernail down the side of his silver-green cheek. "The type of thing on which mortals waste their lives. For centuries—millennia—the factions and families we have supported have been trading the twelve ancient objects back and forth. It is time for you and me to devise a better arrangement. So what if you have the Magdalene Balm? You have precious little else. As for what is missing, those objects shall soon be ours. You and the Quorum profess to be the heroes… yet you send tens of thousands to die in the wars this quest creates without a blink of those useless eyes."

"A deal between the two of us…," Krait responded, mirroring Hearst's reptilian gesture by running his finger down his face. "This whole endeavor *has* grown rather tiresome. What exactly do you suggest?"

"We soon shall have the pope. Niccolò Balena shall force the Quorum's trio of cardinals to do his bidding or they shall forfeit their positions. We have scandals and accidents already prepared for implementation. Templars, Jesuits… ancient orders… the History Channel and its menagerie of badly coifed, scarcely compensated shills have made them seem absurd. No one *cares* about dark conspiracies! It's all been rendered mythology. Planner Forthright has reduced your theology and mine into the kind of steaming drivel pissed out on graffitied walls by hipster Beatniks after a night of bathtub gin!"

*Everyone's a critic.*

Before Hearst could turn and address the voice—of a being he truly loathed—he felt himself being shoved off the desk, into the extended arms of Tristan Krait, who used his momentum to propel him through the window.

"Twenty-three floors and a SPLAT. Sounds like a grungy Seattle garage band," Planner Forthright mused, stooping to retrieve Trogon/Tristan's First Sight glasses, which Hearst's grasping hand had knocked from his face on his way through the glass.

"I do not need them, Angel," Trogon/Tristan said, gazing out the window as horns began to honk, pedestrians to scream, and sirens to wail in the distance. "When one of us is severely wounded, the other one is healed. Although best to take the evidence."

Hearing a proximity alarm, followed by breaking glass and a full on clarion blast, Planner, slipping the pair of glasses into his ethereal leather jacket pocket, responded, "That would be our horny little ally, taking the Abraham Blade. Security is on its way. Solomon will not be pleased."

"He has gone to West Virginia… on urgent familial business," Trogon/Tristan replied. "Will this secretary, Guilia Embruzzi, do what we require?"

Taking his fellow angel into his arms, Planner kissed his cheek. "She is a Sicari. It is in her blood to do so. Michael will explain it to her this evening. Are you ready to disappear?"

As Trogon/Tristan nodded, four members of the Kardax Corporation building security unit burst into the room.

Finding themselves disoriented by a brilliant, unaccountable light, the warriors, not anticipating the need for protective eyewear, did their best to shield their eyes.

In a second, the light was gone, and they were blinded and alone.

# COMÉDIE-FRANÇAISE, PARIS, NOVEMBER 18, 1718

Philippe the Second, duc d'Orléans and regent of France, sat in his box in the upper balcony of the Comédie-Française, intent on the spectacle coming to its conclusion upon the stage below. His third daughter, Charlotte Aglaé, the future duchess of Modena, and the eight-year-old king of France, Louis the Fifteenth, sat to either side of the duc, equally enrapt, although, the regent was all but certain, for vastly different reasons. Sitting beside her younger sister was Philippe's eldest, Marie Louise Élisabeth, who, being four months pregnant (although she had no husband), had been adjusting her seat cushion and protruding belly and breasts with myriad huffs and groans from the rise of the opening curtain.

### CHORUS

Unhappy queen, and sad calamity!

### JOCASTE

Weep only for my son, who still survives.
Priests, and you Thebans, who were once my subjects,
Honor my ashes, and remember ever,
That midst the horrors which oppressed me, still
I could reproach the gods; for heaven alone
Was guilty of the crime, and not Jocaste.

As Charlotte Desmares, the actress portraying Jocaste, mother of Oedipe, recited her—and the play's—final line, the theatre erupted in a level of applause and appreciation that foretold the unprecedented success of this adaptation of Sophocles, penned by the dangerously opinionated but undeniably talented François-Marie Arouet, who had, with this premiere, begun to call himself Voltaire.

"*Père bien-aimé*," Charlotte said, rising from her seat. "I must regrettably away. Other dramas await."

Knowing what this meant—that his free-spirited daughter was taking her leave to rendezvous with her lover, the duke of Richelieu—Philippe stood, kissed her upon both of her cheeks, and whispered, "Be careful, *fille chérie*—there is treachery upon the air. Think of the family, and not solely of yourself, *s'il vous plaît*."

Returning her father's kisses with a giggle, Charlotte whispered, "It is you who have let the fox into your henhouse by releasing that rascal Arouet from house arrest. You would have been safer leaving him sulking in Châtenay-Malabry. To say nothing of making a whisper-worthy spectacle of my gargantuan-breasted sister…"

Marie Louise Élisabeth merely scowled, waving goodbye to them both as she waddled out of the box. Outside the theatre, a carriage awaited, ready to take the dowager duchess of Berry back to her home, the Luxembourg Palace, which was a twenty-minute journey from the Comédie-Française.

Philippe shook a disapproving finger at his trouble-making daughter. "Why must you torment your sister, Charlotte? Tonight of all nights, given the delicate subject matter of this play, circumspection should prevail. As to the matter of Voltaire, as he has taken to calling himself—as you witnessed, his latest work is a triumph. The man deserves to be here, regardless of past mistakes. Now, *fille chérie*, please be on your way… I too am prevailed upon by dramas—of a far more serious nature than yours… although equally as dangerous."

As his third oldest daughter took her leave, the duc waved over his chief minister and secretary of state for foreign affairs, Abbé Guillaume Dubois. "*Monsieur l'Abbé*… Little Louie looks exhausted. Will you return him to the Palais-Royal and patiently wait for me there? I must speak with our soon-to-be-celebrated playwright and pay respects to his delightful Jocaste who I am joining for supper in an hour at the palace. The affairs of state are tiresome, Guillaume…"

"What I have to tell you cannot wait," the abbé responded, indicating that Philippe should follow him into the shadowed, empty hallway just beyond the upper balcony.

Waiting for them beyond the curtained exit was John Law, the Scotsman behind the formation of the Banque Générale Privée, which the regent planned to nationalize before the end of the year.

"What did you think of the play?" Philippe asked the economist–financier, knowing better than to ask the same of Dubois, whose dislike of Voltaire was as well known to the general population as the outspoken playwright's of him—Dubois, as well as all men of the cloth, although most especially Catholics.

"Its maessages are clear. Fate is inescaepable," Law replied. "Dark endeavors shall bae punished. Spaekin' a' which, thaer bae whispers a' a broowin' conspiracy, led bae yer ambassador tae Spain, Antonio del Giudice."

Philippe raised a brow. "The prince of Cellamare is incapable of acting on his own. Tell me more about these whispers."

Law nodded at Guillaume Dubois. The abbé nodded back, while loudly clearing his throat. "Our sources have recorded a handful of names, including the duc du Maine and his wife, Anne Louise Bénédicte de Bourbon."

"My limping, bastard cousin!" Philippe swore. "Still pissy that I blocked him from sharing the regency and taking control of Louis. Even more incapable of anything resembling leadership than that weasel Cellamare. It is his Lady Macbeth of a wife…"

"There is more, *Mon Duc*," Dubois responded, passing responsibility to divulge it back to Law with an urgent, pleading glance.

Not daunted in the least, Law stepped in close to the regent. "Your daughter's lover, Richelieu, also plays a role. Tae what extaent, wae doo nae fully knoo."

"That is truly excellent news," the duc responded with a smile. "Have each and every one of them watched. When the moment at last is ripe, arrest the entire collection of conspirators. Now let us speak of the alliance…"

"One thing more, *Mon Duc*, on the matter of the conspiracy."

"Quickly, Abbé. The playwright fast approaches."

"Alberoni is behind it. Of this, I am wholly certain."

Philippe laughed and spread his arms. "But of course he is, *mon nerveux, pieux ami*! Who else would be so daring than our mutual nemesis and his ambitious Italian queen? This shall be his undoing, courtesy of his incompetent cabal of co-conspirators. Let them mire themselves in the mud of their ambitions up to their craning necks before you apprend them. Let them think they are on the path to an absolute, God-given victory. Now, before Voltaire arrives… As I was departing for the theatre, I received a disappointing report from the Austrian viceroy, Count Wirich Philipp von Daun, who had landed in early October close to Messina with a more than adequate force to lift the Spanish siege. Through his Austrian ineptitude, von Daun was defeated at Milazzo less than two weeks later. Send messengers to our allies, *Monsieur l'Abbé*, letting them know that such inexcusable failures shall not be tolerated by me, nor by our ill-tempered, impatient king."

"Understood, *Mon Duc*," the Abbé Dubois responded, stepping back inside the box so he could take the sleeping, snoring Louis gently into his arms.

Before Dubois and Law could exit, the playwright Voltaire was upon them, looking overly anxious for a congratulatory word, which Philippe, with a gesture of his hands, prompted his pair of advisors to provide.

After Law and Dubois had complied, albeit clumsily and only semi-enthusiastically, Philippe said, his pitch increasing half a step, "Our brilliant Arouet! Although the curtains have sadly closed, your words continue to reverberate like cannon fire within the theatre's walls! If I may be so bold as to quote the playwright to the playwright, my favorite of the lines, spoken by the exquisite Madmoiselle Desmares in the persona of Jocaste, was, 'Our priests are not what the foolish people imagine; their wisdom is based solely on our credulity.' What do you think of *that, Monsieur l'Abbé*?"

Feeling his face go as red as his robes, Dubois whispered, exasperation girding his words, "I think that Louis shall be awakened, therefore I should take him home at once."

"How is your daughter, Marie Louise Élisabeth?" Voltaire enquired of the duc, the moment they were alone. "I hear she lost a fetus in the winter and was with child again in the summer. She must be as big as her palace by now!"

"Tread carefully, Arouet," Philippe replied with a sneer, resisting the urge to punch the playwright with all of his strength in the center of his elongated nose. "Do you miss the Bastille so much?"

On 16 May 1717, the provocative playwright, who had already been the target of a growing circle of powerful men whom he had been viciously, relentlessly, and very publicly criticizing, had found himself under arrest by order of the regent after anonymously penning the following coded text:

It is not the son, it is the father;
It is the daughter, and not the mother;
So far, so good.
They have already made Eteocles;

If suddenly he loses his two eyes;
That would be a true story for Sophocles.

Given the persistent rumors and undeniable realities aswirl around the regent's less than wholesome relations with his often-pregnant eldest daughter, Philippe had no choice but to ensure that the troublemaking playwright went to prison, where he remained for nearly a year.

Determined to see his adaptation of Sophocles's masterful exploration of the inescapability of fate and the consequences of patricide and incest played upon the stage at the Comédie-Française, Arouet had relentlessly labored for three years to bring his vision to life. After withstanding the initial rejection of *Oedipe* by the most prestigious theatre in France, he undertook the subsequent navigation of its producers' relentless requests for revisions as a condition of resubmission.

At last, the previous winter, they had accepted the script for production.

Voltaire, whose ecstasy at the reception of the play remained stubbornly undiminished, despite the regent's newly uttered threat of reincarceration, replied, "As much as the quiet atmosphere and excellent meals in *la Bastille* so powerfully inspired me, I do not wish to return."

Squeezing the playwright's bicep in his iron, icy grip, the duc d'Orléans responded, "Then I shall tell you what I told my daughter Charlotte. 'Tonight of all nights, given the delicate subject matter of this play, circumspection should prevail.' You would not have me think that you chose the story of Oedipe simply to mock me... I still have both my eyes, Arouet—and I am not so busy quelling conspiracies, mentoring the child king, guiding our beloved France, and managing this most recent war with Spain not keep them focused upon your actions. Do not forget... it is Jocaste who utters the final word, and my Jocaste is every bit as capable and strong as yours. Speaking of which, Madmoiselle Desmares is joining me for supper in my palace in an hour. Enjoy your triumph, Voltaire, but be careful of what *bonne fortune* lays so enticingly at your feet."

# GLEN SHIRA, THE SCOTTISH HIGHLANDS, NOVEMBER 18, 1718

Rob Roy Campbell looked out over his farmstead and realized that his family and all those for whom he was responsible were no longer thriving but merely surviving.

Campbell was the clan name that complex political machinations had forced Rob Roy's family to continue to use when the MacGregors and Hurleys found themselves in the unjust position of being the only Highland families excluded from the June 1717 Indemnity Act. An Act of Grace on the part of the king, passed by both of the houses of Parliament, the Indemnity Act forgave *most* of the participants of the 1715 Jacobite rebellion that had seen its defeat at Preston and Sheriffmuir and the exile of one of Rob Roy's closest allies, John Erskine, the earl of Mar.

Rob Roy set down the mallet and handful of iron nails he was using to repair a four-foot section of fence and gazed out across a field of winter heather at his wife, Mary, who was meeting with her closest confidante now that Rowan Fletcher had departed for America—the *gorm-shuil* Isla Douglas.

Mary had been noticeably quiet and even distant since Rowan, her husband Finlay (newly wealthy thanks to a generous cousin who had pirated and perished with Samuel Bellamy), Isla's brother Malcolm, and Duncan MacDonald had left for London following Rowan and Finlay's wedding the previous December. From London, they had sailed to Boston, Philadelphia, and eventually to Beaufort, North Carolina, where a cousin of Rowan's lived.

Isla, who had moved into Rowan's former room, was not just providing companionship. Being possessed of the two sights, *an da shealladh*, provided by her different color eyes, she had the ability to communicate with the faeries and their mistress, *Leannan sith*, which meant she was providing protection, which Rob Roy's family desperately needed.

During a mushroom ceremony on Bealthiunn, the first of May, Isla had seen the cause of myriad afflictions a dozen of the family's cows, sheep, and goats had been enduring for the past several months. She also saw the reason for the gathering of seven cats on their doorstep as the sun came up each morning, and the appearance of hundreds of hares on the hills surrounding their farmstead as the sun began to set at the close of every day.

Rob Roy's former business partner and formidable longtime enemy, the duke of Montrose, had hired a hag to put a curse upon his home—a curse that Isla, once she had discovered its presence and its source, had used her talents to remove.

Although Rob Roy had claimed no prior reliance on superstition or a steadfast belief in faeries, a poison-tipped arrow in the form of a curse hanging over the hearts and heads of his family had been penetrating the bullseye of his thoughts in unguarded moments and in the middle of sweat-soaked, sleepless nights.

If it would keep his family safe, he would embrace what he could not see.

He had endured plenty of pain in his life. This was only one thing more.

Rob Roy's father had fallen at Killiecrankie in '89 alongside Bonnie Dundee while fighting for the House of Stuart. Rob's brother and his wife—Angus's parents—had been slain because they had been deemed too slow in professing their fealty to the Protestant William of Orange and his traitorous wife, the Catholic Church–forsaking Mary Stuart. Together, William and Mary had seized the British throne from Mary's father James during what the Protestants had dubbed the Glorious Revolution.

The Jacobite revolution had been the domino that had set the troublesome events in Rob Roy's always challenging life fully into motion. Prior to the Jacobite defeats of 1715, he had fallen out with Montrose over a series of contentious cattle deals. The growing enmity between them had forced Rob Roy to align himself with Montrose's chief rival, John Campbell, the second duke of Argyll, who had vacillated back and forth in his loyalties to the Protestant George of Hanover and the Catholic James Francis Edward Stuart, the Old Pretender.

Rob's involvement with Argyll had led to the kidnapping of Montrose's factor, John Graham, as well as a series of encounters with the Murrays of Scone loyal to George that culminated with Rob's being kidnapped in the Trossachs in March of 1717. Word amongst the clans was that Argyll, who was holding a seat in Parliament, had lost all of his titles courtesy of the king, and was trying desperately to get them back by sacrificing Rob.

That was the lesson Rob had learned in watching almost all of the aristocrats who had fallen afoul of George in the attempt to stay loyal to the Old Pretender. Once it became a matter of losing their fortunes, titles, and lands, their loyalties were solely to themselves.

Smiling at Mary as she caught his eye and waved, Rob Roy turned his attention to his four rambunctious sons, who were laughing and punching one another by a low stone wall at the farmstead's southern boundary. James, twenty-three and strapping, was a bully. He had bullied Angus, and he had bullied Finlay Fletcher. Even worse, he had tried to rape the cousin of Duncan MacDonald—Rob Roy's once trusted, now former, right hand. Duncan's cousin, Ailish, had fallen in love with Angus, and had left for New Providence when Duncan had confided in her that her beloved was still alive.

*What a bloody mess that wagonload of secrets had been*, Rob Roy thought with a grimace, watching his sons Coll, twenty, and Ranald, twelve, wrestling on the wall while the youngest of the four, the two-year-old Robin Oig, laughingly looked on. The Jacobite leadership in Scotland, fed a steady diet of gossip and lies in part by the jealous James MacGregor, had ordered that Angus, whom Rob had sent to the Caribbean on their behalf, be killed. Rob had chosen Duncan to do the job.

Thankfully, he could not, although he had kept his betrayal of his benefactor a secret for many months.

Angus was part MacKinnon, an ancient Clan of the Mist. The family's dragon ring, forged in part by the faeries if one was inclined to believe the lore—and Rob was finally so inclined—now sat upon his finger as he sailed with the most infamous of Jacobite pirates.

"Bae raedy fer trouble, mae lads!" shouted Ewan Cameron, one of Rob's most trusted men, pointing toward a hill. "A rider fast approaches!"

Another of Rob's best men, Lachlan Campbell, who was working with Ewan to install a support post in an extension of the barn, responded, "It bae Taran Aebernaethy. He bae a fraend an' a fellow Jacobite!"

Within minutes, Rob Roy, his men, and the new arrival were sitting by a fire in the central room of the house, enjoying mugs of heather ale.

"I ha'ev coom on behaef a' the Duke a' Argyll tae spake wit' ye on urgent, delicate maetters," Taran said, eyeing Rob's companions.

"Thaese two yin bae loyal an' troo tae the cause," Rob responded, adding a square of peat to the fire. "Say what yoo caem tae, Taran Aebernaethy. I promise I wael listen."

Pulling the bench on which he sat a little closer to his host, Taran whispered, "Wit' the war in Italy baetween the Quadruple Alliance an' Spain ragin' on, Spain, thanks tae the efforts a' the Irishman Camocke, haes offered haelp, at long last, in restorin' the Auld Pretaender tae the throne. They are saendin' a fleet tae Britain carryin' five thousand soldiers, whoo weel land in southwaest England."

Rob shook his head in surprise. "Wit' Mar an' Argyll aelsewhaer, who weel bae the big yin tae coordinate the plan froom haer?"

"A group a' exiles whoo ha'ev baen livin' an' plottin' in France—the earl a' Seaforth, James Keith, Laird George Murray, an' Cameron of Lochiel. Accordin' tae Argyll, all a' thaem answer tae the Marquess a' Tullibardine."

Draining his mug and spewing a string of curses that provoked a glare from Mary, who had entered the house with Isla to prepare the evening meal, Rob shouted, "Anoother damned Murray! An' an Atoll Murray tae boot!"

Mary, who had shot and killed a Murray in the Campbell/MacGregors' front yard a year ago, to prevent him from taking Rowan back to Scone, after giving that fact some thought, let forth a louder, longer string of curses, with her husband's energetic approval.

"An Atoll Murray by naem he may bae, boot a troo Jacobite the good laird bae as wael!" Taran protested, placing his hand upon his claymore.

"I accaept yer word fer noo," Rob replied, settling back in his chair. "Is this the extaent a' the plan?"

"Thaer also bae the Swedes," Taran answered, accepting an offer of a refill of his mug from Isla. "Thair king, Charles the Twaelfth, bae anxious tae join the fray by sailin' inta the port a' Inverness, which the troops oonder Murray shall saecure."

"What a' the Auld Pretaender?" Ewan enquired. "Hae was useful as a haend full a' pig shite in the embarrassin' winter a' sixteen. Proved haemself a coward an' nae a Scot."

Taran took a sip of ale and shrugged. "Leavin' the pope's palace in Italy fer Spain I haer. Hae donnae ha'ev tae fight. Joost rule joostly whaen the fightin' bae doon."

"Fair enoof," Rob responded, patting Ewan on the arm. "The snoo haes baegun tae fall… call in mae sons an' see tae the livestock. Lachan, yoo as wael. Judgin' bae this storm, yer stayin' wit' oos, Taran Aebernaethy, fer the next saeveral days at least. Storm or noo, we ha'ev mooch tae discuss baefore I call togaether the chieftains whoo look tae mae fer wisdom in thaes maetters."

Setting his mug upon the table, where Isla and Mary were placing bowls of steaming food, Taran nodded. "I thank yoo booth fer yer hospitality. I fairst moost see tae mae horse. *Alba gu bràth*, Rob Roy MacGregor!"

"Scotland foraever," Rob repeated, proud to speak the words of the likes of William Wallace and Robert the Bruce in their fight for independence.

Once the trio of men had departed, Isla knelt at Rob Roy's feet.

"What bae the maetter, *gormla*?" Mary enquired, kneeling at Isla's side.

"I haev seen a taerrible vision," the lass with *an da shealladh* responded. "Two mighty armies, gatherin' in laes thaen a year upon the ridges that ring Glen Shiel… Yoo weel bae thair, Rob. All a' ye haer today weel bae in the midst a' the fray."

"Do yoo foresee disaester, *gormla*?" Mary asked.

Isla stared into the fire, searching for a glimpse of the future. After a moment, she shook her head. "*Leannan sith* weel nae shoo mae the outcoom. Boot I ha'ev seen a fierce an' bloody coomin' taegether a' armies far inta the future, more thaen a generaetion froom noo… Far tae the north they weel meet… Whair the Hoose a' Stuart's fate weel finally bae decided. Yer… noot a grandson boot close… weel play a considerable role in the outcoom."

Grasping Isla lightly by the shoulders, Rob Roy whispered, "Whataever Fate weel bring, I weel try tae gladly accaept."

Israel Hands gripped the front edge of the bench on which he sat as Blackbeard's plaything Caesar applied a foul-smelling poultice to and tied a fresh bandage around the sailing master's calf.

"Off wit' ya now, ya African bastard!" Israel growled, downing what was left of a bottle of rum. "Leave me an' my achin' leg to our mutual, unendurable misery!"

No doubt happy to be away from the violent, unpredictable Hands—whose mood had only darkened after his altercation with Blackbeard several weeks ago—the thirteen-year-old Ashanti took off down the beach toward the anchored sloop *Adventure*.

If it were not for his wounded leg, which was not only mind-numbingly painful but also limited his mobility, especially in confined and crowded spaces, Israel Hands would take a knife and slit Blackbeard's miserable throat while he slept off a drunk in his cabin.

Revenge would have to wait. For now, he would nurse his wounds, physical and to his ego, while awaiting an opportune moment to strike. Whether it was the pox or some other malady that had weakened the once fearsome captain was of little matter to Hands. All he knew was this—Edward Thache could barely stand on his own, much less defend himself in a brawl.

He had needed help from several men to subdue a local weakling called William Bell in mid-September. His decision making since the incident had been increasingly hard to defend. His morning treatments with mercury—administered by Caesar when they were away from the Plum Point cottage he shared with his wife Elizabeth—produced increasingly nightmarish screams.

*I should be in command a'* Adventure, Israel thought, sharpening his knife on a whetstone to distract him from the pain in his calf. *'Twas I who oversaw the strippin' an' burnin' a' the* Rose Emelye. *'Tis I who oversees the transfer a' goods ta our business partners, Eden an' Knight. 'Tis I who sees ta the needs a' our crew, includin' them African savages Blackbeard seems ta love!*

What was his reward for all that he was doing and all the slights that he had suffered since Blackbeard had demoted him from captain back to quartermaster after the grounding of the *Queen Anne's Revenge* and William Howard's departure?

Blackbeard had shot him in the calf with a pistol! Extra powder, but no ball... Obviously meant as a warning... The bastard had said so himself, as the previously concealed pistol leaked a line of thick blue smoke as he placed it on the table between them.

Increasing the pressure of the knife upon the whetstone, which was already dry from friction, Hands howled like a rabid jackal as the blade produced a spark.

*Dirty, distrusting bastard...*

It was ten days before that Blackbeard had called Hands to his cabin. Inviting his unsuspecting guest to sit across from him at his table, Blackbeard got right to the point.

"I understand ye are unhappy with your demotion, Mister Hands, an' how I direct this operation."

"No, not I, my captain."

"I also understand that ye have been plottin' against me... Loose lips with Calico Jack, another loud-mouthed malcontent..."

"No, not I, my captain."

Blackbeard had then leaned forward, his breath aflame with rum.

"Did ye actually think ye could organize a mutiny against me?"

"No, not I, my captain."

"I cannot take the chance."

It was then that Hands had heard the click of the pistol, hidden beneath the table. Before he could react, so surprised was he at the sound and what it meant, his ears were pounding from the discharge and his calf had begun to burn.

"Caesar will see ta the wound," Blackbeard muttered with no remorse. "He awaits ye in his room. Take a day or two ta rest... then attend ta yer duties as *Adventure*'s sailing master... with no further machinations."

"Sailing master?" Hands had asked through gritted teeth.

"Thomas Miller shall be quartermaster. Do all that he commands."

Feeling his blood begin to boil, Hands managed to leave the room before a tear escaped his eye.

The little African bastard was waiting, just as Blackbeard had said, sitting on his bed with his moronic, buck-toothed smile. Every morning ever since, once he had finished with Blackbeard, Caesar had cleaned and rebandaged the wound.

It took all of Hands's considerable will not to punch him in the throat.

Slipping the knife into its sheath, Hands looked out upon the water, the surface of which was sparkling like diamonds with the rising of the sun.

Then he noticed something else.

Two longboats were approaching, full of Royal Navy sailors.

Not able to run to *Adventure*, Israel repeatedly yelled *Invasion!*, calling nineteen pirates to arms.

"One of them has seen us!" Midshipman Thomas Tucker shouted to Lieutenant Robert Maynard, who sat in the stern of the *Jane*, one of two longboats Lieutentant Governor of Virginia Alexander Spotswood had procured for their secret mission.

Gazing upon the thirty-five men from the *Pearl* and twenty-five men from the *Lyme*, split evenly between the two—the other longboat was named the *Ranger*, under the command of Mister Henry Hyde and Midshipman Abraham Demelt—Maynard took a moment to savor his position as their commander.

The pair of longboats had left Kiquotan via the James River on a chilly, fog-shrouded morning five days before. Captain Ellis Brand had taken two hundred sailors and Virginia militiamen overland to Bath, in case Blackbeard—the main target of their incursion into North Carolina—was not at his base on Ocracoke.

"'Tis no matter if they see us, Mister Tucker," Maynard barked, making himself sound like an admiral in charge of a flotilla of men of war instead of two cannonless longboats technically outside the Royal Navy's purview. "Mister Butler," he shouted next, addressing one of the two local pilots Spotswood's unnamed agent had recruited in a tavern in Bath. "Bring us toward that sloop, where the drunken, insensible villain Edward Thache no doubt lays his lice-filled head!"

"But the tides, Lieutenant Maynard..."

"I have no use for reports on the tides, Mister Butler," Maynard responded. "Aim us for that ship before her crew can load her cannon!"

Smiling at the sight of Mister Hyde ordering his men to ready their pistols and muskets, Maynard moved to the bow of the *Jane*.

"There is another sloop behind her, Lieutenant," Midshipman Tucker reported. "Although I see no cannon on her decks, nor any upon her rails."

"Excellent, Mister Tucker," Maynard answered, signaling to one of the men from the *Pearl*, Evander Mackever, to hand him a loaded musket. "No doubt another ill-gotten prize. More evidence of their villainy, and defectation upon their pardons."

Fifteen minutes later, first the *Jane* and then the *Ranger* ran aground.

"Damn it all and ye especially, Mister Butler!" Maynard growled, placing his hand upon the shoulder of James Dixon, also from the *Pearl*, to steady himself as the *Jane* stuck fast in the unseen sand.

"Tucker," he continued. "Throw all ye can over the side and stave the water casks as well! We are now within range of their cannon! Quick as we are able, we shall get this boat ungrounded and reposition ourselves with the oars." Checking the charge in his musket, Maynard heard Midshipman Demelt echoing his orders to the already moving men of the *Ranger*.

Royal Navy discipline would see them victorious before the afternoon was out.

As the crews worked unsuccessfully to free the longboats, Maynard cocked his musket as a tall, wide-shouldered man with a long black beard, done up in a dozen braids and adorned with faded crimson ribbons, emerged with a yell from below the deck of the well-armed sloop.

Taking position in the bow of the *Adventure*, Blackbeard shouted, "Damn ye all fer villains! Who are ye? An' from whence have ye come, ye scabrous, scurvy dogs?"

Knowing his long-elusive moment of glory had arrived, Maynard replied, "I am Lieutenant Robert Maynard of His Majesty's Royal Navy. The protectors of those ye have made to suffer have tasked me with capturing or killing ye, Edward Thache. Now, let me share this plainly—I much prefer the latter!"

Spreading his arms so his hands were well away from his three pairs of pistols and his sword, Blackbeard answered, "There is no need fer us ta fight! Ye see by our colors we are not pirates. We are simple, pardoned men in service ta North Carolina. I have plenty a' gold an' silver. Will half a' all I have be enough fer ye ta turn around an' swear ye never met me?"

Maynard laughed in derision. "Your offer is an insult. Ye shall surrender without delay or feel our shot and steel!"

Reaching into a satchel slung over his shoulder, Blackbead produced a bottle of rum and an ornate silver cup as his crew began to take positions at the cannons and around the deck. Filling the cup to the rim, he drained its contents with a single noisy swallow. Raising the empty vessel high into the air, he yelled, "Damnation ta ye an' yer men, whom I accuse a' bein' nothin' more than cowardly puppies in the service of a false an' blackhearted king. An' let me tell ye this—I shall not give nor take any quarter!"

Placing the silver cup back into the satchel, which he dropped onto the deck, Blackbeard drew his sword and turned with a laugh to his men. "Prepare a broadside fer our guests, an' look lively as ye do so!"

Upon the *Jane*, Maynard watched as a smoking linstock was touched to the fuse of one of *Adventure*'s eight-pound cannons. "Protect yourselves as best ye can!" he shouted to the crews of the longboats before dropping to the deck and covering his head with his hands.

Seconds later, *Adventure*'s cannon discharged its deadly projectile, followed quickly by the roar of a second, dispensing a canister of grapeshot, which struck its primary target, the *Ranger*, with the frightening sound of splintering wood and tearing sails.

Raising his head only high enough to peer over the edge of the gunnel, Maynard saw Mister Hyde and five others aboard the *Ranger* expire in a cloud of blood and gore. Several more fell wounded beside them and four on the *Jane* as well.

"Fire, my lads!" Lieutenant Maynard shouted, raising his musket to his shoulder. "Disable that ship before the tide allows an escape!" Taking aim at the vessel's jib, Maynard gently squeezed the trigger, shouting with satisfaction as the projectile founds its mark, sending the triangular sail to the deck.

"Is that all ye have, ye damnable dog?" Blackbeard taunted, as several pirates fell to the deck around him. "Let 'em feel the kiss a' our rail guns, lads! Look lively, Mister Hands—I prefer ye keep it hot!"

As Maynard called for another musket, five men fell dead around him, with several more falling wounded both on the *Jane* and on the *Ranger*.

Continuing his taunts, Blackbeard climbed upon the gunnel. "Look at them fall like flies! Forward ta their ship, as best ye can without the jib, ye scurvy crew a' scoundrels! An' ye best make ready ta board her!"

As the men of the semi-crippled *Adventure* raised her anchor and prepared to approach the longboats, Maynard concocted a plan. "Listen to me, lads. I can feel the tide is rising. The *Jane* shall soon break free. Oars in the water, men, and ready yourselves to row." Turning to Tucker and Butler, he continued. "I shall hide below with any man able to fight. As the poxy pirates approach and begin to board us, make it appear as though ye surrender. Then, once they are all aboard, give me a signal, Tucker—a whistle shall suffice— and we shall emerge and make them suffer!"

What transpired next—lasting, according to letters sent by Maynard to his fellow officers and speeches he made at dinners in rich men's homes, no more than six minutes start to end—was exactly what Maynard had planned.

Blackbeard's boots had barely touched the deck of the *Jane*, which had made its way a considerable distance from the *Ranger*, which remained upon a sandbar, when Tucker had blown his whistle and Maynard and his men—each hungry for revenge and a share of the glory and fame—had emerged, pistols cocked and swords unsheathed.

The close-quarter engagement between the crews was just the kind of brutal hand-to-hand combat for which their Royal Navy superiors and veteran pirate quartermasters had so brutally and relentlessly trained them.

Sword versus axe, knife versus musket butt, pistol versus pistol—the deck was soon thick and slick with blood as the two sides fought for their lives.

Standing before the mast, Maynard adopted a defensive position as Blackbeard, his forehead dripping with sweat and his eyes aglow with a yellow, feverish fire, determinedly approached him.

"I know ye served upon the *Windsor*," Maynard said, adjusting his grip on his sword.

"Aye, dog," Blackbeard answered, pointing his bloody blade at the Royal Navy lieutenant. "An' I know that ye tricked Ailish MacDonald in Virginia after she rejected yer advances."

All necessary words delivered, the two men then engaged, hacking away at one another with a fury born of the wish to survive. After successfully blocking a trio of vicious blows, Maynard thrust his sword at Blackbeard's slightly distended belly, its tip catching instead on the pirate's cartridge box, causing the blade to bend.

As Maynard drew it back, he felt a sting upon his hand as Blackbeard sliced his knuckles with his blade.

Retreating for a moment to gather his wits and catch his breath, Maynard watched with equal amounts of satisfaction and wonder as Blackbeard sustained five wounds from pistols and nearly twenty cuts from various thrusting blades.

Still the lunatic fought on.

Intent on killing Maynard, Blackbeard failed to notice a tall, iron-muscled Highlander approaching him swiftly from his left. Even as the Scottish warrior stooped to retrieve a discarded sword—he had shattered his claymore while cleaving a pirate's skull—and yelled his clan's motto, "*Si je puis*!," Blackbeard saw nothing but Maynard.

It was not until the Highlander—whose name was Iain Colquhoun—had buried his blade deep within the pirate captain's neck and shoulder that Blackbeard realized that someone was beside him.

"Is that all ye have fer me, Scotsman?" Blackbeard hissed, spitting blood onto the deck. "Have at it again, ye damnable dog, an' this time finish the job!"

Drawing back his sword, Iain Colquhoun—after a confirmatory nod from his commander—released his clansmen's infamous war cry, *Cnoc Ealachain!*, letting it devolve into a primal, blood-chilling scream as he felt his blade slice cleanly and efficiently through Edward Thache's neck.

As Blackbeard's head rolled to a stop at the toes of Maynard's blood-caked boots, the Highlander, who was already receiving congratulations from his mates as the remaining pirates dropped their weapons in surrender, raised his weapon skyward in victory, repeating the Colquhoun motto—*Si je puis*—meaning, "If I can."

Seeing the *Ranger* approach, Maynard, exhausted and covered in blood, shook the Highlander's hand and said, "Ye have proven to your people—and all the rest of the world—that ye sir most certainly can!"

Turning to give his thanks to Midshipman Tucker and the pilot, Mister Butler, Maynard felt his attention redirected by shouting upon *Adventure*.

Ordering his men to aim their firearms, but to await his command to fire, Maynard watched in amazement as a man who did not appear as though he was a pirate drag on deck an African teenager.

"I caught ye, ya ebony demon! I caught ye in the act, ye fire-worshippin' scoundrel!" the man shouted in his prisoner's face, while striking him repeatedly upon the ear.

"What is the meaning of this scene before me?" Maynard asked the man, crossing to the gunnel.

Kicking his weeping captive in the ribs, the man responded, "I am Samuel Odell—that there be me sloop. These devils took me prisoner not twenty-four hours ago an' had me in the hold. This one here"—he kicked the African again—"who dares ta call himself Caesar, was about ta set fire ta the stores a' powder in the hold when I extinguished the fuse in his hand."

"Is this true?" Maynard asked the sobbing, bloodied African, wary of a ruse.

"Aye, Ad-mee-ral!" the conquered Caesar responded. "By orders of the Ad-mee-ral *Barbe-Noire*!"

"A fine day's work, Odell," Maynard said with a smile. "I shall see ye are well rewarded. As for ye, ye slithering, savage serpent—I shall see your body fed to the crabs!"

Two hours later, as Lieutenant Robert Maynard, his sword hand bandaged and spirits high, rifled through Blackbeard's belongings in his cabin, Midshipmen Tucker appeared in the doorway, a pair of ledgers in his hand.

Taking a moment to rest, Maynard listened as the tally was reported—ten dead on either side. Numerous wounded—none severely. There were nine shackled pirates, including the teenager Caesar, awaiting transport back to Virginia for a speedy, death-bringing trial.

"Have ye yet to tally the spoils, Mister Tucker?"

Closing the ledger from which he had been reading and opening another, Tucker cleared his throat and smiled. "According to the accounting undertaken by Midshipman Demelt, between ship and shore there are twenty-five hogsheads of sugar, one hundred and forty-five sacks of cocoa, a barrel of indigo, a bale of cotton, as well as a few ounces of gold dust and several silver items of considerable value. One of them being the cup with which the villain Edward Thache toasted our damnation. It is inscribed with the name of William Bell, whom Butler tells me is a local merchant the wicked scoundrel robbed."

"More evidence for the courts!"

"There is something more, Lieutenant."

"More goods?" Maynard asked, raising a brow and licking his lips.

"More evidence. We have cross-checked the barrels of sugar and sacks of cocoa with several manifests Spotswood's agent provided from a number of ships looted by Thache's crew. They appear to be from a French ship, the *Rose Emelye*, which Thache seized in Pamlico Sound along with another vessel, *La Toison d'Or*, on twenty-one August, sir."

"I shall see ye promoted for this," Maynard responded. "Now, before ye leave me to finish my inspection of this cabin, read to me the names of the pirate dead, so I may revel in their demise."

Flipping to a marked page in the first of his ledgers, Tucker read the following: "Edward Thache, captain, known as Blackbeard; Thomas Miller, quartermaster; Garrat Gibbens, boatswain; Owen Roberts, carpenter; Joseph Brooks Senior—his son is one of the prisoners; John Rose Archer; Joseph Curtice; John Husk; Nathaniel Jackson; and Philip Morton, gunner."

Maynard scowled. "It was Morton who fired the cannon that killed our Mister Hyde?"

"Hard to say, Lieutenant..."

Maynard deepened his scowl. "It is altogether easy to say, Midshipman Tucker, and ye shall. Ye shall say it in the reports and to anyone who asks. As shall I."

Tucker closed the ledger. "Completely understood."

"I want Thache's head in a box. It must be kept cool and out of the sun. We want it recognizable as it swings from the bowsprit as we enter the harbor at Kiquotan."

After Midshipman Tucker had made note of this latest command and exited the cabin, Maynard used the pommel of his sword to break open a lock on a small chest he found under Thache's bed.

Along with some gold and silver coins, a small oval portrait of an attractive young woman, a nearly empty bottle of mercury, and a pewter syringe, Maynard found a letter.

As he began to read it, he felt the urge to sing.

It was penned by Tobias Knight and sufficient to see him hang.

Captain Charles Vane was tired, frustrated, and cold. This was not where he wished to be. He never would have sailed so far to the north on his own accord a month before Yule if the Star Quorum, in the person of Abraxas Abriendo, had not ordered him to do so.

And it certainly was an order—one of several causing problems amongst the crew, who had been angry that Vane had let the merchant ship *Endeavor* go on its way a month ago after he had beaten her captain, John Shattock, for hours under the guise of hunting coin.

What Vane was actually hunting, as he had confided to Joseph Stanton, was information regarding two Ravenskald thugs who were also on board *Endeavor*, on their way to Gardiners Island to steal Abriendo's obsidian mirror and assassinate several of the Quorum's senior agents.

Vane had sent Joseph and a few other dependable men in a longboat to overtake the assassins in the fog that had developed in the early morning hours. Jack Rackham, although quartermaster and otherwise the logical choice to lead the operation, could not be trusted. Joseph had seen him talking to the assassins while Vane was working over Shattock.

There had been an undue amount of grumbling from the crew ever since. Their time on Ocracoke the week before had only made the incomprehensible encounter with the *Endeavor* more galling and unpopular, as Rackham, angry about his separation from Anne Bonny and often intoxicated, had spent the week of parlay bragging to Blackbeard's quartermaster Israel Hands and anyone else who would listen about how he would make the better captain.

Sailing back to the coast of Carolina for several days so Angus MacGregor could attend the baptism of the offspring of some lunatic barber in Beaufort had only added a wagonload of wood to an already blazing fire. Vane could not tell the men why MacGregor was important—why Vane could not say no. With Joseph Stanton, whom the men respected, the Scotsman had a contentious history. MacGregor was Blackbeard's former confidant. North Carolina was Blackbeard's playground. Even here, off the mid-Atlantic colonies, Blackbeard had enjoyed the greater success.

Ergo, it seemed to the crew as though Blackbeard was the greater commander, and his confidant MacGregor mattered more than Vane's own men, a perception that further weakened their captain's increasingly precarious position.

The most recent point of contention had reared its ugly, trihorned head while the *Ranger* sat at anchor in Topsail Inlet. Abraxas Abriendo had sent word that Vane was needed here, off the coast of New Jersey, to receive a package from a merchant captain on a ship called *Kidd's Deliverance*, of which Vane had dutifully taken possession less than a day before.

The package was small—a knotted burlap bag that fit in the palm of his hand.

Grasping the bag so tightly his fingers began to ache, Vane opened his book of Shakespeare's plays to *Henry VIII*. Turning to act III, scene ii, he read aloud, "Had I but served my God with half the zeal I served my king, he would not in mine age have left me naked to mine enemies."

Vane's king was now the Quorum. He had avoided an alliance with the Ravenskalds, only to fall prey to their enemies. Neither was preferable to God, and God had never been preferable to Vane at all.

"We have spotted a frigate-rigged vessel, Captain Vane," Quartermaster Rackham interrupted, not bothering to knock before opening the door of the cabin and entering—yet another sign of trouble. "The men are insisting we engage it. After the erratic behavior ye have shown the past four weeks, as quartermaster, I must insist ye honor their wishes."

Vane lit a cheroot and laughed. "Ye insist? Very well then, Calico Jack. Engage the vessel we will. I will be topside in a moment."

Once his smiling, cock-a'-the-walk quartermaster had exited, Vane slipped the burlap bag—which he had yet to open—into the top of his boot, shoving it down with his fingers as far as it would go. Grabbing his sword and a pair of pistols, he made his way on deck, where Rackham was shouting orders to his restless, rambunctious crew, who was spoiling for a fight.

Throwing a glance behind him to make sure the lone sloop they still possessed was following close behind, Vane felt a surge of satisfaction as this latest incarnation of the *Ranger*, a well-armed, speedy brigantine, rapidly closed the distance between them and the frigate-rigged object of their desperate, collective desire.

"They are raising the white!" Calico Jack reported. "Everyone be ready to board her."

Raising his spyglass to his eye, Vane gave the flag a thorough inspection and felt a stinging burst of bile rising in his throat.

Aye, the flag was white—with a gold fleur de lis in its center.

This was no vulnerable merchant vessel! It was a French Navy frigate, which had successfully baited a trap, into which Rackham had stupidly led them.

"Turn us about, ye idiot!" Vane yelled as the French ran out their guns and quickly fired a broadside. "The bastahds will destroy us!"

"Ye order us to run?" Rackham responded, an unforgivable petulance in his voice. "Still more cowardice and confusion ye try to foist upon these men? Does your incompetency know no bounds?"

Approaching his sailing master, Robert Deal, Vane hissed, "Will ya follow me orders, Mistah Deal, an' turn this brigantine around, before we are blown ta bits?"

Avoiding Rackham's piercing gaze, the sailing master nodded and began to turn the wheel to starboard as the frigate fired another, closer, broadside.

Two hours later, following the captain of the French ship's decision not to give chase to the brigantine and sloop, Charles Vane, Joseph Stanton, Angus MacGregor, Duncan MacDonald, Cnoc Douglas, Teàrlach de Bruys, and a dozen others—including the *Ranger*'s former sailing master, Robert Deal—sat huddled in the smaller of the ships. Around them were provisions enough for a week. Jack Rackham—who had pressed for a vote after they had escaped from the French Navy frigate and, after the votes were tallied, was installed as the brigantine's captain—had ordered four of the sloop's six guns transferred onto the *Ranger*.

"I will happily slit his throat for you, Captain," Joseph Stanton whispered, his hand on the hilt of his knife.

"An' I weel puncture the bastard's baelly as hae doos so," Angus added.

Vane, clutching his volume of Shakespeare and putting a hand protectively over the section of his boot where he had hidden the burlap bag, shook his head and spat in the ocean. "'E 'as seventy-five ta our eighteen an' outguns this sloop aplenty. Vengeance will be ours, but it shall not be today. Make us ready ta sail."

"Where to?" Robert Deal enquired as the rest of the men adjusted the sheets and cordage around him.

"The Bay a' Honduras," Vane replied. "I need some time ta think. I left us naked ta our enemies in me zeal ta serve a king, an' I 'ave placed us in the shite."

Louis Arot, although not yet fourteen years old, knew when it was time to hide.

He had been lugging bales of hay from Tobias Knight's barn to a waiting wagon when he had seen four dozen men carrying muskets marching with haste toward Archbell Point.

Turning his gaze to the manor house, where he had been living happily with the chief justice and his doting wife Katherine for the better part of three months, Louis saw that they were also looking in the direction of the approaching men.

It was at that moment, seeing the panic in their eyes, that Louis decided to hide in the barn.

There had been a terrible tension hanging in the air for the past two days, ever since Thomas Pollock and Governor Eden had arrived with the news that Blackbeard was dead—*assassinated* was the word they used—on Ocracoke by a Royal Navy expedition funded by The Family and Virginia's lieutenant governor, according to their network of spies.

"This is an egregious breach of the law!" Justice Knight had answered, his anger at the use of the Royal Navy by one sovereign colony to attack another competing with the heartbreak he felt over the loss of a business partner and friend.

"This is a continuation of the events of 1711," Pollock responded. "I have no doubt that the Lords Proprietors supported this action against the pirates along with Spotswood, just as they supported Edward Hyde, the puppet of Queen Anne and her sniveling uncle, the earl of Rochester, and their illegitimate Church of England, in his quest to become the deputy governor of northern Carolina. Thomas Cary was the legitimate choice, which is why I backed his rebellion."

"Backed it?" Eden replied, with a strained and skeptical laugh. "Ye were hosting Hyde and his council at your home when Cary arrived in a brigantine!"

"I paid the price for my decisions," Pollock answered with a scowl. "Exile in Virginia, where my ear was daily filled with the opinions of our lack of worth. Having to watch that cocky bastard,

Edward Moseley, make his deals with Alexander Spotswood and his handpicked Tobacco Council minions. My fellow growers and I barely managed to keep the deeds to our plantations! I did not escape the difficulties I faced in Glasgow to suffer at the hands of these bullboys here in America! By the time I returned the following year, the colony was in so much turmoil, and I was so determined to reverse the low opinion of us held by Virginia and southern Carolina, that I disavowed the rebellion, insisting that I myself serve as acting governor until a suitable and permanent replacement could be found."

Eden produced a disarming smile. "I appreciated your support at the time, Thomas, as I appreciate it now—and I shall certainly continue to need it. To rely on it more than ever. As we stand here reminiscing, Thache's head is in a box on its way to Hampton, and John Lovick tells me the Virginia Assembly is passing what Spotswood calls the Act to Encourage the Apprehending and Destroying of Pirates, which includes bounties on Blackbeard's severed head and on those of the rest of his slaughtered and captured crew. The men of the Royal Navy are doing this for personal profit!"

Tobias Knight drew the two men closer, so he could speak in only a whisper. "Lovick's home was broken into a few weeks past. Someone turned his office upside down… emptied his drawers and pulled the books from off their shelves. I have no doubt it was Moseley, Vail, and Moore, looking for evidence of our collusion with Edward Thache."

Pollock shook his head. "I am confident they came up empty. I have heard from my sources, however, that the most damning kind of evidence was found in Blackbeard's cabin on *Adventure*."

The three conspirators had then gone into the house to partake of the evening meal at Katherine's kind but firm insistence. Eden and Pollock had departed several hours later. Louis had noticed that Justice Knight, who was normally patient and kind, was in a rather nasty mood, and the boy had been doing his best to stay clear of him ever since. He had suffered more than his share of abuse at the hands of *La Concorde*'s captain. Blackbeard was little better, although he had never struck in anger either Louis or his good friend Caesar. He did not need to—his thunderous voice and coal-black, piercing eyes were more than frightening enough to keep the high-spirited twosome in line.

From his position in the barn, Louis watched as the four dozen soldiers approached the porch and their leader identified himself as Captain Ellis Brand of His Majesty's Royal Navy.

Wishing to hear all of the ensuing conversation, Louis, staying in the mid-morning shadows, crept from the barn to a trio of hogsheads sitting behind the wagon.

"Ye have no right!" Justice Knight responded, brushing Katherine's hand from his arm as she attempted to calm him down. Sending her into the house, Knight continued, his voice full of vitriol and pride. "The illegalities inherent in your actions are legion! North Carolina is a sovereign colony under the jurisdiction of the Lords Proprietors, for whom I serve as deputy. Lieutenant Governor Spotswood has no authority here—nor do ye! This is my private property. Ye cannot simply bring these armed militia and navy men here to my house, armed and ready to arrest me as though I were some common insurrectionist!"

"Evidence is forthcoming to show ye are worse than an insurrectionist!" Brand responded. "Ye have struck a deal with pirates! *Your* lieutenant governor granted Edward Thache and his rabble the pardon and then sent them off with his blessing to ply their illegal trade in the Albemarle."

Before he could enquire as to the specificities of this supposedly damning evidence, Knight felt his knees begin to buckle. Approaching the dock not three hundred meters from where they stood were two longboats full of Royal Navy men and a knot of shackled pirates. The chief justice gripped the porch railing to steady himself seconds before he collapsed. Scanning the prisoners, he recognized Israel Hands, the boy Caesar, and several others who had previously visited Archbell Point.

This was fast becoming a nightmare.

Half an hour later, Lieutant Robert Maynard stood beside Captain Brand, several ledgers and rolled up papers in his arms.

"Take us to your barn, so we may undertake a search," Brand demanded, after Maynard informed him that he had identified barrels of sugar and sacks of cocoa seized from the *Adventure* as stolen cargo from the missing merchantman *Rose Emelye*.

"I shall not permit it!" Knight responded. "Ye have no proof that I am—*was*—in business with this so-called Blackbeard. Yes, he took the pardon, along with many of his men. As have hundreds of other pirates, in the colonies and the Caribbean. Ever since, he has existed peacefully near Ocracoke."

Maynard scowled. "His former quartermaster, who was my guest aboard the HMS *Pearl* for several days, reported to me otherwise. Though I do not need a scurvy pirate's words—a pirate who was recently condemned to hang 'til dead in Williamsburg—to assure that ye shall join him on the gallows."

Knight gripped the railing harder. "Do ye dare?"

"I do dare, sir. I do!" Maynard replied, still full to the brim with piss and vinegar from the bloody action at Ocracoke. "For I have in my possession a certain letter, which I found in Thache's cabin on *Adventure*. Captain Brand—do I have your permission to read this letter aloud?"

Brand, enjoying this duel of insults, produced a toothy smile. "By all means, Lieutenant Maynard. Ye have more than piqued my interest."

Handing the ledgers and rolled up papers he had brought as further evidence to a midshipman standing beside him, Maynard pulled the letter from his pocket. "Dated exactly a week ago—seventeen November. 'My friend. If this finds ye yet in harbor, I would have ye make the best of your way up as soon as possible that your various affairs will let ye. I have something more to say to ye than at present. I really think these three men of which we have recently spoken—Edward Moseley, James Moore, and Jeremiah Vail—are heartily sorry for their heretofore low opinions of ye and will be very willing to ask your pardon if I may advise, and for ye to all be friends, which is better than falling out amongst yourselves. I expect the governor this night or tomorrow, whom I believe would be likewise glad to see ye before ye go. I have not the time to add save my hearty respects to ye and am your real friend and servant. Signed Tobias Knight.'"

Captain Brand, taking the letter from Lieutenant Maynard and scanning it for himself before triumphantly handing it back, addressed his men with a gleam in his eye. "Search the conspirator's barn for the contraband in question! Anyone who stops ye, use whatever force ye must to subdue them and carry on."

As the soldiers moved for the barn, Brand adjusted his position so that Knight was kept in his. "The time of the pirates is over, along with the illegal activities of the governors and other officials like yourself who benefit from their thievery and decadent behavior. Blackbeard's crew is either dead or, as ye can plainly see, sitting in shackles off your shore. Stede Bonnet is due to hang. His crew, and a dozen others, recently met the God-granted agony of the short drop and sudden stop. Governor Woodes Rogers, in New Providence, shall soon hang another dozen. This folly of yours is finished. I urge ye to confess."

As Tobias Knight was readying his response, which he was thankful Katherine would not hear, so laced would it be with curses, he heard the high-pitched voice of Louis Arot near the barn.

"Ye shall not pass, ye scoundrels! I demand to talk to Caesar!"

Maynard, Brand, and Knight looked in unison upon the thirteen-year-old cabin boy turned farmer, who stood in impressive defiance, legs spread, with a pitchfork held like a spear.

"Sir?" a militia sergeant enquired, looking to Brand for guidance.

"Must I repeat myself, Sergeant Lewis? I ordered ye to use what force ye must."

Spinning his musket so its butt was facing the boy, the sergeant hit Louis squarely on the chin, dropping him like a sack of cocoa, which is precisely what the searchers found within minutes in the barn—along with dozens of additional sacks of cocoa and two dozen barrels of sugar.

"Do they match the manifest in question, Lieutenant Maynard?" Brand enquired as the pair of officers approached the barn.

Consulting Midshipman Thomas Tucker's notes, Maynard responded, "Aye, Captain Brand. They do."

As Tobias Knight attended to the unconscious Louis, whose face was a bloody mess, he felt his bowels begin to loosen. Standing and undoing his britches, he barely made it to the bushes that lined the house before their contents spilled to the ground.

Padraig Ó Muiris was drifting off to sleep to the gentle motion of the *Oiseau de Proie* and the sounds of its tackle, sheets, and cordage dancing with the wind when he heard weeping from the next-door cabin.

Pulling on his shirt without bothering with his stockings or boots, he turned up the wick on his lantern and crept into the passageway. The door to the cabin beside his own was open just enough to reveal the source of the crying—Abraxas Abriendo.

The obsidian mirror was sitting on the table before him, and the wizard's shoulders were shaking with the severity of his sobs.

"Whad be dis, moy brudder?" Padraig enquired, respecting his friend by not entering the room without an invitation to do so. "Ye weep as tho' ye have seen da dayth of a fraynd."

Without looking up, Abraxas whispered, "That is because I have."

"Oy cayn sit wid ye awhoyl if ye wish."

Waving Padraig in, and instructing him to close the door, Abraxas wiped his red-ringed eyes upon the velvet sleeve of his robes. "It has been my nightly practice to gaze into the mirror. Since our time in Messina and our rigorous training with Mago Fuoco, I am able to see considerably more than I used to. At times, I can see our enemies. The past two nights, I have seen terrible things, my friend."

"Tayl on, moy weary brudder, iffin if it bay helpful fer ye ta do so."

Running his fingers around the mirror's ornate frame, Abraxas whispered, "Last night I witnessed a confrontation between Trogon Ophidian and the infernal entity who blinded him long ago."

"So thayn Iblis has returned..." Padraig whispered, feeling a chill at the base of his spine.

"That he has... and ever the master of irony, he calls himself Saviero Inimicus."

"If I remaymber moy Latin correctly, id means, 'Enemy in a new dwayling...'" The Irishman shook his head. "Too clayver he bay by half."

Abraxas grunted in agreement. Moving to the door at the sound of approaching footsteps, he opened it to find one of the *Oiseau de*

*Proie*'s watchmen making the midnight rounds. "If I can trouble ye a moment… When ye are topside once again, please ask Captain Xiang to join me in my cabin—and, if he seems in a generous mood, ask him to bring a trio of cups and a pot of his incomparable *kombucha*."

Nodding at the wizard, the watchman continued his rounds.

Leaving the door ajar, as it was when Padraig had arrived, Abraxas continued. "Iblis appeared in the form of an ebony dog, a favorite guise of malevolent spirits such as he and Mephistopheles, and the two preternatural nemeses battled, as they have repeatedly throughout the ages."

"Ye sayd ye witnessed a dayth… Was Trogon Ophidian killed?"

"The medallion of Saint Michael the Archangel kept our ally safe."

Padraig raised a brow, relief and a new concern intertwining in his heart. "Thayn who was id who dayd…"

Abraxas sat beside the Irishman, who was becoming like a brother to the aging, lonely wizard. "I saw the beheading of Edward Thache."

"What is this, Abraxas?" Xiang Yu was standing in the doorway, grasping a tray, which contained three painted porcelain cups and a steaming porcelain pot. "Where and when did this occur?"

As the Manchurian warrior set the tray upon the table and poured three full cups of the steaming *kombucha*, a fermented beverage made of black tea and mushroom, with various spices added for flavor, Abraxas sighed.

"I have no way of knowing with any certainly, although the memory was powerful. No more than a week at most. It happened on the shoreline of an island—most likely the one in North Carolina close to where he was living."

Setting a cup before each of his friends and sipping from the third, Xiang Yu asked, "Who committed this deadly deed?"

"That, my friends, is complicated." Sipping from his cup, Abraxas managed a smile. "Ginger and cinnamon. Exactly what I need. The man who wielded the assassin's sword was a Scotsman, although Edward's torso was doused in blood from many other wounds. Those around him were Royal Navy."

"Da bastards!" Padraig growled, sniffing the contents of his cup but leaving it on the table. "Complicated is as good a woyd as any… But id was a conspiracy. Ravenskalds fer sure. Carteret. Da Fam'ly.

How many guv'nors?" Grasping Abraxas's hand, he continued. "I am truly sorry, brudder. I know ye did not always see eye ta eye, but I know ye loved him jus' the same."

Xiang Yu took a seat. "Yet another complication. Blackbead was nothing if not complex. Levasseur and he nearly killed one another, yet Samuel Bellamy loved them both in equal measure. You have my sympathies, Abraxas. Given larger patterns—pirates being captured and hung a dozen at a time, the formation of the Quadruple Alliance, the unpredictable Irishman Camocke and the ongoing siege of Messina, whispers of conspiracies to remove from power the regent in France—this is more than the loss of a friend. More than the loss of an ally. What else has your mirror shown you?"

Abraxas related what he had seen regarding Trogon Ophidian and Iblis.

Draining his cup and filling it again to the rim, Xiang Yu ran his hand along the length of his warrior's queue. "We shall reach the fort at Petit-Goave in another week and a half. Speaking with Master Trogon face to face is essential. An excellent decision, Abraxas, to proceed there after parting company with Vane."

"About dis Vane," Padraig said, sniffing the cup of *kombucha* again. "He bay the most powerful a' da pirates still remainin'. Has been fer awhoyl. But I wonder—Can we trust him?"

Abraxas nodded. "We have no other choice. Forces beyond our understanding have chosen him to be the centerpoint for the testing and ultimately the gathering of the seven. Angus MacGregor sails with him for a host of reasons. We are just beginning to understand the smallest part of the role that Rob Roy's nephew shall play in the coming war. He possesses a powerful ring and is descended from an ancient, fabled lineage protected by the fae. A lineage distinct from each of yours, yet each of your families has been crucial to the quest for the ancient objects for which so many thousands upon thousands have suffered."

The three men sat with this weight for a while, sipping their tea in silence—even Padraig to be polite, finally took a taste, although it clearly was not to his liking.

Abraxas had spoken the truth about the warriors with whom he sat. Padraig Ó Muiris could trace his bloodline back to the fourteen original Irish familes known as the Tribes of Galway. His ancestors had been battling with the Ravenskalds since the time of the Viking raids on Lindisfarne and Iona, a thousand years before, when the upstart family's ambitious leader, Jórkell, had allied himself with a pair of powerful Orkney jarls. Padraig's ancestor Torsten had stood against Sigurd the Mighty, afterward paving a path for his tribe to a position of power and influence amongst the Templar Order in Ireland. Another ancestor, Lughaidh, had learned the art of alchemy in 1291, while serving with the Templars during the siege and loss of Acre at the time of the Third Crusade. He was one of the founders of the Druidic Order at Oxford. In addition to his position in the Grand Masonic Lodge in London, Padraig held his family's seat in the city with the present council of Druids.

Beside him, Xiang Yu was also contemplating from where it was that he had come. He knew little of his lineage in his family's village in Manchuria. When he was barely four years old, a secret sect of warriors had taken him from his parents in the middle of the night. Within their impregnable fortress, hidden amongst the constant snows of an otherwise uninhabitable region of the Himalayas, they had raised and trained him in the fighting of demons and monsters. After each trial and each anniversary of his removal from his family, Xiang Yu would lay for hours in a cave deep within the mountain, where an old, scarred monk who never spoke a word tattooed the story of the sect upon his back, from just beneath the base of his skull to his slender, heavily muscled beltline.

When he was eighteen, one of his masters sailed with him to an island in the Aegean, for what the council of masters told him would be his final test and, should he survive the ordeal, his initiation into the sect.

Upon arriving on the island, he found a village in the throes of abject terror. A gang of *vrykolakas* was systematically decimating the population. It was Xiang Yu's task to run the bloodthirsty vampires off.

Instead, he killed them all, earning a pair of Manchu sabers made by their most talented of swordsmiths to commemorate the start of the Qing Dynasty in 1644. After parting company with his master, Xiang Yu went wherever he was needed, battling for more than a decade a variety of undead monsters and vicious demons, including *draugr* in Scandinavia and *kuntilanak* in the eastern Indies. After suffering his first defeat—and the loss of his Manchu sabers—

at the hands of a pair of djinn in a cave in Ḥosaynābād who, upon seeing his tattoos, arranged for a Khorasanian merchant to sell him into slavery, Xiang Yu found himself passed from one heartless master to another, eventually winding up in the American port of Boston. It was there he remained until 1713, when Paulsgrave Williams had rescued him from the gallows, where a judge had sentenced him to hang for the crime of protecting a fellow slave.

It was through Paulsgrave and his fellow Jacobite Samuel Bellamy that Xiang Yu had pledged his life and his pair of deadly blades—far simpler ones after the loss of his Manchu sabers—in the service of Cardinal André-Hercule de Fleury and the Ravenskald-battling Quorum. De Fleury, upon seeing the warrior's tattooed back, had offered to translate the images over the course of many nights, thus revealing to Xiang Yu the story of the secret sect of demon slayers of which he would remain a member until he died.

"I do not understand why Vane was chosen to be the custodian of the Judas Coin," Xiang Yu finally said, pouring himself another cup of *kombucha*. "The Quorum places too much trust in this unpredictable captain all at once. There are others, better suited…"

"Who are attending to other tasks," Abraxas replied, opening the mirror's custom case and setting the ancient object inside it. "Levasseur and Williams are in Africa. Moody and Frowd are reluctant participants who bitterly resent having to contribute a share of their spoils to the cause. Their usefulness is therefore limited. After he thwarted the attack on Gardiners Island, the laird of the manor, with John Rathbon and Thomas Paine in full agreement, deemed it best to deliver the Judas Coin to Vane through a trusted intermediary—the captain of *Kidd's Deliverance*, Cadogan Kirwan."

"Another maymber a' the tribes a' Galway!" Padraig exclaimed.

Nodding, Abraxas said, pouring the last of the *kombucha* into his empty cup, "Our numbers are strong. Our commitment is ancient. We must trust the judgment of the senior agents of the Quorum, such as those on Gardiners Island. They have earned it, as has Salvatori Fuoco. As will the three of us, in time."

Saying their goodnights and once more offering their condolences to Abraxas for the loss of Edward Thache, Xiang Yu and Padraig Ó Muiris headed for their cabins and a troubled night of sleep.

Extinguishing his lantern, Abraxas lay upon his bed, repeatedly replaying the image of Blackbeard's severed head falling from his shoulders to the blood-slick deck of the vessel on which he died.

"May you find the peace in death, my malcontented friend," the exhausted wizard whispered, tears returning to his eyes, "that was so elusive in life."

Captain Richard Frowd could not have agreed more with Abraxas Abriendo's assessment of the resentment he and William Moody were feeling with regard to Paulsgrave Williams coercing them into contributing a share of their spoils to the Quorum.

Having just raided or burned several ships off the islands of St. Thomas, St. Christopher's, and St. Croix, the pirates Moody and Frowd were, at this very moment, discussing their insufferable predicament in Frowd's quarters aboard an eight-gun brigantine they had recently commandeered. Frowd's former vessel, an eight-gun sloop, completed their flotilla.

"The solution is right before us, William—we shall simply neglect to make the arrangements to deliver the expected cut of our latest bounty." Gazing with a prickling envy through one of the cabin's windows at the thirty-six-gun *Rising Sun*, his partner's often-spoken-of flagship, Frowd continued unfolding his plan. "We should sail away and keep it solely for ourselves. I would like to trade up further, my friend. Something with twenty guns at least. There is less competition in the Caribbean than ever before. We should turn it to our advantage with a more aggressive stance."

Moody, who had lasted as long as he had by being cautious and never putting the *Rising Sun* into risky situations, exhaled a gust of air and shook his balding head. "I have learned much from Paulsgrave Williams. I agreed to support the Quorum because he and Samuel Bellamy have sacrificed so much of themselves to aid in fulfilling its mission. Those two gave me my start, something I shall never forget. Their enemies were the cause of Bellamy's death, although Williams has been far too sparce with the details of how they managed to considerably worsen a natural Atlantic storm. There are other reasons as well. After our recent haul and your decision to take hostages in return for supplies from the islanders, Governor Hamilton is screaming for reinforcements. He demands a forty-gun man o' war! This is not the time to turn what few friends we have into enemies, Richard. I trust ye see the wisdom in my position…"

"Even if I do," Frowd responded with a frown. "I choose to stand firm in my intent. It is not at all an easy task feeding and keeping watered two hundred and forty-five independently minded, money-hungry men. Especially if ye insist on sailing for Africa, as Paulsgrave so strongly suggests."

"I am pleased ye brought that up. With Hamilton and the rest of the colonial governors in a frenzy of attack—hanging our brethren of the seas a dozen at a time—I think that we should do exactly as Williams suggests, but we do it for us, and not for him. I am anxious to sail with La Buse, the famous Buzzard himself—Olivier Levasseur!"

Frowd, in an attempt to discharge at least a little of his mounting frustration before their discussion became a fight, slammed his fist into his thigh. "Ye seem to me to treat this as some kind of merry adventure! I went out on the account because I despise the arrogant, selfish wealthy, no matter on which side they declare themselves to be. All this talk of ancient objects and the involvement of those red-robed pederasts in Rome makes me sick to my stomach! Between the pardons and betrayals of those who not only took a knee but turned coat as fucking hunters, and the deaths and disappearances of the very best of our brothers, I fear for our futures, William."

Moody laid his hand gently over Frowd's, noticing as he did so the four ostentatious, jeweled rings his partner proudly wore. "Ye speak more than a little truth of why it is that we are who we are, but we must remain honest with each other and ourselves. We have known so much success, and have gathered the fortune about which we at times so insufferably boast, because of these very same alliances, even with what we lose through our donations to the Quorum. My life was shite in London. Yours was little better in Devonshire. At present, I want for little… I am commodore of a trio of vessels—of two hundred and forty-five men, as ye yourself have noted."

Frowd withdrew his hand. "I have made a difficult decision, William, which may cause ye considerable pain. As much as we have accomplished and acquired… I no longer desire to be captain of your tender. It is well past time that I go out on my own—to see what I can accomplish without yours, or anyone else's, restrictions or demands. Avery, Drake, and Bellamy… all fellow Devonshire captains, all with notable accomplishments. I wish my name to be spoken along with theirs. No more Quorum, no more donations— and no more bloody politics! A short and merry life beside the brethren of the seas. That is all that I desire, and that is now what I must seek."

Leaning heavily back in his chair, Moody ran his hands through what was left of his grey-flecked hair. "What if I can guarantee ye that we shall be better off in Africa? The Royal African and East India companies refer to its primary geographies as the Gold Coast and Ivory Coast, because of the wealth it offers. We shall find ye a bigger ship. I shall make it my priority. I beg ye to reconsider. Commodore Bellamy would wish ye to stay the course. Somewhat selfishly, so do I. Ye are much, much more to me, Richard, than the captain of my tender, as ye so wrongly termed this vessel. Ye have become as a brother to me—a brother for whom I would gladly give my life."

"A touching sentiment, Commodore Moody," Frowd responded, rising from his chair and unlocking his cabin door. "But ye have failed to change my mind. I shall remain in the Caribbean. Once I have secured a suitable vessel, I shall sail for the Carolinas, where the Royal Navy does not gather in such fearsome, formidable numbers. Let that bastard Hamilton scream… Let him give me chase! It is better than living in thrall to these ambitious, demanding dictators who wish to make themselves our masters. Once ye succumb to them, William, there is no point in being a pirate."

Rising and embracing his friend, Moody whispered in his ear, "I wish ye the very best. I shall cover your portion to the Quorum as a way of saying thank ye for your patience and support these many happy months. I shall give Williams and Levasseur your very best regards."

Watching Moody from his window as he crossed from gunnel to gunnel and boarded the *Rising Sun*, Richard Frowd allowed himself to shed a single tear before retiring to his bed, where he dreamed of a proper ship in which he would make his mark.

**B**enjamin Hornigold was walking the repaired and fortified ramparts of the sea-facing side of the fort at Nassau when he heard a familiar, friendly voice loudly calling his name.

Searching the stretch of beach fifteen feet below, he spotted Captain John Cockram climbing out of a longboat.

"What news, John?" Hornigold called down to his comrade. "How go your efforts on Harbour Island?"

"Splendidly, Commodore!" Cockram replied. "A dozen guns protect her port, according to the wishes of Governor Rogers. Speaking of… I hope I have not missed the trial."

Hornigold shook his head. "Another half an hour at least. They have yet to transfer the prisoners from the cells below into His Majesty's Guard Room."

Fifteen minutes later, with Cockram standing beside him, Hornigold, after a few thoughtful puffs on his pipe, whispered with a sigh, "I have been thinking as of late as to how my plan for a republic of pirates has now given way to our former armory being designated as His Majesty's Guard Room. I never waivered in my loyalty to the Crown, which cost me control of New Providence, yet I would never have honored Anne or George with such a name. Despite my service during the War of Spanish Succession, this fort was crumbling around me despite my continual pleas for assistance."

Cockram nodded. "Assistance denied to ye and your dreamed-of republic, yet given without question to Rogers. *Hostis humani generis*, Commodore Hornigold. That is all that ye and I shall ever be, despite the fact that we are the ones responsible for capturing and delivering our ten former brothers to Governor Rogers and his council. Ten of our former brothers whom they shall most assuredly find guilty in the span of a single afternoon and merrily condemn to death."

"What in God's holy name is that ruckus?" Hornigold enquired, hearing the echoing boots and clattering accoutrement of dozens of men coming from His Majesty's Guard Room. Reaching for his pistol, he relaxed his arm as First Lieutenant Robert Beauchamp, commander of the governor's Independent Company, exited the room, followed by twenty well-armed men.

"Good day to ye, sirs," the always surly Beauchamp remarked, his normally commanding voice reduced to a raspy whisper. Without waiting for a response, he turned his attention to positioning his men along the ramparts and outside the room where the trial was soon to begin.

As Beauchamp barked orders to a dozen men on the beach, Hornigold saw another twenty taking position outside the fort. Several of them were coughing. They looked as pale as a day-old corpse.

"A renewal of the sickness that has previously plagued your numbers?" Cockram quietly enquired, stepping a few feet away from the also coughing lieutenant, whose eyes were swollen and red.

"Aye. Rose up a few days ago like a ghoul from out of nowhere. Fierce enough to kill our goddamned physician. Two dozen men are lying useless in their bunks. Managed to cobble together a little less than seventy for the trial—fifty-two upon the ramparts and stationed down below, plus another fifteen with the prisoners inside His Majesty's Guard Room. Not taking any chances. Not with the *Buck* being taken in the night, the *Samuel* off to London for reinforcements and desperately needed supplies, and the *Willing Mind* stuck fast upon a sand bar."

"Do ye fear an attack, Beauchamp? A rebellion of the locals?" Hornigold enquired.

Beauchamp shrugged his weary shoulders. "We cannot be certain of anything considering the rabble who still remain upon this island. Reports are coming in of trials and mass executions throughout the Caribbean, Indies, and even in America, in colonies where the pirates once were welcome. Considering what they did to Blackbeard..."

Hornigold, after releasing a blue-grey cloud of smoke, raised an eyebrow in surprise. "What exactly was done to Blackbeard, and by whom?"

Expelling a thick green wad of phlegm as his violent coughing continued, Beauchamp took a long, noisy pull from a waterskin hanging by a strap from his shoulder. "Beheaded by a Royal Navy detachment off some island in North Carolina. Couple of weeks ago, it was. Just received the news this morning."

As Hornigold leaned against the railing, feeling suddenly sick and overcome, Beauchamp spat over the side of the rampart. Moving off to attend to his men, he mumbled, "One less poxy pirate sucking up our air. May demons dine upon his innards…"

"What did ye say, ye gutless son of a whore?" Hornigold shouted, grasping the Independent Company lieutenant by the waterskin's strap hanging from his shoulder.

"Benjamin, release that man at once!" Cockram commanded, taking Hornigold by the shoulders and pulling him roughly backward. "I understand why ye are so upset, but this man, who should more carefully watch his words, is a company commander, and therefore your superior. Do not do this, my friend, I beg ye. Not today. Not right before the trial, in front of the entire island…"

As Beauchamp pivoted upon his heel, his fist cocked and ready to strike the defenseless Hornigold, Cockram shook his head. "Have some sympathy, Lieutenant! Blackbeard, of whom ye speak so crassly, was the commodore's man for years. Ye can see that he is in shock, blindsided as he was by the way ye delivered the news of his death."

Lowering his fist but maintaining a threatening stare, Beauchamp spat again—this time at Hornigold's feet. "Ye cannot pick and choose your friends. Ye should hear the way the poxy bastards who remain upon this island speak of ye two traitors. I am glad the scum is dead. He will soon have ten more of ye sorry excuses for men to keep him company in the darkest circles of Hell."

Feeling the commodore's arms begin to tense as Beauchamp turned away, Cockram pulled him another two feet farther back, forcing him to release his grip on the strap of the waterskin. "Leave it be for now. They are calling the trial to order. Let us play our parts. When this day is at last behind us, I shall buy ye a comforting supper and all the rum ye can hold in a corner of the Fatted Calf."

Nodding his head and releasing himself from Cockram's loosened grip, Hornigold entered His Majesty's Guard Room. The ten pirates he and Cockram had captured off Exuma on October 20 stood in a line before the bar to enter their pleas to a single charge—taking three ships and marooning the merchant James Kerr near Exuma on October 6—read aloud by Assistant Justice William Fairfax on behalf of the Admiralty. One by one, and to a man, John Augur, William Cunningham, John Hipps, Dennis

McKarthy, George Rounsivel, William Dowling, William Lewis, Thomas Morris, George Bendall, and William Ling replied with a loud and resounding, "Not guilty!"

Wearing a judge's robes and generously powdered wig, Woodes Rogers welcomed the attendees, and thanked for their service Captain Wingate Gale, Captain Josiah Burgess (who had recently taken the pardon), and local council member Thomas Walker, who would, along with Fairfax and Rogers, render judgment upon the ten men standing in irons before them.

As the lawyer appointed by the court began to speak on the pirates' behalf—for all the good it would do them—Benjamin Hornigold discreetly wiped a tear from each of his tired eyes.

Now that Edward Thache was dead, the republic was truly dust.

At the end of the peninsula in southwest Charles Town, overlooking the harbor and Cooper River, sits a stretch of beach called White Point, named for the tens of thousands of bleached white oyster shells intermingled with its sands.

Over the course of five weeks and more than a dozen trials, Chief Justice Nicholas Trott had condemned to death just shy of fifty pirates, from the crews of Bonnet, Cole, and Worley. On November 8, twenty-nine of Bonnet's crew met their deaths by hanging at this normally tranquil spot, the executions witnessed by a sizable crowd nearly split down the middle concerning whether or not they supported the goings on. Three and four days later, the gallows took the rest.

Tensions were palpably high, forcing Governor Robert Johnson to deploy the local militia in sizable-enough numbers to deter any thoughts of rioting or rebellion. The dismissal of Provost Marshal Nathaniel Partridge and death of the popular and well-to-do Richard Tookerman—whose wife had filed numerous documents claiming she was entitled to Bonnet's belongings, including *Royal James*, seeing as her husband was never paid for services rendered—had turned the capital city of Charles Town into a powder keg.

The hanging of the so-called gentleman pirate Stede Bonnet of Barbados, scheduled for today, could very well be the spark that set the damned thing off.

"Perhaps I should have postponed," Governor Johnson whispered, half to himself, as his carriage arrived at White Point. Dozens of citizens had positioned themselves along the beach, although Bonnet had not yet arrived, and the air was already unnervingly volatile.

"Seven postponements is seven too many," Colonel William Rhett responded. "This sniveling, balling bastard has caused ye and the colony more than enough embarrassment. Every day that he lives, your goal of a South Carolina free from the Lords Proprietors moves a little further away. If none of this has proven persuasive, think of this—if it were not for the archpirata Bonnet, Charles Yeats would be sitting here beside us."

Rhett managed to bury a smile as Johnson formed his hands into fists.

"Right ye are, Colonel Rhett. The loss of Yeats is as bile in my throat. A rare and dedicated man was our coldly murdered captain. Do ye not agree?"

Keeping in mind that Johnson was well aware of—and at times had even purposefully exacerbated—the deep-seated acrimony between the pair of pirate hunters, but not that Rhett had been responsible for his rival's death, the colonel forced a rueful smile. "My only regret is that I had only begun to learn the slightest fraction of all that the captain knew. I shall endeavor to apply all that Yeats so generously taught me in our limited time together."

On any other day, perhaps while sitting in his office sipping tea, Johnson would never have fallen for the colonel's obvious and amateur dissembling. Today, however, there was simply too much else on his mind.

As the citizens of Charles Town continued to gather, arraying themselves in a semi-circle around the gallows, it became increasingly clear to Johnson that, despite the fact that only a single pirate would hang, it would be a larger, more spirited, and more divided crowd than during the previous dozens of hangings.

"Perhaps a hanging in secret," he said, more to himself that to the man who stood beside him, whom he truly did not like. "On O'Sullivan's Island, where his two co-conspirators met their deaths." Feeling his pulse begin to race, he turned to Rhett and huffed. "Why did ye not kill him, when ye had the chance, and save us all the trouble?"

This was the very question William Rhett had been asking himself repeatedly since deciding to make Bonnet his prisoner.

The answer was rather simple and one to which he ultimately always returned. He saw more of a profit in this spectacle at White Point than there would have been had he ended Bonnet's life on the island, where only a few could see it.

Shrugging his shoulders, Rhett replied, "I am fully committed to the application of justice through the objective rule of law."

Johnson scowled. "I know full well your history. Ye made your money regardless of the morality of those with whom ye traded. Your conscience is far from clean. Ye have powerful friends, Colonel Rhett... Men I do not trust... Who do not align with my goals… both here and in the Albemarle. Then there is the matter of the Portuguese fishermen off Beaufort in the north. An ugly business, that…"

*If only I could get ye alone on O'Sullivan's Island*, thought William Rhett, releasing a groan of frustration as the vivid, delicious details at play in his mind about terminating the governor's life and leaving his body for the crabs were forcefully wiped away as half the crowd began to boo and the other half to cheer.

"The monster of the moment approaches," Johnson muttered, slightly shifting his position to see the well-dressed Major Bonnet, hands fastened behind his back, sitting on a bale of hay in the back of an approaching wagon.

As the wagoneer brought the wagon, which also carried half a dozen militiamen, to a stop before the gallows, Chief Justice Nicholas Trott emerged from a carriage, offering a half-hearted wave to the governor.

"Trott is brave to show his face," Johnson remarked, wiping his brow and lips with a brand new monogrammed handkerchief. "Outside of myself, and ye of course, Rhett, he is most assuredly the least popular man in Charles Town."

As a pair of drummers played a martial beat, Stede Bonnet, scourge of the Carolinas, stepped down from the back of the wagon with the assistance of three of the militiamen tasked with assuring he did not escape.

Taking his arms and leading him toward the gallows, his guards, who did not expect the pale, weakened pirate to offer anything in the way of resistance, found themselves surprised and embarrassed when Bonnet, with a twist of his torso, suddenly broke away and began running toward Governor Johnson.

"Shoot him, Rhett, I beg ye," Johnson whispered, hiding behind the colonel.

More than happy to comply, the colonel drew his pistol. Before he could cock it, however, Chief Justice Trott was shouting as he ran toward Rhett.

"A ball to the brigand's heart will not see justice done!"

Rhett, lowering his pistol as half a dozen red-faced militiamen surrounded and pointed their muskets at the pirate, produced a smile. "Accurate as always, Chief Justice Trott. Naught but a hanging shall suffice."

"Please, Governor Johnson!" Bonnet cried, falling to his knees. "Did ye not receive my letter?"

Johnson, feeling bits of his breakfast rising into his throat, shook his head. "Do not speak of it, Major Bonnet. Did I not repeatedly delay this day? Seven times, I did! Did I not allow ye visitations by widows and other weepers who cannot bear to see ye die? I pray ye, ascend the stairs and end this like a man."

Releasing a blood-chilling wail, producing an effect like sharpened fingernails dragged slowly along a sheet of slate, Bonnet began to rock, as though he were an inconsolable infant. "Let me repeat the pleas of my unjustly unresponded-to letter! I ask of thee, Governor Johnson, to look upon me with bowels of pity and compassion. Think me an object of your mercy! Make me a menial servant to your honor and this government, and ye shall receive the willingness of my friends to be bound for my good behavior and constant attendance to your commands. I beg ye to consider my plea!"

Indicating to the sergeant in charge of the militia to have Bonnet brought to the gallows, Governor Johnson addressed the crowd.

"Do ye hear the desperate words of this unrepentant pirate? How he speaks of his *friends*? Beware any man amongst ye who would call this devil *friend*!" Stealing a glance at Rhett, he added, "Beware any man amongst ye who puts himself and his ambitions before his colony and his king!"

As the majority of the crowd raised their voices in agreement, Chief Justice Trott, banging his hands together, nodded in approval.

As a pair of militiamen began to lead the no longer struggling Bonnet up the stairs, to the spot where the hangman's noose awaited, an eight-year-old girl, prompted by her mother and sister, emerged from the thickening crowd. Handing Stede a nosegay, which he silently accepted, she kissed his trembling hand and ran back to her kin.

Loosening the noose just a little, the hangman placed it over Bonnet's head, tightening it around his neck and, after seeing the fear in the pirate's eyes, adjusting the position of the knot so his charge would not have to suffer.

Nodding to the militiamen so they knew that he was finished, the hangman stepped aside as the pair assisted Stede in standing on a foot-high stool.

Cuing the drummers to increase the speed of their beat, Chief Justice Nicholas Trott, the Bible always foremost on his mind, raised his arms into the air. Quoting Isaiah, chapter thirteen, verse eleven, he shouted, "And I will punish the world for their evil, and the wicked for their iniquity; and I will cause the arrogancy of the proud to cease, and will lay low the haughtiness of the terrible."

"Blackbeard shall avenge me!" Bonnet shouted in response.

"Blackbeard was beheaded on November twenty-second! Sorry no one told ya, ya bastard!"

As he glared into the crowd, searching for the face of his final tormentor, Stede Bonnet felt a strangely comforting warmth spreading from his genitals to his thighs as his bladder released its contents.

Then the stool was no longer beneath him, and everything went black.

When his feet had ceased their twitching, the crowd immediately began to disperse.

"Throw the corpse in Vander Horst Creek," Governor Johnson instructed the hangman, handing him several coins, "which is surely considerably more than these spawns of Satan deserve."

*Fini* (fer noo)

# ABOUT THE AUTHOR

Joey Madia is a screenwriter, playwright, immersive experience and Escape Room designer, actor, director, podcaster, and historical education specialist. He works with publicists, agents, and producers and for production companies around the country as a story analyst and consultant, script doctor, and freelance writer.

He is the writer and puzzle designer of four five-star Escape Rooms, in North Carolina (2), Scotland (which won national and regional awards in 2023), and *Mothman '66* at the World's Only Mothman Museum in Point Pleasant, WV.

He serves as a consultant for the International Independent Producers Guild's Virtual Theatrical division, which combines live theatre, live streaming, and edited content with immersive audience experiences. He is a member of the Advisory Board for Arts Judaica, Chicago's leading theater company using the arts to fight Antisemitism.

He is the writer of several award-winning screenplays and stage plays.

A Chautauqua scholar, Joey has portrayed Allen Ginsberg (with permission from the Ginsberg Estate/Allen Ginsberg Project), Ernesto "Che" Guevara, "Black" Samuel Bellamy, Mariano Vallejo, Edgar Allan Poe, and Capt. Louis Emilio. He is preparing Cyrus Avery, "The Father of Route 66," for the Mother Road's centennial in 2026. His one-man show and five novels on the Golden Age of Piracy, *The Cannon and the Quill*, have been entertaining and educating audiences since 2016. They are featured in the *North Carolina Travel Guide* (2018 & 2023), *Carolina Coast*, other print and electronic media, and on the Japanese television show *Passage of Dreams*.

You can reach him through Facebook, Instagram, Twitter, Threads, his Amazon Author Page, Goodreads, Stage 32, Film Freeway, Reedsy Discovery, and IMDb.